PATH
OF LUCAS

THE JOURNEY HE ENDURED

SUSANNE BELLEFEUILLE

BALBOA
PRESS
A DIVISION OF HAY HOUSE

Copyright © 2015 Susanne Bellefeuille.

All rights reserved. No part of this book may be used or reproduced by any means, graphic, electronic, or mechanical, including photocopying, recording, taping or by any information storage retrieval system without the written permission of the author except in the case of brief quotations embodied in critical articles and reviews.

Balboa Press books may be ordered through booksellers or by contacting:

Balboa Press
A Division of Hay House
1663 Liberty Drive
Bloomington, IN 47403
www.balboapress.com
1 (877) 407-4847

Because of the dynamic nature of the Internet, any web addresses or links contained in this book may have changed since publication and may no longer be valid. The views expressed in this work are solely those of the author and do not necessarily reflect the views of the publisher, and the publisher hereby disclaims any responsibility for them.

The author of this book does not dispense medical advice or prescribe the use of any technique as a form of treatment for physical, emotional, or medical problems without the advice of a physician, either directly or indirectly. The intent of the author is only to offer information of a general nature to help you in your quest for emotional and spiritual well-being. In the event you use any of the information in this book for yourself, which is your constitutional right, the author and the publisher assume no responsibility for your actions.

Any people depicted in stock imagery provided by Thinkstock are models, and such images are being used for illustrative purposes only.
Certain stock imagery © Thinkstock.

Print information available on the last page.

ISBN: 978-1-5043-4290-2 (sc)
ISBN: 978-1-5043-4292-6 (hc)
ISBN: 978-1-5043-4291-9 (e)

Library of Congress Control Number: 2015916711

Balboa Press rev. date: 10/26/2017

CONTENTS

Acknowledgements ix
Special Thanks xi
Chapter 1 1
Chapter 2 10
Chapter 3 19
Chapter 4 29
Chapter 5 38
Chapter 6 46
Chapter 7 55
Chapter 8 63
Chapter 9 73
Chapter 10 81
Chapter 11 92
Chapter 12 101
Chapter 13 111
Chapter 14 122
Chapter 15 131
Chapter 16 140
Chapter 17 149
Chapter 18 160
Chapter 19 169
Chapter 20 177
Chapter 21 186
Chapter 22 198
Chapter 23 206
Chapter 24 215
Chapter 25 224
Chapter 26 234
Chapter 27 242
Chapter 28 253

Chapter 29 263
Chapter 30 273
Chapter 31 284
Chapter 32 295
Chapter 33 304
Chapter 34 317
Chapter 35 329

ACKNOWLEDGEMENTS

I want to express my deepest gratitude to my family and to the friends who have supported me while I wrote this book. Thank you to every person who has encouraged me throughout this process!

Above all, I want to thank my husband, Ron. You have been an inspiration throughout this journey and have always believed in me, even on the days when conveying this story became difficult. With your smile and great energy, I was able to achieve my dream of becoming a writer.

Thank you to my boys, Andre, Alain, Alexandre, and Mathieu, for believing in their mom and encouraging me every step of the way. Thanks, boys, for keeping me focused and believing in me especially after Grandpa passed away, so soon before the last chapter of the book was completed.

To my two daughters-in-law, Dominique and Tanya, I express my deep appreciation for all the times you listened to me and always motivated me to continue my pursuit of becoming a writer. To my precious grandchildren, Annabelle, Jacob, Samuel, and Xavier, I am grateful for your wonderful smiles and the great amount of joy that you bring to me.

To my brothers, Andy, Marcel, and Robert, who have also suffered through the loss of our parents and of our oldest brother, Richard. You have always been my greatest supporters, through childhood and my adult life; thank you! My sisters-in-law, Diane,

Christine, and Chantal, I am so grateful that you were there for me. You are my dearest friends!

Writing this book has been a wonderful ride, yet sometimes it has been a difficult one. Traveling through the chapters of my parents' lives was a very emotional, though rewarding, experience. It gave me a precious gift; more time with my father before he passed on. We laughed a lot about the good times; however, there were moments when I saw tears in my father's eyes as he talked about the hard life he and my mother endured.

I'd also like to express my gratitude to the following people for their magnificent support and sharing of their wisdom: To my editors, especially Richard Bellefeuille and Jelena Sisko, thank you so much for your kindness and patience. Thank you to the Editorial Team at Balboa Publishing as well as to my copy editor and revisionary writer, Sigrid Macdonald; thank you for all your hard work. Thank you to all my nephews and nieces for believing in me. For offering great words of encouragement, and for being the first person to read my manuscript, thank you to my dearest niece, Robin Sampson (daughter of my deceased brother, Richard). Jeanne Pedersen, thanks for believing in me.

Finally, to my great friends, Melissa Fontaine and Natalie Lalonde, thank you for sharing your time and knowledge. I am extremely grateful to all my friends who have encouraged and had confidence in me throughout this wonderful journey.

God Bless

Special Thanks

Editors
Richard Bellefeuille
Jelena Sisko
Editorial Team at Balboa

Copy Editor
Sigrid Macdonald

****

Cover Design
Mathieu Ouimet

*Cry when you're happy.
When you're sad, fight it.*
—*Roger Bellefeuille*

CHAPTER 1

Lucy wraps up the day and says goodbye to her associates. She is heading from Kingston, Ontario, to her hometown of Alexandria for the weekend, to see her father. She visits her dad one weekend a month as she enjoys his company and is devoted to him. She also loves to visit her childhood town as it makes her feel more closely connected to nature and family. Alexandria is in the country, about an hour away from Ottawa. When she was growing up, the town was very small, with only 1,000 inhabitants. Lucy makes a quick call to Mark, her husband. She tells him not to work too hard, to have a great weekend and that she will see him on Sunday night. As she leaves her office, she notices that her secretary, Wendy, is still at her desk.

"See you Monday morning," she says to Wendy.

"Enjoy the weekend with your dad," Wendy replies with a smile.

"Thanks, Wendy!"

Leaving the parking lot, she feels tired and decides on a coffee before she starts her two-hour journey to her dad's house. She stops at the nearest coffee shop for a caffeine jolt and to buy her dad's favorite donuts. The liquid instantly warms her chest and kicks her into gear as she heads out on the highway. About an hour into her drive, thick white fog starts rolling in, affecting her visibility; Lucy reduces her speed to be safe. Out of nowhere, she sees headlights coming straight at her. She tries to avoid a head-on collision as the other vehicle swings toward her lane. Instinctively, she quickly veers to the right, and her car swerves from side to side. Panic creeps in as she is unable to steer the car back on the road; Lucy loses control of the vehicle. At that moment, everything around her begins moving in slow motion: images of her family flash like a picture show in her mind as she heads right for the electrical pole. Within seconds, the car slams head-on into the pole. Deafening sounds of bent metal and shattering glass fill her with dread. The airbag deploys, knocking the wind out of her as it hits her square in the face. Her head crashes into the headrest, jerking her neck hard with the impact; she loses consciousness. The other vehicle stops for a split second and drives away.

Several minutes later, a man driving by notices car lights in the ditch against the pole. He stops and calls 911. Then he proceeds toward the car. He fears what he might find as he rushes to help. He observes an unconsciousness woman, unresponsive to his comforting attempts. He stays with her while he waits for help. An ambulance, two police cars, and fire trucks rush to the scene. Sounds of sirens fill the air as flashing lights appear. Within minutes the paramedics are at the scene to help the victim. The policemen redirect traffic as the firemen pull Lucy from the mangled vehicle that is imprisoning her. After about ten minutes of painstaking care, the fireman is able to free her from the wreckage. The paramedics instantly take over and work tirelessly to keep her alive, while the police question the man who found her. They investigate the crime scene, verify her license plate and check the vehicle to identify the victim. The paramedics strap her into the gurney, and in one swift movement, they load Lucy into the ambulance. They rush her to the emergency room, with police in tow ready to meet with the next of kin.

At the hospital, a policeman takes the information to the nurses station to call Lucy's husband. The nurse dials the number and listens as the phone rings, but there is no response at home. Lucy's husband, Mark, is working late on a huge court case. He is a defense lawyer and has to finish putting together his case before court on Monday morning. The paramedics roll Lucy into the emergency room as directed; the nurses rush to get the room ready for her, and doctors charge in. Everything is hurried. They transfer her from the ambulance gurney onto a hospital gurney and check for vital signs; a faint pulse gives them hope even though Lucy remains unresponsive. Nurses carry out the orders from the doctors, connecting her to intravenous and an electrocardiograph to monitor her heartbeat. There is very little hope, but Lucy still clings to life. Doctors order an MRI scan right away because of head trauma from the collision. They know that Lucy is in a comatose state and that there is swelling around her brain from the severe impact.

As they prepare her for the MRI, Mark calls, and the nurse informs him what happened. Disbelief leads to panic as his heart rips free of his chest. With no time to spare, he hangs up the phone and dashes out of the office to his vehicle. The General Hospital, which is located about an hour and a half away from his work, seems unbearably far. Unwanted images cross his mind's eye as he makes his way to his beloved wife, tears streaming down his face. He needs to focus and tries to shake the sadness from his heart to no avail. Mark calls his father-in-law, Lucas, on his Bluetooth from the car. The phone rings, but there is no answer. *Lucas must be off doing errands,* thinks Mark as he pushes the switch to hang up the phone. Lucas doesn't have an answering machine, but he does have call display, so Mark knows he will call back shortly.

Still in shock, Mark feels twice as sad as he thinks about Lucy's four children from her previous marriage. She is an extremely fulfilled mother and grandmother; her family is her life. *How will he break the news to them?* he thinks. They are such a close-knit family. He becomes increasingly anxious as he phones Danny, the eldest, with the devastating news of his mother's condition. He hears Danny cry at the end of the line, and his heart breaks for Danny and his wife, Emily.

"Emily and I are going to call Ryan, Dwayne, and Johnny. You're closest to the hospital, so just go be with Mom. We'll be there as soon as we can."

"Okay, Danny, I'm almost there," replies Mark.

After Danny makes the calls, all her children head to the hospital, distressed and shocked about what has happened to their mom.

Mark is about ten minutes away from the hospital when Lucas returns the call Mark placed earlier.

"Hello," answers Mark.

"Hi, Mark. How are you doing? Lucy hasn't arrived yet, but she should pull in anytime," Lucas informs him. "Do you want Lucy to call you back when she comes in? I ordered her favorite supper, and everything is set on the table for her to eat when she comes in," Lucas says with excitement in his voice.

"No! No! Lucas, please listen to me," he responds with a quivering voice.

Lucas suddenly recognizes the distress in Mark's voice.

"What is it, Mark? Is Lucy sick or something?" he says, sounding confused.

Mark's heart shatters. "There's more to it than that, Lucas." The tears are rolling down his face as he tries to find the directions to the hospital and realizes there is no easy way to tell a man his daughter is in critical condition. What can he say? Mark pauses.

"What is it? What is going on?" Lucas cries.

"Lucas, I don't know how to tell you this, but Lucy had a horrendous car accident, and she's in a coma at the General Hospital. I am headed there right now; I should be there in five minutes. I also called the boys, and they're going to the hospital as soon as they can."

Terror grips him, as he cries, "No! No! Not my little girl." Realizing the urgency of the situation, Lucas attempts to regain his composure. "All right, I'm heading to the hospital right now."

"Okay, I'm just arriving; I'll see you in a little while. Bye, Lucas, and please, drive carefully."

"I will. Goodbye, Mark." Lucas hangs up in a state of shock. He rushes out, leaving everything behind. Driving to the hospital, he can't stop thinking of his little girl. *This can't be happening,* he thinks. His mind is racing. *What if?* He fears the worst. He shakes his head. *No, I can't think like that!* He tries to convince himself that everything will be all right. He prays and begs God to be merciful to his sweet daughter who does not deserve this.

Mark parks his car and hurries to the emergency doors. He runs in and dashes to the nurses station. "Can I help you?" asks the nurse.

"Yes, can you tell me where Lucy Ferguson is? I'm Mark, her husband. She was in a car accident and was transported to this hospital."

"Oh, yes! She was sent to the second floor for an MRI, and she should be back shortly in the ICU. You can wait in the room to your right, and a doctor will see you as soon as they have further information," answers the nurse.

Mark says, "How long do you think that will take?" Mark is feeling increasingly tense; he paces back and forth impatiently.

"Sorry, sir, I don't know. But if you want, I can get you a cup of coffee or something to drink," replies the nurse.

"No, no!" Mark retorts. "Sorry, I'm so stressed out right now," he apologizes as he runs his hand through his damp hair. "No coffee, thanks."

As Mark is apologizing, the nurse notices Lucy being escorted to the ICU room. She tells Mark to follow them. He looks to his right and sees Lucy on a gurney being wheeled into the room. He stumbles and loses his breath as the doctor approaches him.

"Are you Mark Ferguson?" asks the doctor.

"Yes," he stammers.

"Hi, I'm Dr. Wright, the neurologist," he says as they shake hands. "I was assigned to assist with your wife's traumatic brain injury. Lucy is in a coma. She just had an MRI, and it shows severe swelling around her brain. She has a serious head injury from the impact of the accident. The next twenty-four hours will be critical."

"How severe is her injury? Will she be paralyzed?" Mark can feel a tremor in his hands.

"Until she wakes up from her coma, we won't know the extent of her injury. We need to see the swelling go down before we can give you more information. You can see her right now," replies Dr. Wright as he pats Mark on the shoulder.

Mark tries to pull himself together as he walks into his wife's room. The beeping of the heart monitor, the wires connecting her to machines make him feel numb. Instantly, as he sees her, an overwhelming sorrow replaces his numbness. He walks toward the bed and stands there for a few seconds as he quietly breathes in and out. He reaches for her hand and clutches it tightly. *Why is this happening to an incredible person like Lucy?* He ponders as his thoughts ramble. He lifts her arm toward him and kisses her hand several times; he's overwhelmed with emotion and breaks down.

When Lucas arrives at the hospital, he gets out of his car and storms in. He runs through the emergency doors and rushes to the nurses station.

"I'm looking for Lucy Ferguson; she was in a car accident. I'm her father," says Lucas, feeling his heart race.

"Lucy is in ICU. That's the door to your right, sir," replies the nurse. "Her husband is with her."

"Thank you," he gasps.

"Are you okay, sir?"

"I've seen better days," he replies as he rushes for the door to his right.

Lucas makes a sudden stop with his hand outstretched; he stares at the door and tries to catch his breath. He slowly opens the door, with no idea what to expect. His daughter is lying on the bed, motionless. Lucas stands there stunned at the sight of his baby girl.

"Hi, Lucas," says Mark with a trembling voice. His eyes are red from crying.

Lucas goes to Mark and gives him a firm hug, trying to comfort him. Lucas is at a loss for words as he reaches for his daughter's hand.

He just stares at her, attempting to see past the wires and machines to envision his little girl. She has so much inspiration and love to give to the world. Mark reiterates to Lucas what the doctor told him about the next twenty-four hours. Lucas brushes Lucy's hair back and kisses her forehead. Then he sits by her side; he grasps her hand.

A nurse comes in and tends to Lucy's intravenous and monitors her heartbeat. She informs Mark that he needs to go to the nurses station to sign some paperwork and that the police have new information regarding Lucy's accident. Mark nods, pats Lucas on the shoulder and makes his way out.

"See you soon."

"Right," replies Lucas softly, never taking his eyes off Lucy.

Mark leaves the room with the nurse.

Lucas clears his throat. Lucas leans in closer to his daughter and whispers in her ear. "I love you so much, Lucy. Please wake up for me, sweetheart." Lucy lies motionless as Lucas begs her to wake up. Past sorrow creeps into his mind as he stares at his beautiful daughter.

"I will stay here as long as you need me, except you have to promise you will wake up for your incredible children, grandchildren, and husband—but, most of all, for me." Bargaining with her is futile as she continues to lie still and silent.

"Lucy… can you hear me? I *know* you can hear me. I'm going to talk to you all night long if I have to. I'll do whatever it takes. I want you with us because your children and husband need you. Most importantly, I refuse to go through this pain all over again." Lucas bows his head, trying to shake the past from his thoughts.

Lucy lies quietly, not making any sounds except for the reassuring sound of her breath going in and out. It is the only sign of life.

"Lucy! Oh, Lucy! You know that I had a wondrous childhood. My parents were amazing to me. But when I was a young man, after I met your mom, my life didn't turn out at all the way I had anticipated," says Lucas as he gazes back at Lucy looking so frail and vulnerable in her blue-green hospital gown.

7

He sees past her bruised and broken body, to her mother's beauty so clearly present in her features. He starts to envision himself as a young man as he recounts the story of the day he met his stunning wife, to his precious little girl while she lies there silently.

Deliberating before he begins his story, instead of talking about himself in first person by saying, "I, Lucas," Lucas decides to tell his daughter the story of his life and his courtship with her mother in third person as though it happened to someone else. He knows Lucy will know that it is his story and, as a result, her story as well.

CHAPTER 2

On a late summer afternoon in 1956, as the sun sets on a hot day, seventeen-year-old Lucas is proudly washing his first set of wheels. He is proud of his 1949 red, two-door Studebaker. Every chance he has, he shines the body and chrome bumpers of his vehicle until they reflect like a mirror. As he finishes shining the hubcaps, he sees his father approaching.

"Lucas, can you go to town and pick up these tools and materials before six o'clock?" He hands a list to his son. "We need to fix the barbed-wire fences first thing in the morning," John says.

"Sure, Dad," he replies with excitement. This is the perfect opportunity for him to ride his beauty through his beloved town of Alexandria.

John is a dedicated farmer with a strong build and deep voice. He stands five feet seven inches and has piercing blue eyes and strands of silver in his hair. As one of the most respected farmers in the community, John owns over four hundred acres of land, as well as the house next door, which is occupied by his eldest son, James, his daughter-in-law, Debra and their three children: Paul, age ten; Donna, age eight; and Scott, age four. His grandkids, Donna and Scott, both have developmental disabilities. Donna had a twin brother, Donald, who died when he was only three months old; he too was severely developmentally challenged. James supports his family by working on the farm with his dad and little brother, Lucas.

In addition, John and his wife, Elizabeth, have a daughter, Mary, who is married to Joe. They have five children: Sandra is nine, Brenda is eight, Jeffery is seven, Darcy is six, and Janet is five. John also helped Mary purchase a farmhouse with thirty acres of land just a few miles away from the farm, when she got married ten years ago. Sadly, John and Elizabeth lost their third child, William—named after his paternal grandfather—a few hours after he was born. They took his death incredibly hard, but six years later, they were blessed with the birth of Lucas, their fourth and last child. He was considered the miracle child, born thirteen years after Mary. Lucas's mom would pamper him, but his dad made sure to keep him in line.

A serious man, John likes to constantly shuffle his money around; he has extensive investments. He is an industrious man and never relaxes until things are completed just so. His goal in life is to help his children grow and become as wealthy as he is. He often shares these dreams with Elizabeth on the porch at night, sipping iced tea while they stare at their crops and admire their daily accomplishments. Elizabeth is a housewife who helps on the farm and loves being a mom. She is a delightfully gentle and soft-spoken woman with stunning dark-brown eyes. She may stand only five feet tall; nevertheless, she is an impressively strong woman, emotionally and physically.

As John walks toward the barn, he sees Lucas driving away with a proud smile; he waves at him. "See you later, Dad," shouts Lucas.

John grins as he shakes his head; he beams with pride at what an incredible son he has.

Lucas's looks rarely go unnoticed; his smile lights up a room, his hair is as black as ink, and he has his mother's deep dark-brown eyes that one can get lost in. Unlike his dad, Lucas is six feet tall and slim; however, he has a strong build like his dad's. He's also a gentle young man, a quality that he inherited from his mother and an attribute that people notice most about Lucas. He is soft-spoken and compassionate.

Lucas makes his way down the laneway slowly, his rolled-up shirt's sleeves showcasing his muscular bicep as his elbow jets out the window. Heading down the lane past the farmhouse, Lucas waves again, but this time he's looking at his mom. He smiles at how magnificent life is; he truly adores his parents.

Just before he turns onto the road, Lucas runs his hand through his hair, puts on his sunglasses and jacks up the stereo. Hank Williams and Johnny Horton are his favorite male vocalists; Kitty Wells and Patsy Cline are his favorite female singers. As he pushes the buttons to change the stations, one of Hank's songs comes on, "Jambalaya (on the Bayou)." Lucas starts swaying to the melody, drumming his fingers on the steering wheel, feeling the harmony in his soul. He enjoys music and loves this song. Lucas slowly starts heading down the country road. He is a proud young man, and the only thing on his mind right now is the love of his Studebaker. That is, until he notices two girls walking down the road; they look familiar. *Are they Mr. Bourgeois's daughters?* he thinks as he slows down. *Mr. Bourgeois is the man from Quebec City that I heard Dad talk about. I'm sure they're his daughters because they just came out of the old farm where the house burned three years ago. I wonder if they would like a ride home,* he ponders. As Lucas approaches them, he gets a glimpse of a gorgeous young woman; his heart starts to thump. The closer he gets, the more of her fine features he sees, the more anxious he gets. He has never felt this way before, and he wonders, *what is going on with me?*

As he brings his car to a stop, he notices that the true beauty seems to be the younger of the two; she looks shyly toward him. Lucas decides to offer them a ride home. He stumbles with his words, which is not normal for him.

Sheepishly, he says, "Hi, ladies, isn't it a beautiful day today?" The pretty girls nod in agreement. "I'm Lucas. I live up the road at the Clarkson Farm, would… would you like a ride home?" he asks.

His incredible smile makes up for the fact that he's struggling with words. The girls look at each other, not knowing what to say. The younger girl is shyly trying to hide behind her older sister.

The older one replies, "You don't mind taking us back to our farmhouse?"

"I don't mind at all," responds Lucas as he smiles at the younger sister. She blushes under his gaze.

The older sister forces her sibling into the car first, pushing her toward Lucas. The younger girl tries to resist but to no avail; her sister is stronger. She has no choice but to sit beside Lucas. The older one then gets in and shuts the car door.

Lucas looks at the younger girl, his dark eyes gleaming with hope, and he displays his amazing white teeth. The girl can't help but notice how handsome he is as she settles herself in his car. She lowers her head and tries to grin, but bashfulness prevents her lips from forming the smile she wishes she could flash. Instead, she feels a knot in her stomach. As for her sister, she is happy to rest her tired feet and have someone take them home after a hard day of working in the fields.

"Nice car," says the older sister, who speaks with a French accent.

"Thanks," replies Lucas. "Sorry, I didn't get your names."

"Oh, my name is France Bourgeois, and this is my little sister, Isabelle," says France. She reaches over Isabelle's lap to shake his hand.

Lucas takes her hand quickly; *after all, he is driving.* "Hi, France, nice to meet you. I'm Lucas Clarkson." He smiles at Isabelle and greets her nervously. "Hi, Isabelle." Silently, Isabelle nods but keeps her head down; the smile she envisions giving him escapes her.

"My sister is very shy," France says apologetically.

"That's okay—we all have days like that," he says, trying to make Isabelle feel more at ease.

"We moved from Quebec City because our father wanted to farm, and he knew friends that lived around here. We used to live on the old farm, but the house burned a few years back. Our father purchased this other farm, and that's where we live now," explains France.

"Yeah, my father told me about a farmhouse that burned down a few years back. I think my dad knows your father somewhat," replies Lucas. "So odd that we never met until now."

"We don't go out much," explains France. "Only to the farm and back."

As Lucas nears their house, he asks, "Which farmhouse is yours?"

"The log house far from the road, next to the big house on your left," says France as she points in that direction.

Lucas slows down and signals to turn left; he turns in their laneway and brings them right up to the house. He notices there are many children milling around the property.

"Are they all your siblings?" asks Lucas curiously as the little tots run toward the car.

"Yes, Isabelle and I have six siblings," says France with a smile as she opens the door to greet them. "Thank you again for the ride."

Isabelle has remained inordinately quiet during the ride. She now looks at Lucas as she gets out of the car, and with a timid smile, she says, "Merci."

Lucas looks back at her, and for a split second, their eyes meet; immediately, he knows he wants to get to know her better. There is something about her that he has never experienced with another girl.

"Welcome," whispers Lucas. His jaw drops, and he feels his mouth get dry.

Lucas turns his Studebaker around, watching carefully for the children. He heads to town after waving to France and Isabelle. Lucas can't stop thinking about Isabelle as he cruises along, trying to remember the reason why he went to town in the first place. Suddenly, the general store comes to mind—*he has to pick up items for his father*. Still fascinated by Isabelle, he enters the store.

As Lucas approaches the counter, Mr. Brown, the clerk, asks him, "What can I do for you today?"

Still in a daze, he hands Mr. Brown the list of items that his father needs for the farm. Mr. Brown reads the list and gathers the items.

"Will that be all for today, young man?" asks Mr. Brown.

Lost in reverie, Lucas snaps out of it. "Oh! Sorry… yes, thanks!"

Mr. Brown puts everything in a bag and says, "That will be five dollars, son."

Isabelle still on his mind, Lucas smiles as he clumsily pulls out his money. Mr. Brown chuckles and says, "What's the matter, boy?" He is insinuating that something is wrong. "Well now, son, I've seen that look before. Looks like you saw an angel from heaven!"

Lucas's eyes light up. His hands rest on the counter, and he gazes toward the ceiling as if picturing her floating down from the heavens. "Oh, did I ever! Today, I met the most beautiful girl I have ever set eyes on."

"Why, son! You look as though you are in love," expresses Mr. Brown with a big smile.

Love? That could very well be, Lucas acknowledges as his stomach is doing flip-flops. He takes his parcels and says goodbye to Mr. Brown. With a bounce in his step, he gets into his Studebaker, buys gas at 22 cents per gallon and drives home for supper. As he drives by Isabelle's house, he slows down to take a good look, hoping to see her again. He's too far to see inside the house. From the road, her house is at a standstill. The front lawn is quiet compared to the way it was a few hours ago; the children are nowhere to be seen. For a split second, a dreadful thought takes hold of his heart: *What if I never see her again?*

Lucas arrives home, puts his Studebaker in the garage and takes his father's materials out to the workbench; then he heads for the house. As Lucas walks into the house, he can smell his mom's cooking, and he hears Elvis Presley on the radio. His mom is setting the table for supper.

"Hi, Mom," he says.

"Hi, precious," replies Elizabeth as she kisses Lucas's cheek. "Can you please wash up? Supper is ready. Can you ask your dad to come also? Thank you."

Lucas gives his mother a big smile. "Yes, Mom. I'm starved."

Lucas walks toward the washroom and at the same time calls his dad, who is sitting in the living room, to go for supper. His dad gets up from his chair and thanks him.

"Welcome, Dad," responds Lucas with gentleness in his voice.

John wonders why Lucas is in such a good mood. Elizabeth is putting the food on the table as John walks in.

"Did you notice something strange about Lucas?" asks John his wife. "He seems mighty happy."

"You know how he loves that Studebaker! It must be the car ride," replies Elizabeth.

John raises his brows as he sits down. He's seen that look before, and it's usually related to love and romance, not cars. Elizabeth smiles at her husband as she sits beside him. Lucas walks in with a big grin. He kisses his mom and dad.

"What's for supper? It sure smells good," says Lucas in a soft-spoken tone.

John and Elizabeth look at each other.

"Lucas, did you go to the store for me?" asks John as Lucas joins them at the table.

"Yes, everything is in the garage," replies Lucas. "You'll never guess who I met today!"

"Who?" Elizabeth asks as she passes the potatoes to him.

"Dad, do you remember when you told James and me about the farmhouse that caught on fire? You said it was a man from Quebec City, and his name was Mr. Bourgeois," explains Lucas as he scoops the mashed potatoes onto his plate.

John nods yes as he thinks about how hungry he is and how delicious the food looks. Elizabeth is such a good cook.

"Well, I met his two eldest daughters and gave them a ride to their house. They're nice. Especially the youngest daughter, Isabelle.

She's very pretty!" says Lucas while he passes the mashed potatoes to his dad in exchange for the fried chicken.

"That explains your behavior," responds John.

"Is it that obvious?" asks Lucas, blushing slightly.

Elizabeth smiles and says, "Your father reacted in the same fashion when he bumped into me, and so did your brother when he met Debra."

"Tell me more about your courtship with Dad."

"Your father went to town by horse and buggy with his cousin Charles, to pick up my brother Ralph, whom you never got to know. When they came to the door and asked for your uncle, your father took a liking to me. He came back the next day on the pretense of visiting Ralph, but he really came to see me. Within a month, we were courting."

They all laugh. Elizabeth has a way of making Lucas feel good; she knows exactly what to say and when to say it. John smirks and looks at his wife with sparks in his eyes as he scoops up his food. Lucas is fortunate to have such a loving family; his parents taught him well. He hopes that one day he will find genuine love, like they did.

CHAPTER 3

Three weeks creep by at a snail's pace; Lucas still has not seen Isabelle. He has driven by her house multiple times, but Isabelle and her family are never around. Lucas's thoughts permeate with images of their first encounter, her smile, how their eyes met, the way she said "merci" when he dropped her off. His brother, James, notices a change in him. One day, as they are milking the cows, James decides to talk to Lucas about it.

"Lucas, have you heard from Isabelle lately?" he asks.

"No," replies Lucas. "I've driven by her place often, but she's never around, and I don't see her siblings outside."

"Have you ever thought of just knocking on her door and asking her on a date?"

"I can't see myself driving to her house unannounced and asking her out," explains Lucas, frustrated.

"Yes, but how else will you see her? Just muster the courage and do it," his brother urges.

"No! Not ever! I wouldn't feel right going there unexpectedly. I have feelings for her, but I don't know how to see her again," says Lucas in a heartrending voice.

"I went to town last Saturday, and I saw some of her family members walking to their old farm; it must have been nearly seven in the morning. Have you ever gone to town on a Saturday morning early?" James asks.

"No. You know I'm always with Dad in the barn at that time," replies Lucas.

James and Lucas stop talking and continue to work as if the discussion never happened. James can see that Lucas truly wants to meet this girl, and he will do anything to help his little brother. As for Lucas, his mind is also engaged in trying to find ways to bump into Isabelle again. He tries to keep his mind off the situation by working harder. Just then his dad enters the barn. John observes Lucas being non-talkative. *It's not like Lucas to act like this,* thinks John as he lets the cows out of the barn.

"Are you okay, son?" asks John.

"Doing just fine!" he snaps, annoyed by his father's question.

At that point, John knows he has to give Lucas his space. They all continue their work and go home to wash up afterward. James hugs his dad and his little brother; then he waves goodbye and sets off home to his family. John talks with Lucas about what is on the agenda for the next day as they walk toward the house. He wraps his arm around Lucas's back and clutches his strong hand onto his shoulder.

"I'm mighty proud of the work you did today, son!" Lucas barely acknowledges his father's praise. He is too preoccupied with thoughts of the elusive Isabelle.

For the next several days, Lucas focuses all his energies on work because he misses Isabelle, and at night he takes his Studebaker for a spin. One evening, just as Lucas is going into the house to wash up, Elizabeth runs up to him and informs him that Steve is back from his training, and he's staying in town for a few days. Lucas's eyes light up, and his smile widens, showing his beautiful teeth.

"Seriously—Steve's back?" he responds in disbelief. "I thought he wouldn't be coming home for another few months!"

"Yep, he just called. Apparently, he finished his training early and wanted to surprise his parents," replies Elizabeth.

Lucas and Steve have been inseparable since grade three; they developed a mutual love of sports and cars. Steve struggled growing up in a poor family; it affected his self-esteem and dreams, but Lucas always helped Steve believe in himself. Steve worked hard to build confidence for his training as a pilot. When Steve left for Trenton Air Force base, Lucas shared his excitement and felt incredibly proud of him, but he was saddened when Steve left town last year.

Lucas can barely contain his excitement at the thought of seeing his friend again. He quickly gets cleaned up before he sets out for town. He kisses his mom and thanks her; then he jumps into his Studebaker and heads off. When he reaches the house, Steve is sitting on the front porch with his mom and dad. Lucas parks the car and runs over.

"Hey, Steve!" says Lucas. "How are you doing?" He greets him with a great big bear hug. "It's so good to see you, buddy!" Then he nods to Mr. and Mrs. Lewis and says hello.

"I'm great! Did you hear? I should get my pilot's license by next week. I'm not sure exactly where I'll be stationed; the Air Force will notify me soon, within the next week or so."

Mrs. Lewis is sitting next to her husband, Arthur, and she takes it hard as she weeps on his shoulder. Arthur comforts her with sadness in his eyes as he listens to his son. Arthur's sorrow does not overpower his pride for his son. He, like any other father, simply fears for his son's safety and wonders when he'll be coming home again. Fortunately, the country is not at war. No one has to fight the evil Nazis, the way Steve's uncle Tom did in WWII, and the Korean War is over. Tom gave his life for his country, but this is not something that the Lewises talk about, and Steve has never mentioned Tom's death to Lucas, simply the fact that he fought in the war. Despite living in peace time, Steve's parents pray that no harm will come to their precious boy during his stint in the army.

Steve tries to change the subject, as he sees it is painful for his parents and Lucas.

With fresh excitement in his voice, Steve says, "Love your set of wheels, Lucas! Where the heck did you ever find a car like that?"

Lucas looks back with pride. "Remember Mr. Gordon? He sold it to me, and James helped me repair the engine. She's a beauty."

"Can you take me for a spin?" Steve asks with eagerness in his voice.

"Sure. Let's go," answers Lucas.

The two young men say good night to Steve's parents and run to the car with boyish excitement. Riding along, they feel as though no time has passed at all, just like the old days, going for a cruise: the wind tousling their hair, their arms out the window, savoring the freedom.

"Where do you wanna go? Anywhere special?" asks Lucas.

"Not sure," Steve mumbles, thinking for a moment. "How about the Alexandria Hotel, where I drank my first beer?" He laughs.

"I remember," replies Lucas. "I had to take you home in my dad's truck you were so wasted." He laughs out loud recalling Steve stumbling up the front porch.

"Good old memories. I enjoyed those days," says Steve.

"What do you mean? Those memories aren't that old," Lucas shouts as he throws a playful punch at Steve.

Steve starts to laugh and punches Lucas back. Lucas pulls into the parking lot of the Alexandria Hotel. They are still playfully punching each other as they get out of the car.

"I could sure use a cold one," says Steve.

Lucas shoots a quick look at Steve. "Only one?" He grins.

As they enter the hotel, they continue joking and hacking around. They walk toward the bar greeting the other patrons with smiles and nods. Steve orders the beers while Lucas grabs a table. They settle down and tap their glasses of beer together before they take their first sip. Steve starts the conversation by telling Lucas about his training in the Air Force. He tells Lucas how thankful he is that Lucas was always there to support him through his trials and errors when he was a teenager. Steve also tells Lucas how he loves flying. The freedom he feels when he is up in the air—there are no words to describe it.

"What ever happened to your dream, Lucas?"

"Steve, you know I can't just leave the farm. My dad and brother need me. I still think about becoming a mechanic but not just yet," responds Lucas as he takes a gulp.

"Someday you will, right?" asks Steve.

"Yeah, someday. I do get to fix farm equipment now, which is something," Lucas replies positively.

They are both silent for a few minutes as they sip their beers.

"Oh!" Lucas says changing the subject. "I have to tell you about this beautiful French girl I met. She lives close to my house. I gave her and her sister a ride home one day. Her name is Isabelle. She has the smile of an angel, and I've heard that she's sixteen years old. Just one year younger than I am—how perfect!" he describes longingly.

"Have you seen her since?" asks Steve.

"No, that's the problem. I haven't seen her since that day," replies Lucas. "I drove by her place a few times, but I didn't see anyone around. James said that he saw some of her family walking to their old farm in the early morning a few Saturdays ago."

"Why don't you go for a ride early Saturday morning?" Steve asks.

"I work with my dad milking the cows; you know my schedule, Steve," replies Lucas. They continue drinking their beers.

"You'll find a way. I'm sure you'll see her again soon," Steve assures him as they tap their glasses. Lucas smiles. "Cheers!"

Steve puts his beer down. Someone walks up and stands in front of him. He looks up to see Kris, the mayor's son. *Ah, crap. Not Kris!* thinks Steve. Kris was very spoiled as a child; he always got what he wanted from his parents. Kris is, to this day, the town bully; nothing stands in his way. No one has the courage to stand up to him, or his mayor dad, who keeps bailing him out of trouble. Kris is a petty criminal who owns fasts cars, wears fashionable clothes and has too many girls to count. There is nothing standing in his way in that small town.

"What brings you back to town, loser?" chuckles Kris.

"Well, well, well! If it isn't *little* Krissy Cameron, Daddy's little rich *boy*," replies Steve tauntingly.

"Don't you talk down to me," Kris shouts.

"Seems like I just hit a nerve," Steve smirks calmly.

Lucas looks at both of them and says, "That's enough, guys. Kris, go back to your table. We don't want trouble."

Kris heads back to his friends. Lucas and Steve continue to talk and order more beers. Kris angrily glares at Steve over his shooter glass and feels threatened by Steve's arrogance. Five shots later, his frustration soars. Kris mumbles to his friends, gets up, and walks toward Steve.

"You're a worthless piece of dirt, poor boy." Kris is so intoxicated, he slurs his words.

"Watch your mouth, pretty boy," replies Steve and carries on with chatting with Lucas.

"Lucas, why do you lower yourself to his level? He's not a friend; he's a good-for-nothing dirt bag," says Kris as he takes a swing at Steve.

Steve takes the blow, touches his upper lip and notices blood gushing down. *This is the last time this guy will get the better of me,* Steve thinks. He swiftly gets up and swings right back, throwing his punch so hard that Kris falls to the floor. Steve jumps on Kris, punching him left and right with no remorse, every punch filled with pent up rage against his childhood tormentor. The crowd cheers him on from a cautious distance. Lucas has to do something; Steve is out of control. He grabs Steve by the scruff of his shirt collar and lifts him up; Lucas's muscles flex. Lucas has a strong grip, like his dad's. He pushes Steve back, telling him to stop before he kills the man. Kris groans as he rolls on the ground. Steve backs off.

"He's not worth it," says Lucas.

"You're right, Lucas," responds Steve as he tries to pull himself together. "I have more important things to do in life."

Lucas helps his friend out of the bar. Everyone cheers Steve for standing up to the town bully. Hopefully, Kris has learned his lesson and will be more considerate to folks around town.

"I'm sorry to say this—but that felt great, after all these years. He needed someone to bring him down. Always hiding behind his father's title," says Steve as he wipes his bloody lip.

"That's so true, and I'm proud of you, Steve. After all these years of being pushed around, you got him good. Hope he got the message," replies Lucas. "Let's go home."

They get into the car, and Lucas heads to Steve's parents' house. Steve starts thinking about their friendship; he feels that they're like brothers.

"Lucas, you know I'll most likely be stationed far from here when they call me, and I will eventually make my way overseas. I know it's hard for you, but it's just as hard for me. I hope you understand; I have to do this. I'm somebody there. It makes me feel proud to serve my country and follow in my uncle Tom's footsteps." Steve pauses after he mentions his uncle Tom and looks sad. After a few sips of beer, he continues. "My passion is the Air Force. I know it comes at a price, being away for so long from my family and friends," explains Steve.

"Of course, I don't want you to go, but I also don't want to stop you from achieving your dream. You have to do it; you have to follow your heart. Just make sure you don't forget me, and come back to visit when you can," says Lucas, his eyes watering. "Better yet, promise me a plane ride someday."

They both stare out of the car in silence, parked in Steve's driveway.

"Lucas, don't give up on your dreams. Become the mechanic you always talked about. Go find that pretty French girl. I wanna meet her when I come back." He opens the door to get out. "Oh, by the way, love your wheels! You did a great job on that engine."

"Thanks Steve. See you later," says Lucas.

"Bye, buddy. Call you when I get the news." Steve smiles as he throws a shadow punch at Lucas.

Steve closes the car door, and Lucas watches as he enters the house. He turns his Studebaker around and heads home.

The next morning, Lucas and James are tending to the cows, Lucas is finishing milking the cows, and James is getting the cows out to pasture. James hears his mother calling. James shouts to Lucas, "Mom is calling you!" Lucas runs out of the barn toward his brother, and Elizabeth meets them in the pasture.

"What is it, Mom?" asks Lucas, coming up beside James.

"Steve just called, and he's leaving soon," says Elizabeth.

"How soon?" James asks.

Elizabeth looks at her two sons with a trembling lip. "He said he has to leave early tomorrow morning. The Air Force called him today," she replies.

"Where is he stationed?" asks Lucas.

"I'm not sure, son. He didn't say, but he is coming over."

Lucas asks James if he can go to the house and wash up before Steve arrives. James nods yes. Then Lucas heads to the house with his mom. Lucas has known that this day was coming. His mind is in turmoil, but he is certainly impressed by his friend.

Soon after Steve knocks at the door, Elizabeth welcomes him. She offers him a chair at the kitchen table and sets coffee and a treat in front of him. Steve accepts her scrumptious chocolate cake. Elizabeth turns to get the forks for the dessert as Lucas walks into the kitchen. Steve stands and shakes Lucas's hand. Lucas gives Steve a knowing nudge. They sit down, and Elizabeth brings them utensils and sugar for their coffee.

"I'm stationed in Cold Lake, Alberta. Have to leave tomorrow at five a.m. I'm taking the train to Toronto and then flying to Alberta," explains Steve, pausing to savor the taste of chocolate perfectly combined with the strong, black coffee.

"How long will you stay there?" asks Lucas.

"I don't know. They didn't give me much information."

They are silent for a few seconds.

"Delicious cake, Mrs. Clarkson," says Steve. "Thanks for the food. I have to rush back home; my folks are waiting for me. They want to spend as much time together as a family as we can before I leave. My sister and brother-in-law will be there for supper with their kids."

"I understand. You're welcome back any time, Steve. Be safe and write often," says Elizabeth as she gives him a big hug. "Say hello to your family for me, please, dear."

Lucas gets up and gives Steve a huge hug. "Take care out there, Steve," he says.

"Yes, buddy," replies Steve as they head for the door. "Remember, your dreams, Lucas, and go find the pretty French girl."

Steve walks to his car, with Lucas in tow. They give each other another gigantic hug. Steve reaches into his car and hands Lucas a piece of his sports memorabilia from his high school football. Steve smiles and says, "Remember me, friend." As Lucas thanks Steve for his kindness, there are tears in his eyes and a lump in his throat. He won't find another friend like Steve. That kind of intimacy takes years to build, and Lucas understands how lucky he is to have a best friend like this. Sorrowfully, Lucas watches Steve drive away, praying for his safety and hoping that he does indeed have the courage to seek out the beautiful Isabelle.

CHAPTER 4

As the summer draws to an end, and autumn leads the way with bursts of bright colors, Lucas is occupied working on the farm. He still can't believe he hasn't seen Isabelle yet; she's always on his mind. After a long day of work, Lucas picks up the mail from the mailbox at the side of the road. There is an envelope addressed to him. It's a telegram from Steve! He says that he's being stationed overseas. That afternoon, Lucas heads to town, hoping to get more information from Steve's parents.

The joy of driving his car with his country tunes blaring distracts Lucas from the sad news of his friend's deployment. Then up ahead, like a mirage, he sees two people walking. He can barely believe what he's seeing, as his heart skips a beat. Could it be? Is it? His excitement builds, as he gets closer. *By golly! It's Isabelle and her sister!* Lucas slows down as he approaches the young women and turns down his music.

"Hi, France! Hi, Isabelle!" Lucas can't contain his happiness and flashes his handsome smile, looking in Isabelle's direction. "It sure has been some time since I've seen you last! How are you doing?"

"We're doing fine, Lucas," replies France in her French accent, grinning.

Isabelle, with a shy look, nods and responds, "Oui." She does not know how to speak English but can comprehend a few English words.

"Do you want a ride home?" asks Lucas nervously.

"You do not mind?" asks France, her long day clearly showing by the slump in her shoulders.

"No, I don't mind at all. Sure looks like you both had a long, hard day," says Lucas as he glances at Isabelle and smiles.

Isabelle notices his charming smile and good looks instantly as she scoots over on the front seat. Her timidity doesn't prevent her from beaming her perfect smile this time around. Lucas can't help but look over his shoulder any chance he gets as he slows down his speed, subconsciously trying to make more time with her by prolonging the drive.

Isabelle feels Lucas glancing at her once in a while. She is starting to like the fact that he appears interested in her, but shyness keeps her from expressing her feelings for him. Lucas asks Isabelle whether she likes working on the farm. She looks at him and responds, "Oui," as she nods her head. France intervenes and tells Lucas that Isabelle does understand a little English but has a hard time speaking it. Lucas thanks France for the information; he tries to think of ways to communicate with Isabelle.

"France, can you help? Please ask Isabelle if it is okay if we communicate through you," Lucas inquires as he looks at both sisters.

"I can try to help," France replies with her lovely French-Canadian accent. She then looks at Isabelle, asking her little sister in French if she would like to speak with Lucas through her. Isabelle agrees. Lucas listens and tries to make sense of the words. He loves the sound of the French language because he has heard his mother's family speak French to each other, and he can pick up some words.

"Yes, she's interested in speaking with you also," confirms France. "What would you like to say to her?"

A few hundred feet from their laneway, he wonders how to ask her out, but he is at a loss for words. He is trying to get the words out; it is harder then he thought. France asks Lucas again if there is anything he'd like to say to her sister. France is wondering why

Lucas has become so quiet. Even Isabelle has noticed that Lucas is dumbfounded.

He sets the car in park, turns and looks right at Isabelle, and in his low charming voice he asks, "would you go on a date with me?"

France smiles at Isabelle and start speaking French. He tries to watch Isabelle's expressions from the side as she faces her sister the other way. He hears her mutter *"oui"* in the middle of a sentence, and he grins. He sits in anticipation. "She wants to know where you want to take her," France translates.

"Oh, yeah, of course," he replies sheepishly. "I was wondering if she would like to go to the Mama Jean's diner in town for supper."

Isabelle accepts.

In all his excitement, he almost forgets to say when. Suddenly, it comes to him. He yells, "SAMEDI" out the window. They both turn, and he puts up seven fingers.

The girls laugh. "Okay. Seven p.m. on Saturday," replies France.

"Oui! Seven," repeats Isabelle.

Proud of his cleverness, he responds, "thanks for your help, France." He turns his attention to Isabelle. He can't stop looking, having missed her all summer. "Bye, Isabelle." The sisters wave as he drives away.

With pride and an enormous smile, Lucas heads to Steve's parents' house. Steve's mom, Stella, is working in her garden, and Arthur is cutting the grass. He parks and saunters over to Stella.

"Good evening, Mrs. Lewis. How are you doing?" asks Lucas.

"Lucas, what a pleasant surprise. I'm well, thank you," she replies. "Let's go in for a glass of fresh lemonade. Arthur is just about finished with the lawn."

"That would be great. Thanks," Lucas says as he watches Arthur putting away his grass cutter in the garage. He helps Stella gather her garden tools. Arthur, on the other hand, doesn't even notice him and seems confused as he moves his grass cutter in three different places, as if he forgot where the equipment belongs. *Arthur is always so organized and a creature of habit. He should know exactly where his grass cutter goes,* Lucas ponders.

"Is Mr. Lewis okay?" Lucas asks her with a puzzled look. "He seems—I don't know, confused by the way that he was storing his grass cutter."

Stella shakes her head in disbelief. "Arthur hasn't been himself since Steve left for Cold Lake."

"Let's go to the garage and help him out, and then we can have some of your famous homemade lemonade," he says with a wink. Lucas supports Stella by the arm, and they walk gingerly toward the garage.

"Hi, Mr. Lewis!" he exclaims as he pats Arthur on the back. "Mrs. Lewis tells me she has some fresh-squeezed lemonade in the house."

"Oh, good evening, Lucas. How are you doing? Keeping busy on the farm?" says Arthur as he shakes Lucas's hand. He wipes his brow with his pocket square. "Let's go inside. I could sure use some of that lemonade; I worked up a sweat!"

Lucas lets Arthur take Stella's arm and walk with her. Lucas walks beside Arthur, telling him that working on the farm is hard; it's a physically demanding job. As they enter the house, Arthur invites Lucas to the sitting room, while Stella heads toward the kitchen for the drinks.

The men sit, and Arthur immediately speaks of Steve. "He's always been a great son and has even helped us pay our bills. We're so proud of what he's doing with his career." Stella walks in and sets a tray of lemonade and a delicious-looking lemon meringue pie on the table. She prides herself on the fact that the boys have loved her pies since they were youngsters. Stella has been selling pies at the general store ever since they moved into town; she is famous for her award-winning baked goods.

"A slice?" asks Stella with a smile, knowing it is practically impossible for Lucas to turn down.

"Yes, please!" insists Lucas. He knows how good the pie is.

"You're very welcome, Lucas," replies Stella as she hands him the pie with a smile. "Enjoy, honey."

She hands Arthur a slice and serves herself one too. They sit silently for a few minutes, relishing every bite.

Lucas sets down his plate. Thank you. I enjoyed that so much. The reason I came over is that I received a telegram from Steve; he said he's heading overseas."

Arthur explains to Lucas, "Steve, as you know, has no limits. He strives for excellence no matter what he does. He reminds me very much of my younger brother, Tom. They both like to live on the edge. Tom was only twenty-four when he died in the war. Steve was just three years old back then; he doesn't remember his uncle, but he knows everything about him. One day he found the stack of telegrams and letters from Tom. He read about his heroic missions and spent hours poring over old photo albums." Arthur reaches for an album off the shelf. "Like this one." He points to a handsome young man, dressed in uniform standing by a fighter plane.

"Wow! I see it now. Steve only told me about his uncle once, but he never mentioned how he died. I know how much he admired Uncle Tom. Now I understand why Steve was so determined to serve. He had an idol to live up to," says Lucas in a subdued voice as he continues to scan through the pictures.

"Steve knew that Arthur struggled with the death of his brother, so we seldom talked about the war," interjects Stella as she picks up the plates and then serves more lemonade.

Lucas hands Stella his glass. "I assume you already knew about Steve going overseas?" he asks.

Arthur takes a sip of his drink as he responds. "Yeah. He sent us a lengthy letter explaining why he wants to go abroad. I really don't want him to go because I already lost Tom. I have to respect Steve's wishes, but it's tearing me apart," says Arthur as he holds back his tears.

"Do you know how long he'll be gone and why he's going overseas?" Lucas asks tenderly, the pain apparent on all their faces.

Arthur straightens his back and places his big hands on his knees. He sighs and says, "We don't know how long he'll be there, but he's going for a practice run. That means a group is going to Europe for a top-secret mission, which Steve was appointed to go on because he's very knowledgeable about aircrafts."

"You must be extremely proud of him; it takes courage and determination to do what he does."

"Of course, we're honored to have him as a son," replies Stella as she looks intently through the photo album. She stops at a photo of Steve and Lucas. The boys are standing in a tree about ready to jump in the lake below. She laughs and shows it to Lucas.

"Oh, yeah, I never did jump out of that tree; Steve was always a live wire when we were growing up and was never afraid to try new things. I wish I were half as brave as he is," Lucas states affectionately. His thoughts wander to times when he was hanging out with his friend. Stella nods and smiles knowingly.

Arthur takes the last sip of his cold drink and says, "Steve has so much to offer. I will never hold him back from his life dreams even though it's really hard for me. I've had many sleepless nights since he left. I can't help but think of Tom and fear the worst for Steve." Arthur takes a deep breath and runs his hand through his hair. He stands and looks the other way, anguish apparent on his tired looking face.

Lucas looks at his feet, then back at the grieving pair. *How difficult it must be for them to be apart from their only son,* he thinks solemnly.

He stands, makes his way over to Arthur's side, and places his hand firmly on his shoulder. "Mr. Lewis, Steve is like a brother to me. If you need anything, or if I can help in any way, just let me know."

"Steve thinks highly of you also. You were always such a good friend to him, especially growing up in hard times like we did, living on my father's old farmhouse. You are like a son to us. Please visit any time." He takes Lucas's hand in his. "Thanks for your concern and for coming over. If I hear from Steve, I'll call you."

"Please do. I gotta go now; it's getting late, and my folks will worry about me."

Stella reaches up and wraps her slender arms around his neck. "You're part of our family, and we love it when you stop over. Please come again—and yes, you must get going because I know how it feels for a parent to worry," she replies with tenderness.

"Thanks again for the lemonade and pie. You've always been so kind to me. I'll wait for your call when you get news."

Driving home allows Lucas time to clear his mind and to temper his emotions. His thoughts gradually shift from Stella and Arthur's pain to his lovely angel Isabelle, her smile so bright and soft, caring eyes. His angel lifts his spirit instantly. Suddenly, a thought occurs to him. *How am I going to communicate with her on our date?* He drives by her house, and it comes to him. *I can get Mom to help me with my French,* he thinks.

He walks into the house and sees his parents sitting in the living room sipping tea. Elizabeth gets up and greets her son.

"How was your evening with Mr. and Mrs. Lewis? Is Steve going abroad?" she asks anxiously as John walks toward them and wraps a comforting arm around his wife. They know the answer to that question, but Elizabeth's hand wringing and hopeful stare beg Lucas to tell her otherwise.

Lucas bends down and gives his mom a kiss on the cheek. "Yes, Steve *is* going abroad; he's leaving next week to do practice runs. Clearly, his parents are feeling very emotional. Did you know Mr. Lewis had a brother who died in the war? Steve never mentioned him to me except once in passing. And even then, he only told me about Tom's service, not his death." He trails off as they walk back to the living room. "I feel so sad for Steve's parents. Thankfully, Steve is a strong man, so I have no doubt he'll be a great asset to the Air Force. He's also helping his parents financially; he's such a generous and caring guy, so I'm not surprised he would do that."

John nods his head in agreement. "He' s a smart and determined one. He'll be okay and back in no time for a visit, I'm sure," John says, noting the worried look on his son's face and doing his best to reassure him.

Lucas smiles at his parents and tells them about what else happened to him on the way to Steve's parents' place.

"I finally got to see Isabelle again, and we talked, well, with the help of her sister France, that is. We're going to Mama Jean's diner on Saturday. Mom, can you help me learn some French words before I go? Isabelle hardly speaks any English," he asks with excitement.

"That's great, Lucas!" says Elizabeth. "Of course, I'll help you with your French."

John chuckles and gently teases his son. "Well, this should be fun."

CHAPTER 5

For the rest of the week, Lucas is preoccupied thinking about his date with Isabelle. Lucas tries to learn a few French words; he practices his French daily while he works, and then he rehearses in the evening with his mom.

Saturday is unbearably long; he's nervous yet excited about his dinner plans. He finally finishes his chores and heads to the house. Lucas takes a peek at his car, making sure everything is okay; he took the extra time to wash and shine his Studebaker the night before. James walks up to Lucas and wishes him the best on his big date; then he heads home to his family.

After his shower, Lucas carefully shaves and combs his hair neatly. He goes through his wardrobe and chooses a pair of nice jeans and his best plaid shirt and cowboy boots. He goes downstairs and his mother beams at him. She straightens his collar, kisses him on the cheek and gives him a hug.

"Do I look all right?" he asks.

"You look very handsome," she says as she brushes his hair with her fingers.

Lucas kisses her on the forehead. He hopes Isabelle thinks the same. "Thanks, Mom," he says quickly and grabs his keys from the hook by the door.

John arrives just in time to see Lucas off. He greets his wife as he normally does, with a kiss and a hug. "Sorry I'm late honey. Lucas, you look grand. Have fun tonight!" Then he shakes Lucas's hand with one hand and pulls him in for a hug with the other.

Lucas bounds off the porch and thanks them as he waves back. He can't wait a second longer. They watch him leave, standing in the doorway, as if they knew this night would be pivotal in their son's life. Lucas lowers his window and waves back with a big smile. He heads onto the road, turns on the music and tries to calm his nerves about having to communicate in French. Still, he's excited at the thought of just being with Isabelle. She has mesmerized him with her beauty.

Isabelle is sitting on the front porch with France, waiting anxiously. France helped Isabelle get ready for her date by picking out her clothes for the evening with her younger sister and doing her hair. Isabelle doesn't need makeup to look pretty; she is a beautiful young lady. She has long, dark-brown curly hair, a dark complexion, a slim face with high cheekbones and beautiful, big brown eyes. She has a very tiny physique, standing only about five feet two inches tall.

France reassures Isabelle by teaching her a few English words. Isabelle tries hard to speak but becomes frustrated because she wants to be more proficient like her sister. France tells Isabelle to wait a minute. She leaves as Isabelle practices some English words. Within minutes she is back. She tells Isabelle to close her eyes and hold out her arms. France places a book in her hands and tells her to look.

"Wow! Merci," says Isabelle as she looks at the book intently. "This is the book that helped you learn English," she says in French as she glances through the pages. Isabelle notes that it is not a large book.

"You're welcome. You can put it in your purse, in case you need it later," says France in French as she sits beside her sister.

Isabelle and France are going through the book together when Isabelle hears a sound and looks up. She can see a car coming up

39

their long, narrow laneway, and she knows it is Lucas. Isabelle's heart starts racing as she stands up and tells her sister that Lucas has arrived. France gets up and stands beside Isabelle. She reaches around her sister's shoulder and steadies her as they watch Lucas approach the house.

"You'll have a great time. Now, breathe," she coaxes with a little elbow nudge to her side.

Chuckling, they both whisper about how handsome he is as Lucas sits in his bright, shiny car. Lucas sees Isabelle and France standing on the front porch as he parks his car and begins to feel that his mouth is a little dry. He steadies his nerves while he opens the car door. He walks toward the porch, smiling tentatively as he looks at Isabelle. Isabelle smiles back at Lucas.

"Hello, Isabelle; you look very pretty tonight," Lucas says uncertainly in French.

"Good evening, Lucas. Thank you," she responds.

They coyly smile at one another. Enraptured, he almost doesn't see France. He apologizes. "Good evening, France; nice to see you again."

France nods his way. "Nice to see you too, Lucas."

"Are you ready to go?" asks Lucas, with a gentle voice to Isabelle.

"Oui—I mean, *yes*," says Isabelle, trying to speak English. She puts the book in her purse.

"Have a great evening, you two. See you no later than 9 p.m. if you don't want Papa to be mad at you," she reminds Isabelle and winks.

Isabelle hugs her sister and walks with Lucas to the car. Oddly, Lucas hasn't seen her siblings or parents around. He holds the door open for Isabelle and makes his way to the driver's side. He proudly takes in the visual of this beautiful girl in the passenger side of his Studebaker. He smiles at her as he crosses the car, and her insides soften like taffy left in the sun. She watches him get into the car until they make eye contact; then she averts her gaze quickly. Her cheeks flush as they both wave to France.

Silence fills the car for the next few minutes as Lucas maneuvers onto the quiet country road. Isabelle is looking toward the passenger's window, feeling shy. Lucas is entranced by her beauty and trying hesitantly to speak in French.

"Have you been at Mama Jean's diner?" he asks in his broken French.

Isabelle looks toward Lucas and says, "No, but I hear she serve good food." She speaks very slowly in English and does not conjugate her verbs correctly as one might expect for a newbie.

Lucas looks at Isabelle with an astonished expression on his face. Even Isabelle is amazed at the way she is conversing in English.

"Wow, your English is very impressive," says Lucas in a gentle voice. He is relieved that they will be able to communicate.

"Your French is not so bad either," replies Isabelle as she smirks at Lucas and begins to feel more at ease.

Isabelle looks at Lucas; they make eye contact for a few seconds, and they both feel mesmerized. Lucas coughs as he brings his attention back to his driving, and Isabelle gazes toward the dashboard as she blushes. She is becoming fond of him already. Lucas glimpses at Isabelle and feels his heart rushing. He knows his feelings for her are becoming deeper.

As the couple pull into town, they are both silent, just listening to Patsy Cline on the radio. Lucas parks, opens his door and goes around the front to open the door for Isabelle. He holds out his hand to help her. Isabelle reaches for his hand, and when they clasp hands, they feel each other's energy. While Lucas is closing her door, Isabelle stands there looking very pretty. She is dressed in a pink floral cotton dress, with buttons from top to bottom, white lace around the neckline and a white belt that emphasizes her tiny waist. She carries her white purse and white cardigan. Isabelle smiles at Lucas and says, "Thank you."

Lucas smiles in return and replies in French, "Bienvenue," as he puts his hand on the small of her back and guides her toward the restaurant. They both laugh as they walk toward Mama Jean's, enjoying each other's company. Lucas opens the door for Isabelle again as they go into the restaurant, and as she thanks him, their eyes meet, and there is silence for a few seconds. Isabelle feels a deep and pleasurable feeling that she has never been aware of before; it is breathtaking. As for Lucas, his affection for Isabelle is soaring. His heart pulsates rapidly with joy.

Lucas reaches out his arm and directs Isabelle toward a window seat for two. Isabelle walks toward the table, and he follows; he pulls the chair out for her as any good gentleman would do. He waits until she sits down and helps push her chair back in. Isabelle thanks Lucas, and as she looks up, they both smile. Lucas settles himself across from her, takes the menus from the table and offers one to her. The waitress comes over and asks if they want anything to drink. Lucas orders a Coke, and Isabelle nods yes for a Coke also, keeping her head down demurely.

As they wait for their drinks, Lucas peruses the menu and asks Isabelle what she would like to eat. Isabelle flips through the menu but feels unsure of herself and what to order. She has never eaten at a restaurant before but is too embarrassed to tell Lucas. Nonetheless, Lucas observes her body language and senses that Isabelle is uncomfortable. He tells her that Mama Jean's is famous for their hamburgers. This makes Isabelle feel more at ease; she cannot help but smile at him. When the waitress returns with their drinks, Lucas orders for both of them. He orders the Mama Jean's hamburger special: the best burgers in town. Isabelle thanks Lucas for ordering. Lucas holds up his drink and makes a toast; they both laugh as they take a sip of their Cokes.

When the plates arrive, Lucas grins and says, "I'm starving." Isabelle is overwhelmed by the platter but strives to conceal her feelings. She takes pleasure in watching Lucas's face sparkle with satisfaction as he picks up his hamburger. Lucas tells Isabelle how tasty the burger is. She nibbles gently and agrees with him, while she says, "Delicious." They both enjoy their supper, even though the portions are too large for Isabelle, and she can't finish her entire hamburger and fries.

Isabelle enjoys being pampered, and she loves the ambiance that fills the air around her. She is unaccustomed to such treatment as a poor farmer's daughter; her parents would never take her and her siblings out to this kind of restaurant for a meal.

Lucas notices Isabelle's contemplation. "Are you okay, Isabelle?" he asks.

Isabelle comes out of her mood and replies, "I'm fine. I'm taking in the atmosphere of this beautiful place."

Lucas smiles at Isabelle. He has already finished his burger and enjoyed every morsel of the meal, which was only surpassed by the company. Lucas looks around the restaurant. There are a number of couples similar in age to Isabelle and himself. He wonders if any of them are as happy as he is right now. He asks Isabelle if she is ready to go. She nods yes; Lucas gets up and pulls out her chair. He pays the waitress and gives her a generous tip. Then he puts his hand around the small of Isabelle's back and leads her to his Studebaker. He opens the passenger door and helps her in again. Isabelle sits in amazement as she watches Lucas get into his car, and then she thanks him for a wonderful supper. At that moment, Lucas knows he is falling in love with Isabelle.

Lucas starts his Studebaker and heads to Isabelle's home. As he is driving, he asks Isabelle, "Did you enjoy your evening?"

She responds, with a huge smile, "Oui, it was lovely." She thinks how much fun she had and what an achievement it was to speak in English all night, rarely consulting her little book.

Lucas is grateful. He wants to ask her for another date but is afraid that if she says no, he will be terribly disappointed. He looks at Isabelle and knows deep in his heart she is the woman he wants to marry. This has been only their first date, but he has known since early summer, the first time he set eyes on her, that she is the one. Lucas doesn't want to overwhelm Isabelle, but he also doesn't want to lose her. He tries to work up his courage to ask her for another date. Lucas looks at Isabelle the second time around, and she notices him looking back. She turns toward him and smiles. Lucas starts to say the words, but nothing comes out. His heart starts to beat faster.

Isabelle is very quiet; she notices Lucas is struggling with something, but she's not sure what that is. She asks, "What is on your mind, Lucas?"

"Nothing—why do you ask, Isabelle?" replies Lucas in a soft voice as he tries to calm himself.

"I am no sure, but I think I hear you try to say something!" responds Isabelle, looking puzzled.

Lucas changes the subject by asking Isabelle whether she has to work the next day. She tells him that she works every day. As they approach her home, Lucas slows down and turns in, driving slowly up the lane. When he gets there, he stops the engine and looks at Isabelle's beautiful, big brown eyes. He tells her it was a wonderful evening, and he had an excellent time. Isabelle thanks him again; she also says it was a beautiful evening as she reaches to open the door.

Lucas begins to perspire; he knows now is the time to ask again. "Isabelle… Isabelle, do you want to go on another date with me?" he asks, his voice trembling slightly.

Isabelle looks down and then looks at Lucas and replies, "Yes, I like to go back out with you." She lowers her eyes.

Lucas is greatly relieved and gives her a hug. Isabelle hugs him back.

"Next week, at the same time, how about a movie?" asks Lucas as he looks at her with excitement.

"That is great!" replies Isabelle, proud of herself for speaking English and not needing the book much, despite a few mistakes here and there. Isabelle steps out of Lucas's Studebaker and walks toward her door. When she reaches the top porch step, she turns and waves. *He is so handsome*, she thinks in French as she steps into the house, eager to tell France all about their evening.

CHAPTER 6

The beeping of the heart monitor reassures Lucas as he holds his daughter's hand while she lies there motionless. Tears fall from his face; he wipes them away. He repositions himself on the chair and attempts to comfort her, or is it himself who he is trying to comfort? he wonders. He continues to recount his life story in the hope that Lucy will wake up and hear every detail of how he met her mother.

"Your mom was a beautiful woman, and you look exactly like her," Lucas says as he brushes his fingers through Lucy's long, dark-brown hair. "Your mother was so proud of you and your brothers; she used to tell me all the time how lucky she was to have such a wonderful family."

He puts his head down and closes his eyes. His mind is filled with images of his children playing in the front yard and Isabelle on the porch beaming with joy. He catches himself drifting deep in memories and refocuses his attention back on his motionless daughter. He massages her hand and carries on with his story.

Lucas inhales deeply. "I knew on our first date that I was in love with your mom. The question was, would she fall in love with me?" He smiles remembering the uncertainty. His memories of sweet, young Isabelle were as clear as if they had just happened last week. "…and then there was the second date."

Path of Lucas

The week passes slowly, but Saturday finally arrives. Lucas hasn't stopped thinking about Isabelle all week. He rushes his chores, and hurries to get ready for his date. He is home alone as his parents are babysitting for his sister, Mary, since she's not feeling well. The house is quiet. When Lucas is done getting ready, he looks at his watch and notices it is time to go; he rushes off to his car.

He arrives at Isabelle's house and parks in the driveway. The front yard is quiet, and the house appears the same way, he notices. He is puzzled. This is quite unlike earlier in the summer when he dropped off Isabelle and France, and he saw so many kids running about in the front yard. Where are they now? Isabelle runs out and jumps in his car before he has the time to spend any more time thinking about her siblings or to even open the door for her. He chuckles. "Well, hello there! Is everything okay?" She smiles and says, "Yes, I am good," as she settles in his car.

He is still wondering where Isabelle's family is, but he dares not ask in case he sounds too nosy. He puts the car in motion and off to the theater they go.

"Is there any particular movie you'd like to see?" Lucas asks, briefly looking into her beautiful brown eyes before bringing his attention back to the road. She returns his look.

"No, and you?"

"Well, tonight there's a John Wayne movie playing called *Legend of the Lost*. The critics say it's excellent," Lucas says. "Hope you like John Wayne."

"I not know movies much, and I not know who is John Wayne," Isabelle says, in her perfectly charming broken English. "I never been to a movie."

"No? Well, this is great. I get to be the first one to take you," he says with the brightest smile. "You're in for a treat!"

Feeling shy, Isabelle asks, "Who is John Wayne?"

"John Wayne is a good actor, and he's very famous. He plays in cowboys-and-Indians type of movies. I'm sure you've seen him. He does a commercial for Camel cigarettes. Surely, you've seen that, yes?" asks Lucas as he enters the theater parking lot. Isabelle shakes her head. "Well, I hope you enjoy the show. His movies are usually pretty good."

"Oui," says Isabelle, looking down again despite her best intentions. She wants Lucas to know that she likes him and appreciates how much trouble he is going to, to make her comfortable, but she is too shy to convey that.

He helps her out of the car, reaches down and grabs hold of her hand. She looks up at him hesitantly, smiles and holds on to his hand tighter. They cross the road holding hands all the way to the theater. Their joy radiates. Anyone passing by can instantly sense the fondness they have for one another. He buys the tickets at the ticket counter. They step in, and her eyes grow wide as she takes in the sights and smells of the theater. Just like restaurants, her family is not in the habit of taking the kids out to the cinema, so this is quite an experience for Isabelle. The carpet is bright red with gold swirls, and there is red velvet rope next to an usher who is taking tickets. The smell of popcorn fills the air, and she can't help but grin like a kid at Christmas. Lucas buys a large soda and large popcorn to share.

Amused by her fascination, Lucas asks, "You like it here?"

"Oh, yes, it is so great! I am happy," she tells him. With stars in her eyes, she devours everything she sees.

They make their way to the theater where the movie is showing. Then they find a seat at the top, last row, in the middle. Lucas likes to sit up high to watch movies. They sit down just before the show starts. She turns and, with childlike excitement, says, "Thank you, Lucas." Her smile says it all.

"It's my pleasure, Isabelle. Really," replies Lucas, feeling his heart fill with pure joy.

The show begins. Isabelle is in awe. Her eyes are glued to the screen. She is sitting on the edge of her seat, and her hand reaches in and out of the popcorn box. Lucas need not have worried about whether or not she was going to like John Wayne. She is captivated. He can't help but sneak glances her way throughout the movie. He clearly adores everything about her; her presence simply reinforces his fondness for her.

Once the movie ends, he leads Isabelle out of the theater. On the sidewalk, with the fresh night breeze in the air, people are pouring out of the theater and talking about the picture, but Lucas only has eyes for Isabelle. He takes both her hands and brings them toward him; they gaze at each other. She can feel her heart beating faster; she is falling in love with this wonderful man who shows her new things and treats her like a princess. *Can this be true love?* she asks herself. She doesn't even try to hold back her emotions or to slow her rapid heartbeat. She wants to feel it all. She looks down for a split second, then back up at Lucas.

Lucas is still attempting to bring her hands toward him. Not wanting the night to end, he flashes his gorgeous smile and asks, "would you like to walk to the diner for a soda pop?"

She grins back at him; she can't help but notice the innocence of his smile. She steadies her emotions enough to speak. She takes a deep breath and gently exhales. "Yes, that would be wonderful." She wishes this night could last forever. She feels so good when she's around Lucas. They walk to the diner holding hands. Her eyes keep gravitating back to his full lips and piercing, white smile. She has never been so joyful as she is at this very moment.

As they enter Mama Jean's diner, Lucas guides Isabelle toward a table for two near the window. It overlooks a small stream with gigantic oak and maple trees, and he asks her if she likes the setting. Isabelle nods yes and looks pleased, as she sits down, and Lucas pushes in her chair. Lucas orders two Cokes and then takes hold of Isabelle's hands and gently kisses them.

"It was such a great night for me. I hope you enjoyed the movie," Lucas says. He releases her hands as the waitress comes and sets their drinks on the table. "Thank you," he responds to the waitress.

"You're welcome," says the waitress, and she glances at the young couple, aware they are falling in love. She walks away feeling content.

There is nothing like watching young romance bloom. Lucas takes his glass, holds it up and makes a toast: "To us!"

Isabelle grabs her glass and toasts with Lucas: "To us!" as she smiles and taps his glass. They each take a sip and gently put their glasses down as they stare into each other's eyes. Lucas reaches out for Isabelle's soft, petite hands as he continues to gaze at her. Isabelle slowly closes her eyes in disbelief at what has occurred in such a short period of time. A few weeks ago, she didn't even know Lucas. She had only seen him once, but now her mind is full of fanciful thoughts about the two of them. As she reopens her eyes, she softly says to Lucas, "Thank you so much for a beautiful evening; you are so kindhearted. Thanks for everything you have done for me, especially your kindness."

Lucas thanks her in return, and their eyes meet again for a moment before Lucas takes another sip of his soda. "Isabelle, I have to admit that I've been amazed by you ever since I first set eyes on you." He kisses her right hand gently. "I want to ask you if you would be my girlfriend. Isabelle, do you want to go out with me?" Lucas shyly smiles as he looks at Isabelle; his stomach has butterflies as he intently waits for her response. Many thoughts go through his mind—what if she doesn't feel the same way? What would his life be like without Isabelle? He hardly knows her, but she has become the center of his world—and he waits anxiously for her reply.

"Lucas," Isabelle begins as she looks into his eyes, and her own eyes start to water, "Yes! Yes! Lucas, I would love to be your girlfriend." She looks at Lucas with true passion. She has never thought that this night would lead from a date to going steady; it is like a dream. Lucas reaches over and kisses Isabelle gently. She feels his warm lips touching hers. Isabelle opens her eyes slowly after the wonderful kiss, and realizes it is true. Lucas wants to be with her. This is Isabelle's first kiss on the lips, and she has never experienced such an exhilarating feeling.

Lucas feels elated; he could not help but kiss Isabelle like that; it felt right. He grins at her broadly after the breathtaking moment.

It felt perfect! Lucas is thinking to himself how he could not resist the kiss and how wonderful it felt.

They look at each other in silence, both overwhelmed by what has just transpired. They are still smiling at each other, both maintaining eye contact. The waitress comes over and asks Lucas if he would like more soda pop. Lucas responds no with a headshake and then says, "No, thanks." The waitress feels happy for the two of them. She hopes they last as a couple. *How romantic*, she thinks. *That looks like true love.*

Lucas asks Isabelle if she is ready to leave. Isabelle nods yes; she is still swept away from his kiss. They get up, and Lucas pays the waitress. As they leave, the waitress thanks Lucas and tells him that they look like a perfect couple. Lucas, proud to be with such a beautiful woman, inside and out, thanks her and escorts Isabelle to the door. They walk hand in hand, smiling at each other, in the direction of the Studebaker. As they get to the vehicle, just before Lucas opens the door for Isabelle, he stops, turns Isabelle toward him and kisses her again. This time it is a passionate kiss, and Isabelle puts her arms around Lucas's neck as Lucas embraces Isabelle around her tiny waist.

He finally opens the door for her, and she gets in, wishing the night didn't have to end. She can feel the love Lucas has for her. *She is incredulous. She is magnificent,* he thinks as he sits next to her in the car. He starts the engine, glances once again at Isabelle, and heads to her place. As he drives, he puts on his radio and then puts his hand on her lap. Isabelle tries to get as close to him as she can while holding onto his big, strong arm. They sit quietly as they drive out of town. It is a perfect moment, one that Lucas will look back on in later years with nostalgia for a time when their love was so pure and blissful.

At her place, Isabelle turns to him and says, "Thank you, Lucas. It was a great evening." He notices that her English is improving each time they meet. She leans forward and gives Lucas a fast kiss on the cheek, hoping that nobody from her family will see, especially her parents. Lucas gently touches her face and gives her a soft kiss on her lips. Isabelle enjoys his kiss but is afraid that a family member will see them.

"I have to hurry. My father will be mad if I take too long," she says sounding worried.

"I understand. See you next Saturday, around five o'clock?" asks Lucas.

"Oui… je veux aller avec toi," replies Isabelle as she opens the car door, ready to rush to the house and not noticing that she is speaking in French. He watches her run up the steps and into the house, and then he slowly leaves. Lucas hates pulling away from Isabelle's house. Every minute with her is a minute that he wants to savor.

Lucas parks his car in the garage and floats into the house. His parents are back, sitting in the living room. Elizabeth is knitting and John is watching television. He tries to sneak to his bedroom, but they catch him and ask about his night. He returns to the living room grinning from ear to ear.

"It was an incredible date; Isabelle and I are going steady," he informs them.

"Wow… Wow!" John says, winking.

"John, stop teasing!" demands Elizabeth as she nudges her husband on the shoulder with her elbow.

"Okay, okay," replies John with a smirk.

"Stop it, both of you," says Lucas. "Mom and Dad, I'm thrilled. I enjoy being with Isabelle," he tells them. "She has a wonderful personality, and I especially love her big, beautiful, brown eyes."

"Sure like to meet this girl," says John.

"Don't be so anxious, John. Lucas will know when the time is right to bring Isabelle over to meet us," responds Elizabeth as she waves good night to her son. She and John are delighted that Lucas is hitting it off so well with Isabelle. Lucas waves back, blows a kiss to his mom and closes his bedroom door gently.

"He looks so happy. I think he's in love," Elizabeth says.

"Yes, he's growing up. I know he will make an excellent husband one day, just like his dad," he chuckles and leans over to kiss Elizabeth.

"Oh, John, you're fishing for compliments, are you?" she laughs and kisses him back.

Lucas lies in bed, staring at the ceiling. He recounts every moment of the night. He is so lucky to have found such a beautiful, sweet woman. He listens to his mom and dad joking around, just enjoying each other's company. He hopes to have that kind of marriage one day … maybe with Isabelle? He wishes. He wears a permanent smile as he thinks back to his perfect evening with her. He is grateful to be happy and in love and that it seems to be reciprocated.

Lucas settles into bed to have a restful sleep because he has to get up early. Life as a farmer's son means that he has to dedicate his time to the farm. Lucas tries to sleep, but thoughts of Isabelle dominate his mind.

CHAPTER 7

Lucas and Isabelle have been courting for several months when he introduces her to his family. Lucas's family adores Isabelle, who is now a beautiful seventeen-year-old. She is wonderful with Donna and Scott, James's two children who have developmental disabilities. However, Isabelle is not ready to have Lucas visit her parents. Lucas wants to get to know her family, but Isabelle keeps finding excuses when he probes for a time to meet them; she doesn't want Lucas to come into her home. Lucas tries to figure out why Isabelle doesn't want him to meet her family, especially her parents. He is mystified.

Winter is over, new spring days arrive, and Lucas picks up Isabelle at her house. As usual, Isabelle rushes to the vehicle. This time she is agitated and appears frightened by something. Lucas looks at Isabelle with concern and asks, "What's the matter, Isabelle?"

"Nothing! It is nothing… Just a bad day," replies Isabelle. "Please, can we just leave!" she pleads, tears running down her cheeks.

Lucas slowly leaves her place, with hundreds of questions going through his mind. Isabelle just sits there as she wipes her tears. Lucas drives to their favorite place, a campground called Loch Garry Park. This is where Lucas goes swimming with his family and friends. It is not far from his parents' place. The park is empty because it is early spring. Lucas stops the car and turns toward Isabelle, who is visibly shaken.

Lucas anxiously demands, "Please, Isabelle! Tell me what's happening."

"Lucas, don't worry. Everything will be fine now that you are here with me." Isabelle tries to smile, but all she can do is cry.

When Lucas holds Isabelle, he can feel her shaking intensely. "Isabelle, please tell me what's wrong."

"No! I can't; it's too hard to talk about." She pauses. "It's complicated," replies Isabelle, feeling better now that she is in Lucas's arms.

Lucas tries to figure out what is happening in Isabelle's family. Why does she continually find excuses for him not to meet her parents? "Isabelle, is it your parents—is there something wrong?" asks Lucas.

"What makes you think that?" Isabelle replies, looking offended.

"Just everything that's happening: you not inviting me into your home, the way you reacted coming out of your house," responds Lucas. "I've only seen France a few times, and that's it."

"France has gone back to Quebec City with my grand-mere. She left before Christmas. Sorry I did not tell you, but I thought it not important to you. She no like country life and want to go back to Quebec City. France is ambitious; she always say that once she turns eighteen, she will leave this place. She turn eighteen last October and leave the farm. Lucas, I miss France a great deal, but I respect her wishes. I no know when I see her again," Isabelle says sadly. Lucas feels her pain. She must miss her sister a great deal, but he still thinks that she is hiding something about her parents.

"Is this the reason you feel this way, not letting me in your family because your sister is gone—or are you ashamed of me?" He is starting to lose his patience because he doesn't understand the situation and can't figure out why Isabelle is miserable.

"No! Lucas, it's not because my sister left for Quebec City and definitely not because of you. I am not ashamed of you, Lucas. I love you! Lucas, you got to believe me," Isabelle responds, upset, as she tries to hug him, but Lucas doesn't embrace her back. He is frustrated because Isabelle is not opening up to him. She is holding something back, and he fears that something is important and that he should know because he could help her with it. Also, how can their relationship progress if he doesn't meet her parents?

"Isabelle, one more time, tell me: what is going on? Why do you always try to hide your family from me? Is it because they don't like me?" Lucas feels his temper starting to rise. "If you don't tell me, there isn't any reason for us to be together," he says, becoming increasingly frustrated over the situation and the pain it is causing Isabelle and, consequently, him.

Isabelle looks at Lucas in surprise. "What did you just say?"

"Sorry, Isabelle, but you have to talk to me about your family and why you don't want to introduce them to me." Lucas lowers his voice; it isn't like him to lose his temper. "The way you looked when you came into the car… you were scared, yet you wouldn't talk to me about your feelings. What do you expect me to think?"

Isabelle puts her head down. She becomes silent as Lucas's words repeat in her mind: "If you don't tell me, there isn't any reason for us to be together." She loves Lucas so much, and the thought of losing him makes her feel numb inside. As tears start to flow, she tries to stop crying so Lucas won't notice. She remains quiet as she looks around at the beautiful trees and starts thinking how this situation is tearing them apart.

"Listen, Isabelle. I love you, but there is one thing about a relationship that I truly believe: couples need to be honest with each other. We cannot go on this way. We both enjoy each other's company, but if we want to be strong and grow together, we need to be straightforward. Even if it hurts inside, you have to talk to me so we can resolve the problem," Lucas says, trying to gain control and make sense of the confusion.

Isabelle is still in shock over Lucas's words and is feeling completely lost.

"Isabelle, have you listened to anything I said?" Lucas looks at her but still receives no response. Lucas gets out of the car for some air; he feels as if his world is falling apart. Lucas has never felt this way before. Everything had been so perfect with them up until now, but the situation with her parents is important to him and obviously is making her unhappy. Something is wrong in that household. What could it be? There is so much emotion running through him that he just wants to walk away from this entire dilemma. As he turns around, he catches a glimpse of the very fragile young woman. So many thoughts run through his mind about what kind of family she has; their problems must be very serious. He wants to get away from this situation entirely, but something holds him back.

Lucas gets back in his car, where he stares at Isabelle for several minutes. "Isabelle, I want to understand your agony, but you don't want to talk to me. Is it that bad?" Lucas makes an effort to speak in a low voice.

"Lucas, I wish it was that simple. I no have wonderful, loving family like you do. I live totally different life compared to yours." Isabelle desperately tries to make Lucas understand her family. "I know is very hard for you to understand this. To start, we are very poor. I have to work hard on the farm, and I just start to work for Mr. Thomas, doing housecleaning to help buy food for my brothers and sisters."

"There's nothing wrong with being poor," says Lucas. "Debra was very poor when she married James. My family doesn't judge people's income, and neither do I; don't be ashamed." Lucas clutches Isabelle's hands. "That's not a reason to prevent me from meeting your family; I don't care if you're poor. I love you, Isabelle, and I want you to believe in me. Let's go meet your family today!"

"No! No, Lucas!" Isabelle shouts, and she starts to panic.

"Why?" Lucas asks, shock written all over his face.

Isabelle tries to find an excuse. "We can't. My parents may have gone to town."

Lucas raises his voice. "Stop making excuses, Isabelle. This time I'm going to meet your family, and I'll wait until they arrive if I have to."

Isabelle starts to cry uncontrollably.

"Isabelle, we need to do this; it's not that hard. You need to trust me; it doesn't bother me if your family is poor," Lucas says in an effort to reassure Isabelle.

"You no understand! My family is no like yours," Isabelle shouts at Lucas as she continues to cry.

"Isabelle, that's enough! Don't yell at me." Lucas is getting upset. "Maybe I don't understand, but someday I will have to meet your family if you want us to continue our relationship," Lucas explains as his temper rises. He still doesn't understand her reluctance, but doesn't know how else to get Isabelle to open up about the situation.

"Lucas, can we stop talking about this?" Isabelle jumps out of the vehicle, but feels she has nowhere to run. She starts running toward the trees and into the forest, crying. She feels so much pain, so much torment, thinking of her childhood and her future. *How can I hide my horrendous life from Lucas?* she thinks as she runs faster, still ruminating about her past. Things are too painful to talk about; and she feels that by talking about the situation, she would disrespect her parents. Isabelle keeps thinking about her family as she continues to run. Her heart pumps faster as she gasps for air; she's starting to run out of breath. She stops, throws herself down on the ground near a tall maple tree, and sobs again uncontrollably. Her past is so painful that even she can't bear it.

"Isabelle! Isabelle!" Lucas yells at the top of his lungs. "Isabelle! Where are you, Isabelle?" he continues to shout. Lucas searches between trees; she is nowhere to be found. Lucas stops, as he is getting tired. He is bent in two, clutching his stomach and trying to catch his breath, he hears sobbing sounds toward his left. Lucas stands up straight and listens intensely. He hears the sounds again and slowly walks toward them. He sees Isabelle with her head down in her arms, sitting by a tree. Lucas is happy to find her but disturbed to see her so unhappy; he gradually walks in her direction. As he reaches for her, Isabelle looks up and sees him. She swiftly gets up and tries to run, but Lucas instantly grabs her arm and holds her close. Isabelle makes every effort to fight back but has no energy.

"Let me go!" she screams at the top of her lungs.

"Stop fighting, and I'll let go," Lucas replies, desperately.

Isabelle calms down, and Lucas keeps his promise. Isabelle puts her head down in shame, so as to hide her tears. Lucas is silent for a few minutes, and then he puts his arms around Isabelle's small waist.

"Isabelle, I don't want to hurt you. I didn't think that your family issues were that bad. I'm so sorry for what I put you through. I just believe that we should be able to confide in each other," Lucas says softly.

Isabelle stares at Lucas, not knowing what to feel as they make eye contact. She is still in denial about her past. As she thinks of her family, Isabelle pushes away from Lucas. She is overpowered by strong emotions. She looks at Lucas and sees how kind, gentle, thoughtful and considerate he is, but still she doesn't believe she could ever open up to him about her family problems. It would be too embarrassing, too private. And he might leave her if he found out, and she cannot stand the thought of him disappearing at this stage in their relationship. She has grown too attached to Lucas. But what choice does she have? She cannot tell him about the turmoil in her family and the way her parents have treated her. No matter how wonderful he is, he will not understand. No one will understand.

She stumbles for her words. "Lucas, I can't go through this. I just want to go home now." She turns and starts to walk away.

"Isabelle!" says Lucas as he senses that she no longer wants to be part of his life. "Isabelle, I don't have to meet your family if it's too painful for you." He attempts to reassure Isabelle as he walks behind her.

"No, Lucas, is too late. You say before that if we commit to each other, you have to meet my family, and is too hard for me, as you can see. I just want go home and forget this day ever happen," Isabelle explains as she continues to walk.

Path of Lucas

"I'm sorry I brought up the topic! Can we at least talk about us?" Lucas tries hard to gain back Isabelle's affection.

"No!" Isabelle refuses to talk. "Please take me home." Isabelle walks toward the vehicle.

Lucas follows behind; he is speechless. There are no words to utter. Isabelle walks to the passenger side and climbs into the Studebaker. Lucas doesn't even have a chance to open the door for her. He gets in the driver's side, and as he sits down, he takes a quick look toward his sweet but miserable Isabelle. She is staring out the passenger window looking sorrowful. Lucas starts to drive Isabelle back home in total silence that lasts throughout the ride.

When they arrive at her house, Lucas stops his engine, and Isabelle opens her door and walks out without saying another word. Lucas tries to say something, but Isabelle runs away without any explanation or goodbye. Lucas is completely heartbroken and dumbfounded. He does not know what is happening or why Isabelle is hurting so much and why she must keep this terrible secret from him. How bad can it be? What on earth could be happening in her family that she feels that she cannot tell him about? There are so many unanswered questions.

As Lucas drives off, all he can think about is Isabelle. He now believes the relationship is over. Heading home, he stops at a gravel road near an empty lot, puts his arms around the steering wheel, leans his head forward and closes his eyes. Lucas feels that he has lost the love of his life, and the pain is excruciating. He doesn't know where to go from here.

CHAPTER 8

The summer passes, and Lucas doesn't hear a single word from Isabelle. He never gives up; every time he drives by her place he always looks for her. He also thinks that maybe someday he will see her walking back to her house from her father's old farm, but Isabelle is nowhere to be found.

Lucas continues working for his dad on the farm with his brother, but he has changed. Lucas is a man now; he is no longer a young, optimistic, infatuated boy. Life has dealt him a terrible blow. He keeps to himself often as he doesn't want to go places or socialize as much anymore. However, he does go swimming at the lake during the summer. Now that autumn is here, Lucas stays at home more and works the fields with his dad, harvesting the crops. He has withdrawn from society and is very unhappy.

Weeks go by, and John hears that a Mr. Thomas is selling his land. John wants to see the property for himself, and he asks James and Lucas to go with him. They all hop into John's pickup truck and set off just a few miles to their destination.

John stops and parks his truck on the side of the road. They all jump out and look across the road at the land.

"Ken Johnson told me there's about forty acres Mr. Thomas wants to sell," says John.

"Why do you want to buy this land in particular, Dad?" asks James.

"Son, don't you see it is a gravel pit? Lots of money can be made here."

"Why is Mr. Thomas selling land if there is money to be made?" asks James, again.

"Well, Mr. Thomas is getting old and wants to move to the city. He has no need to make money anymore; he's a wealthy man and wants to move near his daughter."

As Lucas listens to their conversation, he remembers Isabelle saying something about Mr. Thomas. *What did Isabelle say about that man?* He searches in his mind. *Mr. Thomas, Mr. Thomas,* Lucas repeats in his mind.

"Lucas! What do you think about this transaction?" asks James.

Lucas is startled, as he is deep in thought. "Sorry, what did you say?"

"Are you okay, Lucas?" inquires John. "You seem so distant."

"I'm all right," he replies. "Yes, the land is vast, and I think a gravel pit would be profitable." Lucas's comeback is quick. "Where does Mr. Thomas live, Dad?" he asks, getting involved in their conversation.

John pauses. He doesn't want to bring up Isabelle's name for fear of causing Lucas additional pain. But he was asked a direct question, and he must answer. "Not too far from Isabelle's dad's house, son. He lives two houses away from Mr. Bourgeois," John replies. "Are you both ready to visit Mr. Thomas?"

"Yes!" they both reply.

They all jump back into the truck and head to Mr. Thomas's house.

As John is driving, Lucas suddenly remembers the connection. Isabelle has told him she works for a man named Mr. Thomas. His heart starts to pound as he thinks about their conversation last spring. So many thoughts race through his mind, especially the thought that maybe Isabelle will be there.

John arrives at Mr. Thomas's house and parks the truck near the barn. They all get out. Lucas's heart is still racing as they approach the barnyard. There is no one around as John yells Mr. Thomas's name. "Let's go to the house and hope he's home." They knock at the door, and it opens.

"Yes, can I help you?" A young woman answers the door, but it is not Isabelle.

"Hi, Mademoiselle. My name is Mr. Clarkson," says John as he shakes her hand. "These are my sons, James and Lucas. We're looking for Mr. Thomas."

"Come on in. I'm Mr. Thomas's granddaughter, Julia. I'll get him for you," she says, and she lets them in.

"Thank you, Julia," says John with a grin as they walk in.

Mr. Thomas appears; he is a fragile, old man but has a swift mind. He is nearly ninety years old. "Good day. What can I do for you, sir?" he asks.

"Good day, sir. My name is Mr. Clarkson, John Clarkson, and these are my sons, James and Lucas," replies John as they all shake hands. "We're here to see about the land you have for sale."

"Yes, yes, I'm selling forty acres just down the road, and soon I will sell this house. I want to move to the city with my daughter," Mr. Thomas replies.

John and Mr. Thomas converse about the price, and they make a deal in less than an hour. John shakes Mr. Thomas's hand and tells him he will get his lawyer to prepare the documents and bring them back to him to sign as soon as possible with the check. The deal is completed, and Mr. Thomas is very happy as they all get up and walk toward the door.

"Thank you kindly, Mr. Clarkson," says Mr. Thomas as he shakes their hands one more time. He opens the door for them and then waves goodbye.

"Let's go to town to see my lawyer," says John. "It will only take a few minutes. Then we can go for a coffee at Mama Jean's diner."

James and Lucas both nod yes, but Lucas is quiet. He was so hoping to have seen Isabelle at the house.

As John sees his lawyer, Mr. Douglass, he instructs his sons to go to the diner and wait for him there. James walks in first. They sit down, and the waitress comes for their order.

"Good day, fellas. Can I get you something to eat?" She is a friendly, middle-age woman with pale brown hair and glasses.

"No, thanks. Just coffee, please," says James.

"Just coffee for me also," says Lucas as he looks around at the other patrons. The shop is pretty quiet at the moment except for a few men enjoying their meals.

The waitress looks at Lucas, and she asks, "are you the one that used to come here with the pretty young lady?"

"Yes," replies Lucas.

"We don't see you or her very often anymore; you both looked so in love," the waitress says.

"We were," Lucas says in a sad voice, and he puts his head down.

The waitress notices that this is a touchy subject, and she apologizes for causing him such obvious pain.

"No harm done," says Lucas, but he starts to remember all the fun times here at the diner and the special place where he and Isabelle sat together. He looks at the crew-cutted man to his left and watches him put catchup on his hamburger. He is obviously enjoying the food, and this reminds Lucas of Isabelle trying her first burger at Mama Jean's.

The waitress comes back with their coffee. "I am so sorry," she apologizes again.

"It's okay," Lucas tries to reassure her.

As the waitress leaves, they both take sips of their coffee. James looks at Lucas and sees the anguish on his face.

"Lucas, are you really okay. Seriously?" asks James.

"No, but what else can I do?" says Lucas, feeling defeated.

"Is it possible to just go see her?" James questions.

Path of Lucas

"No! Let's drop the subject, all right?" Understandably, Lucas is sensitive about the topic.

"You're right. Sorry." James pats Lucas on the shoulder, and they each take another sip of the strong brew. Not long after, John walks in and orders coffee with cream and two sugars. As they all sit around the table drinking their beverages, John tells them the deal is done. The only problem is that the documents won't be finished until Friday morning.

"What's wrong with that, Dad?" inquires James.

"I won't be here on Friday. I have to leave early with your mom to see Aunt Sarah at the General Hospital in Cornwall and visit Aunt Rita. I promised your mother," John explains to James. "You can't go either because you and Debra need to go with Donna and Scott to their doctor in the morning."

"That's okay, Dad. I'll get the documents and bring them to Mr. Thomas for you. It'll all be good," says Lucas, taking charge of the situation.

"That's great, son, because Mr. Thomas is leaving on Friday night with his granddaughter to go to his daughter's place in the city for a month. He wants the forms signed before then, if possible," John says. He is happy the problem is solved.

Friday morning comes. Lucas is already in the barn, starting to milk the cows. John walks in and asks if everything is all right. He tells his dad to have a great day with Mom and to say hi to his aunts for him. John smiles when he sees that Lucas has everything under control.

"Don't forget to see Mr. Douglass for the documents and bring them to Mr. Thomas with the check I have signed; it's on the kitchen table," says John as he starts to leave. Then he stops and says, "Thank you, Lucas."

"No problem. Love you, Dad," replies Lucas. He has a big day ahead of him, working the farm alone, but Lucas is happy to be of use to his father. It makes him feel good to be helpful. And the task will take his mind off Isabelle.

Lucas finishes his chores and then goes home to wash up. He has to head to town as soon as possible. He grabs the check from the table, gets into his Studebaker and drives off to town. He parks his car and gets the documents from the lawyer's office. As he leaves the office, he looks across the street and ruminates about the good times he had with Isabelle at the theater and Mama Jean's diner. He brushes off his thoughts and heads for his Studebaker. As Lucas drives to Mr. Thomas's house, he is thinking of Isabelle, of her beauty and her gentleness. He was wrong—completing the task for his father did not prevent him from thinking about her. Nothing does.

Lucas arrives at Mr. Thomas's house, picks up all the documents and makes sure he has the check. He gets out of his car and walks toward the house. When he knocks on the door, Mr. Thomas's granddaughter opens it.

"Hi, Lucas," says Julia as she lets him in and closes the door.

"Good morning, Julia. Is Mr. Thomas here?" asks Lucas. He can smell the aroma of dinner cooking. "It smells delightful in here. Are you cooking?"

"No, not me, my grandfather's maid is in the kitchen, cooking up a storm for us to bring to the city tonight. She's wonderful, with great talent when it comes to cooking," replies Julia. "Grandfather loves her food. He will especially miss her scrumptious fried chicken."

Lucas's pulse starts to race, and he feels his blood rushing to his head. He wonders whether the maid is Isabelle. Lucas tries to relax, but the feeling is so strong. His can hardly catch his breath at the thought that Isabelle may be in the next room.

"Is there something wrong, Lucas?" asks Julia. "Looks like you've seen a ghost."

"I'm fine, thanks," Lucas replies as he tries to stay calm and focused.

"Okay, here—have a seat. I hope you' re comfortable. I'll be just a minute. Grandfather is upstairs getting ready for the trip," says Julia as she heads for the foyer, where the staircase is placed.

Lucas sits down and waits for Mr. Thomas to sign the documents, after which he will give him the check. As he waits, he can hear the sounds of dishes clattering in the next room. Lucas listens quietly and wonders if it is indeed Isabelle. He hears footsteps walking toward him, thinking it will be Mr. Thomas. He looks down the hall and, stunned, he sees Isabelle instead. She doesn't notice him, as she is focused on her work. Lucas doesn't know what to do. He wants to reach out and hug her, but he knows it's probably not the best approach at this moment. His thoughts accelerate as he tries to think of ways to talk to her without startling her.

Isabelle starts to walk again, coming toward the sitting room with tea and cookies for Mr. Thomas and his guest, which Julia has requested before going upstairs. Lucas can only stare as he watches her enter the room. Isabelle has her head down as she concentrates on setting the tray on the sofa table. When she looks up to greet Mr. Thomas's guest, a look of disbelief crosses her face when she sees him.

"Hi, Isabelle." He smiles and quickly stands up, feeling extremely nervous as he greets her.

"Lucas! What are you doing here?" Isabelle asks, her beautiful brown eyes wide with surprise.

"I came to do business with Mr. Thomas for my father," Lucas explains in a soft voice.

"You never say you know Mr. Thomas when I tell you last spring that I work for him."

"I didn't know him until last week, when my father bought land from him," Lucas replies. "Look, Isabelle, I forgot you worked here until my father mentioned Mr. Thomas's name, and then it dawned on me. I'm here because my father couldn't come; he had to go with my mother to visit her sister at the hospital. Mr. Thomas wants the deal to be finished before he leaves with his granddaughter."

"Is there something wrong with Mrs. Clarkson's sister?" Isabelle is concerned because she adored Mrs. Clarkson.

Lucas notices a slight improvement in her English, but she is still speaking in present tense much of the time. He pauses. The conversation is so unsettling and unexpected. "Aunt Sarah had a minor operation last Monday, and Mother wanted to visit her," replies Lucas as he walks closer to Isabelle. "Look, Isabelle, I wanted to see you again, but I didn't know how you felt about us. These past months have been nothing but misery for me. Can we talk?" Lucas asks politely.

Isabelle can't help but admire Lucas; she also misses being with him. Still, this is neither the time nor the place to have a serious discussion with him. "I no can talk to you right now. I working," Isabelle replies.

"How about after you finish work? I can pick you up, and we can talk then. I can take you home," suggests Lucas, looking at her tenderly.

"I don't know." Isabelle hesitates for a minute. "Okay… I finish at four. Just for a little while, though, because I have to be home before dark."

"Great! I promise you'll be home before dark sets in," says Lucas as he openly beams with joy.

They hear footsteps coming down from the staircase; it is Mr. Thomas approaching to greet Lucas.

"Good morning, Mr. Thomas," says Lucas.

"Good morning, young lad," replies Mr. Thomas. "I see that you met Isabelle, my wonderful maid."

"Yes, sir," responds Lucas and smiles at Isabelle.

Isabelle smiles and thanks Mr. Thomas as she pours them both a cup of tea and puts cookies out on the coffee table. Mr. Thomas and Lucas sit down. Isabelle excuses herself and goes back to finish her work in the kitchen.

"Where is your father, may I ask?" inquires Mr. Thomas.

"He had to take my mother to see her sister at the hospital, and he will be back too late to meet with you," Lucas explains. "I have all the documents here for you to sign, and I have your check."

"Thank you, son," Mr. Thomas says, and he signs the documents. Julia enters the room, pours tea for herself and sits beside her grandfather. She also thanks Lucas and says to thank his father for buying her grandfather's land.

"Welcome," replies Lucas.

They drink their tea and talk for a while. Mr. Thomas and Lucas eat the delicious chocolate chip cookies Isabella made. Lucas tells Mr. Thomas and Julia that it was nice meeting them, but now he has to leave to finish his work at the farm. They all get up, and escort Lucas to the door. They thank him again for bringing the documents and shake his hand; standing at the door, they wave him off as he sets out for home.

CHAPTER 9

Lucas rushes to finish his chores early enough to have time to prepare and clean up before picking up Isabelle. Nobody is home at the farm, and everything is quiet in the house. Lucas feels very anxious but also excited to see Isabelle again. He tries to keep calm as he goes to the garage to make sure his Studebaker is spotless. He grabs a cloth and buffs the car until he is satisfied with the way it shines. When he looks at his watch, he sees it is time to get Isabelle.

Isabelle is just coming out of the door of her house as Lucas arrives. He stops his car and goes to greet her. He gives her a gentle kiss on the cheek as he says hello.

Isabelle is surprised by the kiss but enjoys the moment. "Hi, Lucas," she replies.

Lucas walks Isabelle to his vehicle and opens the passenger door for her. "Thank you," she murmurs. She is grateful and thrilled to be with him again. She has missed him so much during the summer. Just being in his car again is a dream come true, and Isabelle cherishes the moment and gives Lucas a contented look as he closes the door.

Lucas grins and says," Welcome." He gets in the driver's seat instantly. "Is there any special place you want to go?" He looks at Isabelle eagerly as he asks the question.

Isabelle smiles at him, and their eyes meet as she says, "Your choice, Lucas, as long as I'm home before dark."

"How about going to my place? Everyone is gone, and they won't be back until late," suggests Lucas.

"Are you sure is okay for me to go to your parents' place even if they not there?"

"It will be fine. Based on the few times they've met you, my parents care deeply about you, and it's not too far from here. It would give us a chance to talk privately instead of being out in a restaurant, if that's okay with you. I want you to feel comfortable," Lucas replies as he starts the car.

"I'm okay as long as you are sure your parents won't mind," says Isabelle in a soft voice. She feels wonderful just being near Lucas again.

Lucas heads to his house; they drive away and both look happy, but they are quiet for a short time, just listening to country music on the radio. Lucas knows Isabelle's favorite station and has it on already.

"Isabelle, what will happen to your job when Mr. Thomas leaves for a month?" asks Lucas.

"Mr. Thomas paid me a month in advance for the upkeep of his house, to make sure everything is well kept. Mr. Thomas is a blessing in my life; he is such a kind man, with a big heart. I will miss him when he sells his house and moves to the city."

"He really likes your cooking." Lucas is pleased to be able to pass on this compliment to her.

"How you know that?" exclaims Isabelle.

"He told me. When I brought over the documents, and we had tea together," Lucas says as they arrive at his place.

Lucas stops the Studebaker near the house instead of in the garage.

"Do you want to go in the house or sit outside near the big oak tree?" He knows that Isabelle adores being outside, especially near the oak tree. They have often sat there in the past, and she always seemed so happy. Maybe she will feel more comfortable alone with him outdoors rather than inside, which might feel a bit too intimate for her at this stage in their relationship and given all the tension that has occurred.

"You know that big oak tree is my favorite place, especially on a beautiful day like today," replies Isabelle in her sweet French accent.

They get out of the vehicle, walk over to the oak tree and sit down under it. Lucas asks if she wants anything to drink, but she declines. He often carries soda pop in his car.

"I just want to sit here forever," she says as she looks up at the oak tree and admires the leaves changing colors. The autumn leaves can be spectacular. Isabelle particularly likes the orange and red leaves and the notion that nature is cyclical, much like life. Everything dies and is born again.

Lucas keeps staring at Isabelle, admiring her beauty. He knows she is the only person who could ever make his life complete. Everything about her is perfect in his eyes. The way she loves nature makes him want her even more.

"Isabelle, I'm very sorry for the way I pressured you. I didn't mean to hurt you. I don't need to know your past or your family. I just want to be with you," he explains when he gains the courage to talk about the issue that tore them apart.

She looks at him; it makes her nervous to talk about that day. She would rather put it behind them and never revisit that terrible evening, but it is a hurdle that they must pass together to move forward. "I think hard about the reason I can't talk to you about my problems... It is because I am in denial," Isabelle explains. "As you can tell, I have a terrible childhood. Even to this day, I have a hard time to talk about it."

"You don't have to say any more. I don't want you to have to endure any additional pain for my sake. I'd like you to be my girlfriend again. I enjoy your company, and you're too important to me to go through that again," he says, looking serious. "Isabelle, I love you."

He moves in closer, puts his arms around her and pulls her toward him. Isabelle lets herself lean in toward him. With his hands holding her face, he kisses her passionately, like a long-lost love. Isabelle melts into him, allowing herself to feel the joy from being in his arms again. But then she remembers their dilemma. She suddenly stops and becomes serious.

"Lucas, there are many things I want to tell you about my family," she says.

"You don't have to, Isabelle. I just want you, not your family, and I surely don't want to see you hurt again," he expresses with love, still holding her.

"Lucas, is okay. I want to confront my demons. I want to tell you!" Isabelle is very committed and strong, and she is finally ready to open up.

"Are you sure?"

"I think about it all summer. I miss being in your arms. I love you, Lucas, and I do not want anything—not even my family—to stand in the way of our future together." Isabelle is determined to make him understand her.

He listens intently to her as he continues to hold her in his arms. Then he says, "I am here for you, if you want to talk about your past." He is surprised to see her strength and determination.

Isabelle repositions herself as she tries to get comfortable; he keeps his arms around her as if he never wants to let her go. She snuggles into him; his arm cradles her small frame. Her legs outstretched and crossed at the ankles, she stares at her feet, mustering up the courage to say what she must.

"I no know where to begin; is so much to reveal." She sits quietly for a few seconds as she composes her thoughts.

"You don't have to do this, Isabelle, if it's too difficult for you," Lucas says while he runs his fingers through her long, gorgeous hair and tries to support her.

She turns to him; tears roll down her cheeks. "Just bear with me, Lucas. I have to do this. It will be challenging, but I can do it,"

Isabelle confesses as she goes deep into her thoughts. "When I was small child, I was abuse by both my parents. My father emotionally abused me since the age of seven, and my mother physically abuse me right up till last spring." Isabelle begins to cry uncontrollably. Finally, she has voiced the pain that has built up for so many years.

Lucas just holds her tight and tries to comfort her as best he can. He is shocked. *How could this happen to a beautiful little girl?* he thinks to himself. *What kind of parents are they?* he ponders as he tries to reassure the love of his life that he will take care of her.

"It's okay, Isabelle. I'm here with you. I won't let you go!" he says as he attempts to console her. "Now I understand your reaction last spring. We hadn't known each other well enough for you to tell me. The topic was just too emotionally raw for you to discuss even though you cared about me."

"Please don't hate me or my parents," she begs, blowing her nose.

"I will never hate you; it was never your fault. For your parents, it will be a long process, but we will work through it." He tries not to be hard on her, but he can't lie about how he feels at that moment about her family. How can he ever respect them, let alone learn to love them, if they treated his precious Isabelle so badly?

She sits up beside him and holds both his hands as she continues, "my father was a drunken man. He use to drink so much! That's when the abuse start. But he hasn't abuse me for years now. He also doesn't drink anymore, ever since he get emphysema. He is very sick man today and cannot work much. That's why I work to help buy food for my siblings."

"What about your mother? Does she still hit you?" Lucas is concerned as he strokes her face gently.

"Not for a while. The last time she did that was last spring, when you picked me up, and I was very upset."

"Was that why?" he responds, piecing it together.

Isabelle rests her weary head on his shoulder and takes a deep breath. "It was because I supposed to give them all the money I make working for Mr. Thomas. One day, Julia goes shopping, and she buys lots of new spring clothes. She shows me what she buys. Julia has this beautiful spring jacket, and she knows that I like that jacket. She tells me to try it on, and as I put on the jacket, Mr. Thomas walks in. He looks at me and admires my clothing." Isabelle smiles as she thinks back to how she felt when Mr. Thomas thought the jacket was hers. "Mr. Thomas actually thinks jacket is mine, so Julia is so kind enough to let me buy the jacket from her."

"That's the gorgeous jacket you wore on the last day we saw each other?" questions Lucas as he thinks back to that day.

"Yes, Lucas. I want to wear it for you," replies Isabelle. "That was the day I give mother my pay, and some money is missing. She ask me where is the rest of the money. I politely tell her I purchase a jacket with it, and she suddenly gets very angry and starts to hit me. That is when I run out in your car. I am very upset, and I am scared, Lucas." Isabelle wrings her hands. "Also, on that day, I lose you. That rip me apart more than the beatings."

"I'm extremely sorry, Isabelle," he says as he kisses her cheek and hugs her. "I was torn apart too. You mean so much to me, Isabelle." He kisses her again, passionately. She sinks into his arms; their unquestionable love for one another spills into the fall air, rustling the leaves of the big oak tree above.

"I love you, Isabelle," whispers Lucas.

"I love you, Lucas Clarkson, forever."

"Do you want to still be my girlfriend, Isabelle Bourgeois?"

"Yes! Yes!" she exclaims with tears of joy streaming down her face.

They kiss again and again with so much rapture. Their hearts beat together as one at that moment.

Isabelle stops. "Lucas, everything that I say is between you and me. You don't tell your parents or anyone."

"Yes, I understand. I promise you, Isabelle," he swears. Then he inquires. "Can I ask questions about your abuse?"

"Yes, anything you want to know. I want to feel free from my painful past. I want you to be part of my healing," replies Isabelle as she looks directly into his eyes. She understands the concept of catharsis and knows that she must talk about the demons that have terrorized her with the man she loves in order to try to free herself from that old prison. It won't be easy, but it must be done. She will try.

"Were your other siblings also abused by your parents?" questions Lucas.

Isabelle put her head down. "Yes. My father abuse my older sister, France, but not the young ones, ever." She heaves a sigh. "My mother always beats on either France or me; again, never my younger siblings. We both try to protect them."

"Is that why France moved back to Quebec City?" he asks, holding her tighter.

"That's part of the reason and also because she never liked living in the country," she replies cuddling in closer. "Please do not hate my family. I know at this point, everything seems awful. But they do have good points… believe me, Lucas," she pleads with him.

"Isabelle, I love you, and even though your parents did something dreadful and unacceptable, I will respect your wishes," he replies, pulling her into his arms.

"Thank you," she exhales in relief, and then she kisses him on the cheek.

Lucas looks down at his watch. "Looks like it's time to take you home, like I promised. We don't want it to get dark." He smiles at her as he gets up. Then he extents his hand and helps her up.

They both stand motionless for a few minutes, just staring into each other's eyes and embracing one another, making up for lost time. She thanks him for not giving up on her. He says that it's a miracle that they met again through Mr. Thomas, and this time he will never let her go. He almost lost her once, and that won't happen again. He reassures her that he is there for her. They walk toward the Studebaker holding hands. As Isabelle gets in, he kisses her again, and then he closes the door. They head back to her place.

CHAPTER 10

A year passes, and Lucas and Isabelle's relationship grows stronger. They continue to be incredibly happy together, and Lucas is extremely impressed by how much her English has improved. He has also picked up a few more French words. Isabelle's eighteenth birthday is coming up; Lucas wants to do something special for her. He plans to buy her an engagement ring, which he has thought long and hard about. He wants her to know how much she means to him. The question is, what kind of ring would Isabelle like?

One morning, Lucas asks his father if he can take the morning off to go to Cornwall. He wants to go to the city to buy a ring for Isabelle. His father agrees to take over the work so that Lucas can go to a jewelry store in the city. Lucas shines his Studebaker and waves to his parents as he heads off to locate the perfect ring.

Lucas arrives in Cornwall and parks his car near Ford's Jewelry. He takes a deep breath before getting out of his vehicle. Lucas wishes to find the perfect ring for the love of his life. He walks across the street and stares at the jewelry store's sign for several minutes before he enters.

"Good morning, young man! What can I do for you this beautiful morning?" asks the owner as he observes the young man's nervousness.

"Hi, sir," Lucas says shyly as he approaches the storeowner. "I would like to purchase an engagement ring for my girlfriend."

"My name is Mr. Ford," the owner says.

"Lucas, sir—Lucas Clarkson, sir." He shakes Mr. Ford's hand, and Mr. Ford notices that Lucas's hand is damp.

"Is there a specific kind you're looking for?"

"I'm not sure. I've been thinking about it, but I have no idea really," Lucas replies.

"Come with me, son, and I'll show you different types of engagement rings," says Mr. Ford. "You can have a seat right here, and we can examine our display."

Lucas looks at all the rings in the showcase and is overwhelmed. Mr. Ford takes all the rings out. Most of them have the wedding set, which makes Lucas even more anxious. He wants the perfect ring. *Which one would Isabelle choose?* he thinks. His stomach lurches, as he glimpses the various selections.

"Is there one that grabs your attention, son?" Mr. Ford asks as he puts all the rings on the glass counter.

"Not sure," he responds, feeling even more confused.

"That's okay; take your time, and tell me which one catches your eye. I have seen many young men struggle over the years, just as you are now," reassures Mr. Ford. "It's perfectly normal. This is a big decision for you, and you want to choose the right ring for your little lady." Mr. Ford has owned his jewelry store for several decades. He has seen this scenario many times before.

Lucas scans through the selection. "They are so beautiful. I don't know which one," he says; he is baffled, but Lucas takes his time and looks at the rings and price tags, making sure to stay within his budget. Then, unexpectedly, one ring captures his eye; it stood out most of all for its elegant simplicity. "This one!" He picks up the ring, gently holds it up and turns it around as he admires the diamond.

"Are you sure that's the ring you'd like?" asks Mr. Ford. "What is her ring size?"

"Yes! Yes! That is the ring I want. She wears a size four," he answers quickly. He had managed to get the size from his mom. She had been showing Isabelle her rings one day and had her try some on. Cleverly, she had taken note that they wore the same size. A four! He hopes Mr. Ford has the exact size.

Mr. Ford checks, and he does have the exact one in the right size. "Right here is a size four," he says.

Lucas is no longer nervous; he has found the perfect ring for his love. He hands back the ring to Mr. Ford and, proudly, he smiles.

"That is definitely the ring; it will look stunning on Isabelle's dainty finger," he says assuredly.

"That is a gorgeous ring," replies Mr. Ford as he puts the others back in the showcase. "A wise choice, young man."

Mr. Ford sets the ring in a beautiful blue velvet box with gold trim. He takes the ring to the cash register, and Lucas follows. He is so happy to have found the perfect ring and to have purchased it. His life is changing for the better since he met Isabelle. He shakes Mr. Ford's hand and thanks him for everything. Mr. Ford smiles and wishes Lucas the best on his upcoming engagement.

He leaves the jewelry store; sitting in his car, he opens the blue velvet box and stares at the stunning diamond ring again. Now that it is away from all the other rings, it looks even more spectacular. He is sure that Isabelle will love it. As he stares at it, he ponders how he shall propose to his love. Friday being Isabelle's eighteenth birthday, he decides that's when he will pop the question. He will take her to Mama Jean's place for supper, to reminisce about their first encounter, and then they will take a stroll in Loch Garry Park where he will propose. It will be a very romantic evening, one that neither one of them will ever forget.

When Friday arrives, Lucas feels nervous all day as he works on the farm. Isabelle is the only thing on his mind. He tries hard to work, but he merely fumbles everything. Noticing the difference in Lucas's behavior, John remembers back to when he proposed to Elizabeth, which brings a smile to his face.

"Lucas, take the rest of the day off," says John.

"Why, Dad?" responds Lucas, looking puzzled.

"Son, you have been fumbling all morning, and you might get hurt," replies John with a wink. "Go home and relax. You clearly have Isabelle on your mind; you have a big evening tonight. I've been in your situation, and I know what you are going through."

"Thanks, Dad!" pronounces Lucas with an immense smile.

He heads home to relax and gets ready for the big event. He walks into the seemingly empty house. He calls for his mom, but she isn't there. Suddenly, he remembers that she has gone to help Debra care for Donna and Scott at the doctor's office. He goes into his room to pick out what to wear for the big night. He goes through his first drawer and comes across the little blue velvet box. He opens the box slowly and admires the ring again. "Wow!" he says with a smile. In his mind, he envisions different ways to propose to Isabelle. Rehearsing and trying to put into words what he will say to her, he becomes nervous again, but at the same time he is excited. He gently places the velvet box on his dresser and continues to search for the right outfit. He wants to look his best for Isabelle because he wants this night to stand out in her mind forever.

He fixes his hair in the mirror, exhales and checks his pocket for the ring. Proceeding toward the door, he reexamines his pocket, assuring himself again that the little blue box with the ring is secure. He gets into his gleaming Studebaker and heads out to Isabelle's parents' house.

When Lucas arrives at the Bourgeois home, he notices Mr. Bourgeois sitting outside on his front porch with his oxygen tank. Lucas thinks, *that's odd. What is Mr. Bourgeois doing sitting on the front porch? He never sits there.* Lucas parks his Studebaker and walks toward Isabelle's father.

"Bonjour, Mr. Bourgeois," says Lucas as he shakes his hand. He is feeling overwhelmed and unsure as to why Mr. Bourgeois is sitting there.

Path of Lucas

"Bonjour, Lucas," replies Mr. Bourgeois as he takes off his oxygen mask. "I have not sat on front porch for years, but today want to sit here." Mr. Bourgeois speaks in broken English. "When you dying, you remember you have so much you take for granted. Now I want to admire nature." Mr. Bourgeois puts his oxygen mask back on.

Lucas forces a smile at Mr. Bourgeois. "It is a beautiful evening and a great time to sit and enjoy the scenery as the sun sets," he responds. He feels very uncomfortable around Mr. Bourgeois because of all the pain he has caused Isabelle in the past. Lucas is still angry at him, and his wife for that matter. How could they have treated his sweet, undeserving daughter so badly? Lucas does not understand. Still, he tries to be polite to the old man because it is not like Lucas to be rude. And it means a great deal to Isabelle for him to at least be civil to her family. He will honor that wish of hers.

Mr. Bourgeois takes off his mask again, and as he is gasping for air, he tells Lucas that Isabelle is in the backyard with her younger siblings. Then he puts the mask back on. Lucas thanks him as he walks down the steps and goes toward the back to see Isabelle. He always feels tense around Isabelle's parents, but he respects them because they are her family.

He walks around the corner, and as he turns toward the back of the house, he hears Isabelle laughing and telling stories to her brothers and sisters in French. Lucas takes a peek, and he sees her sitting on a big rock with her siblings scattered all around her. Her little sister is sitting on her lap listening attentively while the other children are laughing and full of joy. He imagines her, his future wife, playing with their children in the yard. His heart melts. *Isabelle will be a great mom,* he thinks. She often tells him how she loves being around children, and she especially adores Donna and Scott. He knows that children love being around her too. Lucas can't wait to be married and start a family with Isabelle.

He tiptoes behind Isabelle; as he sneaks up, the children notice him, but he smiles at them and puts his index finger up to his

85

mouth as if to say, "Sshh." The children giggle but don't say a word to Isabelle as they watch. He puts his hands over Isabelle's eyes and kisses her softly on the cheek. She is completely startled and puts her hands over his.

"Lucas, is that you?" she exclaims through laughter. Her siblings are laughing even harder as they say, "Yes, yes!"

"Happy Birthday, Isabelle," he says as he kisses her again; then he turns to entertain the children. They all love Lucas.

"You're early," she says, standing up from the rock, still holding her little sister.

"*Allo*, Lucas," says Isabelle's little sister as she cradles herself in Isabelle's arms.

"*Bonjour*, Sylvie," replies Lucas. He reaches out and strokes her cheek gently as the others stand all around them.

"I will just bring the children into the house, and then I will be with you—or do you want to come in with me?" she asks with a smile.

He looks at her with happiness in his eyes and replies, "I'll just go to the car and wait, if you don't mind."

"I don't mind at all," she says as she herds the children to the house. "Say bye to Lucas, children." They say goodbye and follow her in.

"Bye," he responds and waves to them.

He walks to the vehicle, grinning. He is standing beside the passenger door waiting for her when he notices that Mr. Bourgeois is no longer sitting on the front porch. Within minutes, he sees Isabelle walking toward the Studebaker. Lucas kisses her on the cheek and then opens the car door. She thanks him as she gets in, and he closes the door behind her. After Lucas enters the car, they both stare at each other and smile. He wishes her a happy birthday again and reaches over and gives her a gentle kiss.

"Thank you, Lucas," says Isabelle, shyly.

They head out to Alexandria for supper at Mama Jean's restaurant.

"How's your dad doing? I talked to him briefly on the front porch," he says, out of genuine concern for her family.

"He has his good days and bad days," she replies. "He saw his doctor this morning, and Dr. Bourdon said he has only a few years to live because his lungs are damaged, and his emphysema has worsened. Lucas, my dad is not the same man. He looks at life in a more a positive way now; he notices small things he used to not care about, like the blue sky, the wind, the birds and so on. He told me he wants to live and make amends for all the problems and mistakes he's created. To my great surprise, he ask me for my forgiveness four days ago. It tore me apart, but after I forgave him, it felt like a ton of weight lifted off my back. I feel so much better! I know I will never be close to my father, but I do forgive him, and it feels great."

Lucas beams in her direction. "I'm so happy for you, Isabelle." He kisses her hand. "But to tell you the truth, I had a hard time looking your dad in the eye when we talked earlier. I do respect him; he is a human being, but I will never respect his actions."

"I understand, Lucas, and I am very grateful for your understanding. With my crazy life, I value your composure for being able to even talk to my parents. You do not have to love my parents because of what they did, but the fact that you still respect them makes me feel that I don't have to pick sides. After all, they are my family," replies Isabelle. She stares at Lucas with true love in her eyes. She is relieved that he understands her unstable past.

He smiles at her as she reaches over and gives him a kiss on the cheek.

"I love you Isabelle," he whispers with sparks in his eyes.

"I love you so much, Lucas. You are my true love," she replies with the shy gaze that Lucas finds irresistible.

They arrive in town; he parks the car in Mama Jean's parking lot. He reaches over and kisses Isabelle passionately as if they are the only two people in the world. Isabelle suddenly realizes they are in a public place. She becomes self-conscious.

"Lucas, stop! People are watching," she says, laughing.

"We will be the talk of the town." He laughs as he tries to continue kissing her.

"Lucas, let's go. Stop—stop." She pushes him playfully while loving the unbridled attention he gives her.

"I agree, Isabelle—let's go." He gives her one last kiss.

He climbs out of the vehicle, dashes around to the passenger door and opens it for her.

"Thank you," she says with a grin.

"Welcome, my love," he replies as he reaches for her hand. Together they walk to Mama Jean's.

They look so much in love as they walk into the restaurant. Lucas notices the table they sat at on their first date is not occupied; he directs Isabelle to the table and pulls a chair out for her. Sitting there brings back beautiful memories.

"Thanks," she says as she glances at him with love, adoring his good manners.

He looks at her tenderly as he sits down. He reaches to hold her hand; the waitress comes over with menus.

"Good evening, Lucas and Isabelle. What brings you two here tonight?" asks the waitress, whom they have now gotten to know.

"Good evening, Pauline," they both reply in unison.

"It's Isabelle's eighteenth birthday, and we decided to come here for supper because this is where we had our first date. This is the same table we sat at just a little over a year ago," he says proudly.

"Yes, yes, I remember. You both looked shy but adorable, and you," Pauline says to Isabelle, "were carrying a little French translator book with English words in it in your purse that you glanced at occasionally. What a coincidence, sitting in the same place. Wow!" She smiles at them. "You two are meant for each other."

"Thank you, Pauline," responds Isabelle softly.

"You're welcome," replies the waitress. "Do you want something to drink before you order?"

"Yes, I'll have the usual, a Coke, please," says Lucas.

"The same for me, thanks," answers Isabelle.

"Welcome… I'll be back with your drinks in a few minutes." And Pauline disappears into the back of the restaurant to the kitchen to get their drinks.

He puts his hand on Isabelle's; they both smile and gaze into each other's eyes. The waitress comes with their Cokes and takes their order. Lucas orders Mama Jean's special: homemade vegetable soup and a "hot hamburger" with coleslaw. The hot hamburger is made with two slices of bread with a hamburger patty in between and gravy, peas, and fries on the side. Lucas loves this specialty! Isabelle just orders a regular hamburger. They listen to the sweet sound of country music playing in the background and talk as they wait for their meal.

Soon their meals arrive. They enjoy their food silently. Lucas has one thing on his mind—when to propose to her? Isabelle notices that he has become a little quiet and distracted.

"What is it?" she asks with concern.

He smiles as he sees the waitress coming with the cake.

"Sorry, Isabelle, my mind was drifting for a minute," he replies as he watches Pauline coming closer.

All of a sudden, Isabelle hears the song "Happy Birthday" as the waitress brings the cake. Then everyone in the restaurant starts to sing along. Isabelle feels very shy; she turns red as she looks at Lucas, but she is smiling. The waitress puts a beautiful cake on the table, and Isabelle sees it is trimmed in pink, her favorite color, with eighteen candles beautifully set around her name.

"Happy birthday, Isabelle," says the waitress, and everyone in the restaurant sings the Happy Birthday song and wishes Isabelle the best.

"Thank you, Pauline," she replies, and then she nods to thank everyone else.

"Happy birthday, my love," Lucas says. "Make a wish, and blow out your candles."

Isabelle makes a wish as she blows her candles out. He claps his hands and reaches over and kisses her—and everyone claps.

"Did you plan this?" asks Isabelle. She slices the cake and hands one piece to Lucas and serves one for herself on a small plate.

"With a little help," replies Lucas, smiling as he reaches over for his plate. "Thank you, darling."

"You're welcome, Lucas," Isabelle says, grinning, as they both dig into the delicious cake that Mama Jean made.

Lucas starts to think about the ring again and how he wants to ask Isabelle to marry him at Loch Garry. Another thought crosses his mind as he reaches in his pocket to make sure the ring is still there. *Maybe I shouldn't wait for Loch Garry. This seems like the perfect moment to ask.* Lucas glances over at Isabelle as she takes the last bite of her cake. Anxiously, Lucas goes down on one knee beside her chair and pulls out the ring. For a few seconds, Isabelle wonders what on earth he is doing.

"Isabelle, will you marry me?" Lucas says, feeling nervous but proud. So many different emotions are going through him. The diamond glitters as he presents the ring in the pretty little blue velvet box.

Isabelle is totally shocked. *Is this really happening?* she thinks. It takes a minute for her to process the scene. She reaches for Lucas's arm, and tears come to her eyes. "Lucas, yes! Yes!" she exclaims. "I'd love to marry you! Yes, of course." Now Isabelle's tears start to flow as Lucas hugs her.

Lucas puts the ring on Isabelle's ring finger, and they kiss passionately. Every person in the restaurant claps and cheers for them. They're so much in love that everyone can feel the passion in the air. It is a happy evening for all and one that they will remember for a long time.

CHAPTER 11

Lucas and Isabelle plan to get married but don't have a definite date because Isabelle has to help support her family. Lucas is ready to start his life with Isabelle, yet he respects the fact that she loves her siblings and wants to do the right thing by continuing to help them financially and otherwise. This is one of the things that Isabelle adores about Lucas; he has extraordinary respect for others, along with enormous understanding and patience.

Lucas always likes to tease Isabelle and tell her that one of these days he will capture her, take her hostage and bring her to a chapel somewhere out east. He will travel through the countryside with her until they reach Prince Edward Island, where the sand is red, and the fields are a luscious green. The wide ocean washes the sand, and there are beautiful scenic views and picturesque lighthouses. Isabelle laughs and says she would be his confined wife forever. They are so much in love, and Lucas is so content and delighted to be Isabelle's fiancé.

One late summer afternoon, Lucas picks up Isabelle at work and takes her to his parents' place. He surprises Isabelle with a home-cooked meal. When they enter the kitchen, Isabelle is amazed. She smells a delightful aroma filling the air.

"These couple of years I've known you, I never knew you could cook, Lucas," says Isabelle.

"My mother taught me how to cook, especially when there wasn't much work on those blistering winter days," replies Lucas as he pulls out a chair for Isabelle.

"Where are your parents?" asks Isabelle, intrigued, as she sits down.

Lucas is busy preparing the plates and says, "They decided at the last minute to visit my uncle Joe in Toronto for the weekend."

Isabelle enjoys every bite of the meal that Lucas has prepared for her.

"Do you want any dessert? My mother made an apple pie for me this morning," offers Lucas as he brings over the pie and puts it on the table.

"Yes, for sure. I love your mom's baking!"

They each eat a piece of the pie; then Lucas cleans up, and Isabelle helps with the dishes. He can sense how it would feel to be a married couple. Isabelle thinks much the same thing as she happily washes the dishes. She can't believe what a wonderful man Lucas is for her. She is so grateful to have him as a fiancé.

When they finish tidying up the kitchen, Lucas asks Isabelle if she wants to go for a walk in the forest. Lucas knows how Isabelle loves to walk in the woodlands.

"You can also read my mind," says Isabelle with her French accent. She kisses him on the cheek. "Thank you, Lucas, for a delicious supper."

"Welcome, Isabelle," replies Lucas as he reaches over and hugs her tightly and then gives her a kiss. He loves the sound of her accent, and that is enough to awaken his passion for her.

They kiss for several minutes, until Isabelle reminds him about the walk. Lucas stops and agrees with her—they both chuckle. They head outside, holding hands and enjoying the freedom of life. Lucas stops at the barn to check on the animals. Everything is fine there. He gets his dog, Lassie, and they stroll along the open fields before entering the forest. They're holding hands, and Lassie is following behind them, running back and forth and sniffing all the different scents. Lucas grabs a stick and throws it far, and Lassie runs to retrieve the stick. Isabelle enjoys her time with Lucas; she feels protected in his presence. They both derive so much pleasure from the simple things in life: just being together, eating a good meal, and being outdoors.

As they walk around the forest, Lucas runs around the trees and hides. Then Isabelle finds him, with the help of Lassie. Lucas captures Isabelle and kisses her as she tries to run from him. He carves Lucas & Isabelle Forever on a big oak tree. Then they kiss, and he tells her how important she is to him. Isabelle kisses Lucas again and tells him he makes her feel worthy. She has never felt that way before.

The sun is starting to set, so Lucas asks Isabelle if she wants to head back home before it gets too dark. She agrees, and they head back with Lassie. Lucas tells jokes on the way to the farm and makes Isabelle laugh. Soon they arrive home, where he takes Lassie back to the barn; Lucas and Isabelle both kiss Lassie good night.

Lucas asks Isabelle if she wants to go in the house for a glass of lemonade, and she accepts. They sit in the great room with their drinks. Isabelle adores that room; she feels the beauty and love surrounding them there. This is where the family enjoys special occasions and where they gather every Sunday afternoon.

"Lucas, this is my favorite room. I love your mother's décor and the way she has accented the room," says Isabelle as she looks around, adoring every corner of the room.

"Yes, I'm very proud of my mother's work and the way she puts love into everything she touches. My grandfather Duval was an artist. He would paint freehand designs on horse carriages; it's from him that she inherited her great taste for colors and design."

"Incredible!" says Isabelle as she snuggles toward Lucas. They sip their lemonade and cuddle a bit.

"Come with me," says Lucas. "I want to show you a painting my grandfather did for my mother before he died. She gave it to me to put in my room." He gets up and helps Isabelle up. "I also have pictures of my grandfather painting the horse carriages and pictures of my grandmother holding me when I was a baby."

"I love to see your grandfather's art," replies Isabelle with excitement in her voice. She wants to know everything about Lucas and his family, which is so different from hers.

Lucas opens his bedroom door, and as Isabelle enters, she is astonished at the painting.

"Wow! Lucas, your grandfather was an amazing artist." She can't stop staring at the painting. It is a beautiful summer forest scene, with horses pulling a carriage on a trail. In the carriage are a boy and girl in the backseat, and up front, a man is taking the reins, with his wife sitting beside him holding an infant.

"Yes, Mother said he died just before I was born. She wants me to keep this painting. It is an honor, and I promised her that I would always keep it safe," says Lucas as he sits on his bed.

"Lucas, your grandfather put in so much detail—even the dog running behind the carriage. And the family. It looks like your family."

"Grandfather Duval knew that my mother was pregnant with me and did this painting for her a few months before I was born," says Lucas, emotionally.

Isabelle sits beside Lucas. "Your grandfather must have been a wonderful person."

"According to my mother, he was a great man," replies Lucas as he looks at Isabelle. "Do you want to see photos of my mother's family and the art my grandfather painted on horse carriages and town signs?"

"Yes. Your mother certainly has an interesting family," says Isabelle.

Lucas gets up, goes over to the bottom of his dresser and digs up the albums. He returns to sit beside her. She enjoys looking through the albums, and once they are done, Lucas carefully puts them back in his dresser. He sits beside Isabelle.

"Lucas, you are so blessed to have a fantastic family," expresses Isabelle. "Your family has so much to offer and are very kind."

"Thank you, Isabelle. That's very sweet of you to say," says Lucas in a soft voice.

Lucas hugs Isabelle for a few seconds, and then they both stare into each other's eyes. Within minutes, they are kissing. They can't stop kissing; it is like a bolt of energy going through them. Lucas gently puts Isabelle down on the bed and continues kissing her passionately. Isabelle feels only a strong love for Lucas as they carry on. Lucas can't stop himself, and Isabelle doesn't want him to stop. They continue as their passion overcomes them. It is the first time they have gone this far; their love for each other is extremely powerful physically. Soon after that, they both doze off.

Lucas suddenly awakes and sees Isabelle lying by his side; he turns around to his clock and sees it is three o'clock in the morning. He brushes his fingers through his hair in confusion as he turns back and looks at her sleeping peacefully beside him. In a panic, Lucas shakes Isabelle.

"Isabelle! Isabelle!" he whispers. "Isabelle, wake up! Wake up!"

"Mmm... what?" Isabelle says, sounding baffled as she tries to wake up.

"Isabelle, it's three o'clock in the morning! We fell asleep, and we're late! I have to take you home, right now, before your parents wake up," insists Lucas, feeling very anxious.

Isabelle gets up fast as she realizes what has happened. She should have been home before midnight! Lucas also puts on his pants and kisses Isabelle gently on the cheek. Isabelle looks at him with joy, and they take a few minutes to caress each other.

"Will you get into trouble with your mother?" asks Lucas, sounding very worried.

"If we hurry, I can sneak into the house because my parent always sleep until six o'clock in the morning, and their room is upstairs in the far back," replies Isabelle as they continue to hug each other. "Just drop me off at the end of the laneway. I will walk up to the house and creep in from the front door because it is near my room."

"Isabelle, I hope everything will be okay with your family because I know how upset your mother can be," Lucas says, in a very frightened voice. "I love you, Isabelle, and I don't want anything bad to happen to you on my account."

"It will be fine, Lucas. Don't worry about me; I can handle my mother nowadays. Let's leave now, and I will sneak softly in the front door to my bedroom," says Isabelle with confidence as she continues to embrace Lucas. "I love you, Lucas." As Isabelle puts on her dress, she is glowing with joy as she recalls the wonderful night.

Lucas kisses Isabelle. "You are such a tremendous person, and I want to spend the rest of my life with you," he says softly, while he grabs his shirt.

They hurry to the car. As always, Lucas opens the passenger door for Isabelle, closes it after her and then runs to the driver's side and accelerates away. Lucas holds on to Isabelle's hand as he drives. Isabelle does not stop glowing. She knows in her heart that Lucas is a terrific guy, and she wants so much to start her life with him. Lucas looks at Isabelle with a tender smile. He adores her and is proud to have her by his side.

Lucas soon arrives at Isabelle's parents' house; he stops at the end of the driveway so Isabelle's parents do not hear the engine. He parks his vehicle and hugs and kisses Isabelle.

"I love you, Isabelle," says Lucas. "Thank you for such a marvelous evening." He can't stop hugging her.

"I love you, Lucas, because you are so gentle and kind," replies Isabelle. "But I must go before my parents hear me come in." She opens the car door and smiles at him. "Bye, Lucas."

"Bye, Isabelle. I'll see you later—around six o'clock, for supper," responds Lucas as he watches her leave.

"Yes. I can't wait." Isabelle closes the door and blows Lucas a kiss.

Lucas watches Isabelle run up her laneway and enter the house. She waves goodbye and blows him a kiss as she goes in. Lucas slowly leaves and drives back to his place. He thinks of Isabelle and the amazing evening they had together. She said yes! Isabelle is going to be his wife. He is beside himself with joy. What a life they will have.

Saturday morning, Lucas heads out to the barn thinking only of Isabelle. He is counting the hours until the evening arrives. Lucas meets James.

"Good morning, James," says Lucas. He is still glowing.

"Good morning, little brother," replies James. He smiles at Lucas, seeing the glitter in his eyes. "You seem so cheerful this morning."

Lucas laughs. "I am," he responds. "Isabelle and I had a fantastic evening last night, and she enjoyed my cooking. She's coming back tonight, and she will cook my favorite meat, sirloin steak."

"We better hurry then and get the work done so you can have an early start to your night," says James. Then he pats Lucas on the shoulder.

The evening arrives. Lucas picks up Isabelle at her parents' house, where he greets her parents and takes the time to play with her siblings as Isabelle finishes her duties.

"Ready to go," says Isabelle finally.

Lucas says bye to her family as they depart and head toward the Studebaker. Lucas looks at Isabelle with admiration and kisses her on the cheek as she enters the vehicle and they settle in. Isabelle is feeling confident that she is a great cook because her grandmother taught her French cooking from Quebec.

"How were your parents? Did they hear you come in last night?" asks Lucas, nervously.

"Everything was incredible. My parents didn't hear me come in, and everything went as normal for a Saturday morning," replies Isabelle.

"Great! I feel much better now," says Lucas with a sign of ease. "I don't want your parents to think badly of me. Now, I can't wait to eat. After a big day, I'm very hungry."

With a smirk, Isabelle responds, "It may take a while before you eat."

Lucas is still laughing as they arrive at his parents' place. Isabelle proceeds to the kitchen to start supper. Lucas helps her find all the things she will need to cook her specialty: tender sirloin steak with caramelized onions and fried mushrooms, baked potatoes with sour cream and chives, glazed carrots, and cream puffs for dessert.

"Do you have everything you need?" asks Lucas, nuzzling her neck.

"Lucas, I need to concentrate on the cooking or we will not have supper," replies Isabelle as she kisses him.

"You can be my dessert," Lucas whispers in Isabelle's ear.

"Yes!" exclaims Isabelle as Lucas gives her a passionate kiss.

Isabelle can't resist him, and they continue to kiss. Lucas lifts up Isabelle and takes her to his room. He lays her on the bed gently and continues to kiss her. Isabelle feels his gentle hand on her body.

"Lucas, I promised you supper tonight," says Isabelle. She is cherishing his tenderness.

"Eventually, we will get there," whispers Lucas, and then he nibbles on her ear.

Isabelle smiles as she kisses Lucas. "I love you, Lucas."

"I love you, Isabelle; I have from the first day I set eyes on you." Lucas continues to touch Isabelle softly, and then he gently brushes his hand across her face. Their passion and love are unstoppable.

CHAPTER 12

At the General Hospital, Lucas is still sitting in the chair by Lucy's side, holding her hand. Lucas massages Lucy's arm, and then he puts his head down. He lifts it back up to stare at Lucy. She is still motionless. He stands up and walks around the room because he is feeling some discomfort in his chest. A nurse walks into the room to monitor Lucy's intravenous line and check her heart rate. Lucas sits down beside his daughter. He smiles and thanks the nurse, and then he takes hold of Lucy's hand.

"Lucy, it was an amazing weekend. Your mom and I were deeply in love, and we wanted to be together. Unfortunately, your mother was dedicated to her family, which I totally respected, so it took some time before we could get married. She was wonderful with her siblings, and that gave me confidence that she would be a great mother to my children one day," says Lucas. "But not that soon," he says, and he chuckles as he continues his story.

A few months pass, and Isabelle starts to feel ill. Every morning, she wakes up nauseous and vomiting. She cannot look at food; it makes her gag. This is not like Isabelle. She doesn't want to tell anyone, not even Lucas, about her morning sickness. Isabelle is in a panic. She has no one to talk to—especially not her mother. Isabelle feels scared and alone.

Then, one morning, she is walking to Mr. and Mrs. Smith's house to work; it's two houses away from Mr. Thomas's old house. Mr. Smith was Mr. Thomas's cousin, and he hired Isabelle after Mr. Thomas moved away. Julia is driving by and, seeing Isabelle walking, stops to offer her a ride. Isabelle is very happy because it has been over a year since she has seen Julia.

"Hi, Isabelle! So nice to see you," says Julia. "You must be going to work this early in the morning."

"Yes, how did you guess?" Isabelle says flashing a big smile at her friend.

"Hop in, my dear friend." Julia pats the passenger seat.

"Thank you, Julia," says Isabelle as she gets into the car. "What brings you down this way?"

"I've come to pick up my grandfather's cousin, to bring him to Ottawa to visit with Grandpa for a few days," says Julia with excitement. "Uncle Victor and Grandpa will be celebrating their ninetieth birthdays; they were born just two days apart. I'm planning a special party for both, but they don't know yet. It will be fun!" Julia was laughing.

"Yes, Mrs. Smith mentioned they were leaving for a few days. How is Mr. Thomas doing?" asks Isabelle.

"Grandpa is doing great—but you, Isabelle, you look very pale. Are you ill?" Julia looks at Isabelle with genuine concern.

"I'm doing okay," replies Isabelle. "I'm just tired lately."

"Sorry to say, Isabelle, but you look beyond tired; you look drained and dehydrated," explains Julia. "Do you need to go to the doctor's? I can take you there."

"No! No! I'm fine," says Isabelle, but then she starts to cry uncontrollably.

"What's the matter, Isabelle? Is something wrong?" asks Julia, extremely concerned for her friend's wellbeing.

"Julia, I think I'm pregnant, and I'm too afraid to go see Dr. Bourdon in Alexandria. My father is always there because of his emphysema."

"Isabelle, does Lucas know about this?" asks Julia, shocked by what she's heard.

"I haven't told anyone but you," replies Isabelle; she is still weeping. "I don't know for sure, but every morning I get sick, and I can't stand the look of food. I missed last month's cycle, and I'm always regular."

"I have a few hours to spare. I can take you to see my grandfather's old doctor in Alexandria. His name is Dr. Bates; he is a very caring doctor. I used to see him when I was a little girl. I'll tell my aunt that you're not feeling well, and I have to take you to see the doctor," says Julia.

"Julia, I'm so afraid. I don't know if I should go see the doctor. What if Mrs. Smith asks questions about my health?" responds Isabelle with fear in her voice.

"Isabelle, you have no choice; you have to see a doctor. My aunt is a very understanding person, and she loves you like a daughter. She never had children, and she always tells me how wonderful you are. She loves your personality. You are lucky that I drove by and picked you up so I can take you and help you through this. Isabelle, I'm here for you, and I'll support you because you're like a little sister to me," says Julia as she drives into her aunt and uncle's driveway.

"Julia, I'm so afraid," cries Isabelle, trying to wipe her eyes.

Julia looks at Isabelle. "I understand your fear, Isabelle; that's why I want to help you. I don't want you to go through this alone," she explains as they arrive at Mr. and Mrs. Smith's house.

Julia parks the automobile and tells Isabelle to wait for her in the car. When Julia leaves, Isabelle puts her head down and cries. The pain of fear just bolts through Isabelle as she thinks about Lucas and how he will react to the news that she is pregnant. Most of all, she is worried about her parents, especially her mother. This will mean shame and embarrassment to both parents and Lucas's parents as well. Isabelle feels she let everyone down, starting with Lucas, and moving on to his family and her family. She holds her stomach and weeps.

Julia comes back to the vehicle, sits down, and sees Isabelle with her head down, crying. She reaches over and hugs Isabelle. She tells her that everything will be okay, and she will help support her in any way possible. Isabelle thanks Julia as they continue to embrace. Julia informs Isabelle that she has called the doctor's office, and that he will see her now. Also, Mrs. Smith has told Julia to tell Isabelle to take the day off and come back to work on Monday because they will be gone for the weekend.

Julia starts her engine and heads for Alexandria. When they arrive, Isabelle's heart starts to beat rapidly. She gets out of the vehicle, takes a deep breath, and wipes her tears. Julia walks in with Isabelle, and Isabelle takes a seat to wait her turn. Julia then walks to the secretary and announces the appointment with Dr. Bates for Isabelle Bourgeois. The secretary nods and tells Julia to go to room 2 with Isabelle, and Dr. Bates will be there shortly. They both walk toward the room. Julia opens the door and tells Isabelle to go in and sit down; Dr. Bates will be in shortly, according to the secretary.

"Can you come in with me? I'm really scared right now. Please!" begs Isabelle.

"Are you sure you want me with you in the room?" questions Julia.

"Yes, I definitely need you to be there with me. I can't do this alone."

"No problem. I will stay with you, my friend."

"Thank you so much for everything; you are my angel," replies Isabelle as she gives Julia a huge hug.

They both sit down to wait for Dr. Bates. It is the longest five minutes in Isabelle's life; so many thoughts race through her mind. Julia takes hold of Isabelle's hand; she can see her friend trembling. Isabelle keeps staring at the door and waiting restlessly for the doctor.

Slowly the door opens. Isabelle's heart starts pounding, and her hands begin to sweat as she sees the doctor walk into the room.

"Good morning. My name is Dr. Andrew Bates," says the doctor.

"Hi, Dr. Bates," replies Isabelle, looking very shy.

"Hi, Julia. Nice to see you here again," says Dr. Bates as he shakes Julia's hand.

"Nice to see you too, Dr. Bates," replies Julia.

"Well then, Isabelle, what can I do for you?" asks Dr. Bates.

"Dr. Bates, I think I'm pregnant," says Isabelle in a very low voice. She feels vulnerable and humiliated about her disclosure.

"Do you have any signs of being pregnant, such as feeling tired, sick to your stomach in the mornings, vomiting, or missing your monthly cycle?" asks Dr. Bates very gently. Noticing Isabelle's embarrassment, he tries to make her more comfortable.

"Yes, I have all those symptoms," replies Isabelle as she struggles for her words.

"I will need you to take a urine test, and my secretary will call you in a few days to come back to get your results," says Dr. Bates as he hands Isabelle a container. "Just go to the bathroom with this bottle and provide a sample. Then give it to the secretary, and she will put your name on it."

Isabelle takes the container, thanks the doctor and goes to the washroom. Just before Isabelle leaves the room, Julia asks the doctor if it is possible to make the appointment for next Tuesday because she will be back in town that day. She explains to the doctor that Isabelle doesn't have any other way to come into town. Dr. Bates understands and makes a note to rush the results for Tuesday.

Once Isabelle is done and the secretary has scheduled Isabelle's appointment for early afternoon the next Tuesday, Isabelle thanks the secretary, and they leave the office. As they walk to her vehicle, Julia asks Isabelle if she still wants to go back to work. Isabelle nods yes, so they head to Mr. and Mrs. Smith's house. Isabelle is unusually quiet for a while as they drive back.

"Thank you so much for your help, Julia. I couldn't have done this without you," says Isabelle. She keeps her head down, feeling ashamed.

"I'm very happy to help you," replies Julia. "Isabelle, when are you going to tell Lucas about this?"

"Only after I get the results. I feel terrified to tell my parents because I help support my siblings. They have no money. They need me," replies Isabelle. There is abject fear in her friendly eyes.

"Isabelle, if you're pregnant, you must think of yourself and Lucas; your family comes second. You are engaged, and he wants to marry you. You and Lucas can get married and have your baby. Start your own family, Isabelle, with Lucas. You are so lucky to have a wonderful fiancé like him. He is a magnificent person, not to mention how handsome he is, with that famous smile," explains Julia, directing a grin at Isabelle.

"Julia, you are such a beautiful friend," says Isabelle as she finally lets out a smile. "I know Lucas is a terrific person, and he will be a great father."

Julia arrives at her aunt and uncle's place. As she parks the vehicle, Isabelle hugs Julia for being there with her and thanks her. They walk together into the house, and Julia asks her aunt whether they are ready to go to the city. Mrs. Smith greets them and tells Isabelle not to work too hard. Mr. and Mrs. Smith get their luggage, give Isabelle a goodbye hug, and they leave with Julia. Julia tells Isabelle she will be back on Tuesday. Isabelle smiles, thanks Julia again, and waves goodbye to them. Then she closes the door to get back to her housecleaning.

Isabelle spends some time with Lucas on the weekend, and she can feel the love he has for her, but the only thing on her mind is her potential pregnancy. Lucas notices that Isabelle is often inattentive and looks exhausted.

Puzzled by Isabelle's appearance, Lucas asks, "Isabelle, are you okay? Is something wrong?"

"Everything is fine, Lucas. What makes you assume there is something wrong?" questions Isabelle. She looks fearful and hopes that she has reassured him.

"It's just that you look so tired that I worry about you. I love you, Isabelle," replies Lucas as he puts his arms around her and gives her a gentle kiss.

Isabelle hugs him back and tells him that she loves him too. But even his love for her cannot quell her worries. She wonders what Lucas will think when he finds out she is pregnant. Isabelle is certain she is pregnant and that the results will come in positive on Tuesday. Despite the pain and shame of having an unplanned pregnancy, especially before marriage, Isabelle is proud to carry Lucas's baby. She knows that this child is conceived through love.

Isabelle walks to work early on Tuesday morning because she knows Mr. and Mrs. Smith are coming home, and she wants everything ready for them. Also, this is the day that she will receive her test results, and she is feeling extremely nervous. When she arrives, she does the dusting and starts to prepare lunch for the Smiths. But the only thing on her mind is her visit to see Dr. Bates.

Suddenly, she hears a vehicle roll in. Isabelle looks out the window to see who it is. It is Julia, with Mr. and Mrs. Smith. Isabelle drops her apron and runs to the door to greet them.

"Good day, Mr. Smith! Hi, Mrs. Smith!" says Isabelle as she hugs them. "Happy belated birthday, Mr. Smith." Isabelle gives him a kiss on the cheek.

Smiling, Mrs. Smith replies, "Good day, Isabelle."

"Hello, Isabelle," says Mr. Smith. "And thank you. It was a great party."

"Hello, Julia," says Isabelle as she reaches out to hug her.

"Hi, Isabelle!" replies Julia with an immense grin and genuine happiness.

"Lunch will be ready soon," Isabelle tells them and picks up the luggage.

"Thank you, Isabelle," replies Mr. Smith. "I'm hungry—especially for your food!"

They get settled in, and Isabelle returns to the kitchen to finish preparing lunch. Julia enters the kitchen and watches Isabelle setting the table. Julia can smell the aroma of Isabelle's cooking infusing the room.

"Hey, Isabelle, what are you cooking?" asks Julia as she takes a good whiff. "It smells fabulous in here."

Isabelle is startled; she jumps up and turns around, almost dropping the dishes she is holding.

"Julia, you frightened me!" she says, clutching her chest. "Oh, I'm so happy to see you."

"Did you tell Lucas that you may be pregnant?" asks Julia. She comes over to help Isabelle finish setting the table.

"No, but Lucas is a little suspicious about me; he thinks I looked tired. Besides that, we had a great weekend, although he was busy working," replies Isabelle as they finish the table together.

"Are you nervous about this afternoon, going to see Dr. Bates?" questions Julia. She lifts lids and looks in the pots on the stove, tasting Isabelle's corn chowder.

"Yes, very scared," replies Isabelle. She is feeling edgy. "I wish this was all a dream, and I would just wake up, but it's not. I may not be pregnant, but that is a small chance. I still have morning sickness, and I have not yet started my monthly cycle."

"Isabelle, I'm sorry! I'll stay with you until you get your results, and we'll figure something out together. I want to help you through this, and I hope if the answer is positive that you don't wait too long to tell Lucas because he's a great man. You know that Lucas loves you," states Julia.

"Thank you, Julia, for your advice and understating," says Isabelle through tears.

Soon Mr. and Mrs. Smith come into the kitchen for their lunch. They all sit together and have a delightful meal. Mr. Smith always enjoys Isabelle's cooking. Once they finish, Isabelle starts cleaning up, and Julia offers to help. After everything is cleaned up, Julia takes Isabelle to see Dr. Bates.

Entering the office, Julia and Isabelle identify themselves once more to the secretary. She directs them to room 3 and tells them the doctor will be with them soon. Isabelle is very quiet, feeling again that time has stretched—it feels elastic—and an ordinary minute now seems like an eternity; waiting is long and excruciating. Julia stands beside her, holding her hand as she attempts to quell her own anxiety.

They hear the sound of the doorknob and watch apprehensively as the knob turns. The door opens, and Dr. Bates enters the room with Isabelle's file.

"Good afternoon, Isabelle and Julia," says Dr. Bates as he opens the file. "Isabelle, I just received your results this morning. You are pregnant."

Isabelle stares at the doctor in shock. Even though this is exactly what she has suspected, particularly because she has missed her cycle, she feels numb to have this reality confirmed. Then she puts her head down in her hands and cries. Julia massages Isabelle's back to support her and asks the doctor whether there is a chance the results could be wrong.

Dr. Bates shakes his head. "No, I'm sorry," he says with empathy as he closes the file. "Isabelle, your next appointment will be in four weeks. Ginger ale and dry toast or crackers with tea may help with the nausea. Eventually, the morning sickness will pass, but meanwhile just eat light. When your stomach calms down, add some milk. Calcium is important for the baby. And get some rest. Remember that you are carrying a new life. Take care of yourself, Isabelle," the doctor says kindly.

CHAPTER 13

Two weeks pass, and Isabelle keeps her secret. Fortunately, the doctor is right; her morning sickness starts to diminish. She tries to find the best time to tell Lucas, but Lucas is always busy at the farm. Isabelle is advancing toward the end of her first trimester. She wants to tell Lucas, but the timing is always off, until one day after work Lucas picks her up to go out to a social event in Greenfield. Greenfield is a small village that holds a community event every year, and Lucas's family always volunteers to help their church raise money.

Lucas is excited to go to the social because this year the guest star is Maurice "Rocket" Richard. Maurice was a great hockey player for the Montreal Canadiens, and hockey was Lucas's favorite winter sport. Lucas is so excited that he mails a letter to his buddy Steve and tells him about Rocket Richard coming to the event.

Lucas heads to Mr. and Mrs. Smith's house, and as he enters the driveway, he sees Isabelle and Mrs. Smith outside tending the flower gardens. Mr. Smith is sitting on the front porch swing and looking at the beauty of the gardens that Isabelle kindly helps nurture. Isabelle loves the colorful flowers. They make her feel alive.

Lucas parks his Studebaker and walks toward the gardens. He waves to Mr. Smith with a big grin, and Mr. Smith waves back happily. As he walks closer to Isabelle, Lucas says hello to Mrs. Smith and gently kisses Isabelle on the cheek.

"Hi, Lucas," responds Isabelle in a soft voice and a shy smile as they hug.

"Good day, Lucas," says Mrs. Smith, sounding cheery. "You look to be in great spirits today."

"Yes, I'm happy because tonight when I volunteer at the social event, I will meet Rocket Richard, a famous hockey player for the Montreal Canadiens," replies Lucas, flashing his award-winning smile.

"Isabelle, you can go freshen up while I keep your handsome fiancé company," says Mrs. Smith with a wink.

"Thank you, Mrs. Smith," replies Isabelle. "I won't be long, Lucas," she adds, as she gives him a kiss on the cheek and then walks toward the house. Lucas thinks how well Isabelle does with contractions and her English now. He remembers back to her broken speech and how formal it used to sound. Isabelle has come a long way in terms of being bilingual.

"Take your time, Isabelle," says Lucas. "I have Mrs. Smith here to keep me company." They all laugh.

Lucas assists Mrs. Smith to the front porch, and she sits with Mr. Smith while Lucas stands there enjoying their company. Mrs. Smith offers Lucas lemonade that Isabelle made for them. Lucas drinks his lemonade while listening to Mr. and Mrs. Smith reminisce about their youth. Lucas smiles; he enjoys hearing their stories and hopes that he will be able to tell his children happy tales about his younger days.

Soon Isabelle opens the screen door, and as she comes out, Lucas finds it hard to catch his breath. She is stunning—she is wearing the most gorgeous dress. Julia brought this dress from Ottawa and gave it to Isabelle for her birthday last month, and Isabelle has kept it at the Smiths' for safekeeping. It is a sleeveless, silky, flower-print dress that follows the contours of her body. It has orange print flowers and green leaves on a brown background and gold buttons.

It reflects the beautiful colors of autumn, which Isabelle loves so much, and reminds her a bit of the falling leaves on the big oak tree. There are matching shoes and accessories. Isabelle is wearing her hair down, and she has put on some makeup, which Julia has taught her to apply.

"Wow! I'm speechless. Isabelle, you look so beautiful! The dress looks wonderful on you," says Lucas as he approaches Isabelle and gives her a kiss on the lips.

"Thank you, Lucas," responds Isabelle bowing her head. She is still not used to his compliments, although she enjoys receiving them, but Isabelle is modest.

"You look wonderful," says Mrs. Smith with delight.

"You are like my daughter." Mr. Smith makes this clear with a proud look. "Lucas, take good care of her."

"I promise," replies Lucas with a wave goodbye.

Isabelle kisses them and says goodbye. Lucas and Isabelle head out for Greenfield. Lucas is happy tonight and proud to have Isabelle by his side. When they arrive at the event, James and Debra are there with Paul, while Donna and Scott are being looked after at Debra's sister's house. Mary is there with her five children; she is due anytime with her sixth baby. Joe, her husband, is not with them. Isabelle and Lucas greet them, and Isabelle makes a fuss over the children; they all call her Aunt Isabelle. Lucas talks to his brother and father about the dart-game booth, so Isabelle stands there with Debra and Mary, talking about the event. They tell her that Elizabeth will be back soon; she has gone to bring her prize-winning pumpkin pie to the pie contest booth. Isabelle feels comfortable with Lucas's sister and sister-in-law, although when she looks at Mary's belly, she starts to panic wondering how on earth she will tell Lucas he will be a dad in six months.

"Isabelle, do you think Mary is having a boy?" asks Debra as she feels the baby move. "Here, Isabelle, touch Mary's belly. The baby just moved; I felt his little feet."

Isabelle is nervous as she reaches out to touch Mary's belly; Mary directs her hand toward the kick.

"Can you feel the kick?" Mary asks Isabelle.

"Yes—wow!" says Isabelle. "It must be a boy because he is very active."

Lucas walks toward them and puts his arm around Isabelle. He asks Mary about Joe's whereabouts.

"Joe had to work late tonight," replies Mary with her head down.

"Where is he working now?" asks James. He knows that Joe is not a good provider for his family.

"James, please stop asking Mary that silly question," mutters Debra. Then she tells the children to help Grandpa bring the boxes to the dart-game booth.

"Sorry, Mary," James apologizes. Then he gives her a hug to try to make amends.

"It's okay, James," says Mary as she tears up.

They head to the booths; Lucas and Isabelle get to work at the dart-game booth, putting balloons in place and arranging prizes around the booth. James, Debra, and Mary are barbecuing hotdogs and hamburgers to sell in the next booth. John and Elizabeth are selling tickets for the grand prize.

Lucas smiles at Isabelle as they set up the booth. "In about five minutes, the people will start coming in," says Lucas. "Bet you my Uncle Bob will be the first to come to our booth."

"What makes you say that?" asks Isabelle while she puts the biggest prizes in the back row.

"He comes every year to help out, but before he volunteers, he has to play the dart-game," explains Lucas. "Remember last year he won the big stuffed dog and gave it to Mary's children?"

"Oh, yes. Now I remember," says Isabelle. She starts to blow up balloons.

"My father told me Rocket Richard will arrive around seven o'clock; in about a half hour, I will see the pro hockey player that Steve and I always dreamed of when we were young. I sent a letter to Steve last week to tell him all about Rocket Richard," says Lucas as he finishes putting all the darts in place. "I wish Steve were here. He would get such a kick out of meeting Rocket Richard."

"Did he respond to you?" asks Isabelle.

"No, but I'm sure I'll receive a letter soon. Oh! Here comes Uncle Bob." People are beginning to enter, and the music is starting to play. Just as Lucas predicted a few minutes earlier, Uncle Bob walks right to their booth.

"Hi there, young lad," says Uncle Bob to Lucas as he shakes his hand and hugs Isabelle. "Good evening, Isabelle. You're looking pretty, as always. Isabelle, I love this game." Uncle Bob pulls out his change. "Lucas, I want six darts, please."

Lucas grins as he hands Uncle Bob his six darts.

They watch Uncle Bob shoot the darts. Lucas and Isabelle clap their hands each time Uncle Bob bursts the balloons. He wins a big stuffed teddy bear.

"Oh! Hey! I love this game," repeats Uncle Bob as he chuckles. "Lucas, can you give the prize to Mary's children for me? I have to help your mother place some chairs before the star guest arrives." Uncle Bob winks at Isabelle, and then he leaves to assist his sister Elizabeth.

"Your uncle is a wonderful man," says Isabelle as she replaces the prizes.

"Never a boring moment with Uncle Bob," jokes Lucas as he gazes at his lovely Isabelle.

Isabelle smiles back. Without Lucas noticing, Isabelle puts her hand on her belly and reminds herself that Lucas needs to know she is pregnant. He has the right to know about his baby. She is still afraid of his reaction, and she feels ashamed because of social mores and what their parents might say, but deep inside she is happy to be starting a family with Lucas. Isabelle looks at Lucas and tells herself that this night will be the right time to tell him.

"Look! Isabelle, look near the gates, there he is—Rocket Richard!" shouts Lucas with excitement in his voice.

Isabelle acknowledges the famous player and watches Lucas's shining face as he sees Rocket Richard entering the gates.

"Wow!" says Lucas. "I have to get his autograph later!"

"It's not too busy right now. You can go, and I will attend the booth," Isabelle suggests with a joyful smile, with her slight French accent.

Lucas asks, "Will you be okay?"

"Yes. Go see Rocket Richard, and get his autograph. I can take care of the booth. Go! Go!" she says laughingly, pushing Lucas out of the booth.

"Thank you so much, Isabelle." After a kiss, Lucas hurries off to see his idol.

"You forgot your pen and picture of Rocket Richard," yells Isabelle with amusement; she can see the joy in Lucas's face as he spins back to get his pen and photo.

"Thanks again for your help." Lucas gives Isabelle another quick kiss and races off.

When Lucas approaches Rocket Richard, his mouth goes dry as he sees Rocket walking his way. They are soon face to face. Lucas can't believe his eyes—he is actually near Rocket Richard! Steve and Lucas used to talk about Rocket when they played hockey on the pond as they were growing up.

"Hello, young man," says Maurice as he reaches to shake Lucas's hand.

"Good evening, Mr. Richard." He is wearing a huge smile and is thrilled by the opportunity to meet this great athlete. "My name is Lucas Clarkson. It is an honor to meet you, sir."

"Thank you, Lucas. This is a beautiful parish, and I am very happy to be here tonight," responds Maurice. "By the way, son, are you related to John Clarkson?

"Yes, he's my father. Why do you ask?" inquires Lucas.

"I'm supposed to meet him near the stage," Maurice informs him as he looks around.

Lucas announces that he will take Maurice to his father. They walk together toward the stage, and there they see John attending to the list of performers. John looks up and sees Lucas walking proudly with Maurice Richard. They greet each other with a handshake, and then Lucas tells them reluctantly that he has to go back to his booth.

"Before I go, can you please sign your autograph for my friend Steve and me?" asks Lucas.

"I sure can, son," replies Maurice as he reaches for the pen and photos.

While Maurice is signing his autograph, John reaches for his camera.

"Maurice, is it all right if I take a picture of you and Lucas?" questions John.

"Of course," replies Maurice.

John takes a picture of Lucas and Maurice. Lucas is so happy; he can't believe that his father has a camera handy and has taken a snapshot of them.

"Thank you, Mr. Richard," says Lucas as they shake hands, "and thank you, Dad." Lucas gives his father a big hug, and then he returns to his booth with Isabelle. He tells her all about his encounter with Maurice "Rocket" Richard.

The night is almost over. Mary and the children have left. Isabelle and Lucas are cleaning up their booth, while James and Debra are packing away the food. Lucas is telling James all about Rocket Richard. Isabelle and Debra are smiling as they watch the two men chatting about hockey. John and Elizabeth walk over to say good night. Soon they all leave. They are pleased that they have assembled another successful social event with the community. Everything has gone exceedingly well.

While Lucas is driving, he recounts to Isabelle his wonderful night, especially meeting Maurice Rocket Richard. Isabelle is happy for Lucas, but her mind is still focused on how to tell Lucas about the baby.

"Lucas, I know it is getting late, but can we go somewhere to talk?" asks Isabelle in a low voice.

"Is something wrong?" replies Lucas with growing concern.

"It's just that I have something very important to tell you," answers Isabelle, with a shaky voice.

"Sure, Isabelle. How about going to the land my father bought from Mr. Thomas? It is just down the road, not far from your place."

"That will be great," responds Isabelle, her voice shaky and revealing her nervousness.

Lucas arrives, parks his Studebaker and turns toward Isabelle. He gives her a kiss and a hug. "What's on your mind, sweetheart?" he asks. "It must be crucial; you have an awfully serious expression. What is it you have to say that is so urgent?" He is very worried about what Isabelle is about to say.

Isabelle struggles to find words, but she cannot speak. She puts her head down and cries.

"What is it that is so painful to say, Isabelle?" asks Lucas. He puts his hand under her chin and lifts her head.

Isabelle looks at him. "Lucas, I don't know how to tell you this." She takes a deep breath. "Remember the wonderful time we had when you showed me your grandfather's painting in your room, and then we made love?" Isabelle hesitates for a few seconds.

"Yes! Yes!" replies Lucas with an uneasy expression. "Did I do something wrong to hurt you?"

"No, Lucas, it is what we did."

"What do you mean?" Lucas is confused.

"Lucas—I'm pregnant!" Isabelle cries out.

"What! Pregnant—" Lucas is further confused. It takes him a while to process the information, and then he looks at Isabelle. "How do you know this?"

"I went to see a doctor, and he confirmed it," says Isabelle as she tries to stop crying.

"How long have you known this, and how far along you are?" Lucas asks. Tears come to his eyes as well when he thinks that she has been suffering with this information alone for so long.

"Julia took me to see her old doctor about four weeks ago. I am almost through my first trimester," explains Isabelle. "Julia was so kind to help me. She was very supportive because I was so scared, and I didn't know how to tell you, Lucas. I felt ashamed, and I didn't know what you and your parents would think of me. I know my parents will condemn me, especially my mother," cries Isabelle while she searches in her purse for a tissue.

"Isabelle, I love you, and we will get through this together." Lucas embraces Isabelle tightly as they both cry. "I am so sorry to put you through this. We can get married as soon as possible, without telling your parents that you are pregnant. I will arrange something soon, if that's okay with you," says Lucas, and he kisses her on the forehead as he gently touches her face.

"Lucas, I don't want you to marry me just because I'm pregnant," says Isabelle as they stare into each other's eyes.

"Isabelle, I love you, and I want a family with you. I am not marrying you just because you are pregnant but because you are the one I truly love." He tries to convince her of this with a passionate kiss. "And I don't want you to feel ashamed, darling. You didn't do anything by yourself. We both made love together, and I don't feel ashamed. I feel overjoyed at the thought of having you as my wife and starting a family with you. So, don't feel bad about any of this. It's not your fault."

"Lucas, I love you so much, and I want to marry you and be your wife," Isabelle responds.

"We can get married in November, just like my sister and Joe—also James and Debra got married in November," says Lucas with excitement. "What a wonderful day!" he declares.

"What do you mean, Lucas?" asks Isabelle as she watches him glow.

"Think about it, Isabelle," replies Lucas with his gorgeous smile. "Today I met Maurice "Rocket" Richard, and now we're planning to get married in a few weeks, and I'll be a father next spring!" Lucas beams. He can't believe his good fortune. Everything is falling together even though they had not planned it this way.

Isabelle feels happy and so relieved that she has told Lucas about her pregnancy. Seeing Lucas happy gives her the best feeling of all. As for Lucas, this is something he has longed for—to marry Isabelle and start a family.

CHAPTER 14

It is November 15, 1958, and Isabelle is putting on a beautiful wedding dress that Julia has helped her buy in the city; the two of them went shopping together, and Isabelle trusted Julia's judgment. Sure enough, standing there in her magnificent dress, she looks so beautiful; it even brings tears to her mother's eyes. France is now living in a small country home near Dalkeith; she has moved back because their grandmother has died, and France has no money to live alone in Quebec City. She married a farmer there the year before and is pregnant with their first child. She doesn't know that Isabelle is pregnant. France is helping put on Isabelle's veil. Then she gives her a beautiful pearl bracelet with matching earrings; it has come from their grandmother. Isabelle is very emotional about the jewelry because their grandmother was always special to her and France.

"That is something old for you to wear, and your dress is something new," says France, lovingly looking at her younger sister.

"Here is something borrowed—it is from my mother," says Julia. It is a gorgeous pearl necklace, and Julia proudly puts it around Isabelle's neck. "Now you need something blue."

Isabelle's mother leans forward, gives Isabelle a gift, and in French, she says, "This is for you, Isabelle."

Isabelle opens the box and inside finds a lacy blue garter to put around her leg. Mrs. Bourgeois has made it herself. Isabelle is overwhelmed with happiness and strong emotion as she hugs her mother, her sister, and then her best friend, Julia. "Thank you so much, all of you, for being with me on my wedding day and helping me," says Isabelle.

"We must get going," says France. "Father is waiting for you downstairs." She makes sure Isabelle has everything before she heads to the church.

As Mr. Bourgeois watches his daughter walk down the stairs, it takes his breath away. Where did his little girl go? It's like the song from *Fiddler on the Roof,* "Sunrise, Sunset." That father is about to prepare his daughter for marriage, and he takes a good hard look at her and wonders where the time went. He remembers when she was a little girl, but those days are long gone. Like Tevye, the dairyman, Mr. Bourgeois is now staring at a young woman. He is extremely ill but is determined to walk Isabelle down the aisle. They all get in Julia's vehicle, and she takes them to the French church in Alexandria.

As they arrive at the church, Lucas anxiously waits for Isabelle to walk down the aisle. Steve is there to comfort him as they stand at the front of the church, which is full to capacity with friends and family. Lucas is incredibly pleased to have Steve there as his best man. Suddenly, Lucas hears a noise; it is Isabelle's little brothers opening the doors for their sister. Lucas watches intently and sees his little nephew, Paul, as the ring bearer and Sylvie, Isabelle's youngest sister, as the flower girl. Right behind them, France is walking down the aisle. Julia is next as Isabelle's maid of honor. Isabelle is proud to have Julia in this special role; she has been there to help her so often in times of need.

Lucas watches and smiles to know that Isabelle will be the next one to walk down the aisle. As the music swells louder, he sees Isabelle entering through the doors. There she is, the most utterly gorgeous girl, wearing an exquisite grown. She is walking with her father, wearing her precious shy smile that Lucas has admired from the first day they met.

When they reach the front, Lucas shakes hands with Mr. Bourgeois and then takes Isabelle's hand and gently kisses it. It is an incredible ceremony, full of love and joy that fills the whole church. Once they have exchanged their vows and the ceremony is done, Lucas kisses his beautiful bride. Everyone feels great happiness as they walk out of the church. After that, they all go to Lucas's parents' house to celebrate. At the supper, Steve makes a toast and a speech about the wonderful couple. Julia also wishes them the best and tells Lucas what a lucky man he is to have such an amazing wife.

Lucas and Isabelle go to Toronto for their honeymoon. Isabelle is thrilled to see such a huge city. She is the one who had never been to the movie theater or to a restaurant; she is not used to traveling outside her small town and is delighted at all the sites in the huge city. Lucas has uncles there, and they stop to visit them while enjoying the city views. Isabelle and Lucas are so much in love; they are ecstatic to be starting their life together. Lucas touches Isabelle's belly and is proud that someday soon he will become a father. No one knows about Isabelle's pregnancy except for Julia.

When they return home, they settle at Lucas's parents' house. Lucas still continues to work with his dad, and Isabelle keeps working for Mr. and Mrs. Smith. Isabelle and Lucas don't mind living with his parents because they all get along well. Isabelle is still shy, but Elizabeth has a way of making her feel accepted in the family, which helps her feel at home. Lucas and Isabelle often discuss when would be the right time to tell the family about her pregnancy. It is almost Christmas, and neither family knows. Isabelle is petite and slim and still isn't showing signs of being pregnant.

On Christmas Day, everyone will head to Grandma's house for supper. Elizabeth always puts on an amazing Christmas supper, and all her grandchildren love to go to their grandma's house to celebrate the holiday with delicious food and presents under the tree. Lucas tells his mother that he will take Isabelle to visit her siblings and parents for just a little while but promises to be back before four.

Once Lucas is done at the barn, he takes Isabelle to visit her family. He always feels uneasy being there, but he does it for Isabelle. There is nothing he would not do for her. Lucas enjoys being with Isabelle's brothers and sisters but is not too keen on her parents because of what they did to her in the past. He is an understanding man; he knows Isabelle values her family and loves her siblings, so he respects her choices. If her connection to her parents is that important to her, he will play his part to maintain the relationship.

Mrs. Bourgeois prepares lunch, which is not fancy but is the best she can do with little money. Isabelle and Lucas stay for lunch and give presents to her siblings. France and her husband, Jean, also give presents to the children. Lucas and Isabelle have brought desserts, and France and Jean have brought ice cream that she made on the farm.

France's pregnancy is now showing. France and Jean are going to buy a farm just beside his grandfather's farm, and they will move into the farmhouse just before the baby is born. Isabelle is happy for her sister but still doesn't tell France about her own pregnancy. Mr. Bourgeois thanks his two daughters and his sons-in-law for everything they have done as they depart.

They arrive at Lucas's place; his brother and his sister are already there. Lucas and Isabelle greet his family and wish them all a very merry Christmas just before they sit down for their meal. It is a delicious meal, golden brown turkey with stuffing, mashed potatoes with glazed carrots, and hot rolls with different kinds of salads. For dessert, lemon meringue pie and black forest cake, their favorite. Once everyone has finished eating, Elizabeth asks the family to go to the parlor near the Christmas tree. As they settle down in the parlor, John waits to hand out gifts. Mary has a new addition to the family: a little boy, George, whom Isabelle holds while they are opening their presents.

Joe looks at Isabelle with a smirk. As he has too much liquor, he remarks in a rude way, "Isabelle, when is it your turn to have a baby?"

"Stop, Joe!" says Mary as Isabelle lowers her head in embarrassment.

Lucas turns around and gives Joe a look. "Joe, you've had enough to drink," he tells him. He sits beside Isabelle, picks up baby George and hands him back to Mary. "I have something to announce." Isabelle looks at Lucas shyly, as she knows what he is about to say. "Isabelle and I are having a baby." Lucas kisses her and proudly continues, "Isabelle is due this spring, and yes, we knew this before we got married."

"Congratulations," James and Debra say as they walk over to Lucas and shake hands.

Elizabeth replies, still in shock, "I'm going to be a grandmother again!" as she gets up and hugs them.

John also rises with Elizabeth and hugs Lucas and Isabelle with joy.

"This is fabulous news, Lucas! Congratulations to both of you," says Mary.

Isabelle is relieved and proud of Lucas for the way he handled the situation. It has been a very merry Christmas, and everyone is happy for Lucas and Isabelle. She is so pleased that everyone has taken the news so well. Much of her worries were for nothing.

Finally, before New Year's Day, Isabelle tells her family, and they are also happy for her. France is especially excited because they will be having their babies only about a month apart. Lucas and Isabelle are relieved to finally announce Isabelle's pregnancy; now they can go on with their lives.

Spring finally arrives, and Isabelle has to stop working because it is getting too difficult. Lucas and Isabelle are not counting months anymore; it is now weeks. Isabelle is getting things ready for the baby in her room when she hears Elizabeth calling her name.

"What is it, Mrs. Clarkson?" asks Isabelle.

"I just received a call from Mrs. LaSalle, France's mother-in-law, and France is having her baby," replies Elizabeth.

Path of Lucas

Isabelle fills with excitement over the great news and asks. "Did she say if France had the baby yet?"

"No, just that Jean will be taking France to the General Hospital soon because she is in labor," Elizabeth informs her. "If you want to tell Lucas, he can take you to see France, and you can also tell your parents."

"Thanks, Mrs. Clarkson!" says Isabelle.

Isabelle hurries out to find Lucas, and quickly, she sees him plowing in the fields. Isabelle starts to walk toward the field, waving her hands to Lucas, but he doesn't see her. Forgetting she is pregnant, Isabelle starts to run and wave at Lucas because she is so happy for France that it does not occur to her to slow down. Suddenly, she stumbles over a rock and loses her balance. She falls to the ground and loses her breath. She struggles to pick herself up but feels too weak. Isabelle can only hold her stomach. With tears, she lies there, hoping she didn't do any harm to her baby.

Out of the blue, Lassie comes running to Isabelle. She licks her face and barks loudly toward the field Lucas is working on. Lassie keeps on barking, but Lucas can't hear. Lassie runs for the field, still barking, until she gets Lucas's attention.

"What's the matter, Lassie?" asks Lucas.

Lucas stops the tractor and starts to follow his dog to see what is wrong. He is surprised and concerned to find Isabelle on the ground. Lucas's heart starts to beat rapidly.

"Isabelle! What happened? Are you okay? Why are you here?" asks Lucas, a puzzled expression on his face.

"I am okay," says Isabelle as she tries to sit up. "I came to tell you that my sister is having her baby. I got excited and started to run; then I tripped over a rock. What if I hurt the baby?"

"Don't worry. Isabelle, I'll carry you home," says Lucas as he cradles his injured wife in his strong arms.

"It is okay, Lucas. I can walk," replies Isabelle.

They head home, with Lucas refusing to let Isabelle walk. He carries her all the way. Isabelle feels safe in his strong arms as he takes her into the house.

"Lucas, what happened to Isabelle?" asks Elizabeth, evidently worried.

"Isabelle tripped over a rock. Lassie found her and came to me, barking," replies Lucas as he lays her on the bed. "Thank goodness for the dog. It would have taken me much longer to find her without him making such a ruckus."

"Isabelle, are you okay?" asks Elizabeth with concern.

"I'm fine. I was scared for the baby, but now the baby is moving," responds Isabelle as she sits up on the bed. "Lucas, my sister is having her baby, and I would like to tell my parents and then see France at the hospital."

"Take a nap while I clean up, and then we'll go," says Lucas. He kisses her on the forehead. "You worried me there, Isabelle."

"I'm sorry. Will you promise to take me to see my sister later?" requests Isabelle.

"Yes, of course," Lucas promises.

Lucas goes to clean up while Isabelle takes a nap.

A half hour later, when Isabelle gets up to go to the washroom, she notices the bed feels wet. It takes her a minute to process this, and then she realizes that her worst fear about the fall was confirmed; her water has broken. She starts to feel a sharp pain in her lower abdomen. Contractions have started, and she is in labor.

"Lucas, I need your help," Isabelle calls as she sits back down.

Lucas hurries into the room. "What's the matter, Isabelle?" he asks when he sees the pain on her face. "Are you in labor?"

"My water broke, and I am starting to get contractions. They are about ten minutes apart. I am not due for another three weeks!" replies Isabelle, her voice rising.

"Don't worry, Isabelle; everything will be just fine," Lucas assures her through he is also nervous, but he must not let that show.

He has to be there for her. Nonetheless, Lucas is extremely concerned about his wife, and he will do anything to protect her.

Elizabeth comes into the room to comfort Isabelle while Lucas is getting his car.

"Mrs. Clarkson, can you and Mr. Clarkson see my parents and tell them?" asks Isabelle as she tries to get up.

Elizabeth nods. "Yes, of course, we can do that for you, Isabelle," as she helps her. Elizabeth gets her suitcase ready for Lucas to bring to the hospital.

Lucas parks his Studebaker near the side door. Feeling apprehensive, he rushes in and helps Isabelle walk to the vehicle. Elizabeth wishes them the best and promises to let Isabelle's parents know that both their daughters are at the hospital giving birth.

CHAPTER 15

Lucas looks at his watch; it is 9:45 a.m. on May 27, 1959. He is pacing in the waiting room. It has been over twenty-four hours, and Isabelle has not yet given birth. The doctor has told them that often first pregnancies have the longest labor, and this labor is early. Lucas is exhausted; he has only gotten a few hours' sleep. Every time a nurse walks by, Lucas becomes anxious and wishes that he would hear what is happening with Isabelle. It is not commonplace at all in 1959 for the father-to-be in the delivery room, so he must do as all prospective fathers do—wait. He continues to walk back and forth with great anticipation. No one ever told him how hard it is for a father-to-be to wait for his child to be born.

Lucas has just returned from getting a coffee because he feels overwhelmed and tired. As he reaches for the cup, a nurse walks in and asks if he is Mr. Clarkson.

"Yes, I am Lucas Clarkson," he replies wide-eyed.

"Congratulations! Your wife just gave birth to a healthy, beautiful, eight-pounds-and-six-ounce baby boy," confirms the nurse.

"Thank you! Wow! My first child, my son!" says Lucas ecstatically. "Can I see them now?" Lucas is so grateful that everything went well even though the baby arrived early. And he is not even premature or underweight. How fortunate they are.

"Of course, you may, but remember that Mrs. Clarkson is exhausted from all the hard labor she went through. She will need her sleep."

"I understand," says Lucas as he puts his cup down. He is feeling like the luckiest man in world at this moment.

"Come with me, Mr. Clarkson. I'll take you to Mrs. Clarkson's room. I'll also get the baby for you," says the nurse as she leads the way.

"Thank you," replies Lucas, overwhelmed with gratitude and excitement.

The nurse directs him to his wife's room, "Right this way, Mr. Clarkson."

Lucas smiles at the nurse; with a nod, he thanks her again as he walks in to see Isabelle.

"I'll bring your baby boy to you any minute now, Mr. Clarkson," says the nurse as she heads the other way.

Isabelle is sleeping as Lucas walks into the room. He just stands there and watches his beautiful wife. Lucas walks closer to Isabelle's bed and continues to stare at her; he then gives her a kiss and sits down beside her.

The nurse walks in with the baby tucked in a blue blanket; Lucas stands up as he watches the nurse carry the baby toward him. He is overcome with joy as she hands him his baby.

"Congratulations, Mr. Clarkson; he is a beautiful boy," says the nurse as she looks at him holding his baby. Then she leaves the room.

Nervously, Lucas holds his son. He smiles at the baby and glances toward Isabelle; she is waking up. Lucas hears a grunt as he continues to look at Isabelle. Then she slowly opens her eyes.

"Lucas. Lucas, we have a son," says Isabelle in a husky voice as she smiles at Lucas. Even after a complicated delivery and through much pain, Isabelle manages to smile. That's the woman he adores.

"Do you want to see your son, Isabelle?" asks Lucas as he approaches her.

"Yes, please," she replies as she slowly extends her arms.

Lucas positions the baby into her arms and gives them both a kiss.

"I love you, Isabelle," he says as he crouches down and cuddles them both.

Isabelle gives her baby a kiss on the forehead and pronounces him Lucas Junior. She looks at Lucas and smiles. "He is a perfect baby," she says.

"Isabelle, there's something I've been thinking about ever since I looked at our son," says Lucas.

"What is it, Lucas?" Isabelle asks, looking surprised.

"Remember when you told me you were pregnant?" he recalls while he gently strokes the baby's head.

"Yes, I remember. How could I ever forget?" she jokes.

"Remember I met Maurice Richard that night?" Lucas is smiling.

"What are you implying, Lucas?" Isabelle smiles back as she starts to catch on.

"I'd love to call our son Richard," says Lucas; then he looks at the baby proudly. He is moved by the potential for greatness his son holds.

"Yes, that sounds like a strong name—Richard Lucas Clarkson," replies Isabelle while she looks at their baby and tries out the name Richard. It fits. She can envision calling him in for supper or cheering him on from the bleachers when he goes to hockey league.

"I talked to my mother, and she told your parents about both their daughters giving birth. Apparently, France gave birth at home because her contractions were too close together; they had no time to take her to the hospital. Her mother-in-law assisted the birth, with a doctor nearby. France had a boy as well. Mother also believed that France had an easy delivery and gave birth even before we arrived at the hospital. Isabelle, I have to call my parents right now; they are anxiously waiting to hear about their grandchild," says Lucas, full of joy.

"Yes, for sure; they have been waiting for a long time. Please tell them. I will be okay here with Richard." She smiles as Lucas kisses her and their little boy and then leaves to call his parents to tell them the great news.

Lucas and Isabelle are proud parents and enjoy their family life together. One year later, on June 3, 1960, Isabelle gives birth to a second son; they name him Johnny William Clarkson after Lucas's father and Lucas's brother who died at birth. They continue to live at Lucas's parents' place, and Isabelle learns to drive and starts to work at a sewing factory in Alexandria. Another year after that, Isabelle gives birth, on September 1, 1961, to a third son. They name him Steve James Clarkson, after Lucas's best friend and Lucas's older brother. The doctor tells Lucas and Isabelle that they should not have any more babies because Isabelle has had three very hard deliveries. If she were to get pregnant again, the chance of losing the baby or even her own life would be high because she has had life-threatening complications in the past. Isabelle wants more children but accepts what the doctor has said, and Lucas does not want to jeopardize his wife's life. Isabelle also comes to acknowledge that her health is important so she can nurture her three beautiful boys. Isabelle is fulfilled as a mother; her children are her joy. Her life, as Lucas's wife, is so wonderful. Lucas is extremely proud of his family and content with life. To him, life is superb.

Lucas and Isabelle talk about the fullness of the house. They enjoy living there, but decide that it is time to make a move to make room for their new addition. They are able to find a nice country house split into two apartments, not too far from Alexandria. In the front apartment house lives an older couple, and in the back, the apartment is bigger, perfect for Lucas's family. James and John help Lucas paint the apartment and then move in the furniture. Debra and Elizabeth assist Isabelle in sewing curtains for their windows and putting boxes of dishes away.

Lucas and Isabelle are happy about their move; they cherish their independence after three years of living with Lucas's parents. Jobs are hard to find, so Lucas continues working with his father on the farm and finds a part-time job working as a mechanic for a garage

Path of Lucas

nearby. He is forced to sell his Studebaker because it needs many repairs and is not suitable for his young family. It is heartbreaking for Lucas when he has to part with his vehicle. But the love for his family is more important to him, and he knows that getting a 1954 Ford station wagon is the right choice.

Practically a year has passed since they lived in their apartment. Lucas is playing with his three sons, and Isabelle is sitting down knitting while listening to Frank Sinatra on the radio. She is admiring her husband and her children playing. Lucas is a great father; he loves to spend quality time with his boys. Lucas gazes at Isabelle with a wink, and then he smiles. He always makes Isabelle feel appreciated. Although the demands of raising a family are great, they always ensure to take the time to cherish their love for each other.

Lucas feels the need to become more than a farmer's son. He has always told Steve, his old friend, that one day he wants to become a Class A Mechanic, but he has never done it because his father believes he should be a farmer like his old man. At this point of Lucas's life, he is starting to work more as a mechanic and less as a farmer. He is hired full-time at the garage, helping Claude Giroux, a Class A Mechanic, repair cars. Lucas is not certified, although he knows a lot about auto mechanics. However, he doesn't make enough money at his job, so he still works part-time with his dad and his brother, James.

John and James have started a logging business, and Lucas helps work in the bush, which is not his favorite trade. But Lucas is a hardworking man and does what he needs to do to provide for his family. Isabelle continues to work in a sewing factory to help pay the bills because Lucas doesn't want to depend on his father's money, and neither does Isabelle.

In the spring of 1962, Isabelle announces to Lucas that she is pregnant again. She knows she is not supposed to get pregnant, and Lucas is shocked. Isabelle is afraid, and so is Lucas, especially after what the doctor has told them about the danger of having another baby. The fear is with them for the next seven months, until

January 19, 1963, when Isabelle gives birth to their daughter. It is an extremely difficult delivery, but Isabelle somehow pulls through. She is hospitalized for two weeks under observation because she has hemorrhaged and is very weak. After the ordeal is over, Lucas and Isabelle are thrilled to have a healthy little girl, a sister for Richard, age four; Johnny, age three; and Steve, almost two.

Lucas sits down near Isabelle's bed, holding his little girl. As he looks at the baby and then at Isabelle, he says, "Isabelle, I want to name her Marybeth."

"Marybeth!" replies Isabelle; she doesn't really like the name, and it shows on her face.

"Yes, my sister's name, with my mother's name mixed in," explains Lucas as he kisses his little girl.

"Lucas, I know your intentions are good, but there is a name that I adore, and I believe that our daughter will carry the name wisely," Isabelle responds.

"What is the name?" asks Lucas.

"Lucy! Yes, Lucy Isabelle Clarkson," says Isabelle as she reaches and gently touches the baby's cheek and then kisses her on the forehead.

"Wow, what a magnificent name!" Lucas smiles, stretches over and kisses Isabelle.

"I'd love our little girl to have part of your name and part of my name also. What do you think, Lucas?" asks Isabelle smiling and joyfully glowing.

"I love the name," he replies happily, as he looks at his little girl and calls her Lucy.

Lucas and Isabelle are starting to save money for a down payment on a home, until one summer day when Debra's sister Diane and her brother-in-law Jim come down for a visit. They visit every summer, and Lucas loves to chat with Jim because he is knowledgeable about cars, inside and out. He knows how to build sports cars from scratch; Jim is a Class A Mechanic. He owns his own garage in Uxbridge, near Toronto.

Path of Lucas

James has told Jim about Lucas and how he works at a garage and is learning a lot about working as a mechanic. Jim is impressed and proud of Lucas; every time he comes down, Lucas is always interested in Jim's expertise about cars. Jim has known Lucas since he was eight years old, when James started dating Debra. Jim and James have become great friends since they started dating the Kennedy girls, Debra and Diane.

Lucas, Isabelle, and the children go to James and Debra's place for a family gathering. It is a beautiful day for an outside event. All of Lucas's family is there. John and Elizabeth are playing with the children, except for baby Lucy, who is sleeping in her carriage. Debra's family is also there, spending time with Jim and Diane before they leave to go back home to Uxbridge.

Debra and her sisters are preparing food with Isabelle and Mary. They are enjoying woman talk as they prepare the meal. The guys are playing baseball. Once the game is over, Lucas volunteers to get the refreshments, and Jim offers to assist him. The two of them walk together toward the garage.

"Lucas, James told me about you working as a mechanic's helper and that you're learning about repairing cars," says Jim, sounding impressed.

"Yes, I'm enjoying my work. Claude has taught me a lot. He lets me work on parts, and then he inspects my work; he gives me a thumbs-up on almost every job. He says I am a Class A Mechanic without the papers," replies Lucas with a smile.

"You've always loved working on cars more than farming, Lucas—I've noticed that since you were about fourteen years old," says Jim as they walk into the garage.

"I never wanted to admit to my father that farming was not for me. I adore my dad, and I don't want to break his heart. So, I work both, doing what I like and always dreamed about and also working with my brother and father," answers Lucas with sadness. "But the fact is, I wish that I could just work full-time as a mechanic; it would be my dream to get my Class A Mechanic's papers and own a garage, just like you, Jim. I love working on engines. I don't like farming, especially working in the bush, cutting logs. It's not for me."

"Lucas, I have a proposition for you," Jim says.

Lucas is reaching to get the refreshments out of the coolers. "What's that, Jim?" he asks with a surprised look.

"I'd like you to come to Uxbridge, go to school to get your papers and work with me. My business is growing, so I'm looking for a good mechanic, somebody I can rely on and trust. There are lots of opportunities out there for you and your family. I can see that you have the passion, and that's what I'm looking for in a mechanic," says Jim seriously as he helps Lucas with the refreshments.

"You're kidding me, Jim!" responds Lucas in shock. "Why would you do that for me?"

"I can see your potential and your passion for automobiles—I can even help pay the tuition cost," Jim says. "There's a country house for rent not too far from the garage. Your family can live there, Lucas."

"Jim, that's a lot to take in right now. I don't know what Isabelle would think about moving far away—and what about my father? I just can't imagine what he would do without me on the farm. I appreciate the offer, and it sounds fantastic, but I need to think about how it affects other people in my life as well. I don't know," replies Lucas looking conflicted.

"I understand, Lucas; there's a lot to think about. I just threw this at you, which can be very confusing. But my offer still stands, Lucas. Take your time, and talk to Isabelle about this opportunity and dream," says Jim, patting Lucas on the shoulder.

"Wow, thanks, Jim! I'll need some time to think about this remarkable offer," answers Lucas as he embraces Jim.

"It's your call, Lucas. I have plenty of work. You can have a job with me because I believe you can become a great mechanic," expresses Jim. "So, let's go have some fun with the guys, and you can think about this opportunity tomorrow."

"Thanks, Jim. You're a great friend," says Lucas with a smile. Then they make their way over to the others with the refreshments.

CHAPTER 16

Two weeks pass, and Lucas is constantly thinking about the opportunity Jim has offered him. He wants to jump at the chance, but he doesn't know how Isabelle would feel about moving to Uxbridge with the children. He knows his father wants him to work on the farm, and he has never known how to tell his dad that farming is not for him. So many things go through his mind, but he doesn't know how to express himself or what to do. He thinks that no one will understand his choices.

One evening, Lucas is sitting on the edge of the bed, watching Isabelle combing her hair before bedtime.

"Isabelle," he murmurs in a very soft voice.

"Yes, Lucas," she replies as she continues to stroke her long hair with her brush. She looks at Lucas in the mirror and smiles.

"Isabelle, there's something I'd like to talk to you about. It's been on my mind for a couple of weeks now," Lucas says with an uneasy look.

"What is the matter, Lucas?" questions Isabelle as she turns around in her chair to face him. "You look so distressed."

"I don't know where to start," he whispers; he runs his hand through his hair and keeps his head down.

"What is it?" she asks with concern in her voice as she gets up and comes to sit beside him. "You can tell me anything, Lucas. You know that."

"Isabelle, you know how much I would love to become a Class A Mechanic," replies Lucas as he reaches for her hand.

"Yes!" says Isabelle. Her eyes are wide open as she looks into his.

"Remember when James and Debra had a party for Jim and Diane before they went back home?" Lucas begins to explain.

Isabelle is nervous and slowly nods.

"Well, Jim was talking to me about his business and how extremely hectic it's turned out to be," says Lucas as he kisses Isabelle's hand.

"What has that got to do with us?" questions Isabelle.

"Jim wanted to know what I did at Claude's garage. When I told him, he offered me a job in his garage and said that he would help pay for my tuition to get my Class A Mechanic certification," answers Lucas with a slight tremor in his voice, not knowing what Isabelle will think or how she will respond.

"Wow! Lucas, what did you say to Jim?" she asks, feeling shocked.

"I told him I needed to think about his offer. That's what I want to talk to you about tonight," says Lucas, and then he gives Isabelle a huge hug. "I've been thinking about this opportunity for a couple of weeks now, and all I can think is that I want to go to Uxbridge and live my dream, Isabelle. Only if that's okay with you, of course."

"If you decide to go to Uxbridge, what about us and the kids, Lucas?" she inquires looking scared.

"We would move there," he replies with a smile.

"Where would we live?" she asks.

"Jim has it all planned for us. All we have to do is call him, and he'll relocate us there. He said there was a country house not far from the garage that's for rent," explains Lucas as he strokes her hair.

"Lucas, this is a big step in our life and for the children. It will be Richard's first year in school come September. We will need to register soon—and what about our furniture? There is a lot to think about, Lucas. What about my job, your father, and the farm?" asks Isabelle as she looks at Lucas with uncertainty.

"I've thought about all that, Isabelle. Believe me, I've thought about the challenges ahead. It won't be easy, but it's my lifelong dream to become a mechanic, and Jim is giving me the chance to do that. I don't want to be supported by my father; I want to live my dream and do what I love to do. I know I am asking a lot from you right now, Isabelle, but isn't working together and reaching our dreams what married couples are supposed to do?"

"Yes, Lucas. I want to support you, and I know deep in my heart that becoming a mechanic is an enormous dream for you, and I want to help you fulfill that goal. I love you, Lucas, and of course, I will follow you. But you will have to tell your father, and that, I know, will break his heart," says Isabelle softly.

"I have thought about Father and the farm, but I have to be true to myself. You know, Isabelle, farming isn't for me. I have to stand up and tell my father the truth about farming. If you are willing to take the next step in our new journey and go forward, I'll call Jim tomorrow morning and confirm with him first to see if everything still stands. Then I'll approach my father and tell him we're moving to Uxbridge," responds Lucas. Then he gives Isabelle a passionate kiss.

The next morning, Lucas calls Jim, and Jim assures him that everything can go ahead as planned. Lucas and Isabelle, with the children, can move into the country home in two weeks, on the first of August. Lucas is excited but scared because the move will come quickly, and he has plenty to do beforehand.

Lucas tells Isabelle all about the plan, and she says she will give notice to her boss that morning. Lucas agrees; this way they will have more time to pack their things for the move. Lucas also tells Claude about his new journey. Claude is sad to lose a good worker but is proud of Lucas and believes that he will become a great mechanic. They shake hands, and Lucas must now visit his mother and father to tell them the news. He is dreading this part of the preparation for the move. Everything else has gone so smoothly, but how will his father take this news? Lucas fears that he will be greatly disappointed.

Lucas arrives at the farm early that morning, while his father and mother are still having breakfast. Elizabeth offers him some pancakes, but Lucas asks only for a cup of coffee.

"What brings you here bright and early this morning, Lucas? Aren't you supposed to be working with Claude?" questions John with wondering eyes.

"There's something I want to talk to you and Mom about, Dad," says Lucas in a nervous voice.

"What is it, son?" asks John.

Elizabeth turns around with the cup of coffee for Lucas to listen to the conversation. She looks worried and assumes that something has happened with his family. "Lucas, is everything okay at home? Is Isabelle all right?" she asks.

"Yes, everything's fine. There's nothing wrong," explains Lucas, and Elizabeth gives a sigh of relief.

"You look nervous, son," says John. "What is so important to tell us, Lucas?"

"Remember when Jim was here a couple of weeks ago? Well, James told him that I'm working in Claude's garage and that I'm learning lots of things about being a mechanic. As a result, Jim has offered me a job in Uxbridge," explains Lucas.

"Uxbridge—Uxbridge!" cries Elizabeth. John, too, is shocked at what he has just heard.

"Mom, Isabelle and I had a long talk last night, and we agreed to move up there," Lucas tries to explain. He sees his parents are saddened to think of him, Isabelle, and the children moving away.

"Where will you reside?" asks John.

"There is a country house not far from the garage. Jim told me we can rent there, and I trust his judgment about the place," answers Lucas. "Also, Jim said that when I work for him, I can take a program at night to get my Class A Mechanic's certificate, and he'll help pay my tuition fees."

"When do you and Isabelle plan to make the move to Uxbridge?" asks Elizabeth looking crushed.

"We need to pack now because we have to move into the house for August first," replies Lucas as he hugs his mother.

"That soon!" John sounds surprised.

"I know it's a shock; it was the same for me. Dad, I have to be truthful about my feelings, and I want to tell you that I'm sorry, but farming is not for me. I never wanted to hurt you, so I didn't tell you this earlier, but I'd much rather work on cars than farm," explains Lucas in a genuine tone. He feels relief at letting down a burden that he has carried for years.

"Son… I would not have ever known because you are such a great worker," says John with a stunned look on his face.

"Sorry, Dad, for not being the man you wanted me to be," responds Lucas with tears in his eyes.

"Don't be so hard on yourself, Lucas," advises Elizabeth. "Your father loves you just the way you are."

"Lucas, I do love you, and there is no way I would love you less just because you don't want to farm anymore," replies John. He gets up and goes to hug his son.

"Thanks, Dad. I love you, too." Lucas is incredibly relieved. Both his parents have taken the news well, much better than he expected. He knows they are disappointed and sad, but they will not stand in his way. And they will not make him feel guilty for leaving.

"What are your plans to move there with all your furniture and the family?" asks Elizabeth.

"Not sure, but I was thinking if Dad and James take their trucks with my station wagon, there should be plenty of room to take all the furniture and the boxes of goods and clothes," replies Lucas. "What do you think, Dad?"

"I'm certain there will be enough room. I'll talk it over with James to make sure he can help you move. Except, before we go any further, are you sure this is what you want, Lucas?" He wants to verify that Lucas has thought this through and isn't making a mistake with his decision.

"I am absolutely confident that this is what I want, Dad. I didn't want to move far away from the family, but this is a great opportunity for me—one that may never come again—and Jim will help me on my journey," says Lucas, excited by what the future holds for his young family.

"Son, I respect your choice and support it even though it's hard for me. We'll help you move," replies John as he tears up and hugs his son again.

"Thanks, Dad. I love you both, but I'm sure you understand how important it is for me to carve out my own way with my new family," responds Lucas as he reaches for his mother and hugs her also.

The time has arrived for the big move. Lucas and Isabelle are exhausted but happy about the new journey. Everything is packed in the two trucks, and Lucas's station wagon is full. The four children are snuggled in the backseat, ready for the journey.

Isabelle and Lucas hug and kiss Mary and Debra, as they get ready to leave for Uxbridge.

"Lucas, I wish you the best," says Mary; she is crying to see her little brother leave. "Isabelle, I hope you enjoy your life with Lucas in Uxbridge. Send me pictures of the children… they grow up so fast."

"Thanks, Mary," replies Lucas.

"I will send lots of pictures," Isabelle promises Mary and Debra.

Lucas and Isabelle enter their vehicle and drive away, as they all wave. James follows with his son Paul, and then John and Elizabeth go next; both their trucks are full of furniture.

It is a five-hour journey to Uxbridge. With a few stops on the way, they all finally arrive at Jim and Diane's house. They stop in for a short visit and so Lucas can get the key and directions to the country home. Jim tells Lucas to take a week off to settle in, and then they will get together to seriously talk about the job and the Class

A Mechanic certification program. Lucas nods and looks extremely enthusiastic about the program, so Jim decides to explain a bit more about it to Lucas. He will start working for Jim the next week, and in three weeks, the program will begin. It will be three evenings a week for three years. Lucas is eager, nevertheless, and also nervous to actually see his dream beginning to come true.

Once they arrive at their new home, Isabelle is impressed with the outside view, and as they enter the house, she is amazed at how it has been kept up. It is a big, beautiful house, and Isabelle and Lucas are happy to be moving into such a grand place.

"Jim was right! It is beautiful," says Lucas as he kisses Isabelle. He is feeling confident about his decision to move to Uxbridge.

"Lucas, it is a wonderful place," replies Isabelle as she holds Lucy and watches the boys touring around the living room. When Elizabeth enters the house, she is also thrilled for Lucas and Isabelle; it is a stunning house.

"Lucas, this house is a beautiful place to raise your children! Isabelle, you have a big kitchen to cook in." Elizabeth smiles as she looks around the house.

"Thanks, Mom," responds Lucas as he gives her a kiss on the check, and Isabelle gives her a hug.

"I'll take Lucy and the boys for a tour upstairs," says Elizabeth. She reaches for Lucy, gives her a kiss on the forehead and then gathers the boys. They run upstairs together.

Lucas and Isabelle are happily standing there kissing as John walks in with James and Paul.

"Lucas, did you see the garage in the back?" asks John sounding excited.

"No," replies Lucas as he walks to the window to see. "Wow! It's great!"

"Let's get the furniture in," says James, while he admires the lovely house.

With absolute delight in his voice, he responds, "Yes, James—let's go!"

The next morning after breakfast, James, Paul, John and Elizabeth are all ready to go back home. It is hard for them to go, especially Elizabeth, but they have to get back to the farm.

"Bye, Dad, and thanks so much for helping us. Love you, Dad," says Lucas with watering eyes.

"Goodbye, son. Love you, Lucas," replies John as he gives him a big hug and waves goodbye kisses to his grandchildren. "Bye, Isabelle," he says as he gives her a gentle hug with a kiss.

"Bye, Mom," says Lucas, "I love you, Mom." He hugs his mother and kisses her on the cheek.

"Bye, son," replies Elizabeth, crying and hugging him tight. "Bye, Isabelle." The two women hold each other and sob. Elizabeth walks over to the children and hugs and kisses each of them.

"Goodbye, big brother," says Lucas with a big hug for James. "Thanks again for your help."

"Bye, little brother, and bye, Isabelle," replies James. "You both take care. And don't be a stranger. Keep in touch somehow." James will miss Lucas. They have always lived in the same town and been close.

Lucas hugs his little nephew and says, "Bye, Paul, and thanks for your help."

"Bye, Uncle Lucas. I'll miss you," responds Paul with a trembling lip.

Isabelle and Lucas wave goodbye from their front porch as they watch his mom and dad leave the yard. They also wave at James and Paul as they leave. Lucas kisses Isabelle and looks at his children with a grin. *My dream is coming true,* he thinks. *Everything I ever wanted in life is right here in this house and this town.*

CHAPTER 17

More than a year has passed. Lucas is now twenty-six years old. He is doing well at his job and proudly working on his mechanic's certification. He is happy to be able to provide for his family at the same time as pursuing his dream. Isabelle stays at home and nurtures the children, which she cherishes. Lucas is capable of paying all the bills and more. They love living in Uxbridge where the four children, ages six and under, have the space to play and grow. It is a wonderful life.

Often, they visit Lucas's aunt Betty and uncle Charles, whom everyone calls Chuck. Betty is John's sister. They are a childless couple, and they love it when Lucas and Isabelle bring the children over. Chuck is a great uncle, and he loves kids. The children also love going over to their place. Lucas has a few uncles and aunts living in the Toronto area. His dad's brothers, Uncle Joseph and Uncle George, both work on the CN Railway.

One hot summer morning, as Isabelle gets up to start breakfast for the children, she seems to feel under the weather; she thinks she may be catching the flu bug that is going around. She heads to the bathroom, feeling nauseous and sick to her stomach. After she throws up, she feels relief, and then she continues her day. As the children wake up, Isabelle prepares breakfast; she is still feeling queasy. By the later part of the morning, she feels better and spends the day outside with the children. It is a beautiful day, and they enjoy a picnic in their backyard, which the children love, especially Richard.

The next morning Isabelle feels her stomach turning, but after an hour or so, she feels better again. She now knows what is happening to her body. She does not have the flu. She is pregnant. This is impossible! Lucas and she take all the necessary precautions because the doctor has told them to not get pregnant again—she or the baby have a ninety percent chance of dying. Isabelle becomes nervous; she calls her family doctor for an appointment and is scheduled that morning. Isabelle knows it will take days before she gets the results, but in her mind, she is convinced that she is pregnant.

Four days pass, and as she is reading a book to the children, the phone rings. It is the doctor on the other end.

"Hello," says Isabelle with her charming accent.

"Hello, is this Isabelle?" asks Dr. Coleman.

Isabelle, in a worried tone, concedes that it's her.

"Isabelle, this is Dr. Coleman speaking, and I have your results on the pregnancy test," responds Dr. Coleman. "Can you come in today?"

"Can you tell me now because I have been worried sick for the past few days," says Isabelle in a trembling voice.

"If you want, Isabelle. According to the test results, you are pregnant. Isabelle, you need to come to my office soon, so we can go through your file because you had a complicated delivery with your last baby. This delivery will have complications with an even higher percentage of risk according to your file. You were not supposed to get pregnant again because of the high-risk factors. For example, hemorrhaging was a problem last time. I don't want to scare you, but we have reasons to take serious precautions with this pregnancy," explains Dr. Coleman. "I'll see you in a few weeks Isabelle, and take good care of yourself."

"Yes, Dr. Coleman. I will," replies Isabelle, and she hangs up the phone. She holds her stomach with both hands and starts to cry.

"What's wrong, Mommy?" Richard asks as he comes running out from the living room with Johnny behind him while Steve and Lucy are still playing in the living room.

"Mommy is okay, sweetie," says Isabelle as she wipes her eyes.

"Why are you crying, Mommy?" asks Richard looking concerned, and Johnny runs to hug his mommy.

"Sorry, Richard. Mommy has a bellyache. But I am better now that you and Johnny came to hug me. My bellyache is gone, sweetie," she says and hugs both of them and kisses their little foreheads. "Let's go see Steve and Lucy, and I will continue to read the story," replies Isabelle.

Later that afternoon, just before supper, Lucas arrives, and the children run to the door and hug their dad. Lucas always loves this moment when his children run to him with excitement.

"Isabelle, you'll never guess what happened to me today," says Lucas, exposing his handsome smile. As he reaches her, he gives her a big kiss and a gigantic hug.

"Lucas, you look as if something tremendous happened to you today," replies Isabelle, feeling safe in her husband's arms. "What happened?"

"You won't believe this, Isabelle," says Lucas; there is excitement in his voice.

"What, Lucas? Don't leave me in suspense." Isabelle looks tenderly at her husband as she kisses Lucas.

"Isabelle, a man came to the garage to get his car repaired, and guess what?" says Lucas as he picks up Lucy, and the boys follow him toward the living room.

"What? What?" Isabelle follows them anxiously.

Lucas sits down on the sofa and sits Lucy on his lap. The boys sit around them.

"The man had an old Studebaker, and Jim put me in charge of repairing the engine," explains Lucas with a twinkle in his eyes. "The best part was that I found the problem and repaired the engine within the day. Jim was very proud of my performance. Isabelle, when I took the Studebaker for a test drive, I felt seventeen again! It was an exciting experience. Also, the man—Mr. Newman—was very happy to hear his engine running smoothly."

"Wow, Lucas!" says Isabelle as she sits down on the sofa chair.

"What is a Studebaker, Daddy?" questions Richard; he is a child with an inquiring mind.

"Richard, my very first vehicle was a Studebaker; that's the car I drove when I met your mom," explains Lucas as he smiles at his son and then winks at Isabelle.

"I love cars," says Johnny very innocently, sounding just like the four-year-old that he is.

"I'm certain you do, Johnny," replies Lucas proudly.

"Johnny is just like you, Lucas," Isabelle says. Then she gets up, saying, "Boys, time to clean up because supper is ready."

As they get up, they can all smell the aroma of their mom's cooking, and they are all hungry.

That evening, after Isabelle and Lucas tuck the children into bed, they go outside to the front porch, each with a cup of tea.

Lucas sits on the front swing, and Isabelle sits beside him. Lucas put his arm around Isabelle and gives her a kiss.

"How was your day, Isabelle?" asks Lucas and grins from ear to ear. Isabelle has always admired Lucas's beautiful smile, and she feels fortunate to have such a warm and friendly husband.

"It was good," replies Isabelle as she sips her tea and looks away, thinking about what the doctor said to her this morning. How will she tell him? He will not be happy about this news.

"Is there something wrong, Isabelle?" asks Lucas with concern. "You seem so distant, and that's not like you."

"I am fine, Lucas, but there is something I need to talk to you about," confesses Isabelle as she looks down.

"What is it, Isabelle?" replies Lucas in a worried voice.

"Lucas, I went to see Dr. Coleman because I thought I was having morning sickness last week. Dr. Coleman called me today, and he confirmed that I am pregnant," explains Isabelle in a frightened voice. "Dr. Coleman examined my file from Lucy's birth, and he told me that this delivery will be riskier."

"What! You're pregnant, Isabelle?" shouts Lucas in confusion as he tries to wrap everything up in his mind.

"Lucas, I am so scared!" cries Isabelle. "I don't know what to do."

"Isabelle, I am so sorry for putting you through this again. What more did the doctor say?" questions Lucas as he hugs Isabelle.

"This pregnancy has a higher risk factor, so he wants me to take serious precautions with this pregnancy and to take good care of myself," replies Isabelle as she weeps. "It is not your fault, Lucas. We were very careful, but things happen for reasons." Isabelle wipes her tears. "Dr. Coleman is an expert obstetrician and gynecologist, and he is looking at my file to better understand my medical status."

"Isabelle, I believe that Dr. Coleman is a great doctor, but I'm still afraid for you and the baby. I couldn't bear it if anything happened to either one of you. I love you, Isabelle," says Lucas. His eyes become moist while he hugs Isabelle.

"Let's take it one day at a time, Lucas. I will be extremely careful and follow the doctor's orders to the letter," replies Isabelle as she kisses Lucas.

Isabelle has a good pregnancy, as she did for all her children; it is at the delivery that all the complications occur. Lucas lives every day worrying about the day when Isabelle will go into labor. During the last trimester of Isabelle's pregnancy, Dr. Coleman has scheduled Isabelle for a cesarean on March nineteenth. He believes this will provide a better chance for both the mom and baby to have fewer complications.

On March 18, 1966, around four in the morning, Isabelle's amniotic sac ruptures in bed. Isabelle quickly wakes up Lucas.

"Lucas, it is time to go to the hospital," whispers Isabelle.

In confusion, Lucas wakes up and exclaims, "What! What!"

"Lucas, my water broke, and my labor pains have started," explains Isabelle as she gets up slowly. "You need to call Aunt Betty and Uncle Chuck to come over to care for the children. We need to go to the hospital right now."

"You're in labor?" replies Lucas as he wipes his eyes. "Wow, it's time to go." Lucas gets up quickly as soon as he realizes that Isabelle is in labor. He has to call his Aunt Betty and Uncle Chuck to come over. Lucas anxiously runs to the phone.

He dials, and the phone rings a few times before they pick up.

In a sleepy voice, Aunt Betty answers the phone and says, "Hello. Who's this?"

"Aunt Betty, it's me, Lucas. Isabelle is in labor; her water broke. Can you and Uncle Chuck come over now?"

"Yes, Lucas, we'll be there right away," replies Aunt Betty and then abruptly hangs up the phone. She knows there is no time to waste.

Lucas helps Isabelle to the car and takes the luggage at the same time as his uncle and aunt are pulling into the yard. They live only a few minutes away.

"Thanks, Aunt Betty. The children are all still sleeping," says Lucas as he rushes to the driver's seat. "Thank you, Uncle Chuck; thank you so much."

"You both take care, and don't worry about the children," replies Aunt Betty.

In the passenger side, Isabelle is having strong contractions, and they are coming pretty steadily.

"Are you doing okay, Isabelle?" asks Lucas. He can see she is in pain as he jumps in and drives off.

Isabelle tries to be quiet, but her labor is overcoming her, and the pain is becoming intense. She begins to moan. "Lucas, I feel like pushing—that means the baby is coming!" cries Isabelle. She starts to shriek.

"Isabelle! We're almost there! Hold on, honey. We'll make it to the hospital," Lucas responds. His heart starts pumping faster with fear of what might happen if Isabelle gives birth in the car and complications occur. His mind is racing, but he tries to keep calm for Isabelle, through his own desperation, to protect his wife.

Lucas arrives at the hospital, stops the vehicle near the emergency doors and helps Isabelle inside.

"Help! Help! My wife is in labor," yells Lucas to the nurses.

One nurse runs with a gurney and helps Lucas put Isabelle on it, while the other nurse calls for Dr. Coleman, as he had ordered. The doctor is getting ready because he knows Isabelle's condition and that she will need an emergency cesarean. Some nurses are getting the operating room prepared for Isabelle and the baby.

The two nurses wheel Isabelle to the operating room. As Lucas watches them take her away, he prays to God to help his wife and baby. Everything is out of Lucas's hands, which makes him feel helpless.

Isabelle is still in great pain; the contractions are more intense and frequent. "I feel like pushing—the baby is coming," yells Isabelle as she tries not to push, but the urge is there.

"Don't push, Isabelle! You need to have a cesarean section," the nurse tries to explain as they put her on the operating table.

Dr. Coleman is waiting to examine Isabelle. His eyes widen as he checks the baby's pulse. "The baby's head is coming," says Dr. Coleman to the nurse. "Isabelle, you have to deliver your baby because there is no time for a cesarean. I will tell you when to push." The doctor looks nervous. "Okay, Isabelle—push… push… push."

Isabelle tries hard to push; the baby is nearly there. Isabelle is getting weaker as she tries to push again, while the nurse guides her.

"Stop pushing, Isabelle," demands Dr. Coleman as he notices the cord around the baby's neck. Dr. Coleman finally gets the baby untangled and tells Isabelle to push again, but Isabelle is losing her strength; she is getting weak. The nurse tries to coach Isabelle to push again; she tries but with no luck. Isabelle has no energy. Dr. Coleman puts pressure against Isabelle's stomach as he feels the contraction. The baby's head is out, but now it is the shoulders.

"Isabelle, one more push, and your baby will be out. Please push, Isabelle! Push! Push!" instructs Dr. Coleman.

Isabelle ultimately finds strength and pushes; the baby thrusts right out. "It's a boy, Isabelle," says Dr. Coleman. Isabelle grins, for she is exhausted. Then Dr. Coleman notices Isabelle has started to hemorrhage. Isabelle is feeling weaker and weaker. Dr. Coleman hands the baby to the nurse and attends to Isabelle. The other nurse hurries and gets pints of blood, as the doctor ordered because Isabelle will need a transfusion. She has lost too much blood. Dr. Coleman eventually stops the hemorrhaging. Isabelle is extremely drained; her pulse is weak, and she is very pale. The doctor orders an intravenous, and the nurse additionally hooks Isabelle to a heart monitor.

The baby is immensely exhausted as well; his cry is weak, and his breathing is shallow. Dr. Coleman calls for backup, and Dr. Davis, a pediatrician, hurries to attend to the baby. With the help of the nurse, the baby is put on intravenous, oxygen, and a heart monitor. As Dr. Davis examines the baby, he sees a very weak heartbeat because of the distress he went through. Only time will determine his condition.

Dr. Coleman and Dr. Davis come out of the room and see Lucas sitting in the waiting room, looking extremely nervous. Lucas looks up and sees both doctors walking toward him. He stands up, waiting anxiously; his heart is pounding hard as he watches them approach.

"How are Isabelle and the baby? Is it a boy or a girl?" questions Lucas in a worried tone.

"You have a son, weighing eight pounds and four ounces. He is very weak, and the next twenty-four hours will be crucial. The cord was around his neck, and he went into distress, which will weaken his heart, and his lungs are very weak. He is stable, being on oxygen, and he is on a heart monitor because he might go into cardiac arrest," explains Dr. Davis, "but by tomorrow, we will know more about his prognosis."

Tears start to flow down Lucas's cheeks. Lucas asks, "What about Isabelle? What is her condition?"

"She is very weak also because of the tribulation. She hemorrhaged, as in her last delivery. I got it under control, but she lost a great deal of blood. We gave her a transfusion and intravenous, and her vital signs are poor. Isabelle is exhausted, and she will need to sleep to recover. The next twenty-four hours are critical for her, also. We are monitoring her; there is a nurse by her side," responds Dr. Coleman. "There was no time for Isabelle to have a cesarean because the baby was already in the birth canal, and by that time, it was too late."

"Can I see the baby and Isabelle?" asks Lucas as he tries to keep strong for them.

"Yes, you can see the baby. He is in an incubator," says Dr. Davis. "The nurse will assist you."

"Lucas, when you are ready, you can see Isabelle too, but she will need her rest," explains Dr. Coleman.

Lucas shakes their hands and thanks them both. Then a nurse assists Lucas to see the baby. Lucas smiles at his little baby boy.

"Hi there, my little one. Daddy's here because Mommy needs her sleep; she will be with you soon."

Lucas watches his son fight for his life with every breath. Lucas puts his finger in the baby's hand, and the baby wraps his hand around Lucas's big finger. Lucas prays as he stares at his son, and he has a lump in his throat.

The nurse comes into the nursery to tell Lucas, "Isabelle is awake but still very weak. She is asking about the baby and if you are with the baby."

"Can I see her?" asks Lucas as he continues to stare at his son.

"Yes, but remember she needs to rest," explains the nurse.

"I just wanted to tell her about our beautiful son."

The nurse feels for Lucas and leads him to the recovery room. Lucas looks at Isabelle's fragile body hooked up to machines as he walks in and walks toward the head of the bed and kisses her on the forehead. She looks up and tries to smile through her weakness.

"Isabelle, we have a beautiful boy. I was just with him," Lucas tries to smile and stay strong.

Isabelle whispers, "Is he okay?"

"He had the cord wrapped around his neck, and he was in distress at birth, but now the doctors are taking good care of him," explains Lucas. "I want you to sleep, and I'll stay beside you, so you can get your strength back. Then we'll see our son together."

"Thanks, Lucas," says Isabelle faintly, as she falls back to sleep.

The next day, Isabelle is getting some of her strength back, and Lucas takes her to see the baby. Although the baby is still in critical condition, the outcome is looking brighter. Isabelle yearns to hold her baby; she and Lucas touch and talk to him but won't be able to hold him for a few days. On the third day, Isabelle starts to get stronger, and the baby's condition changes for the better. Both Lucas and Isabelle are excited to hold their newborn.

Lucas watches Isabelle rock the baby, and he ponders his good fortune even in this dire situation.

"What do you want to name him?" asks Lucas as he kisses Isabelle and their son.

"I was thinking about Thomas Charles Clarkson," replies Isabelle. Then she kisses baby Thomas on the forehead. "Mr. Thomas was such a wonderful person to me when I worked for him."

"I like the names," says Lucas. "Hi, Thomas." Lucas holds his little baby's hand. "Uncle Chuck will also be happy to hear this."

It takes two weeks before they both can go home. Lucas is grateful to have his wife and baby come home to the other children. They have missed their mommy deeply.

It is a wonderful time for Lucas and Isabelle when they have their miracle child come home with them. Aunt Betty is terrific; she takes excellent care of the children and also helps Isabelle with her recovery for a few weeks by pitching in around the house until Lucas comes home at night.

CHAPTER 18

Lucas continues to talk about his life, while Lucy lies there with no indication of movement. Lucas becomes silent and then glances at the heart monitor; he thought he heard the monitor beep faster, but there is no sign of change. Lucas looks at Lucy, wishing fervently that she would wake up. He wipes his tears and picks up his story again.

"Months flew by, and then I had a call from my father telling me that he and Mother were coming to visit. He said he had something very important to talk to me about," says Lucas, still holding onto Lucy's hand.

Lucas goes back in time and recalls the day his father and mother came to visit them in Uxbridge.

It is a hot summer day in the middle of July when Lucas notices a truck driving up his laneway. He takes a good look and sees it is his mom and dad.

"Isabelle! Get the children—my parents are here," shouts Lucas excitedly.

Isabelle gathers the children and picks up Thomas from the cradle. She stands with Lucas on the front porch. John and Elizabeth drive up near the porch, and John parks his truck. As they get out, Lucas runs to them and embraces them. Isabelle and the children follow behind Lucas. They all embrace. Elizabeth is so happy to see the children again and to hold Thomas for the first time. John holds Lucy in one arm, with Richard, Johnny, and Steve huddled around him. Isabelle and Lucas hold each other, watching with big smiles as they see the importance of grandparents to the children.

"Mom and Dad, we can all go inside. Isabelle has prepared the guest room for you," says Lucas. "I'll bring in your luggage."

"Thank you, son," replies John.

Isabelle leads them into the house. Elizabeth brings the baby, John carries Lucy and holds Steve's hand, while Lucas, Richard, and Johnny get the luggage from the truck.

In the house, Isabelle walks them to the guest room upstairs, and Lucas follows right behind them, with Richard and Johnny carrying the luggage.

"You both can get refreshed and settle in while I finish preparing supper," says Isabelle. Then she takes Thomas from Elizabeth. "Supper will be ready in an hour."

"Thank you, Isabelle," replies Elizabeth as she hands over the baby. "I could smell your cooking as I walked in. There always seems to be something delicious in your kitchen."

"Isabelle made your favorite meal, Dad," reveals Lucas, reaching over and taking Lucy from his dad. "Come on, boys. Let's go downstairs and let Grandpa and Grandma get ready for supper."

Richard runs over to his grandma and gives her a kiss on her hand. "I missed you, Grandma."

Elizabeth looks at him lovingly. "You are a sensitive soul just like your dad," she informs him as she kisses Richard and looks gently at Lucas.

Everyone laughs. Then Lucas and Isabelle head downstairs with the children. Lucas takes the kids into the living room to play, and Isabelle lays the baby in his cradle before she continues preparing supper.

Supper is almost ready, and Isabelle is starting to set the table in the dining room when Lucas sneaks up behind her and kisses her.

"Lucas," says Isabelle as she hands him the plates, "your parents will be down any minute, and they will be hungry."

"I love you, Isabelle, and your cooking smells mighty appetizing," replies Lucas as he sets the plates on the table. Then he grabs Isabelle by her waist, and tells her, "You are so wonderful! I'll do anything to make you as happy as you make me, my dear."

"Lucas, I am so happy with you!" says Isabelle as she kisses him.

Lucas continues to help Isabelle as they hear John and Elizabeth coming down the stairs. Elizabeth offers to help, but Lucas tells his parents to sit down and relax while he gets the children because supper is ready. Lucas heads to the living room to gather the children. John pulls out a chair for Elizabeth and then sits down himself. Isabelle brings in the roast beef with seasoned roasted baby potatoes and glazed carrots.

"Isabelle, the platter looks delightful, and the aroma fills the room," says John. "You are our wonderful French chef."

"Thank you, Mr. Clarkson," replies Isabelle as she shyly smiles at her kind father-in-law.

"You have a wonderful talent, Isabelle," says Elizabeth and jokes, "I am so grateful you married my son and that I will never have to worry that he will go hungry."

Isabelle and Elizabeth glance at each other and grin when Lucas enters the dining room with the children. They all gather together and enjoy the fabulous meal Isabelle has prepared.

Once supper is finished, Lucas and his dad sit in the living room with a cup of coffee while Isabelle and Elizabeth get the children ready for bed. Elizabeth is happy being with Lucas and his family. She wants to help Isabelle bathe the children and tuck them into bed.

Lucas and John are talking about Lucas's Studebaker. As they reminisce, Lucas can tell that something is wrong with his father just by John's tone of voice.

"Dad, are you all right?" questions Lucas.

John looks surprised at his son's attentiveness and asks, "What makes you think there's something wrong with me, son?"

"I can tell by your voice, Dad."

Isabelle and Elizabeth walk into the living room with the children to say good night to Lucas and Grandpa John. Richard and little Johnny hug Grandpa and then their dad. Steve and Lucy give their dad and Grandpa John a kiss and a hug; they are still in the arms of Isabelle and Grandma Elizabeth.

"Come on, boys. Let's go upstairs, and Grandma and Mommy will tuck you in," says Isabelle as she guides them toward the stairwell. She is holding Steve, and Elizabeth follows carrying Lucy.

John and Lucas smile as they watch them go upstairs.

"Lucas, there is something that's bothering me, and your mother doesn't know," says John, looking down. "I hope I can count on you to keep this just between the two of us for the moment."

"Sure, Dad. What is it? Is it that bad?"

"Yes, Lucas—it is quite crucial," replies John, quietly. "James told me he wants to move to the city so Donna and Scott can have better schooling and more up-to-date therapy."

"That's understandable, Dad; I'd do the same for my family if I were in James's position."

"That's not all," explains John. "James wants to sell the house, and he'll need the money for a down payment on a house in the city."

"Okay," says Lucas, taking everything his father has said seriously. "What's wrong with that, Dad?"

"No, that part is fine; I gave that farmhouse to him," replies John. "James doesn't want to work on the farm when he moves; he found another job, trucking logs."

"You can get outside help," Lucas says.

"It is more complicated than that. Mary needs my help, and my health is deteriorating," explains John, and his eyes glaze over.

"Dad, I'm confused. What do you mean? Mary needs your help? What's wrong with Joe?" asks Lucas with concern. "And what's going on with your health?"

"Lucas, my asthma is getting worse. The doctor told me that within three years, I might need oxygen to breath. The most painful

Susanne Bellefeuille

thing for me is Mary and the children... Joe continues to drink, and he doesn't work. I have to pay her bills, and I also paid off her mortgage. The children need to eat. I always get groceries for them, but now times are hard for me. I sold the land that we bought years ago to pay off Mary's mortgage because she was going to lose everything. Son, I'm scared. I don't know how to tell your mother that I am very close to bankruptcy, and I don't have the energy that I used to," cries John.

"Does James know about this?" asks Lucas. His poor father. He feels for him intensely, but he also feels helpless. What can he do?

"No. I don't want to tell him because he needs to do what's best for Donna and Scott," says John. "James and Debra need to move to provide better care for the children, Lucas."

"I understand," whispers Lucas. "What do you want to do, Dad?"

"Lucas, I want you to move back with us," replies John. "I know this is a shock to you, but I need your help, son."

"Dad, this is my life here, and I have only one more year until I get my mechanic's certificate. Besides, I have a great job, and Isabelle can stay home and be with the children," explains Lucas.

"I realize that, Lucas, but I will be bankrupt soon, and I need you to help me so I don't lose the farm. Your mother would be crushed if she knew we could lose the farm. I have a chance to keep the farm with your help; we can farm and have cash crops. Also, you can cut logs and sell them to the pulp industry. You are young and knowledgeable about farming and the chainsaw. I need your strength because I can't do the hard labor anymore," says John.

"Dad, the house is too small for all of us," expresses Lucas. "The children are growing, and they need space. Isabelle and I love our independence."

"Lucas, I'm desperate. I'm begging you to help me. Please, son— please, Lucas," pleads John.

Lucas becomes quiet for a few minutes as he looks out the window. So many feelings are going through him right now; he empathizes with his father and feels terrible about his situation.

He also feels slightly guilty that he left the farm, but it's not his responsibility to stay anymore. He's a grown man with a large family of his own to support, and he is so close to realizing his dream. Will it all go down the drain now if he goes home to help his father? But what kind of a man would he be if he didn't help his dad? His thoughts whirl.

John just stares at the floor, wondering how this has happened. He feels terrible but has no choice. He needs his son's strength and his ability to work the farm. Lucas turns and sees his father staring down at the floor. Lucas notes how his father is aging. *How could a strong, successful person like my father go bankrupt and become a sick, fragile old man?* thinks Lucas. Lucas wants to stay in Uxbridge and become a Class A Mechanic. He loves living in the country house with his wife and children. He has to make a serious decision. He does not want to give up his dream, but how can he abandon his father in his time of need? Lucas feels he has no option but to go back at his father's farm and try to mend the pieces.

"Dad, I'll need time to talk to Isabelle about this. I want you to promise me that you will tell Mom about your situation because I don't want any surprises if I move back with you," requests Lucas.

"Thank you so much, son! I know you have to talk to Isabelle, and I definitely will tell your mother. I won't leave any details out," John assures him.

"Since I'm putting down ground rules, you have to promise me that you will not continue to provide for Joe's responsibilities. You and I will have a talk with him and Mary about your state. Joe or Mary will have to work to provide food for their children. You're in no position to take care of other people at the moment; you have to put yourself and Mom first right now. Dad, I know that's hard because you have been used to taking care of others your whole life, but they are adults now and will have to make decisions themselves. Of course, I love Mary also, but she chose to be with Joe. As a result, she will have to make her own choices."

"Yes, Lucas, I agree," replies John, but he still feels sad about his daughter's way of living.

"Dad, this will be a huge decision for me because as you know, farming was never my passion, and I will be giving up what I love most. But I love you, Dad, and I'm willing to put my life on hold for a while so that we can get back what you've worked so hard for," explains Lucas. He gets up and embraces his father lovingly.

"You are a great man, Lucas, and a devoted son, and I love you and can't tell you how much I appreciate this," whispers John as he hugs his son back. Lucas sits back down in his chair and the weight of his decision lifts from his strong shoulders. But he still has not told Isabelle. How will she react? And what about the children? It will not be easy to uproot them from their schools and their routine.

Isabelle and Elizabeth walk into the room. "Wow! You two are in deep conversation," says Isabelle with a smile as she carries in the coffee pot. Elizabeth brings the sugar and cream to the living room. "You both want a refill?"

"They say women talk a lot," remarks Elizabeth, smiling, while she sets the sugar and cream on the coffee table, and they all chuckle.

"Yes, Isabelle," replies Lucas as he stands up and reaches out his cup.

Isabelle pours the coffee into his cup, and Lucas thanks her with a kiss. Before she turns toward John, Isabelle grins broadly at Lucas, and it is clear to everyone their love is still strong after all these years.

"John, do you want another cup of coffee?" Isabelle asks.

John accepts graciously, and Isabelle pours his coffee. "Thank you, Isabelle." She then pours coffee for Elizabeth and herself.

They sit there chatting about the children: how they have grown and about the miracle baby, Thomas. As they converse, Lucas and John look at each other, knowing that Isabelle and Elizabeth are not suspicious about their conversation, but they are about to have a bomb dropped in their lap. Neither man knows how his wife will respond to the news. They wish they didn't have to tell them.

Lucas gazes at his watch and then looks at Isabelle. As she smiles back at him, Lucas glances at his parents.

"I'm sure you both had a long day, and you must be getting tired, and so am I," says Lucas as he gets up. "I think I'll call it a night."

"You're right, Lucas. I am getting a little worn out," replies John.

In true Lucas style, he hugs and kisses both parents and says good night. Isabelle follows. They all proceed to their bedrooms, and even though it is a difficult time, there is a general feeling of peace and contentment in the house.

CHAPTER 19

A few days later, John and Elizabeth are getting ready to head back to the farm. Lucas is helping his father put the luggage in the back of the truck.

"Lucas, before I leave, have you had a chance to think about coming back home?" asks John in a nervous voice.

"That's all I've been thinking about in the last few days, Dad," replies Lucas. "I haven't mentioned it to Isabelle yet, but I have to talk to her soon."

"Son, I know I'm asking a lot from you, but I need your help to get out of this mess," John says, his eyes turning red as though he might cry.

"Dad, I want to help you, but it's a lot to sacrifice. I love you, and family is more important to me than anything else in the world, but I'm afraid that Isabelle will be disappointed," says Lucas as he hugs his dad. "Give me a couple of days, and I'll get back to you and give you a firm answer." Lucas reaches out to touch his father's arm reassuringly. "I promise."

"Thanks, son. Please know how hard it is for me to ask you to make this sacrifice," replies John. Lucas knows this to be true. His father is a proud man, hardworking, and self-sufficient. He would not ask this of Lucas if it were not absolutely essential.

"I understand, Dad. Remember to tell Mom about your health and finances," says Lucas. "You can't keep this from her any longer. You're partners. She will understand more than anyone."

"I'll tell her when we get home. I promise, son."

Isabelle and Elizabeth come over with the children. Elizabeth is holding Thomas.

"Are you ready, Elizabeth?" asks John.

"Not really, but we have to go," replies Elizabeth as she kisses Thomas on the forehead and then hands him to Isabelle.

John and Elizabeth hug and kiss the children, and then they say goodbye to Isabelle. They both stand there looking at Lucas, sad to leave him again after their reunion. They miss him so much along with Isabelle and the children.

"Goodbye, Lucas," says Elizabeth and then gets into the truck.

Lucas shuts the truck door and gives her another kiss on the cheek. "Love you, Mom."

Lucas walks toward John. "Goodbye, Dad," he says as he winks.

"Goodbye, son," says John with a smile.

Lucas puts his arm around Isabelle, and they, with the children, wave as they watch John and Elizabeth drive off. Lucas guides the children back to the house, and Isabelle carries baby Thomas.

That same night, Isabelle is in the bedroom, brushing her hair, as she does every night. Lucas is sitting on the bed, staring at her beautiful, long, dark hair. Isabelle notices Lucas staring at her.

"What is the matter, Lucas? You seem so distant," says Isabelle as she looks at him in the mirror.

"Just staring at your beautiful hair," replies Lucas with a smile.

Isabelle gets up, comes over to sit beside Lucas, gives him a kiss on the cheek and says, "but I know you… There is something you are keeping bottled up inside."

"What makes you think that?" asks Lucas as he starts kissing her on the neck.

"Lucas, stop—I'm serious." Isabelle laughs as she tries to push him away. "I think you and your father had an intense talk."

"What makes you think that?" asks Lucas with surprise.

"Just the way you are looking at me. I know there is something troubling you. It is written all over your face, ever since you and your dad sat down in the living room the first night they were here. I did not say anything because your parents were here, and I did not want to upset you, Lucas," explains Isabelle as she brushes her fingers through his hair. "Please, let me know—what's wrong?"

"It's my father, Isabelle. He is in trouble, and he needs my help."

"What is wrong?" asks Isabelle in a more serious tone. Her French accent has decreased over the years but still apparent and although she uses a few contractions, she still tends to speak more formally than Lucas or other Anglophones.

"He's sick; his asthma is getting worse, just like your father, and he has difficulty breathing. Working on the farm is extremely hard for him in this state," explains Lucas, sadly.

"What about James? Can he control the farm himself or maybe hire a person to help him?" wonders Isabelle.

"There's more to it than that, Isabelle," Lucas pauses as he kisses her on the cheek. "James is selling the other farmhouse. James and Debra want to move to the city to give Donna and Scott more opportunities and better care for their disabilities. James also chose to move on with his life and work elsewhere. Dad said James will not work the farm; he got a job trucking logs," says Lucas, shaking his head in disbelief. "And to top it off, my father is going bankrupt."

"What! Why?" Isabelle looks shocked. "How is that possible? He was always so good with money."

"I guess Joe wasn't working, only drinking, and Mary needed money for food and to pay the bills, so Dad paid off her mortgage and kept paying for necessities. He had to sell the land he purchased from Mr. Thomas to pay her mortgage. He is still buying her food, but he needs to speak with Mary and Joe about the issue and be honest about his health and financial situation. He needs to insist Joe take full responsibility for his own family," says Lucas. "My father cannot continue subsidizing them." There is sadness in his eyes.

"Your poor father—what about your mother?" inquires Isabelle.

"She doesn't know what is going on; he's been too afraid and embarrassed to tell her. She thinks everything is great," replies Lucas, shaking his head in disbelief.

"Wow! That is a lot to take in, Lucas," says Isabelle, devastated to hear this about Lucas's parents.

"There is more, Isabelle; it gets worse," Lucas informs her in a low voice.

"What can possibly get worse than that for your father, Lucas?" replies Isabelle.

"It is what my father asked of me," responds Lucas hesitantly.

"Okay, Lucas, my heart is pumping fast now—no suspense. Tell me, what is it?" says Isabelle.

"Dad wants us to move back to the farm," whispers Lucas, who is still in disbelief that he might have to give up on his dream, which he is so close to obtaining after all his sacrifices and hard work.

"What! Did you just say your father wants us to move back to the farm?" shouts Isabelle. Now, the tears are flowing fast down her cheeks as she realizes the impact of John's situation on her and her family and how much they might have to give up.

"I know, Isabelle. I was shocked myself when he asked me," says Lucas in a heartrending voice.

"Oh, Lucas! What are you going to do? We can't move back," exclaims Isabelle; her mind refuses to accept the rearrangement.

"Isabelle, I love it here. This is my life, my world. But my father needs me, and I don't know what to do. I feel torn between my dream and my father's needs. Isabelle, I've thought hard about this, and it's tearing me apart inside. But I believe caring for family in times of need is very important. What kind of a man would I be if I walked away from my father in this desperate situation? I can't do that. You know, Isabelle, that family comes first in my life. I would do anything for you, the children, and my parents. I would set aside my own dreams to make sure my family's needs are fulfilled," explains Lucas while he holds Isabelle's hands.

"Lucas, you are a great man, and that is why I love you so much, but there are times when you have to think of yourself and your dreams and needs," states Isabelle as she tries to convince him.

"I understand what you're saying, Isabelle, but it's even bigger than that. It is about my parents losing the farm. They worked so hard to give their children, including me, a good life, and now they're losing everything. My dad sacrificed his farm to help Mary and her children, and now he needs help. What are my options, Isabelle?" laments Lucas. He stands up and walks around the bedroom while rubbing his forehead, trying to lessen the pressure in his head.

"Lucas, I can see the hurt. I know this is where you want to be. You are almost finished your mechanic's certification. Is it possible to stay here for just one year until you get your papers, and then we can move to the farm? Maybe you can get a part-time job as a mechanic, especially in the winter. You know, Lucas, there's not much to do on the farm but feeding and milking the cow and cleaning the stalls," suggests Isabelle with a concerned look. She repositions herself on the bed to face Lucas.

"I wish it were that simple, Isabelle," says Lucas, pacing around the room. "My father needs me right now, before next month because his bank account is dry. He can't even afford to feed his livestock. He can't wait another year. He could lose the farm by then, and where would he go?"

"It is that bad, Lucas?" asks Isabelle, confused. "What difference would it make if you leave now or a few months from now?'

"It's a real mess, Isabelle. Father wants me to start cutting down trees and hauling the logs to the mill for extra cash, and we can also do cash crops," explains Lucas.

"What do you mean by cash crops?" questions Isabelle.

"After we cut down the trees, we can plant extra crops to sell to the feed mill in different little towns," Lucas informs her as he sits down beside Isabelle.

"Lucas, you don't like to farm, and cutting trees for a living is not you!" insists Isabelle. She knows Lucas is not enthusiastic about farming, especially slaughtering cows or pigs. "Lucas, you have a weakness when it comes to slaughtering animals. It is painful for you. For crying out loud—you don't have the nerve to go hunting! That is not your character. That is not who you are."

"I know—I know I have a weak stomach, and I don't like farming, but my father needs my help. What else can I do?" He raises his voice in frustration, which is contradictory to his usual gentle disposition, but his frustration is apparent. He does not like the situation and is torn between his loyalty to his wife and children and his loyalty to his parents.

"Sorry! I'm sorry… Lucas, I know this is an enormous decision for you to make. Your family is extremely important to you, and I know you will make the right choice. I will stop making you feel guilty and will respect your choice," vows Isabelle as she takes him into her loving arms.

"Thank you, Isabelle, for your understanding," replies Lucas and kisses Isabelle on the forehead. Then he looks her in the eyes as he holds her shoulders. "Yes, this is a huge decision, and I must make it soon. The only solution is to move back to the farm, Isabelle."

"Lucas, are you certain?" asks Isabelle as she frowns. "Is that what you want to do?"

"Yes, Isabelle! I've thought about it a lot, and my father needs my help," replies Lucas, showing the gravity of his dedication to his family.

"Lucas, for the last time—are you ready and willing to give up your mechanic's license for farming with your father?" asks Isabelle, hoping to confirm that Lucas has seriously considered every aspect of what he would be giving up by moving back to the farm.

"Isabelle, if my father was not in hardship and he had good health, then yes, I would continue my mechanic's training. I love it here. But the situation has changed, and I have no choice but to help my father. It's hard for me to make this decision, but it is easy to see that my father's health has drastically diminished. He is not the strong man I used to know, and it hurts me to see him that way.

It is just like your father, Isabelle. He is still living, but his quality of life will never be the same. Maybe it is best for you and me to move back to the old farm so we both can be close to our parents. Look at your father, Isabelle… he was supposed to die four years ago, but he's still alive, so you can spend quality time with him and your mother, brothers, and sisters. Let's be close to them because life is short, and you know how fast the years go by," explains Lucas. He looks at Isabelle sorrowfully.

"I understand every word you are saying, but this was your dream! I know the situation has changed, and I am ready to do what is best for our families. It is just that I do not want you to look back some day with regrets, Lucas," says Isabelle. At that moment, she embraces Lucas and starts to shed tears.

"Isabelle, the most important thing for me is that I have you, we're together, and we have healthy children," explains Lucas. He holds her close and kisses her on the cheek.

Moments later, Lucas says, "I'll call my father first thing in the morning to tell him that we're moving back to the farm soon." He forces himself to smile at Isabelle but is still sorrowful about the whole ordeal.

"Lucas, I would move anywhere, as long I am with you and our beautiful children. With your love and support, I feel that I can overcome any troubles."

The love that they have for each other always shines most strongly in the deepest and darkest moments of their lives. Lucas loves and respects Isabelle; he has always admired her. And Isabelle would do anything for her husband and is always loyal to him.

CHAPTER 20

The morning has arrived for Lucas and Isabelle to move back to the farm. As they watch the trucks with their belongings pull away, they all wave goodbye to Uncle James driving the first truck and his good friend Jeff, in the other truck.

Isabelle is putting the children into the vehicle while Lucas does the final check around the house. Lucas becomes nostalgic as he does his last inspection. He doesn't want to leave, but he feels he has to help his father.

Isabelle finishes tucking the children safely into the vehicle, and then she walks toward Lucas. She notices his sad face.

"Lucas, if this is too hard for you, you can change your mind, and we can still stay here," says Isabelle as she embraces him.

"I promised my father, and I can't change my mind. He needs me, Isabelle, but I have this feeling that life will never be the same," replies Lucas. He feels safe in Isabelle's arms.

"What do you mean, Lucas?" Isabelle looks at him with concern.

"I don't know; it is just this feeling in my gut that life will change for me when I go back to the farm," explains Lucas. He is confused. "There is just something about going back to the farm."

"Lucas, this is your choice! We can stay here if you don't think that going back feels right," cries Isabelle, feeling wary about his negative prediction. *Lucas is usually so positive and certain of himself,* thinks Isabelle.

"No, Isabelle, we're going back; I'm sure of that. Just be strong for me. Believe in me, and everything will be all right," says Lucas, and then he gives her a kiss. "Let's go. The children are waiting in the car, and it's a long drive."

"Okay," replies Isabelle, feeling drained.

They walk to the car with their arms around each other—supporting one another. Lucas kisses Isabelle on the forehead, and she smiles back at him. As they get to the vehicle, Thomas and Lucy are sleeping, but Richard, Johnny, and Steve are sitting up, ready for the journey to see Grandpa and Grandma Clarkson. Lucas opens the door for Isabelle and looks sweetly at her as she sits down.

"Are you ready for our journey?" asks Lucas before he shuts the door for her.

"I am ready to go," Isabelle says with a smile.

Lucas takes a last look at their country home as he draws a huge breath and gets into the car. He recalls all the fun times he has had with Isabelle and his children, the growth he has had while living here, and the dream job that he is leaving behind. This will be all gone once he drives off. Lucas closes his eyes for a few seconds, and when he opens his eyes, he comes back to reality. He looks at Isabelle and grins. Again, he gets a premonition that his life will change, but he brushes it off and starts to drive.

"Let's go live with Grandma and Grandpa Clarkson, boys!" says Lucas with a smile. He hopes that the kids don't sense the sadness in leaving behind his dream and tries to make the move a happy one for them.

"Let's go, Daddy," replies Richard.

Lucas looks back in his rearview mirror and chuckles as he hears Johnny and Steve laughing and repeating, "Yeah! Yeah! Go! Go!"

They drive for two and a half hours because all the children have fallen asleep. As they near Kingston, Isabelle hears baby Thomas fussing as he starts to wake up.

"We'll need to stop soon, Lucas, because Thomas is waking up, and he will be very hungry," says Isabelle.

"Yes, we can stop in Kingston. It's about ten minutes away," replies Lucas with a smile.

"You know how loud Thomas can get when he's hungry," Isabelle reminds him as she looks fondly at Lucas. "He has good lungs, and he will wake up the others."

They both laugh, sharing the love for their children.

When they get to Kingston, Lucas stops at the nearest restaurant and parks the vehicle. Isabelle goes into the restaurant to warm up the bottle as Lucas takes baby Thomas out of the car. His fussing increases to crying now. Lucas walks outside around the vehicle with the baby, and his crying grows louder.

"You're hungry, Thomas," expresses Lucas to his baby as he tries to comfort the little one while rocking him in his arms.

When Isabelle arrives with the bottle, Lucas takes it and feeds Thomas.

Isabelle looks through the car window to see whether the kids are still sleeping. As she peers in, she sees they are all sound asleep. Isabelle smiles to see her precious children nested into the backseat. Then she looks up at Lucas feeding the baby. She feels joy and love for the wonderful father and loving husband Lucas has always been.

Lucas smiles as he burps the baby. "Isabelle, I want you to know that you are a blessing in my life," he tells her, feeling her watchful gaze.

Isabelle feels the love of her husband as she takes Thomas to change him. Lucas opens the car door and wakes the children to tell them it is time to eat. He picks up his little girl, Lucy, as she is half-asleep.

"Daddy, I sleepy," says Lucy as she rubs her pretty little eyes.

"It's okay, Lucy. Once we get inside with your brothers, you will be hungry," Lucas tells her. "Come on, boys, let's feed our bellies."

Isabelle finishes changing Thomas, helps Lucas take the children out of the automobile, and they go into the restaurant for lunch. As they enter, Richard looks around the restaurant with anticipation. The other patrons take pleasure in seeing the young family together.

"Wow! Mommy, can we sit in the booth where we can see out the window?" he asks, his eyes wandering all around the country-style themed restaurant.

"Yes! Richard, you have chosen a beautiful spot for the family to relax and enjoy our lunch," says Isabelle as she hugs Richard with one arm while holding the baby in the other arm. Then Isabelle looks at Lucas. "Lucas, what do you think?"

"That is a great choice, Richard. I couldn't have done better myself," replies Lucas and rubs Richard's shoulder.

Richard, feeling proud, leads them to the booth, and they all follow. Lucas and Isabelle look at each other contentedly because they both see their son becoming a little man. Richard and Johnny sit beside each other with Lucas, while Steve sits beside Isabelle with Thomas in her arms, and little Lucy sits in a high chair.

Lucas places the order, as he knows what they want to eat. Everyone is hungry as they chat over lunch. Isabelle is proud of her family. She always enjoys watching how Lucas interacts with their children. Lucas is a man who appreciates his family, and never for one moment does he take them for granted.

After they finish lunch, Isabelle cleans little Lucy's high chair, Lucas pays the waitress, and he then picks up Lucy and guides the boys to the vehicle. Isabelle is carrying baby Thomas. Once they are all settled in the vehicle again, Lucas prepares to drive the last two hours to the farm. Isabelle feels more comfortable with their new journey with each happy moment that passes on the drive.

They finally arrive. As they pull into the driveway, John and Elizabeth are waiting for them in the house. The children get excited when they see the farmhouse. Richard tells Johnny that they will live with Grandpa and Grandma.

"Forever," says Johnny with an innocent smile. "Is it true, Mommy?"

Lucas and Isabelle look at each other and smile.

Path of Lucas

"Yes, Johnny, we will live with Grandpa and Grandma Clarkson at the farm," says Isabelle as she turns to look at the children. She adds, "Promise me that you will be good boys for Grandpa and Grandma Clarkson."

"We will, Mommy," respond Richard and Johnny together.

"Me too, Mommy!" says Steve's little voice in the background.

They all laugh.

As they get closer to the house, Elizabeth and John hear the vehicle driving into the yard. John looks out the window and calls out to Elizabeth that Lucas and Isabelle have arrived with the children. They both run outside to greet them, and Lucas toots his horn.

Lucas parks the vehicle, Elizabeth runs to meet them, and John follows behind her. After Lucas and Isabelle get out of the car, Elizabeth gives Lucas a big hug and a kiss, while John gives Lucas a handshake with a huge hug. Elizabeth goes around and hugs Isabelle; then she reaches out for Richard as he comes out of the backseat.

"Grandma, we will be living with you," says Richard as she hugs him.

"Forever, Grandma!" shouts Johnny as he comes out and hugs her.

"Yes! Johnny, I redecorated your daddy's room just for you boys," replies Elizabeth cheerfully.

Isabelle is helping Steve jump out, and he runs to hug his grandma.

"Hi, Grandma Clarkson," says Steve in a shy four-year-old voice as he bites on his fingers.

"Hello there, Steve," replies Elizabeth as she picks him up and gives him a kiss.

Isabelle reaches into the backseat and picks up Lucy, who is still sleeping. Lucas takes out baby Thomas and hands him to John. John gives the baby a kiss and walks over to Elizabeth.

"Wow! Our miracle baby is growing," says Elizabeth as she continues to hold Steve while bestowing kisses on the baby and little Lucy.

Elizabeth is happy to see her son back home with his family, and John is relieved to have his son back to help him save his farm.

"Let's go in the house, boys. Grandma has homemade chocolate chip cookies with milk," says Elizabeth as she puts Steve down with his brothers.

"Yeah!" yell the three boys as they start to run to the house.

They all head toward the house, with Isabelle carrying Lucy and John carrying Thomas as they sleep. Lucas walks arm and arm with his mother. As they walk into the house, the boys are sitting waiting for their grandma to give them milk and cookies.

Lucas takes the baby to their room and puts him on one of the beds, and Isabelle lays Lucy on the other bed. John prepares the coffee while Elizabeth gets the snacks. Lucas and Isabelle sit down with the children and enjoy Elizabeth's homemade cookies. John pours the coffee and sits down with Elizabeth, near the children.

"I see that James and his friend have put all our belongings in the garage," says Lucas as he looks out the window and sees the garage with its doors open.

"Yes," replies John. "If there's anything you need, I'll help you later."

"No, not tonight! There are a few things that we will bring in the house, but there's no rush," Lucas says as he watches his children enjoying their cookies.

"James had an offer on his house, and there is a house in Cornwall that they're interested in," says John as he takes another cookie.

"James told me the house is close to the school for Donna and Scott," adds Elizabeth as she takes a sip of her coffee.

"That sounds wonderful," replies Isabelle. "I am happy for Debra; she has been praying for this for such a long time."

"It's sad to see them move to Cornwall, but it's best for the children," says Elizabeth. "Do you want more coffee, Isabelle?"

"No, thanks, Mrs. Clarkson," replies Isabelle.

"More for you, Lucas?" offers Elizabeth.

"Yes, please, Mom," replies Lucas, and he winks at Isabelle. Lucas is constantly showing his love to her, and it never ceases to make her feel special.

"How about you, John?" asks Elizabeth as she pours Lucas's coffee.

"No thanks, love," replies John as he takes his last sip.

"Mommy, can we see Daddy's bedroom that Grandma decorated for us?" asks Richard when he has finished his snack.

"Yes, Mommy, please," begs Johnny with a big smile.

"Okay, boys, but wash your hands first," says Isabelle. "Do not wake up Lucy or Thomas."

"We promise, Mommy," Richard and Johnny declare, with Steve following them.

Isabelle and Elizabeth get up to clear the table, while Lucas and John go out to the vehicle to get the luggage.

"Son, thank you so much for moving back with your mom and me," says John as he grabs the handle of some luggage. Lucas sees a tear in his eye.

"Dad, we are family after all, and I am here to help you get through your difficult times," replies Lucas as he closes the trunk and pats his father on the shoulder.

They walk together toward the house. Lucas looks at his luggage and thinks of the new journey. John opens the door, and Lucas sees his children, happy to live at their grandparents' place, and his beautiful wife feeding their baby. *This will be a new chapter in my life*, he thinks. *Maybe that gut feeling was wrong. Maybe everything will turn out all right after all.*

Lucas works the fields, helps his father farming, and works logging trees. Lucas often thinks about what kind of life he would have had in Uxbridge. Sometimes Diane and Jim come down from Uxbridge to visit James and Debra. James calls Lucas and Isabelle, and they visit with them. Lucas is always happy to see Jim. Jim talks about how his business is growing and tells Lucas that he is always welcome to come back to work for him. Lucas just smiles and tells Jim that his father needs him most.

Isabelle goes back to work at Brown Shoe Company, sewing designs on leather shoes. It is not her choice of work, but she wants to help Lucas bring in an income because farming does not provide enough money for them to feed the children and pay the bills. Life is challenging for Isabelle and Lucas, but they manage to take the time for themselves, to keep their love alive. Lucas always knows what to say to make Isabelle smile.

CHAPTER 21

A few years go by, and Isabelle's father passes away on a cold winter night in 1969. Isabelle, France, and their mother are by his side. France and Mrs. Bourgeois have gone to get coffee while Isabelle is sitting by her father's bed. Mr. Bourgeois slowly opens his eyes and looks at his daughter through tears. His last words, in a very low voice, are, "Isabelle, please forgive me." With heavy tears herself, Isabelle nods yes as he takes his last breath.

After the death of her father, Isabelle has a hard time coping with her childhood issues. All the painful memories of her physical and mental abuse come back to haunt her. She never speaks a word to anyone about her feelings, not even Lucas. She starts to eat more because of her emotional state and becomes quite heavy. Even with Isabelle's weight gain, Lucas still loves her and always shows his love for her even though he's not sure what is haunting her.

As for Lucas, he is now thirty years old and has taken over the farm completely. He does not like working the farm; he feels it is losing money. Lucas has a serious talk with his father, and they decide to sell all the livestock. It is a big decision for both John and Lucas, but people can't make any money farming anymore. Lucas continues to haul logs to Domtar in Cornwall; he works long hours. He buys timber from other people's land and cuts down the trees to make ends meet. John's health has deteriorated until he can no longer work. Elizabeth helps Isabelle care for the children, as she continues to work at the shoe company. Lucas does not like his work, but he does what he has to in order to survive. He derives his happiness from the time he spends with his wife and children and the knowledge that he has been a good son to have come back to the aid of his father.

One autumn day, Lucas's best friend, Steve, calls to say he is home. Steve has come down from Alberta for a surprise visit to see his parents, whom he has not seen in years. Lucas has not seen him since his and Isabelle's wedding day. He is extremely happy and excited to hear from his longtime friend. Steve arrives at the farmhouse and is surprised to see no cattle in the fields. As he is parking his car, Lucas rushes out of the house to greet him.

"Hi, Lucas!" shouts Steve as he exits the vehicle, and he waves with an enormous smile.

"Hi, Steve!" calls Lucas excitedly as he runs to greet him.

The two guys hug when they meet and look at each other for a few moments in disbelief that they have finally gotten together after so many years.

"Lucas! It's so great to see you again, buddy," Steve exclaims with joy. "How is married life treating you?"

"Married life is great! Isabelle is a wonderful wife; we have five children. Did you know we named our third son after you? Come inside, and I'll introduce them to you. Also, Isabelle made a delicious dessert," replies Lucas as he tackles Steve.

"Yes! Let's go!" says Steve as he fights Lucas like in the old days. "Hey Lucas, by the way, how are your parents doing?"

"Mom is great, but Dad's health is not so good. He can no longer work," explains Lucas, sadly.

They walk to the house together and The Beatles are playing on the radio. Elizabeth is the first to greet Steve as he enters.

"Well, well! Steve, it's such a surprise to see you again," cries Elizabeth, and they embrace. "It has been years since I last saw you. You look good."

"Great to see you, as well, Mrs. Clarkson," says Steve with joy as Elizabeth finishes hugging him. Steve extends his arms and puts them on her shoulders. "You're like a mother to me, Mrs. Clarkson."

Steve notices John sitting down in a nearby chair. Stunned, Steve closes his eyes and reopens them. Mr. Clarkson is hooked up to an oxygen tank. Steve casually smiles and walks toward John.

"Hi, Mr. Clarkson!" says Steve as he shakes John's hand and gently pats him on the shoulder. He sees a fragile man sitting before him.

"Hello, Steve—how are you, son? How is the Air Force treating you out there in Alberta?" asks John as he looks up at Steve with a grin.

"The Air Force is swell. I just bought a 1966 Beechcraft C23 Musketeer four-seat airplane from a friend in Alberta—she's a beauty," says Steve in a joyful voice. "This is my dream come true, Mr. Clarkson." Lucas is happy for his friend to have realized his dream, but it only serves to remind Lucas about how much he wanted to become a certified mechanic and that he hates farming.

"Young man, your father must be very proud of you," replies John, as he repositions his oxygen mask.

"Wow! Steve, you've done so much with your life. I'm so happy for your success, and I'm very proud to be your friend," expresses Lucas, with a huge smile of joy at seeing his friend so happy. Lucas is standing beside Isabelle, with his arm wrapped around the small of her back.

"So nice to see you again, Steve," says Isabelle as she walks toward him and gives him a hug.

"Lucas is a lucky man, Isabelle, to have such a great wife," replies Steve as he gives Isabelle a kiss on each cheek.

"Thank you, Steve," says Isabelle shyly and then walks toward Lucas.

"Steve, do you want to meet our children?" asks Lucas, knowing the answer already. He smiles and calls the children into the kitchen to meet, "Uncle Steve."

"I'm extremely excited to see them, especially little Steve," replies Steve as the children run in.

Lucas introduces Steve to his children. Steve is so honored to know that Lucas has named his third son after him, and the kids are delighted to finally meet their uncle. John and Elizabeth are thrilled to see Steve again, as they sit there admiring their son and his best friend reuniting. Isabelle prepares dessert, coffee for the adults, and milk for the children. After their snack, Isabelle excuses herself and tells the children to say good night. They all hug their daddy and say good night to Uncle Steve. Isabelle takes them to their room, reads a story and tucks them into bed. John is getting tired, so he and Elizabeth say good night and head to bed. Lucas asks Steve if he wants a beer, and Steve nods yes. Steve gets up and goes to sit in the living room as Lucas brings them each a beer.

Lucas settles down on the sofa and tells Steve about his adventure in Uxbridge and how he had to come back for his dad. Steve is an independent man and has never understood why Lucas would sacrifice his life for his father.

"Lucas, there's so many changes in your life! Your dad is not the same man, and where is your brother, James?" asks Steve sounding puzzled. "I thought James would handle the farm. You, Lucas, you are a mechanic, in my mind, because you have so much knowledge about engines."

"Being a mechanic was my passion, but I gave it up to help my father, and that was a few years back. Today we don't farm because there is no money to be made. I started logging trees to Domtar in Cornwall. James gave up farming to move to the city for his two children with special needs, so they could get better care," explains Lucas. He takes a sip of his beer.

"Lucas, you were always such a good-hearted man. That's the quality I most admire about you: so gentle, yet so strong." Steve is happy to have the opportunity to share his admiration for his good friend. He drinks his beer and genuinely enjoys the moment.

"Enough about me, Steve. Tell me more about your airplane and the Air Force!" says Lucas with great interest.

"The Air Force is great. I am now ranked lieutenant, and I teach the troops how to control the aircraft before they can register to fly planes. I'm very busy with my work; I don't have time for a social life. The best thing I've ever done is purchased my own plane; I love flying on my free time. I know that is my passion, and when I fly my plane, it is so relaxing—I love the feeling of freedom! Someday I'd love to take you up in my plane," says Steve, sounding excited. His eyes glow with joy as he looks at Lucas.

"Wow! I'd love to take a plane ride with you, Steve! That would be super," replies Lucas, thinking about how amazing it would be to be flying above the skies.

They both feel like teenagers again as they laugh and sip their beer.

At that moment, Isabelle enters the room, and she grins when she hears their laughter. Isabelle is happy for Lucas, for they have so much to share. She sits beside Lucas as the men continue their conversation. Then Lucas kisses Isabelle on the forehead and tells her that someday Steve is going to give him a ride in his plane.

Isabelle asks Steve, "How does it feel flying planes?"

Steve explains to Isabelle about the freedom he feels every time he is up in the air. Then he takes a look at his watch and tells Lucas and Isabelle that he has to leave because he has to catch the first flight in the morning to go back to Alberta. They all get up, and Isabelle and Lucas accompany Steve to the side door.

"Goodbye Isabelle," says Steve as he bends down a bit to give her a kiss.

"Goodbye Steve," replies Isabelle. "Thank you for visiting us; it was a pleasure to see you again."

"Thank you, Isabelle, for your kindness—and you make such a delicious dessert. How could I resist?" says Steve, who is appreciative of the hospitality.

"Steve, my buddy, thanks so much for visiting us, especially my kids. They've heard a lot about you, and now they got to meet you," explains Lucas as he shakes Steve's hand and gives him a huge hug. It is through this embrace that they prove what they have both suspected—that even through the distance, they are still best friends.

"Lucas, I'm so happy to finally meet your children. I'm very proud of you—you are a marvelous father and great husband. I hope someday to settle down and have a family," says Steve as he squeezes Lucas in a bear hug. "We are best friends with totally different lives. Thank you again, for always being there for me, especially when we were teenagers. You always encouraged me and helped me believe in myself, Lucas. You're the best."

"Steve, you'll always be my best friend," replies Lucas. He feels emotional knowing that Steve is leaving. "Come visit us again, and next time bring your plane. There is a small-plane landing near Alexandria."

"Yes! I'll do that, and like I promised, I'll give you a plane ride," expresses Steve with excitement in his voice. "You too, Isabelle! Come for a joyride in the sky."

They all laugh and savor the jovial moment.

"Goodbye, Lucas," says Steve as he opens the door.

"Take care, Steve," replies Lucas as he watches him leave.

Isabelle stands beside Lucas as they watch Steve drive away. He holds her in his arms and gently kisses her on the cheek. Lucas is emotional at seeing his friend leave, but he feels extremely joyful at having his wonderful family. He hopes that Steve will meet someone as wonderful as Isabelle someday and have a family. Steve may have his dream job, which Lucas lacks, but Lucas is rich when it comes to marital and familial happiness.

Three months pass, and Lucas is returning home after a long, hard day working in the bush cutting trees and loading them onto the truck. Even though he is physically fit and has a well-muscled build, he still gets very tired. Lucas just wants to relax and spend the evening with his children and Isabelle. As he sits down to watch television with the kids and Isabelle, the phone rings. Elizabeth answers the phone.

"Lucas, the phone is for you," she calls. There is an uneasy expression on her face as she gives the phone to Lucas.

"Who is it, Mom?" asks Lucas as he takes the phone.

"I don't know, Lucas," replies Elizabeth.

"Hello! Lucas speaking." He wonders who it could be.

"Hello, Lucas Clarkson?" asks the person on the line.

"Yes… May I ask who is speaking?" The voice is unfamiliar.

"Mr. Clarkson, my name is Colonel Howard Smith, from the Air Force. There has been a tragic accident concerning Lieutenant Steven Lewis. He was flying his plane yesterday morning. The plane malfunctioned, and Lieutenant Lewis lost altitude, crashing onto the side of a mountain. In his files, Lieutenant Lewis wrote that Mr. Lucas Clarkson was to be notified if anything should happen to him. I am terribly sorry to have to inform you about this tragedy. If you need more information, the Air Force will be glad to answer any questions or concerns you may have, Mr. Clarkson."

Lucas just goes silent in disbelief at what he has just heard. *This cannot be… he was here a few months ago and was so happy to be following his dreams,* thought Lucas.

"Mr. Clarkson! Are you still there?" asks the colonel.

There is silence for a few moments as Lucas fumbles to find his voice and say the right words. His heart is breaking, and he is in too much pain to speak.

"Yes, sir. Sorry. I'm still here," says Lucas. His face is soaked with tears, and he can't believe what he is hearing.

"Sorry, Mr. Clarkson. I've had to deliver this kind of tragic news before, and I can't imagine how you must be feeling, but Lieutenant Lewis's wishes were for us to inform you about what happened to him immediately, and that's what I've done. Also, his parents just learned the news about their son and are very emotional. Lieutenant Lewis stated that you should be in charge of his funeral. Everything is all prearranged at the Alexandria Funeral home, and his body will return to Alexandria next week. Is it possible for you to do that for Lieutenant Lewis? Those were his wishes, and he talked highly of you, Mr. Clarkson. I don't know you personally, but believe me, Mr. Clarkson, you were like a brother to him," assured Colonel Smith.

"Thank you, Colonel Smith," says Lucas as he gulps and tries to stay strong. "Yes, we were like brothers. He was the ambitious one."

"Yes, Lieutenant Lewis was very ambitious and a very knowledgeable person when it came to aircrafts," replies Colonel Smith.

"Who will contact me when his body arrives here so that I can make the final arrangements and contact family and friends with details of his funeral?" asks Lucas. He takes a deep breath to maintain his strength; he feels his knees getting weak.

"I can do that for you personally, Mr. Clarkson," Colonel Smith informs him.

"Thank you again. I appreciate your kindness, Colonel Smith," says Lucas. He is grateful for the colonel's genuine words of sympathy.

"You're welcome, and please give Lieutenant Lewis's parents and family my deepest condolences," says Colonel Smith.

"I certainly will," replies Lucas.

"You take care of yourself, Mr. Clarkson," says Colonel Smith. "I'm very sorry for your loss. Goodbye."

"Thank you. Bye, sir," replies Lucas. He feels his heart tearing apart when he hangs up the phone. He morosely wonders to himself, *how can a person endure so much pain in life and yet continue to live?*

Lucas dreads telling Isabelle and the children. After all, they just had such a beautiful celebration with their uncle Steve. How on earth is he going to tell them that Steve, so young, so vital, is dead and will never be taking them for a joyride in the sky?

Isabelle is still sitting in the living room with the children. When she sees the look on Lucas's face, she can tell that the phone call was bad news.

"What is it, Lucas!" asks Isabelle with desperation on her face, bracing herself for the worst.

Lucas just looks at Isabelle. There is overwhelming sadness in his eyes. "Isabelle," says Lucas in a very low voice, "the call was from the Air Force."

Instantly, Isabelle knows that something has happened to Steve. "What happened to Steve?" she asks. She knows the answer but does not want to hear the truth. She looks at Lucas with terror written all over her face.

"Steve... Steve, he died yesterday in a horrible plane crash... Isabelle," says Lucas as he walks toward her. He holds her and starts to weep and shake with the same intensity of his mounting grief. "Steve is gone, Isabelle! I can't believe this is happening to me. My friend!"

"Lucas, I am so sorry," replies Isabelle, crying, as she holds him tight. "There are no words I can say to appease the pain of what you are going through right now."

"Isabelle, I feel like I have a knife stabbing me, and the pain is excruciating—it burns like fire inside me," says Lucas as he continues to hold on to Isabelle, hoping to ease the heartbreak. For the first time in his life, Lucas is out of control.

Elizabeth returns from her bedroom to see what the commotion is about.

"What happened, Isabelle? What's wrong with Lucas?" asks Elizabeth in a worried voice. She can see that something serious has occurred.

"The call was from the Air Force, Mrs. Clarkson," replies Isabelle with a disturbed look on her face. "Steve was killed in an airplane accident."

"What! No, not Steve!" cries Elizabeth. Her stomach clenches as she feels the pain of what she has just heard. She weeps for the loss of a life too soon.

Path of Lucas

Lucas looks at his mother and goes to hug her. He needs to be consoled by his mother because he feels like a baby again—totally helpless.

"Steve... My best friend, Steve... Mom, it seems unreal! He was just here a few months ago looking great and feeling happy," says Lucas, feeling his mother trembling.

"Lucas, I can't believe this is happening," expresses Elizabeth as she continues to sob. "I have to go tell the news to your father ..."

Lucas watches his mother go to the bedroom and then sits beside Isabelle in the living room as she tells the children what has happened to their uncle. Lucas thinks back to times when he and Steve were young and carefree. He remembers how his best friend stood up to the bully at the hotel all those years ago and how proud he felt to be by his side. Now, he realizes that was the day that his friend became a man.

Lucas honors Steve's wishes and makes all the arrangements for the funeral exactly a week later. He finds enough strength to write the eulogy for his best friend. At the funeral, Lucas reads the eulogy and feels a warm sensation, as if his buddy Steve is giving him strength to carry on. He talks about how brave Steve was to have followed his passion in life and how fortunate he was to have known him. Lucas feels this inner strength even at the burial; he is able to keep strong and give support to Steve's family, especially Mr. and Mrs. Lewis.

One month later, tragedy strikes the Clarkson family in a devastating way. Mary's child Darcy is killed in a terrible accident; he was taking a cow across the road when a car hit him. Darcy was rushed to the hospital but was pronounced dead on arrival. Mary is devastated, and the accident makes Joe drink even more. It is tearing the family apart. Their marriage is falling apart, and Joe is becoming increasingly abusive toward Mary.

John and Elizabeth are heartbroken over losing their grandson and witnessing their daughter's painful, tormented life. They try to help her and advise her to leave her husband, but she refuses. Lucas remembers his fear that life would change for the worse before moving back to the family farm and realizes that his prophecy has come true. He knows that there is more to life than just the physical world and vows to do everything in his power to make life better for his loved ones.

Lucas tries to support his sister even if he does not agree with her decision to continue living with Joe. Lucas can see the pain his parents are going through, and he is feeling hurt himself, but he must stay strong for his family. He also notices Isabelle slipping away because of her anguish. Lucas tries desperately to keep Isabelle from feeling the hurt from her past, but it often resurfaces now that her father has passed. She and Lucas frequently go out to enjoy time together to make her feel the bond of their shared love, but his love for her is not enough to heal her.

CHAPTER 22

Four of the children are now in school, all under the age of twelve. Only little Thomas has one more year to go before he can start school. Isabelle continues to work at the shoe company; she is still feeling the burden of her childhood issues but never confides in anyone, not even Lucas. She continues to put on weight as she tries to cover up her painful memories. Lucas carries on with logging, even though his heart is not in it. He often wonders what life would have been like for him and his family if he had received his mechanic's certificate and Steve and Darcy had lived. Lucas needs to live in the present, but the past was so much easier and filled with such joy that is now diminished.

Lucas has always been a loving father and husband; he has never disappointed his family. He has dedicated his life to his parents, his children, and most of all, to Isabelle, in spite of all the weight she has put on. Lucas loves to stare at Isabelle with a charming smile, a quality that Isabelle adores. John is still hanging on, but he needs his oxygen tanks with him at all times. Elizabeth is starting to slow down as she ages.

Summer is approaching, and Richard's class is going on an end-of-school-year trip to Upper Canada Park. Richard is excited to be going swimming at the beach with his friends. It is a cold June morning in 1971, and Isabelle is reluctant to send his swimsuit because it is so chilly. Somehow, Richard persuades her to let him take his swimsuit in case the weather changes. Isabelle finally gives in and says yes, but she writes a note to the teacher stating that if the weather does not warm up, Richard should not go into the water. With all the hustle and bustle of the day, the teacher does not read the letter, and Richard does go into the water, even though it is still too cold. Isabelle is upset that evening when she finds out Richard has swum in the cold water; she is afraid he will catch a bad cold.

A few days later, Richard does become sick, with a high fever. Isabelle and Lucas take him to the hospital emergency department. The doctor examines Richard and tells them that Richard has a virus. The only thing to do is to give him Tylenol and plenty of fluids. They take Richard home, and Isabelle gives him the best care she can, but Richard's fever does not subside. The next morning, Richard becomes extremely weak and dehydrated, to the point that he can't even stand up. Isabelle definitely knows that this is not the flu—it is far more serious.

Lucas and Isabelle rush Richard to General Hospital in Cornwall. Isabelle holds back tears as she sits in the backseat watching her son getting weaker by the moment and seeing his eyes sunken by dehydration. Lucas is driving and worrying about his son's condition; he constantly looks in the rearview mirror. Isabelle holds her son as he goes in and out of sleep. At this point, Richard has no energy to speak. When they arrive at the emergency parking lot, Lucas carries Richard into the hospital, and Isabelle follows. As they enter the emergency doors, Lucas shouts to the nurse at the nurses station, "Please help us! My son is very sick!"

The nurse runs out of the nurses station and grabs a gurney to put the young boy on. "Here, sir—I'll bring him into the ER right away to see the doctor, and you can go to the nurses station for information on his condition," she states.

"Thank you, ma'am," says Lucas nervously as he lays his son down on the gurney with the nurse's help.

Isabelle stands beside Lucas, and just before the nurse takes Richard to the emergency room, Isabelle gives him a kiss, while Lucas holds his hand.

"We will see you in a little while, Richard," whispers Isabelle, but Richard does not respond.

Isabelle starts to cry as she watches the nurse take him away, and Lucas holds Isabelle. He also feels the pain and helplessness of watching his son being wheeled away and not knowing what is happening to him.

Isabelle and Lucas go to the nurses station to fill in a report on Richard. When the nurse asks questions about Richard, Isabelle has a hard time answering, so Lucas sits down with her and holds her as he answers all the questions.

The administration nurse tells them they can sit down in the waiting room until further notice.

"As soon as I hear from the doctor, I'll let you know about your son's condition," says the head nurse.

"Thank you, ma'am," replies Lucas, as he helps Isabelle get up to go to the waiting room.

It feels like forever as they wait for an answer from the head nurse. Isabelle sits there sobbing, and Lucas holds her and tries to stay strong. Suddenly, Lucas sees the emergency door being opened by the head nurse. She is walking toward them with a doctor. Isabelle, with reddened eyes, sees them coming also. She feels something bad is happening to her child because both the nurse and the doctor are walking so seriously toward them, and the doctor is carrying a file. Lucas has a lump in his throat. He swallows hard when he sees the faces of the doctor and the nurse approaching him. Lucas helps Isabelle as they both stand up to hear what the doctor has to say.

"Mr. and Mrs. Clarkson?" asks the doctor.

"Yes," answers Lucas, his voice trembling.

"I am Dr. George MacDonald," says the doctor. "Your son is very ill. I took some tests, and the reports tell me that Richard's high fever, headaches, lethargy, and feeling of nausea are caused by meningitis."

"Meningitis!" repeats Isabelle. "That can be deadly!" She starts to cry harder in Lucas's arms.

"How serious is Richard's condition, Dr. MacDonald?" asks Lucas, holding onto Isabelle as she is having difficulty standing. Lucas tears up too.

"Right now, Richard is in critical condition. His fever is extremely high, and we are giving him strong doses of antibiotics through intravenous. We are working on bringing his fever down. He has severe swelling in his head that we are trying to control. We need to bring the inflammation down from around his brain," explains Dr. MacDonald.

"Inflammation around the brain? Will that damage his abilities, or can he develop brain damage?" asks Lucas as he inhales deeply and tries to retain his composure for the sake of the family.

"Mr. Clarkson, at this point, we have no answers on what your son's outcome will be. We need to continue the antibiotics and bring down his fever," says Dr. MacDonald as he pats Lucas on the shoulder for comfort. "Your son is in very serious condition, and he has a fifty-fifty chance to live at this point. As Mrs. Clarkson said, meningitis can be deadly. But we have a good team of doctors here, and they are working on him now, doing the best they can," Dr. MacDonald assures him.

"When can I see my son?" asks Isabelle, suddenly feeling exhausted. She is trying hard to keep from falling apart.

"We need you to sign some more forms, and then I'll take you to the intensive care unit, where your son is in a private room," replies the nurse.

"I'll go with the other doctors to look at your son's brain scan, and as soon as I have more answers, I promise I'll give you the update," says Dr. MacDonald as he heads toward the door to leave. "I know this sounds impossible, but try to rest if you can. You're going to need all the strength you have over the next few hours and days," he adds.

"Thank you, doctor, for all you are doing for our son," says Lucas, maintaining his respect toward others even through his own trying times. He looks at the nurse and says, "Please, let us sign the forms, so we can be with our son."

"Yes, Mr. Clarkson. Just follow me to the administration office, and they will help you there. After that, I'll take you to see your son," says the nurse with warmth in her voice.

Lucas and Isabelle walk arm in arm, supporting each other, as they follow the nurse. The nurse takes them to the admin office and explains to the administrator why they are there. Lucas thanks the nurse as they both walk in.

"It won't take long, and I'll wait for you both at the nurses station. After you're done, I can take the two of you to see your son," explains the head nurse as she tries to make them feel comfortable.

"Thank you so much," says Lucas.

"Thanks," repeats Isabelle in a low tone. She is feeling very weak and nauseous at this point.

The head nurse nods and tells them, "I will wait for you."

Once Isabelle and Lucas finish signing the forms, they go to meet the head nurse. As soon as she sees them, she gets up to greet them.

"Your son is on the second floor, in the ICU, room 224. He is in a private room until the doctors can stabilize his fever," says the head nurse as she walks them to the elevator.

They get into the elevator, and she presses the button for the second floor. They are silent for a few seconds.

"Expect to see lots of wires and tubes around and on your son because the intensive care unit nurses have to monitor him every second. There is also a nurse by his side at all times," says the head nurse as she prepares them for what they are about to see.

"Is he in any pain?" asks Isabelle, her voice shaking.

"He is very ill, but the doctors have given him medication to make him comfortable," replies the head nurse. The elevator reaches the second floor and the door opens.

The nurse heads for room 224 with Lucas and Isabelle following anxiously. As they reach the room, Lucas takes a deep breath, and Isabelle focuses on opening the door to be with Richard.

The head nurse reaches to open the door for Isabelle and Lucas. Lucas thanks her as they walk into the room.

Isabelle hurries to be by her son's side. She kisses him and begins to pray for him to get better, as she sits there holding his precious little hand. Lucas stands there for a few seconds—to absorb what is happening and to find strength for his son and wife. Then he walks over beside Isabelle and gives Richard a kiss.

"Richard, Daddy is here. I love you, son. Stay strong—you're my little fighter," says Lucas as he gently strokes Richard's hair.

Lucas sits beside Isabelle as she holds Richard's hand amid all the wires and machines surrounding him. Within minutes, Dr. MacDonald walks in to inform them about Richard's condition. Lucas stands up and puts his hand on Isabelle's shoulder. Isabelle looks at the doctor, knowing he has the worst news to tell them.

"We got back the results from the lab, the x-ray, and the CAT scan," says Dr. MacDonald as he opens the files.

"Please tell us," replies Isabelle as she holds onto Lucas's hand on her shoulder.

"Your son is a very sick little boy. We are doing everything in our power to help him through every step. The next twenty-four hours will be crucial, due to his high fever and the inflammation around his brain. The most important thing right now is to stop the swelling and bring his fever down," explains Dr. MacDonald.

"Can we stay with him through the night?" asks Isabelle.

"We want to be with our son," explains Lucas. He looks at Richard lying there, with no signs of life.

"I'll make sure the nurses are notified that you are staying the night, and they'll get you blankets," replies Dr. MacDonald.

"Thank you so much," says Isabelle with as much energy as she can muster. Her mind is swirling with thoughts about her son's condition, and she is finding it difficult to concentrate on the others in the room. *He simply has to get better, otherwise, I'm not sure how I will recover from this*, she thinks.

Lucas and Isabelle stay overnight at the hospital, but there is no change in Richard's condition. His temperature remains high, and the swelling does not go down. It is extremely hard for Isabelle and Lucas to watch their son lying in a hospital bed clinging to life. Doctors and nurses are doing everything in their power to keep Richard alive. There is nothing that Isabelle and Lucas can do except pray.

Finally, one week later, Richard starts to show signs of recovery. His fever breaks, and the swelling around his brain subsides. One of the first things he says is, "Mommy, I'm hungry." Isabelle will never forget those words! It brings her such joy to hear her son speak again, and Lucas is also there to witness the miracle moment. It takes several months for Richard to fully regain his health. Every day, Lucas and Isabelle go to the hospital to visit their son, and on the weekends, they take the other children to visit their brother.

Isabelle and Lucas feel blessed every day as their son regains his strength. Richard is a survivor and is thrilled when he can come back home to his family. Lucas and Isabelle thank God for a second chance to have their son home in great health. That night, they watch the other children huddle around their older brother as he tells them how wonderful the doctors and nurses were to him, especially Dr. MacDonald.

Lucas smiles at Isabelle and then kisses her; he is so happy to see his children together. He knows very well based on what happened to Darcy that the outcome here could have been different. Lucas and Isabelle are grateful. John and Elizabeth sit with them in the living room, admiring the whole happy family.

CHAPTER 23

Lucas and Isabelle don't have much money, but they are extremely happy together, and their love for each other continues to stay strong no matter what obstacles they go through. The children are growing and healthy; they are full of life, and they love playing outside. Lucas enjoys playing football with his boys, while Isabelle sits back and watches the men with Lucy as she plays with her dolls. Elizabeth and John do their best considering their poor health.

One day when Lucas goes to town to get new parts for his chainsaw, he enters the hardware store and encounters a friend. They converse about their families and then about work. Ron, Lucas's friend, says he has heard that a cable company is hiring people in the area. He is seriously thinking about going; applications will be available at the town hall. Lucas becomes interested in the topic and wants more information about the work.

"Hey, Lucas, do you want to come with me next Monday to the town hall when they give out applications?" asks Ron.

"Wow! What a great opportunity!" says Lucas. "I'll talk with my wife about it and get back to you soon."

"They say the pay is great, and they have lots of work around here for a few years," adds Ron, clearly excited about the new possibility.

"I'll definitely get back to you as soon as I talk to Isabelle about this," says Lucas with an interested look.

Path of Lucas

Ron hands Lucas a small piece of paper. "This is my phone number. Hope I hear from you soon," he says. He is confident that he is going to apply for a job.

"Thanks, Ron," responds Lucas, and they shake hands.

Lucas walks over to purchase his chainsaw parts. He smiles, deep in thought regarding his conversation with Ron. He feels this is a second chance to increase his income for his family.

On the drive home, Lucas can think only about working for the cable company. How great it would be to have better employment to provide his family with a richer quality of life. Lucas thinks about Isabelle and how she works so hard and puts in a lot of overtime to help make ends meet.

Lucas soon arrives at home and sees his children playing in the backyard. As the children see him, they all run to him for hugs.

"Where is your mom?" he asks.

"Mommy is cooking supper," replies Richard with a smile; he has his father's handsome smile.

"Thank you, Richard," says Lucas as he tousles his hair. "Continue playing outside, and I will go see your mom, okay?"

"Yes, Daddy," replies Lucy with a giggle.

Lucas kisses his little girl on the cheek and then heads for the house. As he enters, he sees his wife and mother happily preparing supper together. His father is sitting in his favorite chair, watching them cook.

Lucas walks toward Isabelle and kisses her, along with a big hug; then he goes and kisses his mother and father.

"Hey, Dad, can you smell that delicious food?" says Lucas as he puts his hand on his father's shoulder.

"Yes! I've been watching the cooks for a while, and they're doing a great job," says John as he winks at Elizabeth.

Lucas laughs with joy to see the love his parents have for each other. He walks toward the stove, peeks into Isabelle's pots on the range and takes a spoon to scoop up and taste her special barbecue sauce that will go with her roasted chicken.

"Lucas!" says Isabelle as she strokes his hand and smiles. "You know the rules!"

"I know, but I can't resist your barbecue sauce—you know it's my favorite," replies Lucas. He blows on the sauce to cool it down and then samples it. "Wow! That sauce is out of this world, Isabelle."

"Lucas, get the children for supper," says Elizabeth as she sets the table.

"Yes, Mom," replies Lucas as he gives his wife a kiss.

"You seem in such good humor, Lucas," says Isabelle as she reaches out to stir the sauce.

"Just being with you, Isabelle, puts me in wonderful spirits," replies Lucas with a radiant smile.

Lucas continues smiling as he leaves the kitchen to tell the children that supper is ready. They run in, and Lucas helps them clean up as Isabelle and Elizabeth prepare their plates.

Later that evening, once the children are settled in and Lucas's parents have gone to their room, Lucas and Isabelle are sitting in the living room together, and Lucas reaches out to hold Isabelle's hand. Isabelle looks at Lucas with a smile, and he smiles back.

"You are such in a cheery mood tonight. Is there something you know that I don't?" asks Isabelle with a squeeze of his hand.

"Yes! Yes!" Lucas says eagerly.

"What is it, Lucas?"

Lucas moves closer to Isabelle and steals a kiss. "Remember my friend Ron?" he asks.

"Yes," she replies, still in suspense.

"Well, I met him at the hardware store today, and he told me about a great opportunity."

Isabelle is thoroughly curious and asks, "What kind of opportunity?"

"A job opportunity," says Lucas, "working for a cable company!"

"Cable company! Where?"

"Here. Ron told me there will be a lot of jobs putting cable around here, and they are hiring locals," Lucas says in an excited voice. "Ron asked me if I would go with him to apply for a job on Monday. He's certain that he is going for the job, and he wants me to go with him. I thought about it all day, and my conclusion is that I want to go, if it is okay with you, Isabelle."

"Well, I don't know what to say," replies Isabelle with concern. "Is there lots of traveling, or would you be home every night?

"According to Ron, the job is just nearby, so I would be home every night. There may be nights I would come home late, but that's all I know. Working in the bush is hard work, and I often come home late as it is," Lucas reminds her.

"That's true. If this is your decision, Lucas, I'll stand behind you. I'm a bit nervous about the change, but I respect you and your decisions," says Isabelle as she gently touches his cheek.

"Isabelle, I have given it a lot of thought, and I believe we would be better off financially, and there would be a chance for growth in the future. I always wanted to work as a mechanic, but it didn't work out for me. Now I have a second chance, and I want to take it, Isabelle," Lucas replies. "I love you and our children, and I want to be able to give you all a better future."

"Lucas, you are such a wonderful husband. You always put us first, and that is what I love about you," says Isabelle. "I have always believed in your decisions."

"I love you so much, Isabelle, and I want to give you a wonderful life. I want us to grow old together happily, and I want our children to have greater opportunities. The extra money I make will help us get all of this," says Lucas as he hugs her. "Thank you, Isabelle, for believing in me."

"Lucas, I love you too, and I want us to have a wonderful life together and watch our children grow," replies Isabelle with tears of happiness rolling down her soft cheeks.

"I'll call Ron, and on Monday, we'll go together to apply for the job," says Lucas. He kisses her, and then he gets up to call Ron.

Monday soon arrives, and Lucas gets ready to go with Ron to apply for the job at the town hall. Lucas has butterflies in his stomach, but he is eager to embrace this chance for a new opportunity.

"Good luck, Lucas," says Elizabeth as she hugs him and kisses him on the cheek.

"Thanks, Mom," replies Lucas, holding on to her like a child on his first day of school, feeling nervous.

"Wishing you the best, son. Knock them dead, like I know you can," says John as he gives his son a tender hug.

"Your support means so much to me, Dad. Without your example, I wouldn't be the man I am today," replies Lucas as he squeezes John's shoulder.

Lucas looks at Isabelle with his handsome smile, which always makes Isabelle proud to be his wife. She is grateful to be a part of such a caring and warm family and has never taken it for granted that her circumstances have changed so much for the best since her tumultuous childhood.

"Lucas," says Isabelle as she walks toward him, smiling back. "I believe in you, Lucas. I believe in your kindness and generosity and in your intelligence and hard work. You'll be great!"

"Thanks, Isabelle," replies Lucas. He kisses her passionately and then waves kisses at all of them as he leaves to meet Ron. "See you all later."

Lucas picks up Ron, and they discuss the job opportunity while Elton John plays on the radio. They are nervous but also excited to have a chance to work for a cable company. Lucas wishes Ron the best and thanks him for telling him about this opportunity as they walk toward the town hall.

Three days later, Lucas and Ron have interviews for the job with the cable company. Their interviews are about an hour apart. Lucas has the first interview, and he is hired on the spot to start work the following week. Ron also is hired the same day, and the two go to the Alexandria Hotel for a beer to celebrate.

"I'm so happy that you told me about the job. I really appreciate what you've done for me," says Lucas as he takes a sip of his beer.

"You're welcome, and I'm happy to know that I'll be working with you, Lucas. We're on the same crew and working the same hours; that is so great!" Ron exclaims and gives Lucas a thumbs-up sign.

Lucas is thrilled. "Yes, Monday! Can you believe it, Ron? We'll be working for the cable company!"

"Wow!" says Ron as he sips his beer.

"Ron, I have to go... I want to tell Isabelle the news as soon as she gets back from work," Lucas says as he drains his glass.

"I have to go also, Lucas. Janet is waiting at home to hear the outcome of the interview. She will be very happy for me because this is the only thing that was on my mind all week long," Ron responds as he picks up the bill. "This beer is on me, Lucas."

"Thanks, Ron. Next time, it will be me picking up the tab," replies Lucas. He gets up and puts on his jacket with a smile. "See you Monday!"

"Bright and early, Lucas," says Ron cheerfully as he pays for the beers.

Lucas arrives home before Isabelle and tells his parents that he got the job. Elizabeth is delighted for her son, and she hugs him. John shakes Lucas's hand and puts his hand on his son's shoulder. Soon the children come home from school. Lucas hugs them and tells them about his wonderful day. He says Mommy will soon come home, and they will celebrate this wonderful day by taking Mommy out for supper. The children get very excited and jump around Lucas, giving him tons of kisses and hugs. When Lucas hears a car coming into the yard, he tells his children to keep the news a surprise and to go with Grandma and Grandpa into the living room until he talks with Mommy.

Elizabeth and John take the children to the living room as Lucas walks to the door to greet Isabelle. Lucas watches for Isabelle to approach the door and then opens it for her.

"Hi, Isabelle," says Lucas with a huge grin. "How was your day at work?" He helps Isabelle with her jacket.

"Busy day but good," responds Isabelle as she kisses Lucas. "You sure look happy. How was your interview?"

"Great—very good news!"

"You got the job!" replies Isabelle sounding thrilled. "Lucas, you did?"

"Yes, I did! I start on Monday," says Lucas as he grabs her and swings her in the air.

"Congratulations, Lucas," replies Isabelle as she holds him tight. "That is exciting news!"

"Ron also got a job, and we will be working on the same crew. I feel absolutely amazing—like I got a second chance at a great job!" says Lucas as he puts her down.

"I am so happy for you, Lucas," she responds with pure delight. "We can tell the children and your parents, and then I will make your favorite supper to celebrate your new journey."

"They already know, Isabelle." Lucas smiles as he continues to kiss her. "They're sitting in the living room, waiting for us to get ready to go out for supper."

"What! Supper!" Isabelle smiles. "You and the kids had this all planned."

"Yes! I want to celebrate this day with my family, and I don't want you to cook. I want you to enjoy and celebrate with us. I plan to take all of us to Mama Jean's," explains Lucas. He then shouts out, "Mom, Dad, are you and the kids ready to go?"

The children run to the kitchen, yelling, "Yes! Yes!" and Elizabeth and John follow them. Isabelle bends down and hugs the children as they greet her.

"Thank you, Lucas," says Isabelle as she looks up. She suddenly has a feeling that her husband deserves only the best in life since he is such a good person.

Lucas grabs her hand and helps her up. "I love you, Isabelle."

"I love you too, Lucas," replies Isabelle. She tells the children, "Get your jackets, kids. Daddy is taking all of us out for supper."

Isabelle looks at Elizabeth and John lovingly and helps them get their coats. The children scramble to put on their jackets. Lucas opens the door, everyone rushes out, and the children run to the vehicle.

After only a few months, Lucas gets a promotion. He also now drives a company truck. The children are astonished the day their dad comes home with the truck, which has a CB radio in it. As they are riding their bikes, they hear voices coming from the empty truck, and they run to their dad to tell him about the sounds. Lucas laughs and explains that the CB radio is a way of communication. The children are amazed and proud of their father. With Lucas's bigger paycheck, the bills are now being paid. Isabelle continues to work, and they are able once more to save money. Life is wonderful for Lucas and Isabelle now that they have more financial freedom.

CHAPTER 24

Lucas stares at Lucy in the hospital bed. He is silent for a few minutes, and then he shakes his head in disbelief. "Why is this happening to my beautiful daughter?" he asks rhetorically. His shoulders heave as he looks at Lucy barely clinging to life. Lucas feels a sudden tension around his chest. As he gasps for air, the pain becomes more intense. He rubs his chest with his hand. After a few minutes, the pain finally subsides, and Lucas continues to tell Lucy his life story as she lies there as still as a ragdoll.

"Lucy, I wish you would wake up now because this is where my life takes a turn," says Lucas. He wishes she would just look at him and say "Dad" again. He tells her, "I love you, Lucy."

Lucas takes a deep breath and readjusts himself before he continues his story.

One year has passed, and Lucas is enjoying his work for the cable company as well as his family life. Isabelle, who is now thirty-one years old, is very proud of her husband. Their marriage is heaven on earth; Lucas and Isabelle are meant for each other, and they are fulfilled parents who enjoy watching their children grow. They are becoming financially secure, and Lucas has been able to pay off the farm. Lucas has become a supervisor; he has a huge responsibility but also a great crew. His workers all love to work for him, as Lucas is such an overall great person. He has managed to make his parents happy and fulfill his responsibilities as a dutiful son, to make his wife and children happy and create a better life for them financially and to be happy himself working in the cable company instead of the farm.

Everything is great until one day when Isabelle gets a phone call from Jean, France's husband, telling her that France is not doing so well. France had become obese and had developed type II diabetes. She has to inject herself with insulin, but she has gotten worse and her heart is in overdrive. Jean is very concerned and confides in Isabelle to ask for her help.

"Isabelle, France just came from the doctor's, and he said that she needs to lose weight because her heart cannot take the stress. Carrying that extra weight could be very dangerous for her," says Jean in a trembling voice.

"This is terrible, Jean. How can this be—she is so young! Where is France now?" asks Isabelle.

"She's at the hospital. She has to stay there for observation for a few days, and the doctor will conduct various tests on her," replies Jean. Isabelle can hear him crying. "She had chest pains this morning; that's why I took her to the hospital."

Isabelle is worried for her sister. "How is she feeling now?"

"She was doing better when I left the hospital because they gave her medication for her pain, and she was sleeping," explains Jean.

"Where are the children?" asks Isabelle.

"They're at my mother's place, and they will sleep there tonight because I have to work early tomorrow morning on the farm," explains Jean, who is still sniffling.

"I am glad to hear the children will stay at your mom's place. Tomorrow, I will visit France after work," says Isabelle. "Take care of yourself, Jean, and I will see you tomorrow evening at the hospital."

"Thanks, Isabelle," replies Jean, relieved.

Isabelle is crushed by the news; she can't believe her sister's failing health. France is too young to be worried about heart problems. Isabelle tells Lucas about the phone conversation. Lucas feels heavyhearted for France. He suggests that Isabelle take time off to help France with the children and to help nurse her back to health. Isabelle is happy to have the support of her husband.

Isabelle works hard helping France to improve her health. Within a month, France loses twenty-five pounds, and she is so proud. She continues losing weight, and Jean renovates her whole kitchen as a reward for her great accomplishment. Jean wants his wife to bring herself back to health for him and, above all, for their children. Isabelle is extremely proud of her sister's hard work and dedication.

A few months later, France is doing extremely well. Isabelle is impressed with her positive attitude. Isabelle goes back to work, believing that France is on the right track. France has lost over fifty pounds, and the doctors are amazed by the improvement in her health.

Six months later, France takes a turn for the worse; she is gaining weight again—even more weight than before. She is extremely sick and has lost energy. Isabelle does everything in her power to help her sister, but at this point, there is nothing Isabelle can do. France often goes to the hospital with health issues, especially her heart, which causes her extreme pain when overworked.

Isabelle becomes exhausted trying to help France with her obesity. She tries hard to help her sister lose weight and is concerned about her. Isabelle is often at the hospital with France because Jean needs to work on the farm, and his mother is helping to care for the children. France again tries to help herself but always seems to fail. It is such a difficult task. Jean has also tried hard to help his wife, but nothing seems to work for her. Everyone who loves her is frustrated and worried.

One day at the hospital, as France is lying in bed, she starts to cry when she is alone with Isabelle. Isabelle consoles her and tells her it will be okay, but France knows it will not. She knows that her health is failing rapidly, and she is seemingly helpless to stop this from occurring.

"Isabelle, what have I done to myself—but most of all to my children and husband?" cries France. "How could I let this happen to my family?"

"France, stop thinking that way! You did not do this to yourself. Your body has a hard time coping with stress, and so it made you sick," replies Isabelle. She embraces France and tries to console her. The last thing France needs right now is to add self-admonition to her problems.

"Isabelle, I am dying. My children will be without a mom, and they are still so young! Jean works hard on the farm and has tried everything to help me, but I am too hardheaded to help myself," says France, and she begins to weep in despair.

"France, don't blame yourself. Really, that won't help anything," replies Isabelle as she holds her sister's hand tenderly. "You love your family, and you did the best you could under the circumstances."

"I've got to get myself together, Isabelle, for the sake of my children," cries France. "Please help me! Please!"

Isabelle reaches out and holds her sister; deep down, she feels the same terror as she did when she and her sister were children and their mother was in a rage. She takes a deep breath and pushes down the feeling, reminding herself that she is an adult and is no longer powerless.

"France, you and I have always protected each other, and we will do so in this situation as well. I've always been there for you and will try my best to help you get healthy again," says Isabelle, gently stroking France's cheeks.

As France lies in bed, she stares at the ceiling and is silent for a few minutes while Isabelle strokes her hand. Suddenly, they both hear voices in the hall. Jean is bringing the children to visit their mom. They come running in and surround their mom's bed with big smiles. Jean lifts the youngest daughter onto the bed; she is only five years old. Jean kisses his wife and greets Isabelle.

"Mommy, Daddy is taking us to the restaurant after we leave here," says France's oldest son as all the children kiss their mom. They are innocent about what is happening to their mother.

France smiles as she hugs and kisses her children; even at this darkest moment of her life, she gets so much joy just from seeing their happy smiles.

"Wow, Daddy is taking you all to the restaurant," says France, smiling as all the children nod yes and laugh with excitement.

Isabelle gets up from her seat. "Here, Jean, take this chair. I have to go. Lucas will be home soon, and the children are with his parents," says Isabelle as she stands and positions the chair for Jean.

"Thank you, Isabelle," replies Jean, sitting down and embracing his wife.

Isabelle smiles and looks at France. She reaches over and gives her sister a kiss. "See you tomorrow, France," she says cheerfully, not wanting France to know how worried she is.

"Take care, and say hi to Lucas and the children for me. I want you to know that I appreciate your support today and every day," says France. "I am so lucky to have you as a sister, and I know it!" France blows Isabelle a little kiss.

"I'll tell them! Love you too, big sister," responds Isabelle, and she kisses her nephews and nieces goodbye.

When Isabelle leaves the room and closes the door, she leans against the wall with her head up. She prays for her sister to get better, for the sake of the children, as tears roll down her cheeks. Within minutes, Isabelle shakes her head in disbelief. *This is not really happening*, she thinks. Regaining her composure, she heads home believing her sister will get better.

Three weeks later, in the middle of the night, Isabelle gets the phone call that she has been dreading. It is Jean, calling about France's condition. She has taken a turn for the worse; her heart is in distress, and she has had a few heart attacks in the past hour. Isabelle heads out to the hospital in a hurry.

Within a half hour, Isabelle arrives at the hospital. She is wondering whether she will see her sister alive as she gets to the room. She opens the door to see Jean sitting and sobbing. Isabelle walks closer and hears the heart monitor indicating that France's heart is still pumping.

"Hi, Jean," says Isabelle.

Jean nods as he looks up at Isabelle with despair.

"What's happening, Jean?" questions Isabelle as she reaches for France's hand.

"She started to have chest pains late last night. I took her to the hospital, and when we arrived, she had several mild heart attacks, and then it got worse. She had a few major attacks within an hour; the doctors revived her but told me the next twenty-four hours will be crucial. They don't think she will make it through the night," explains Jean, and he starts crying more intensely.

Isabelle tries to console him, but she is also crying.

For three hours, Jean and Isabelle take turns sitting with France as she lies there, with nurses taking turns checking on her. After Jean and Isabelle do not notice any further deterioration, Jean becomes very sleepy, and Isabelle tells him to lie down on the sofa in the lounge. If there are any changes, she will wake him up.

A few more hours pass, Jean returns to the room, and they both sit by France's bed. Suddenly, France moves her fingers and tries to squeeze Jean's hand.

"France, can you hear me?" asks Jean as he sees her try to open her eyes. "France, it's Jean—can you hear me?"

France nods yes.

"Jean… Jean," whispers France in a weak voice.

"Yes, France," replies Jean.

"Jean… Jean," France repeats, her voice so low that he almost cannot hear her. "I… love… you."

"I love you too, France," says Jean as he watches France close her eyes and then take her last breath.

"No! No! France, stay with me," screams Jean as he hears the heart monitor start to beep.

Isabelle looks up and sees the straight line on the screen as the nurses and doctors rush in to try and revive France. They use the defibrillator, but there is no response. The doctor announces the time of death.

Isabelle takes charge as Jean crumbles in despair. The doctor takes Jean aside and gives him some meds to help him through these initial devastating moments.

Isabelle asks the nurses to give her some time alone with France. She sits down besides France's bed, takes her hand and holds on to her tightly as tears splash down her cheeks. France, her beautiful older sister, her protector, her confidante, her best friend in the universe aside from Lucas, is gone. Isabelle does not believe it. Everything about losing her big sister feels surreal and dreadful, as though she has entered the twilight zone.

"France, I love you. I promise you that I will never forget you; I will always think of you. Especially the time I met Lucas... You were there for me, and that was so much fun. And you were always there throughout the hard times we had growing up. France, I could always count on you. What will I do without you? I will miss you intensely," says Isabelle as she places a kiss on France's hand. "I love you so much, sis, now and forever."

Isabelle puts her head down and starts to sob. After a good cry, she gets up and leaves the room. Despite her own heartbreak, Isabelle finds the strength to support her brother-in-law and to tell her family members, especially her mother, about France's passing.

That night, Isabelle is emotional, and so many things run through her mind. Lucas and Isabelle find the kindest way possible to tell the children that their aunt France has died. He also takes time off work to give Isabelle time and support through her grieving.

At the funeral, Isabelle stays strong to help Jean and his children. With Lucas's help, she writes a eulogy for France. When the priest announces the eulogy, Isabelle gets up, walks to the front of the church and starts to read. Lucas is proud to watch his once shy little Isabelle stand up in front of a crowd in the midst of her heartache to give a speech on behalf of her beloved sister.

"France was only thirty-two years old and had so much to give. She was a wonderful mother, great wife, and the best sister that anyone could have. France was not only a sister, but she was my closest friend. She was always there for me; even in my saddest moments, she could make me smile.

"The most memorable times France and I had were when we would go on picnics. France loved life; she loved nature, and our best time was when we would pack a picnic and take a tractor ride in the forest with our husbands and children. France and I talked about how wonderful life was and how blessed we both were with great husbands and beautiful children. We placed blankets on the ground and set out a delicious lunch as we watched our children and husbands play.

"France was known for her pranks. She enjoyed laughing and making others laugh. She always had a smile on her face that would light up the room. France always had a joke or a funny story to tell; she knew how to make people feel right at home.

"Most of all, France had so much love for her family her friends. Caring for others was her first priority. She used to tell me that no matter how bitter a person was, you had to overlook the bitterness and see only the good in that person.

"We will all remember France for her positive attitude, compassion, generosity and her love for life. My sister is a great example to everyone here today to always find in your heart the good in people. I am honored to be France's sister, and I will always look back with fondness on our fun times together as sisters and mothers. France, I will never forget you and the times we spent together. Your memory will always live in my heart."

Everyone is very impressed with Isabelle's speech, especially her mother. Isabelle walks back to Lucas, who hugs her and tells her he is proud of her, in particular for her strength to deliver such a moving talk despite her broken heart.

CHAPTER 25

It is 1974, and two years have passed since France's death. Isabelle has gained even more weight, and she is fearful of becoming obese like her sister and perhaps even having the same problems with her heart. After talking with Lucas, she joins a program to lose weight and to stay healthy. Isabelle works hard, and within the year, she loses a lot of weight. She reaches her goal, and she keeps it off for over a year. Lucas is happy and has been supportive of her from the get-go.

To honor her achievement, the weight-loss program organizers ask Isabelle to go to Toronto for a weekend conference. There, she will have a chance to be crowned among twenty-five contestants from different areas of Ontario. Isabelle is a success story, and they want her to speak out about reaching her goal of losing weight and keeping it off. They want her to encourage others and help them believe in themselves. Isabelle wants to go, but she is afraid to leave her children and husband behind. Lucas is happy for Isabelle, and he convinces her to go. He assures her that he will be fine alone with the children for the weekend. This is the first time Isabelle will go away by herself with the weight-loss committee. She feels excited but also anxious; she will be staying in a big, fancy hotel, the kind she has only seen in photos or magazines. She will have to make a speech about how she has succeeded and offer tips for others to follow. Isabelle wants to do the speech in dedication of her sister France; that will be the topic of her success.

Lucas is very proud of Isabelle's accomplishment because she has done something that means so much to her. He also likes the fact that Isabelle has a fantastic shape again, just as in the days they met. She has bought new clothes, which look fabulous on her. Isabelle is healthier than ever and is feeling proud of her achievement. She knows a dressmaker that will make her a beautiful long gown for this special occasion.

When the weekend comes for Isabelle to go to Toronto, she feels happy yet sad to leave her family. At the train station, Lucas gives Isabelle a big kiss and tells her to have fun; the children give her hugs and kisses. As Isabelle jumps on the train, she waves to Lucas and the children with sadness. She will miss them. The children wave to their mommy, while Lucas smiles as he blows Isabelle a kiss. Then with his lips, he mouths the words, "I love you." Isabelle sends Lucas a kiss with a wave back and repeats, "I love you" as the train leaves the station.

Isabelle has a wonderful weekend, filled with surprises; she has never been so pampered. Isabelle feels like a star, especially that Saturday evening when they announce that she has won the crown. They place the crown on her head, and Isabelle walks down the runway with a dozen red roses. Everyone claps. She has been chosen because she has lost the most weight and kept it off for over a year. The gown Isabelle is wearing is gorgeous; it makes her look like a true princess. Isabelle delivers a fabulous speech; everyone loves her passion about her own success and her dedication to her sister. The audience knows that Isabelle wants the same health and fitness for them. It is a magical evening, with many wonderful gifts and supportive people.

On Sunday morning, Isabelle attends a conference about helping others to reach their diet goals. They learn about nutrition and how to exercise properly. She feels so proud of being with the committee and giving her input about dieting successfully. Once the conference is over, Isabelle takes the first train home. Despite all her success and the thrill of being crowned, nothing feels better than being back home with her family.

Three months later, Lucas is told that his work is moving farther away from home to Kemptville. They ask Lucas to take a more responsible position because they need his knowledge with the company. Lucas would be more than a supervisor; he would take charge of different crews and direct them in job positions. Lucas is proud of the offer, but he doesn't know whether it is a good idea because he would have to leave home during the week. The company tells Lucas that they need an answer before the following week because they have lots of preparing and hiring to do. Lucas respects and understands their position and asks them to give him a couple of days to think about the offer.

That night, driving home, Lucas thinks that he wants to take the offer. He loves his job and is confident about taking a higher position and moving up the ladder. The only thing that concerns him is his family—not seeing his family during the week will be hard. How will Isabelle feel about that? Knowing her strength, Lucas thinks that she will be understanding. The more Lucas contemplates the job offer, the more he wants to take it. He would double his salary, and he knows he can handle the job.

That night, Lucas has a big conversation with Isabelle, who is excited for her husband. She tells him to follow his dream and to take the offer. Lucas is grateful that Isabelle agrees he should take this opportunity. The next day, he tells his boss he would be delighted to accept the offer, and the following week, Lucas is off to Kemptville.

Things go along very well. When Lucas comes home on weekends, he gives his family his full attention; they always have a wonderful time. Lucas finds different places to take Isabelle out on Saturday nights while his mom cares for the children as they sleep. Sunday mornings are family time with his children and his parents, although in the afternoons, Lucas enjoys taking his little family for rides. Often, they drive to little towns, where they teach the children the history of the towns and how settlers survived back in the late 1800s and early 1900s. History is Lucas's favorite subject. They go to restaurants for supper and then back home to settle for the night. The next day, in the early morning, Lucas leaves for the week.

One weekend, Lucas surprises his children by taking them to Kemptville to show them where he works. The children are proud of their dad. Lucas brings them to the apartment where he stays during the week. They stay there for a little while, and he and Isabelle watch while the children explore the place. Lucas takes his family to a barbecue restaurant and tells the children to order anything on the menu—what fun! The children are impressed with their big trip. On the drive home, they are exhausted and sleep all the way. Isabelle and Lucas hold hands and talk about their future. Lucas reaches over to kiss Isabelle on her cheek; their love keeps growing stronger.

Before the end of the first year that Lucas is working in Kemptville, Isabelle starts to gain weight again. She hides her emotional pain from Lucas. As Lucas works hard to support his family, Isabelle slips back into painful thoughts of her childhood and the anguish over the death of her sister. Lucas notices something different about Isabelle, but when he asks her if anything is wrong, Isabelle says she has had a hard week at work.

One weekday, little Lucy walks into her mom's room and sees her crying. "What's the matter, Mommy? Why are you crying?" asks Lucy in a very concerned voice. As she walks closer, she sees her mom putting something under her pillow.

"I'm okay, sweetie, just feeling a little overwhelmed with work," replies Isabelle as she tries to hide the evidence under her pillow while distracting Lucy.

Lucy doesn't mention what she has seen but just goes over and hugs her mother to comfort her.

"Mom, don't be sad. Dad is coming back soon, and we'll have lots of fun on the weekend," says Lucy, trying to make her mother feel better. It really pains the little girl to see her mother in such a sorrowful state.

"Yes, Lucy, Dad will be here soon, and we all will be happy to see him. Thank you, Lucy, for your big hug," says Isabelle as she gets up. "Now, let's go see your brothers and watch television." Lucy and Isabelle go to the living room to join the boys.

The next morning, while Isabelle is at work, Lucy goes to her mom's room to look under her pillow. She finds a picture of her aunt France, her mom's sister. Lucy's little heart stops for a few seconds as she takes a deep breath and tears come to her eyes. This makes her so sad, but she doesn't know what to do about the situation. Now she knows why her mom was crying, but she doesn't know how to tell her dad. Lucy gently puts the picture back under the pillow and wipes her tears before she heads for school.

That evening, Isabelle comes back home from work and goes straight to bed. She tells Elizabeth and the children that she is exhausted and needs to rest for a couple of hours; then she will get up and help them with their homework. Lucy knows it is not her work but rather missing her sister that is upsetting her mom. She is just about to tell her grandmother when, at the same moment, Isabelle calls to Elizabeth for help. Elizabeth excuses herself to Lucy and runs to Isabelle's room.

"What's the matter, Isabelle?" she asks, the worry in her voice evident. She opens the door, and Lucy follows behind her.

Isabelle replies in a weak voice, "I'm feeling really sick; I don't know what is happening to me! My whole body is shaking! I am very anxious, and my head hurts so much."

"Do you want me to call the ambulance?" questions Elizabeth as she sits down beside Isabelle and tries to comfort her.

"Mrs. Clarkson, I'm scared... feels like..." utters Isabelle in a weak voice as she slips away into unconsciousness.

"Isabelle! Isabelle!" says Elizabeth as she gently shakes her, but there is no response.

Elizabeth runs to the living room and calls the ambulance, while Lucy watches her mother collapse with her little heart pounding. Elizabeth runs to tell John and then goes back to be with Isabelle.

John is not in the best of health, but he tries to comfort the children. He tells them their mother is very sick and needs to go to the hospital as the ambulance arrives in the yard. John directs the paramedics to Isabelle's bedroom, and the boys sit in the kitchen and watch as the paramedics rush in. Elizabeth, who is with Lucy, sits by Isabelle's side, comforting her, but Isabelle is still unconscious.

The paramedics take control and ask Elizabeth questions about Isabelle's state. Elizabeth answers the best she can as she steps back to let the paramedics work on Isabelle.

"Her pulse is weak," says one paramedic as the other opens the medical equipment. "She is unconscious and will need medical attention right now."

"Isabelle, can you hear me? My name is Dave; I'm a paramedic. I've come to help you," says the first paramedic at the scene as he shakes Isabelle's shoulder, but she does not respond.

The second paramedic measures the oxygen level. Then he gets the IV ready. They both work on Isabelle, and then they tell Elizabeth that Isabelle is nonresponsive, and they need to rush her to the hospital. The children watch as the medical team wheels their mom out of the house. Tearfully, they ask their grandfather what is happening.

"Your mom is very ill right now, and the paramedics will take her to the hospital so the doctors can make her better," says John as he looks at the sadness in their eyes.

"Will Mom get better soon?" asks Richard in a concerned voice.

"We'll know more tomorrow, after the doctors examine your mom," replies Elizabeth as she tries to comfort the children. "Grandpa will take me to the hospital. Richard, please take care of your brothers and sister for me until we get back. Okay, it's time for bed, children. Go and brush your teeth."

Elizabeth does not have a driver's license, so John has to drive her to the hospital. John is weak, and it takes all his strength to walk to the vehicle to drive Elizabeth. Just before Elizabeth leaves, she tries to call Lucas. The phone rings, but there is no answer. Lucas must be working overtime. There are days during the week that Lucas works over fourteen hours.

John will wait in the car with his portable oxygen tank while Elizabeth goes into the hospital to see what is happening with Isabelle.

"John, will you be okay here until I come back?" asks Elizabeth, looking worried.

"I'll be fine; go see Isabelle. She needs you more than I do right now," replies John as he gasps for air.

"Okay, I'll be back soon," says Elizabeth as she opens the passenger door. She rushes to the emergency door and walks to the nurses station, concerned now about her husband as well as their precious Isabelle.

"Excuse me, I'm looking for Isabelle Clarkson. She was brought here by ambulance," says Elizabeth, feeling out of breath.

"Yes, Mrs. Clarkson was rushed to the emergency room. The doctor is with her as we speak. We have to prepare a room for her; she will be admitted. Her room number is 38; if you want to bring her things to her room, I will see if the doctor has any information I can relay to you," replies the head nurse.

"Isabelle is my daughter-in-law, and my son is away working. I tried to call him, but he works long hours, and he was not at his apartment," explains Elizabeth. "I am the next of kin."

"Nurse Julie will get some forms ready for you, and I will meet you in room 38," says the head nurse.

"Thank you so much," answers Elizabeth in a soft voice as she tries to hold back her tears. As a family, they have endured so much over the years. Elizabeth fears having a breakdown but resolutely decides that she will do her best to stay composed. Much like her son Lucas, she has great inner strength. The pressure is mounting with each passing moment.

Elizabeth signs the forms and goes to the room. She paces as she waits for information about Isabelle. After about twenty minutes, the head nurse and the doctor walk in.

Path of Lucas

"Hi, Mrs. Clarkson. This is Dr. McKenzie," says the head nurse as she presents the doctor to Elizabeth.

"Hi, Mrs. Clarkson," says the doctor.

"Hello, Dr. McKenzie. How is Isabelle?" asks Elizabeth.

"Your daughter-in-law is very ill. We took many tests, and now we have to wait until morning for more answers. We have sedated Isabelle, and she is breathing better. She will most likely sleep all night. We're not sure what is happening to her; after the tests come back tomorrow, we'll have more answers," explains Dr. McKenzie. "I suggest you go back home and call us in the morning."

"Is Isabelle in pain right now?" asks Elizabeth.

"No, right now she is sleeping and should be able to sleep all night," explains Dr. McKenzie. He pats Elizabeth on the shoulder to reassure her.

"Thank you, Dr. McKenzie. If there is any change, please call me at any time," says Elizabeth. "Can I see Isabelle before I go?"

"Yes, you can, Mrs. Clarkson. Your daughter-in-law will be here in her room shortly," says the head nurse as she gets a chair for Elizabeth.

"Talk to you tomorrow," says Dr. McKenzie as he leaves the room, and the nurse follows him.

Elizabeth waits a few minutes, and then she hears the door open. She sees the nurses wheeling in Isabelle on a gurney. They work together, and on the count of three, they lift Isabelle onto the hospital bed. One nurse covers her while the other checks the heart monitor. Elizabeth watches what is going on and worries about Lucas and how to tell him what is happening to his beloved wife. Elizabeth shakes her head and wipes her tears as she approaches Isabelle. She sits beside Isabelle's bed and takes her hand.

"Isabelle, can you hear me? It is Mrs. Clarkson; you're in the hospital, and the nurses and doctors are taking good care of you. I have to go now to see the children, but I will be back tomorrow with Lucas."

Elizabeth gets up and looks at the nurses. "If anything happens to Isabelle tonight, please call me at any time," she reiterates as she leaves the room.

"We will take good care of her, and if for any reason something happens, you will be the first person we'll contact," replies one young nurse to reassure Elizabeth.

"Thank you," says Elizabeth. She ponders Isabelle's immense importance to her young family as she heads out to find John in the parking lot. She is thankful that he is looking stronger than he was when he dropped her off and is no longer gasping.

As soon as Elizabeth arrives home with John, she helps him into the house and thanks him for driving her to the hospital. John is happy to be able to do something for Isabelle and Elizabeth. At that moment, she is thinking of Lucas, who has no clue what is happening to his wife.

"I should call Lucas," says Elizabeth to John as she helps him with his oxygen tank.

"Yes, Lucas definitely needs to know! Our son will be absolutely heartbroken," replies John. He is short of breath again as he lies down on the bed.

Elizabeth makes sure John is okay before she leaves the bedroom, checks the children to see if they are all sleeping and goes to the living room to call Lucas. Lucas answers the phone, and Elizabeth explains what has happened. Lucas tells her he is heading to the hospital, but Elizabeth replies that there is nothing he can do right now. She tells him that Isabelle is heavily sedated, and the doctors will not know what is wrong with her until the tests come in, but Lucas insists he wants to be with his wife when she wakes up in the morning. Lucas rushes off from his apartment in Kemptville to see Isabelle at the hospital.

CHAPTER 26

Lucas sits by Isabelle all night, and the next morning, he is waiting for answers about Isabelle's condition. Isabelle continues sleeping, and Lucas dozes off; he is exhausted by this whole ordeal. Lucas hears the door open, and he opens his eyes. The door shuts behind them as Lucas rubs his eyes to refocus. He sees the doctor and nurse walking toward him.

"Hi, I'm Dr. McKenzie," says the doctor. "The test results just came in."

"What's wrong with my wife?" Lucas interrupts him anxiously. He gazes fixedly at the doctor and the nurse, who both look at him somberly.

"Mr. Clarkson, your wife is very ill; she has fallen into a deep depression. Her body is starting to shut down. She may sleep for days because her body is extremely exhausted from all the stress she has been through," explains the doctor. "Mrs. Clarkson will be transported by ambulance to the General Hospital, on the third floor. It is a ward for patients with clinical depression. They have psychologists and psychiatrists for mental-health disorders. They specialize in treatment and diagnoses to help Mrs. Clarkson."

"What? My wife has a mental illness? Is that what you're saying?" says Lucas, anxious and confused as he runs his hands through his hair. "No, not Isabelle—she is a happy person and a great mother."

Path of Lucas

"I understand what you're thinking, but depression can creep up on a person very fast," replies Dr. McKenzie. "I am not a specialist in that area; that's why you will need to see Dr. Jones at the General. He will help you understand what is happening to Mrs. Clarkson, and he will better diagnose and find a treatment for your wife. Prepare yourself, Mr. Clarkson—it will be a long process. I don't want to discourage you, but your wife is very ill. Please go home and rest. We will have Mrs. Clarkson taken by ambulance to the General, and most likely, she will sleep for days before she wakes."

"No, I want to be with my wife!" shouts Lucas as he holds back his tears.

"Fair enough. Follow the ambulance to the General. Miss Jackson, the nurse, will give you information about Dr. Jones's office and a contact number. I am terribly sorry about your wife's illness," says Dr. McKenzie sincerely. Then he leaves the room.

"Come with me, Mr. Clarkson, to the nurses station, and I will get you all the information you need before you go to the General," explains Nurse Jackson. She holds the door open for Lucas.

"Thank you," says Lucas as he walks out of the room feeling sad and overwhelmed. He looks at Isabelle sleeping soundly in the bed and thinks she looks like an angel.

"You're welcome," replies the nurse, and she leads Lucas to the nurses station.

Lucas gets the information he needs and then watches the paramedics wheel Isabelle out of the room, go through the emergency doors to the ambulance and drive away. Lucas can hardly believe what is happening to his beautiful, loving wife.

So many things go through Lucas's head as he drives to the General Hospital in Cornwall. *What could I have done better to help Isabelle?* He starts blaming himself for what has happened to her. *I should never have taken this job; maybe then Isabelle wouldn't be in this predicament,* Lucas tells himself as he arrives at the hospital. *She probably needed more emotional support after France died, and she was still dealing with her childhood issues,* he thinks. Lucas wishes that

235

he could've been there more for Isabelle when she needed him, but there is no turning the clock back now.

Lucas takes a deep breath and walks into the General. At the nurses station, he asks for Dr. Jones.

"Do you have an appointment?" asks the nurse.

"No, but my wife, Mrs. Clarkson, was brought here by ambulance from the Glengarry Memorial Hospital," says Lucas.

"What is Mrs. Clarkson's first name?" asks the nurse as she looks through the incoming files.

"Isabelle… Isabelle," replies Lucas.

"Thank you, Mr. Clarkson. Oh, yes! Mrs. Clarkson is on the third floor, room 323, but there are forms for you to fill out first. It is hospital policy—please, can you sign them? Then a nurse will direct you to Dr. Jones," she says as she gives Lucas the required paperwork and a pen.

Lucas signs the forms and hands them to the nurse.

"Thank you, Mr. Clarkson. Please have a seat, and I will get the nurse in charge," explains the office nurse with a smile as she gets up.

"Okay," replies Lucas as he goes to sit down. He feels like he is in a bad dream and feels a deep sorrow in his chest for himself, Isabelle, and their children. *Is this really my life?* thinks Lucas. *What could I have done differently?* The thought repeats itself in his mind.

Lucas waits for several minutes, and then a nurse comes over and introduces herself to him.

"Hi, Mr. Clarkson. My name is Mary Sequin," she says as she shakes Lucas's hand. "I am the nurse in charge on the third floor."

"Hi," replies Lucas. He is anxious to hear what is happening to Isabelle as he shakes the nurse's hand.

"Mrs. Clarkson is in room 323; she is sleeping. Dr. Jones is looking through her files and wants to talk to you about what is happening to your wife," explains the nurse. "Follow me. We will go to his office, where he will explain more in detail. If you have any questions, he will be there to give you answers about depression. Unlike strokes or heart attacks, people don't talk much

Path of Lucas

about depression, and they don't often understand what the term clinical depression really means."

Lucas follows the nurse to the elevator. Once they are on the third floor, it feels surreal. Lucas is in a state of disbelief. As he walks toward the doctor's office, he feels a sharp pain in his chest. He senses that he might not hear good news about Isabelle's situation.

The nurse knocks on the door and leads Lucas into the office. Sitting there is an older man with white hair and black-framed glasses; he is looking over his papers as he waves for them to come in. The nurse walks closer to the doctor and then introduces Lucas. "Dr. Jones, this is Mrs. Clarkson's husband," explains the nurse. "I must go now," she states and walks out.

Dr. Jones gets up from his chair and extends his arm to shake Lucas's hand. "Hi, Mr. Clarkson," says Dr. Jones. "Please, have a seat."

"Thank you, sir," replies Lucas as he sits down. He feels very nervous and scared.

"I am going through your wife's file," explains Dr. Jones. He takes off his glasses and puts them down; then he folds his arms and settles them on his desk as he looks at Lucas. "Mr. Clarkson," he begins. He takes a deep breath, puts his glasses back on and glances through the file again. "Your wife's condition is serious; she is suffering from an extremely deep depression. Right now, she has no awareness of who she is or the fact that you are her husband. Mrs. Clarkson will probably not have any recollection of her family; she will believe she is someone else. I can't be exactly sure; I am not certain what Mrs. Clarkson's state of mind is at this point. Right now, she is heavily sedated and will sleep for a couple of days because she was going into shock. We needed to make her sleep to get her to relax her body, so she can get out of the shock she is in. Mr. Clarkson, this will be overwhelming for you. There is much to learn about this kind of depression. There are no overnight cures. It will be a long road ahead—if she ever recovers from this kind of depression," explains Dr. Jones as he flips through Isabelle's file.

"What do you mean—'ever recovers from this kind of depression'?" questions Lucas in a low voice as he leans forward. "You said that Isabelle may not know me as her husband? How is that possible? We've been married for years."

"Mr. Clarkson, sir. Your wife is in a state that we call clinical depression, but looking at her files, and judging by her behavior, I think she will be diagnosed with psychotic depression. What that means is that she will behave in a manner that you will not understand; she may live in a fantasy world. Be ready for anything. For example, in her mind, you may not be her husband; you may be a total stranger to her. The outcome is impossible to determine at this point; we have to wait and see what state Mrs. Clarkson is in when she wakes up. I will need time to work with her closely and find the right antidepressant to treat her illness. If for any reason we are unsuccessful, there are shock treatments—called electroconvulsive therapy, or ECT—but that would be my last resort. In the meantime, I want you to go home and get some rest because you will need all your energy and strength for what is about to come your way. I am not trying to frighten you, Mr. Clarkson, but to tell you the truth about what is to come. I have seen this illness so many times, and I believe you have the right to know what to expect. You will need to be strong for what you are about to endure with your wife," says Dr. Jones as he closes the file. "Do you have any questions, Mr. Clarkson?"

"You are telling me my wife has a mental illness and that she will not know me?" asks Lucas in a petrified voice. "But I am her husband, and we love each other!"

"Mr. Clarkson, your wife is most likely in a psychotic depression. Many patients that I work with have illusions, and they believe or live in their illusions. At this time, I cannot say what your wife's condition will be, but Mr. Clarkson, you need to prepare yourself and your family for the worst because depression is very unpredictable. It all depends on your wife's mental state," says Dr. Jones. He takes some material out of his desk and gives it to Lucas.

Path of Lucas

"Here are pamphlets with information on clinical depression and psychotic depression for you to read."

Lucas reaches out to take the pamphlets. "Thank you, sir," he says and then shakes the doctor's hand as they both stand up. "Is it possible for me to see Isabelle before I leave? I need to see her before I go home."

"Yes, for sure, Mr. Clarkson. I will call the nurse, and she will take you to her room," replies the doctor as he picks up the phone.

Lucas thanks the doctor again and leaves the room. As he looks down the hall, he sees the nurse walking toward him. Lucas walks toward her, anxious to see Isabelle.

"Follow me, Mr. Clarkson. Mrs. Clarkson is just down the hall, in room 323," says Nurse Sequin.

Lucas remembers Isabelle's room number from their pervious conversation as he walks down the hall. He looks at door numbers as he walks there. He notices room 323.

"This is the room, Mr. Clarkson," says Nurse Sequin as she stands near the door. "Mrs. Clarkson is still sleeping."

"Yes, Dr. Jones told me all about what is happening with Isabelle," replies Lucas. He is anxious to open the door and be with his wife.

"If you need anything, Mr. Clarkson, I will be at the nurses station, right down the hall to your right," explains Nurse Sequin as she starts to walk away.

"Thank you for your help with everything, Miss Sequin … thank you," says Lucas as he reaches for the door handle.

Lucas walks into the room slowly and then stands there for a few seconds just watching Isabelle sleep. *She looks peaceful and normal, as if she were sleeping at home*, he thinks. He walks closer as he continues to stare at Isabelle. She is sleeping on her side, curled up, with blankets covering her. It all seems so quiet; the only thing Lucas can hear is Isabelle's breathing. He puts his hand on her shoulder and continues to stare at her in disbelief. He watches her sleep, thinking that everything is a bad dream and that she will wake up with her pretty smile and say, "Hi, Lucas. Where are the kids?"

Lucas gently touches her hair and then gives her a kiss on the cheek. He sits down on the chair beside her bed and holds her hand.

"Isabelle, I love you. Tomorrow, when you wake up, I hope that you will remember us as a family. Please, Isabelle—I need you, and the children need you. Whatever happens, Isabelle, I will stay by your side until you completely recover from this tragic illness. Then we will be back together with our children, at home, like it was," says Lucas as he puts his head down and starts to cry. "Isabelle, Isabelle. I will love you till the day I die. That is my promise."

Lucas continues to cry as he holds her hand. Isabelle just lies there in a deep sleep. Once Lucas is finished crying, he simply stares at Isabelle for a while. He kisses her again and then gets up slowly. He brushes her hair with his fingertips and touches her cheek. He remembers their first date and how shy but carefree she seemed. He recalls how he loved the way she combed her hair and her lovely French accent and wishes he could return to simpler times.

"Bye, Isabelle," says Lucas and then whispers in her ear, "I love you."

After Lucas walks out of the room and closes the door, he leans his head against the door for a few minutes; it is hard to part. He walks to the nurses station to tell Nurse Sequin that he is leaving.

"Thank you, Mr. Clarkson. I'll call you when Mrs. Clarkson awakens," says Nurse Sequin. As she stands up, she sees Lucas's red eyes. "Go get some rest, Mr. Clarkson," she says kindly.

Lucas pushes the Down button and waits for the elevator. He stands there for a few seconds until the doors open. As he walks into the elevator, he sees a man pushing a woman in a wheelchair; she seems so gloomy, as if all the energy has been wiped right out of her. Her eyes are blank, and she is staring straight ahead with no facial expression. The man gently talks to her, but she does not acknowledge his existence. As the doors of the elevator close, Lucas thinks of Isabelle. Is this the path they are about to embark on?

CHAPTER 27

When Lucas arrives home and parks his vehicle, he takes a few minutes to readjust himself; he needs this time to compose himself before he sees the kids. As he walks in, the children run to him crying, "Daddy, Daddy!" Elizabeth stands there watching them all hug their father.

"Hey, it's great to see all you guys," says Lucas as he hugs and kisses them. "But I think it's close to your bedtime. Go to your rooms, and I'll come to tuck you in. Daddy has had a long day."

Richard asks, "How is Mom doing, Dad?"

"Mom is very ill, and right now she is sleeping. The doctor gave her medicine to help her sleep because she is very tired," replies Lucas as he holds back his tears.

"When is Mommy coming home?" asks Lucy. "I miss her already, Daddy."

"I miss her too, darling," replies Lucas. Then he kisses his daughter on the forehead, saying, "The doctor told me that when Mommy wakes up tomorrow, they will call me, and I will find out more about Mommy's illness. Okay, guys, it's time for bed."

"Can we see Mommy tomorrow?" asks little Thomas, with Johnny and Steve by his side, nodding yes—they want to see their mom too.

"I don't think so, Thomas. Not yet anyway. Let's just take it one day at a time. Okay, guys, brush your teeth, and I'll see you later," says Lucas as he tickles them. It takes every fiber of his being to smile, but he knows that he has to keep things positive for his kids. Soon enough they will have to deal with the reality of having a very sick mother.

They run out to brush their teeth, and then Lucas looks at his mom. She gives him a big hug and holds him for several minutes in silence.

"Mom, it is bad—really bad," says Lucas as he continues to hold his mother for comfort. "I'll tuck the kids into bed, and then we'll talk."

"Okay, Lucas," replies Elizabeth in a gentle voice; she can sense her son's pain. She knows Isabelle is seriously ill but does not know it has anything to do with depression. "I'll brew coffee for us."

"Thanks, Mom," says Lucas as he gives her a kiss on the cheek. Then he goes to tend to his children.

When Lucas returns, both his parents are sitting in the kitchen, anxiously waiting for him to update them on Isabelle's condition.

"Hi, Dad," says Lucas as he pats his father on the shoulder. "Mom... Dad... Isabelle is seriously ill." Lucas pulls out a chair and sits with his parents at the table. He needs to sit immediately in order to support the terrible weight that he is carrying on his shoulders.

"What are the test results?" asks Elizabeth in a concerned voice, taking hold of her son's hand.

"They diagnosed Isabelle with clinical depression, which means a deep depression. But Dr. Jones is a psychiatrist, and he went over Isabelle's files, and he thinks Isabelle's actual diagnosis will be psychotic depression," explains Lucas as he holds Elizabeth's hand tightly.

"What does that mean, Lucas? Psychotic? What's the difference between the two kinds of depression?" inquires Elizabeth. Both she and John look blank, never having dealt with any kind of severe depression before.

"Clinical depression is a deep depression, like I said; a person is seriously depressed. It's as if all your energy is pulled out of you, and you have no will power to do anything but cry or sleep, but you remember everything that's going on. As for psychotic depression, that is very different. Psychotic means out of touch with reality. In a psychotic depression, you live in another world. The pain is so extreme that the brain goes on overdrive and then shuts down, and you live in a fantasy world of whatever your mind wants to become," explains Lucas. He shakes his head, still not quite able to believe it. "Oftentimes, according to the pamphlets the doctor gave me, people feel persecuted, as though someone or something is after them. It's a miserable experience."

"That's dreadful, Lucas. They both sound terrible, especially psychotic depression. When will you know which one Isabelle has?" asks Elizabeth with a concerned look on her face.

"As soon as she wakes up, they will work with her and determine where Isabelle is in her depression," replies Lucas as he fights his tears.

"Wow! Son, this is serious," says John. He pats Lucas on the shoulder to support him. "How are you holding up?"

"I'm feeling shocked about all of this; it's too much for me. I'm hoping that it is clinical depression because I don't want to lose Isabelle. Mom... Dad... I want my wife back! It is so hard to think of life without Isabelle," cries Lucas as he breaks down.

"Oh, sweetie! Isabelle will get better; have faith! We have to believe," expresses Elizabeth as she gets up and hugs Lucas for support.

"Mom, I can't go through this... this is too much for me," says Lucas as he breaks down. "And what about the kids? This will be so frightening and confusing for them."

"Lucas, we will be here for you," promises John as he holds Lucas's hand tightly.

"Please excuse me; I need to go to my room," says Lucas, and he gets up and then leaves the room.

Path of Lucas

As Elizabeth and John watch Lucas go, they are overwhelmed with sadness by the information they have just received.

The next day Lucas gets up early, telling his mom that he can't wait for the phone call. He wants to leave before the children wake up, and he asks his mom if that's okay. Elizabeth tells him to go and be there for his wife; she will take care of the children. Lucas does not want his children to see him as a wreck. He also needs to leave early because he really wants to be there when Isabelle wakes up. As Lucas drives to the hospital, he thinks of Isabelle and the children and how he feels about this mental illness, which is robbing him of his family. How fast the illness has crept up! He knows that Isabelle had a hard childhood, but he never imagined that her anguish would lead her to this point.

Lucas arrives at the hospital and sits in his truck for a little while as he tries to pull himself together. He prays that Isabelle is not in a psychotic depression. He gathers all his strength and heads in to see Isabelle. Lucas goes to the nurses station to see what the nurses have to say about Isabelle's night.

"Good morning, Mr. Clarkson," says the nurse as she sees him approach the desk.

"Good morning," he replies. "How was Isabelle's night?"

"Isabelle slept through the night. She is slowly waking up. Dr. Jones and Nurse Sequin are with her, but she is still a little drowsy," explains the nurse.

"Can I see Isabelle?" asks Lucas anxiously. He leans both hands against the desk as he waits for an answer.

"Yes, but before you go in, I will notify Dr. Jones and tell him you want to see Isabelle," replies the nurse. "It won't take long."

"Thanks," says Lucas. He runs both his hands through his hair; he is feeling the stress of the whole ordeal.

Within minutes the nurse returns to the nurses station.

"Mr. Clarkson, you can go into Mrs. Clarkson's room, but before you enter the room, Dr. Jones wants to ask you to be strong for your wife," explains the nurse.

"What does he mean by that?" he asks, feeling confused and apprehensive.

"Mrs. Clarkson is going through a lot right now, and you need to suppress your own fears about the situation and how it will affect you and the family for her sake right now, and act calm, at least in her presence," replies the nurse as she sits back in her chair. "Mrs. Clarkson is slowly waking up, and she may be delusional for a while because of all the medication she has had."

"Thank you for that information," he says as he nods his head and starts to walk toward Isabelle's room. "I have always put my wife's needs first, so you needn't worry that I will upset her," Lucas says to the nurse, with a strained smile, but in fact, he has no idea what he will encounter when he walks in.

Lucas stops at the door and waits a few seconds, taking a deep breath to keep himself together for Isabelle and to deal with the worst if he has to. He opens the door and sees the doctor and the nurse attending to Isabelle's needs. She is restless and crying, and then she becomes totally out of control.

"What is happening?" shouts Lucas as he runs toward Isabelle's bedside. "What are you doing to her?" He tries to comfort her, unaware of Isabelle's state of mind.

"Lucas, you don't understand—" says Dr. Jones. "At this point, I don't know what to expect from Isabelle. Do you understand me, Lucas?"

"Isabelle! Isabelle! It is me, Lucas," cries Lucas as he reaches for her.

"Who are you? Get out! I don't know you! Get out now! You're a monster!" screams Isabelle as she fights Lucas, hitting him with hatred in her eyes.

"Isabelle, I'm your husband, Lucas," repeats Lucas, begging for her to remember what they mean to each other.

"I said, 'Out, right now'! I don't know you! You're a stranger!" yells Isabelle at the top of her lungs, and she becomes even more frantic.

"Mr. Clarkson! Mr. Clarkson! Please leave the room—now," insists Dr. Jones as he tries to calm Isabelle's frantic state of mind by sedating her slightly.

"She's my wife, Dr. Jones! We love each other, and we have children who need their mother!" cries Lucas. He shuts his eyes and covers them with his hands, as he cannot bear to see what is taking place. He once promised to always protect her, and now when she most needs his help, he is powerless. He is enraged and ashamed that he cannot help his wife. The true nightmare has begun.

"Mr. Clarkson, leave this room immediately," demands Dr. Jones. "The nurse will escort you out right now. Do it for Isabelle. We need to calm her any way we can."

Lucas turns toward the door as Nurse Sequin opens it. Lucas takes a last glimpse at Isabelle and then walks out. Nurse Sequin closes the door and goes to help Dr. Jones comfort Isabelle and try to console her. The doctor is analyzing Isabelle's behavior in order to work with her mental illness.

Lucas leans against the door as he grabs his head and then runs his fingers through his hair. He feels the anxiety flowing in every part of his body as his heart pounds in his chest. The pain is so severe that it is tearing him apart. Within seconds, he loses control of his emotions. Lucas weeps like a child who has just lost its mother. He slides down the door, putting his head against his knees as he continues to cry.

A nurse sees Lucas falling apart, and she runs toward him as he is trying to compose himself.

"Mr. Clarkson, are you okay?" questions the nurse.

"No, no, my wife..." says Lucas as he continues to sob. "She doesn't know me. It's not her in that room."

"Mr. Clarkson, your wife is very ill. Mental illness is one of the most delicate situations in which it is hard to predict what state of mind a person is in. Right now, Mrs. Clarkson is living in a fantasy world. She must have suppressed so much pain from her past that her mind could not handle it, so it went on overdrive, and now, in order to survive, she is living in another world. Her memory is lost for now, but with the help of Dr. Jones, she can recover. It will take time and patience, and you, Mr. Clarkson, cannot give up on your wife. Even though she doesn't know you right now, you have to help Dr. Jones understand her issues and past pain, so he can find the right prognoses for her and the right medication to help her recover from the delusion she is in," explains the nurse as she kneels down beside Lucas. "Do you want to go to the lounge? We can talk while we wait for Dr. Jones and have some coffee."

"That would be good; thanks for your kindness and understanding," says Lucas as he wipes his tears, slowly gets up and follows the nurse. "Do you believe my wife will be able to recover from this illness and be herself again?"

"Mr. Clarkson, I'm not a doctor, but I have seen some remarkable recoveries in the past. Dr. Jones will be able to answer your questions better than I," replies the nurse as she leads Lucas to the lounge.

"How long does it take for a person to recover from depression?" he asks as he enters the lounge.

"Everyone is different, and it depends on what type of depression they are in," replies the nurse as she goes toward the coffee machine. "Remember that your wife is in a psychotic depression, which is considerably more complicated than regular clinical depression," she says.

"Right. Dr. Jones told me that's what he thinks—Isabelle has psychotic depression—which sounds bad to me," says Lucas as he sits down and tries to understand about depressions. "What will happen to her?"

"Psychotic depressions are the worst cases, and the recovery period takes longer, say about a year, and there are some that don't recover. According to the Mental Health Institute, they are out of touch with reality, and their behavior changes: they may have hallucination or voices in their heads. They don't want to bathe or change clothes. They want to spend a lot of time in bed during the day and be up all night, and they may get angry for no apparent reason," explains the nurse as she pours Lucas a coffee. "Any sugar or cream?"

"Two sugars and cream, please," replies Lucas. "You must see a lot of different behaviors here on this floor."

"Yes, everyone has a different approach, and we have to learn to understand our patients' behavior in order to care for them. There have been times when people cannot control their actions to a point that we have to sedate them because they can hurt themselves or others; there are even times when we are at risk of being harmed by a patient who doesn't know what's real and what is not real," says the nurse as she gives Lucas his coffee and sits down.

"I had never heard of psychotic depression until yesterday, with Dr. Jones. He even gave me a pamphlet on it. It is scary, especially when there are cases that don't recover. I am very frightened of what might come, and I wonder if I will ever get my wife back," says Lucas. He takes a sip of his coffee and momentarily appreciates the familiarity of the hot beverage.

"Mrs. Clarkson is under an expert's care. I believe in Dr. Jones's work; he is an amazing doctor!" expresses the nurse. "Dr. Jones has helped hundreds of people like Mrs. Clarkson, but you have to help him, by staying strong and focused. Remember what Mrs. Clarkson is going through—whatever she does or says is not her but the illness. Don't take any of this personally. She is not herself at the moment."

"It is hard to understand all that she is going through, but I will stay strong for my wife. It's true her childhood wasn't great, but as a result, she has blossomed into a wonderful person. She doesn't deserve this, and the children surely need their mom. It is hard for me to grasp the magnitude of the situation in such a short time," says Lucas as he takes another sip of his coffee.

"Yes, this is really hard to handle, but the key right now is for you to stay strong for your wife and children," replies the nurse as she pats Lucas on his hand. "You look like a good-hearted man, with a great deal of inner strength. With our expertise, we can help you and

Mrs. Clarkson through this horrible time in your lives and get you back to the happy family life that you both had with your children."

"You are so right. I need to pull through this, for my wife's sake and our children's. She would do it for me if I were in her position," Lucas says. He shakes the nurse's hand. "Thank you so much for talking to me. Thank you!"

"You're welcome. If at any time you need to talk about this issue, there is always a nurse at the nurses station, or if you feel more comfortable with me, they can contact me for you, Mr. Clarkson," explains the nurse as she gets up. "I need to attend to my duties, and I'm sure Dr. Jones will come soon. I'll tell the other nurses where you are if they need to contact you."

"I appreciate that," says Lucas. He finishes his coffee and waits patiently for Dr. Jones, who soon comes into the lounge and sits down beside him.

"Mr. Clarkson, I have the results for Mrs. Clarkson, and it is not looking good. As I suspected, she has been diagnosed with psychotic depression, and she will need some extensive medical treatments. It will be a long haul for both you and your wife. As you just witnessed by her behavior, she has no clue who you are. This behavior is a known symptom in psychotic depression, and there are many more," explains Dr. Jones. Then he opens Isabelle's file. "We will start treatment tomorrow, and we have started giving her antidepressants with antipsychotic medication."

"What should I do now?" asks Lucas, with confusion on his face. "Isabelle doesn't know me, and if I see her again, she will tell me to get out as if I am a stranger."

"Yes, Mr. Clarkson; you will need to go slowly. I will guide you through this. As Mrs. Clarkson's medication starts to work, and with treatment, she will eventually come to terms with reality. Before we commence, I have to tell you that there is a chance that the medication and treatment will not work. In that case, we will have to go another route, which is called electroconvulsive therapy, or ECT, which I talked about yesterday," explains Dr. Jones. Then he closes the file. "I have seen many cases who have come out of their depression, but it can take as long as a year."

"Yes, Dr. Jones. I am starting to understand this devastating illness that took my wife, and I'm determined to fight back. Please, Dr. Jones, help me return my wife to the person she was before," says Lucas as he stands up. His fingers are tapping the table; he is determined to do whatever it takes to get Isabelle back.

CHAPTER 28

Lucas is dedicated to helping Isabelle recover from the destructive illness that is wiping away her mind and controlling her in an ugly world of hallucination. He works night and day with Dr. Jones and all the nurses on the third floor of the General Hospital. Lucas is getting to know the hospital inside and out; on some occasions, he spends more time there than at home. Lucas has also chosen to quit the job that he loves in order to be with Isabelle. He has to make a choice between his job and his wife, and he doesn't have to think twice about the issue. Isabelle is his priority, and at age thirty-four, she has a lot of living yet to do.

Lucas has money set aside so he can be with his wife and raise his children as best he can. Every morning he is with his children for breakfast; it is their time. They listen to the Beach Boys and ABBA together to try to maintain some normality. He gives them updates about their mom, on how she is really sick and they have to be strong for her. He reminds them that she loves them deeply, but her illness has put her in the hospital. When she gets better, she will come home. He also asks them to pray for her and to never believe that they ever did anything wrong, especially never to feel guilty for what has happened to their mom. He understands that children sometimes place the blame on themselves, but their mother's condition was not their fault. He tells them again that it is an illness that has taken her away, and the doctors are working in collaboration to make their mommy better.

Lucas works very closely with the doctors and nurses to understand what Isabelle is going through; about her hallucinations and how to help her to come back to the real world. There is a point at which Dr. Jones thinks of giving up on Isabelle because she is not responding to treatment. He even takes Lucas aside and tells him that Isabelle is not responding, that when a year has gone by and there is no recovery, most patients go into institutions.

Lucas doesn't want to hear what the doctor is saying. He knows there has been no progress, but he is not one to give up. Lucas has always been persistent and placed his family first. Isabelle now allows Lucas to visit her; she has come to trust Lucas but has no recollection about Lucas as her husband, nor the fact that she has five children with him—and a wonderful life.

Nearly a year goes by, and Isabelle shows a slight improvement in her psychotic depression but is not ready to leave the hospital. When Dr. Jones reevaluates Isabelle, he finds little change in her ability to become the person she once was. She has no recollections of her past and believes she is in the hospital because she has just given to birth to twins—a girl and a boy. Isabelle often tells Lucas that her babies are in the nursery, and they are premature; that's why she can't see them.

Lucas tries to tell her about her life and her children, but she denies the truth. She feels comfortable around Lucas, but there are times when she flares up and curses him, saying that he is trying to take her babies away from her. Lucas always stays calm and finds ways to settle Isabelle; she often cries herself to sleep in his arms. Lucas stays strong, but there are nights he cries himself to sleep as well. Still, he doesn't want to believe Dr. Jones that Isabelle might be one of the rare cases that will never recover from her illness.

One morning, after having breakfast with his children and sending them off to school, Lucas talks with his parents about Isabelle and the fact that Dr. Jones is giving up on her but that he is

Path of Lucas

not ready to give up. Elizabeth tells Lucas to do whatever it takes to get his wife back; it is his life. She also advises him to ask the doctor if there are any other options. At that moment, Lucas comes to a conclusion and kisses his mother.

Lucas rushes to the hospital to talk to Dr. Jones about his idea to help Isabelle. As he enters the hospital, he runs toward the elevator. His thoughts are rushing through his mind as he reaches the third floor. Lucas comes out of the elevator and runs toward the nurses station.

"Good morning, ladies," he says cheerfully, flashing his beautiful smile.

"Good morning, Mr. Clarkson. You look so happy this morning," responds one of the nurses while the other nurses smile at Lucas.

"I just got an idea to help Isabelle come out of her depression, and I'm looking for Dr. Jones to talk with him. Have you seen him around this morning?"

"Dr. Jones is in his office. I can call him," replies the nurse sitting nearest to the phone.

"Yes, please!" he says excitedly, and then he waits for the answer with a grin on his face.

The nurse puts the call through, and Dr. Jones answers and tells the nurse to send Mr. Clarkson in right away.

"Mr. Clarkson, Dr. Jones will see you now," says the nurse at the phone as she hangs up.

"Thank you so much," replies Lucas, running off toward Dr. Jones's office.

Lucas knocks at the door, and then he hears the doctor say, "Come in." Lucas opens the door and rushes toward his desk.

"Good morning, Mr. Clarkson. What can I do for you?" questions Dr. Jones as he takes off his glasses and sets them on his desk.

"Dr. Jones, you are giving up on my wife, and I am here to see what else we can do to help Isabelle recover from her depression," he says with confidence as he sits down.

"Mr. Clarkson, I have done all I could to get Mrs. Clarkson to remember who she was, and it didn't work for her. I am sorry to disappoint you, but I am out of ideas," explains Dr. Jones as he puts his glasses back on. "Looking at her file, I see nothing else I can do. We even gave Mrs. Clarkson electroconvulsive therapy, and it didn't work. That was my last option. She should be put into an institution because she may never recover, or it might take many years. This is not easy for me to say, but I've got to be honest with you, Mr. Clarkson."

"It sounds as though you have pretty much given up on my wife, Dr., but I thought about something this morning, and I so much want to believe it will work," replies Lucas as he stares at her file. "This is a long shot, but I have nothing to lose—I am a desperate man, doctor!"

"And what might that be, Mr. Clarkson?" questions Dr. Jones with a puzzled look on his face.

"Well, like I said, it's a long shot, but I have nothing to lose at this point. Isabelle doesn't believe that I am her husband and that she has five children, right?" he says as he leans over toward the desk.

"Right," replies Dr. Jones, no less confused.

"Isabelle has grown to trust me, but she has never responded to the pictures of us and our children when we tried that therapy. I think it was too soon the last time, and this time I want to show her pictures of us again—but this time I want to do things differently. I want to start taking Isabelle out of the hospital into society, so she can feel the real world, not just be isolated on this floor. Then I want her to reexamine the photos but in a different manner. By that I mean to start small, out there, and then start going to stores," he says as he dreams of this happening.

"Mr. Clarkson, I'm sorry to say this, but Mrs. Clarkson is not ready to go out in public —she will only become hysterical. She will get very frightened and might become violent, and without medication, you will not be able to control her actions. This could be very dangerous," replies Dr. Jones.

"Dr. Jones, you want to send my wife to an institution, and you think I will just let that happen? I want a second chance at this. I will take full responsibility for her actions," demands Lucas, his voice growing louder.

"As I said, Mrs. Clarkson is not ready to go out; she has not made anywhere near a full recovery. Mr. Clarkson, you know she is very delicate at this point, and she will only have a breakdown if she goes out in society."

"Dr. Jones, I'm begging you to give me one chance to help my wife—please! I have learned a lot through this journey about psychotic depression, and Isabelle has built trust in me, even though she doesn't believe I am her husband. Please, have mercy. This is my only chance to have my wife back," cries Lucas, pleading with the doctor.

"Yes, she has built trust in you, Mr. Clarkson, but is that enough to allow her out in society?" asks Dr. Jones. He scratches his head and sits deep in thought. *Is this a potential solution for Mrs. Clarkson or a huge risk to her safety?*

"I will take small steps, and eventually I may take her out for supper and then go from there. Dr. Jones, I want to do this; it is my last opportunity. I know it will be challenging, but it is the only thing left that I can do for my wife and my family."

"Mr. Clarkson, if I let you do this, will you report to me every action you take with Mrs. Clarkson?" asks Dr. Jones.

"Every move, sir!" says Lucas, with big bright eyes and an enormous smile as he looks at the doctor, anxiously waiting for a response.

"She does have trust in you for some reason, which is highly unusual, but it could trigger her memory to start working again," answers Dr. Jones with an amazed look. He smiles in amusement. "I will sign the release form—but remember: Mrs. Clarkson is very fragile, and too many people around her could cause her to flare."

"Thank you, Dr. Jones! I believe in my heart that this will work. I know it is like finding a needle in a haystack, but this is my last chance to have my wife back. Dr. Jones, Isabelle is the mother of my children, and I need to do whatever I can to have her back with us and not in an institution for the rest of her days," says Lucas. He takes the signed form, stands up and shakes the doctor's hand. "Thanks again."

"Prove me wrong, Mr. Clarkson, and go get your wife back," replies Dr. Jones as they continue to shake hands. Then he pats Lucas on the shoulder with admiration for Lucas's devotion and undying hope.

Lucas smiles at him in return and leaves the office to take the release form to the nurses station and then to see Isabelle.

"Good morning, Isabelle!" he greets her. "How are you doing this morning?" He smiles as he walks closer to her.

"I am going to see my babies today; they are doing better. I can't wait to see my twins," says Isabelle with a smile. She is sitting down on a chair, combing her hair.

"Isabelle, I have to go home, but when I come back, would you like to go out with me?" he asks as he tries to change the subject. He is wondering how he will ever make Isabelle realize that she is in the hospital because of depression, not having babies.

"Where do you want to take me?" questions Isabelle as she stops combing her hair and looks at Lucas with a serious face. "I have to be with my babies. I have to stay here. You know, Lucas, my babies need me here."

"Isabelle, Isabelle, the doctors and the nurses have told you over and over again that you didn't give birth to twins; it is only a dream. Your children are at home, waiting for your recovery, so you can go back to them," explains Lucas as he has so many times before. "Isabelle, listen to me—it is very important for you to come with me out there to see the real world, not just the walls and hospital beds. And then I can take you to your real children, who are dying to see you."

"Lucas, listen to me! I have two babies out there waiting for me to care for them. They were premature babies, and now they have gained weight, and they are ready for me to care for them—today," shouts Isabelle. Then she gets up, runs to the bathroom and slams the door.

"Okay, Isabelle, let's find your babies. If you had babies, they would be on this floor waiting for you … right. And if not, then these twins are a figment of your imagination. It is just an illusion; it is not real. It is just your depression making you think that way," says Lucas quite sternly as he walks to the bathroom door. "Open the door, and let's go search every inch on this floor for these two newborn babies that you have built in your mind."

"Lucas, stop it… stop it!" cries Isabelle as she puts her hands over her ears to hide from what he is saying.

"Isabelle, open the door! Why are you so scared to face the truth that there are no babies out there? Come out; let's go see. You said to me that you are going to see your babies; well, I want to see them also. Let's go now," shouts Lucas, trying to make Isabelle see reality.

Isabelle opens the door slowly, and Lucas opens it wider. Then he holds Isabelle tightly as she sobs.

"Isabelle, don't be afraid. Let's look for your babies. I can assure you that there are no babies here; there are just people like yourself who are ill—they are all battling depression. We can go around the whole floor, and you can ask questions to anyone. You may not remember your past, but they can help you with the truth about who you really are. If you do this, it will help to free you once and for all to get back to your real life and your real children. You do have children waiting for you. They love you very much. Please listen to me. After our tour, I want you to rest. I have to go home, but then I'll come back. We will go for a little ride, so you can see the real world," says Lucas as he holds her by the arms. "Come with me… I will prove to you that there are no babies here. It's all in your mind; it is not real."

Isabelle stops and listens in confusion to every word Lucas is saying. She slowly walks out of the bathroom with him.

"Come with me, Isabelle, and I can prove my point. I want you to understand that there are no babies. Come, let's go see," expresses Lucas as he gently guides her.

"Lucas, Lucas, I am scared. I want to see my babies," says Isabelle with sheer terror in her eyes. At this point, she's beginning to question what to believe.

"Isabelle, please come with me, and take a good look around. It pains me to see you hurting, but you must believe me when I say that there are no babies," replies Lucas as he takes her hand and starts to walk around the hospital with her. "Look, there are just rooms with people who are fighting different kinds of depression. Just like you, they are here to get better with the help of great doctors and medications. There are no babies. Look around. No babies... No nursery, just people who are trying to recover from depression."

Isabelle cries as she walks around in disbelief, seeing no babies, no nursery, and especially no twins. Lucas continues to walk around, holding her hand and showing Isabelle every corner on the floor to emphasize once and for all that there are no babies in sight.

"Lucas... Lucas, stop. Please stop; this is too much for me. I feel very confused right now. Please take me to my room—please," cries Isabelle as she breaks down. "I want to go to my room."

"Okay, Isabelle, okay. Let's go back," says Lucas as he holds her tight and kisses her on the forehead. "I don't want to hurt you, Isabelle. That's the last thing in the world that I would ever want to do, but I want you to start believing me so that you can be whole again, and we can resume our lives together with your real children."

"I am scared, Lucas. Why do I believe in my mind that I gave birth to twins?" questions Isabelle, crying.

"It's your depression that is confusing you and that makes you feel frightened," says Lucas as he carries Isabelle back to her room. He feels her whole body shaking. "It is your mind playing tricks on you, Isabelle. You need to relax and take deep breaths when you feel confused; that will help you feel less scared."

"Lucas, why are you so kind to me?" asks Isabelle. She feels good in his arms but doesn't know why.

"You may not remember, but as I have told you before, I'm your husband, and we have five children together, who are at our home waiting for their mommy to come back," replies Lucas as they enter Isabelle's room. "Lie down, Isabelle, and go to sleep because you have gone through a lot at this point. I will go home for a while, and then I'll come back, and we'll go for a little ride."

Lucas kisses Isabelle on the cheek as she lies down on her bed. He pulls the blanket over her. Isabelle looks back at Lucas, her eyes red from crying, but she tries to smile.

"Thanks, Lucas, for all your kindness," whispers Isabelle; then she turns and settles her head on the pillow.

"See you later, Isabelle," says Lucas softly as he tucks her in.

Over the next weeks and months, Lucas slowly starts taking Isabelle out in the real world, and she gradually begins coping with reality. Isabelle still doesn't remember her family but trusts what Lucas is telling her. She has become calmer and less delusional, not becoming overwhelmed and flaring out in public as she had done in the past. Lucas is thrilled with the results. Isabelle wants to learn more about her real life. To think that he could've listened to Dr. Jones and just given up on Isabelle—he is so grateful that he did not.

CHAPTER 29

It is nearing the month of December. Lucas is working closely with Isabelle; she is doing well but still can't remember many major details of her life including having children, marrying Lucas, and being his wife. They still get along extremely well, and Isabelle is trying hard to remember her past, but she continues to feel perplexed.

Lucas keeps bringing her places that they have been before, and he always tells Isabelle stories about them being together in the past as a couple. Isabelle listens intently to what Lucas is saying but has no recollection of these events. She continues to see Dr. Jones for therapy, who sees changes in her behavior and is proud of the work Lucas is doing with Isabelle.

The morning of December first, Lucas has another great idea. He decides to take Isabelle out shopping to buy Christmas gifts for their children. Lucas has found a cube picture holder, which little Thomas had given his mom two years prior as a Christmas gift before her depression. Lucas takes the picture cube and inserts a picture of each child and then a picture of himself with Isabelle.

Proudly, Lucas comes out of his bedroom and goes into the kitchen to see his mother. Elizabeth is attending to the dishes, and John is sitting at the table, finishing off his tea, as Lucas walks in.

"Look, Mom. Look, Dad. Remember this picture cube that Thomas gave Isabelle as a Christmas gift?" says Lucas with a big smile.

"Yes, I remember," replies Elizabeth as she turns to look toward Lucas. John nods his head.

"Isabelle never had a chance to put pictures in it, and it just sat there on her dresser," explains Lucas as he turns the cube around and looks at the pictures with joy. "I inserted the children's school pictures, and I put a picture of Isabelle and me together, so Isabelle can see each one of us. I am going to take Isabelle Christmas shopping, and her job will be to find a gift for us, one at a time, to put under the tree for Christmas morning."

"That sounds fantastic! Do you think Isabelle will want to participate?" questions Elizabeth as she wipes her hands and walks toward the coffee pot. "Do you want a coffee?"

"Yes, please," says Lucas as he sits down beside his dad and hands John the picture cube. "Think this will work, Dad?"

"Son, it's amazing what you have done with Isabelle so far; when the doctor wanted to give up, you didn't. You have nothing to lose, and Isabelle has grown to put trust in you, which is a great start," says John. Then he puts his oxygen mask back on. "Believe, and that's when miracles happen."

"Thanks, Dad! I feel like I'm fighting for all of our lives and will do anything for her," replies Lucas.

"Lucas, I think your idea is great, but how is Isabelle going to know what to buy for each child?" asks Elizabeth as she serves him coffee and tops up John's.

"Thanks, Mom," says Lucas and then takes a sip of his coffee. "I will explain one child at a time—their age, their characteristics— and then we will go shopping. That is when Isabelle will have to look at the picture cube of each of the children, and she will have to figure what gift will suit them best. I am hoping Isabelle can get some kind of flashback from beyond her memory blockage and recognize something from her past with us."

"You think that can work, Lucas?" questions Elizabeth as she sits down beside them.

"I hope so," replies Lucas. "Isabelle enjoys Christmas. Watching the children unwrapping their gifts from Santa was always one of her favorite moments. Maybe this could trigger her memory."

"Son, you have a positive attitude, which is something your mother and I greatly admire about you," says John as he takes his mask off and sips his coffee.

"Well, I have to go; wish me luck. Bye, Mom. Bye, Dad," says Lucas as he finishes his coffee. He gets up and gives each of them a kiss.

"Bye, Lucas," says Elizabeth as she smiles at him.

"Bye, Lucas," echoes John as he squeezes Lucas's shoulder. "Wishing you the best, son."

Lucas heads to the hospital, taking the picture cube with him, feeling wonderfully hopeful.

When Lucas arrives at Isabelle's room, he sees she is all dressed up and looking very pretty. She is sitting on her bed, reading a book about depression that Dr. Jones gave her earlier this morning.

"Hi, Isabelle. What are you reading?" asks Lucas with a gorgeous smile. He takes in Isabelle's beauty; she looks just as she used to before she got sick.

"Oh, this is a book about depression. Dr. Jones came to see me; he said I am doing great and that it is time I learn about my illness and what is going on in my brain," replies Isabelle as she smiles back at Lucas. "It is amazing how a mind functions, particularly with psychotic depression."

"Yes, I've also learned a lot about depression, especially as it relates to my wife," says Lucas with a laugh as he sits down beside Isabelle.

"Oh, Lucas, you're so funny this morning! You're beaming!" says Isabelle. She stares at him as he sits beside her, and she closes her book. "What do you have in your hand, Lucas?"

"Yes… this is a picture cube. I put pictures of our children in each slot and a picture of you and me together," replies Lucas as he shows Isabelle the picture of their family. "I want you to do something for me."

"What, Lucas? What do you want me to do?" asks Isabelle as Lucas hands her the picture cube.

"I want you to buy Christmas gifts for these five children," explains Lucas. Then he looks again at Isabelle, seeing her true beauty.

"They are beautiful children," says Isabelle as she turns the cube and takes a look at each child. "I would not know what to buy for them, Lucas."

"Don't worry. I will be with you, and if you have any questions, I will help you. When we were together, you loved Christmas, and most of all, you always enjoyed watching our children open their gifts from Santa," replies Lucas as he gets up. "Let's go Christmas shopping."

"Lucas, I'm afraid," says Isabelle with watery eyes as she looks at the picture of her and Lucas.

"Isabelle, don't be scared. Trust me; we can do this together," patiently replies Lucas as he sits down and hugs her. Months ago, he came to terms with the fact that simple tasks could be terribly challenging for his sick wife. Of course, leaving the hospital after such a long period of confinement would be difficult.

"I wish I could remember being your wife. We look so happy in this picture," says Isabelle as she hugs Lucas back. "I want so badly to remember us and our children."

"You will someday soon, Isabelle. I will not give up on us," explains Lucas. "Don't be afraid. We'll just go with the flow and see what happens."

"Lucas, you are such a wonderful person," expresses Isabelle. She knows she feels good being in Lucas's arms even though she has no recollection of their past together as a couple. "Let's go shopping."

"Yes! Yes! Let's go!" Lucas smiles with anticipation as he gets up off the edge of the bed.

Isabelle is happy to go with Lucas even though she still has no memory of her children and her husband.

Isabelle enjoys shopping for Christmas, and she is great at picking gifts for the children. Richard is thirteen years old, so Isabelle chooses a guitar for him; Lucas is proud of her first choice. For Johnny, who is twelve, Isabelle chooses a realistic-looking train set, and for Steve, who is eleven, she chooses a rod hockey table. For nine-year-old Lucy, Isabelle picks a record player with a Rene Simard Christmas record, and for little six-year-old Thomas, it is a big Tonka truck.

Once they are finished shopping, Lucas buys Christmas wrapping paper to wrap the gifts for their children. Isabelle enjoys this precious moment with Lucas. Back at the hospital, they wrap the gifts together. She thanks him for taking her shopping and tells him that it was fun. Lucas has to leave to have supper with his children and parents, but he promises Isabelle that he will be back later in the evening. Isabelle tells Lucas that she will finish wrapping the rest of the gifts, if he doesn't mind. Lucas is delighted to see Isabelle getting involved, and he encourages her to continue. He kisses her on the forehead before leaving. He is wearing a huge smile as he sees progress with Isabelle.

As Lucas leaves, Isabelle continues to wrap. A split second later, Isabelle has a flashback, a vision of her and Lucas at a restaurant, and it seems he is giving her a ring. Isabelle shakes her head in disbelief and continues wrapping the gifts. Ten minutes later, she has another flashback; this time it is a longer period, and it is her wedding day with Lucas, it seems. Isabelle is bewildered and wonders what is happening to her.

A nurse walks into the room to give Isabelle her medication before supper and sees Isabelle holding her head. "What is the matter, Mrs. Clarkson?" asks the nurse. "Do you need the doctor?"

"No! No!" replies Isabelle as she continues to hold her head. "Something weird is happening to me."

"What is happening to you, Mrs. Clarkson?" questions the nurse, "Can you try explaining to me in more detail what you are feeling?"

"It is strange, nurse. I am getting flashbacks. It seems that I am with Lucas in both visions. The first one was for a split second and very blurry; it was Lucas and I at a restaurant—it looked like he was giving me a ring. In the second vision, I was wearing a wedding dress, holding a bouquet of roses and seeing the groom in the front of the church—he looked like Lucas. These visions feel so peculiar! Do you know what is going on in my mind?"

"That's great, Mrs. Clarkson! It can be scary, but this is your memory coming back. It's important to talk to Dr. Jones about this later when he comes to see you after supper. Dr. Jones will be able to guide you through this special time. Lots of patients who have gone through psychotic depression have flashbacks, and often within weeks, they get all their memories back," explains the nurse as she gives Isabelle her medication. "This is wonderful news, Mrs. Clarkson!"

"Do you think I will remember my children?" asks Isabelle as she grabs the picture cube and turns it to see all of her children.

"Mrs. Clarkson, continue your Christmas wrapping. Supper will be served soon. And don't worry about remembering your children—it will all come in good time. You have made a breakthrough, which is wonderful, so don't be hard on yourself," advises the nurse as she reaches for the door. "I must continue giving out the meds before supper arrives. Take care, Mrs. Clarkson. I think you are recovering—don't be afraid or rush it; just let it all come to you."

"Thanks for your help and taking extra time with me," replies Isabelle. Then she gets up and starts wrapping Christmas gifts again.

Isabelle is having her supper, eating roast beef with mashed potatoes, when she has another flashback. This time she sees herself cooking in a strange house, but when she looks at the picture of her and Lucas, it is the same kitchen as in the vision. Isabelle goes to lie on her bed, and as she closes her eyes, she thinks about what is happening. Everything Lucas has told her is starting to make sense. He has been telling the truth about their relationship. Isabelle lies there, rubbing her forehead with her hands in confusion. She feels exhausted and falls asleep.

Lucas arrives at the hospital and enters the elevator. As he comes out of the elevator doors, he meets Dr. Jones. "Good evening, Dr. Jones," says Lucas as they walk toward each other.

"Hello, Mr. Clarkson. Going to see Mrs. Clarkson?" asks Dr. Jones as he stands beside Lucas while holding a number of files in his hands.

"Yes, that's right! We had a great day together," says Lucas with a genuine smile.

"Yeah? What did you do today?" asks Dr. Jones, looking interested.

"As I told you, I wanted to take her out Christmas shopping, so we did that, and Isabelle did a great job finding gifts for the children. It was wonderful watching her shop, looking for the right gift for each child," explains Lucas. Then he looks toward Isabelle's door. "I left it to Isabelle to wrap gifts, and I promised I would be back this evening."

"Yes, I was just heading to her room for my nightly report," states Dr. Jones as he shows Lucas Isabelle's files in his hands. They have gotten to know each other well over the last few months and act collegially together.

"Let's see if she's still wrapping gifts," replies Lucas. There is excitement in his voice as they walk together toward Isabelle's room.

Lucas opens the door slowly and walks in, with Dr. Jones behind him. They both notice Isabelle sleeping, her supper barely touched and a gift partially wrapped. Lucas looks at Dr. Jones; they are both puzzled at seeing Isabelle sleeping so soundly. *It is not like Isabelle to sleep this early in the evening,* thinks Lucas as he walks closer to her and then gently shakes her shoulder to wake her up.

"Isabelle... Isabelle," whispers Lucas.

"Ah... um... um," mumbles Isabelle as she slowly opens her eyes. "Lucas... Lucas, you're back! ... Dr. Jones." Then Isabelle sits up. "Sorry, I fell asleep."

"Don't be sorry; it's okay. You had a big day today," replies Lucas as he sits beside her on the bed. He does not know what Isabelle went through just a few hours ago.

"Dr. Jones, I'm happy you're here with Lucas because I have something important to share with both of you," says Isabelle. She turns to Lucas and takes hold of his hand, as if she is building confidence in herself. "Lucas, after you left to go for supper with our children, and I asked you if it was okay to wrap gifts—"

"Yes," says Lucas with a nod. He is surprised that Isabelle is holding his hand and is so happy inside to see her take control for the first time since her depression started. He is anxious to hear what Isabelle has to say.

"As I was wrapping the gifts, something happened to me," continues Isabelle as she smiles at Lucas with joy. For the first time, there is no confusion on her face—and it is so beautiful.

"Go on," says Dr. Jones; he, too, is eager to hear what Isabelle has to say.

"Well, after wrapping a few gifts, I had a flashback of Lucas and me. The first vision was very blurry, but it was about Lucas giving me a ring at a restaurant. About ten minutes later, I had another vision. I was wearing a wedding dress and holding a bouquet of roses. It was my wedding day—and Lucas, you were the groom," says Isabelle as she squeezes his hand and looks into Lucas's eyes. "I am married to you, Lucas... I am your wife!"

"Yes! Oh, Isabelle! It is so true—we got engaged at Mama Jean's restaurant on your birthday, and you had a bouquet of roses at our wedding," cries Lucas excitedly as he tears up.

"Mrs. Clarkson, this is a big breakthrough for you! It is the first sign of your memory coming back," explains Dr. Jones with glee. He feels so happy for Isabelle and Lucas.

"But I don't have any recollection of my children," says Isabelle sadly, with tears.

"Don't worry, Mrs. Clarkson. It usually takes a few weeks to get back all or most of your memory," replies Dr. Jones with confidence.

"Are you sure?" asks Isabelle feeling hopeful.

"Yes, Mrs. Clarkson, I am sure. It was great that you went shopping for Christmas gifts, and it must have triggered something to help bring back parts of your memory. I think it will continue now, but don't push too hard. Let it come to you," explains Dr. Jones, "I must go now, but I will see you tomorrow."

"Thank you, Dr. Jones. With that news, you have made me the happiest person alive! I have my wife back, and soon my kid's will have their mother back," says Lucas with joy and disbelief.

"Bye, and thank you, Dr. Jones," says Isabelle with a big grin. She continues to hold Lucas's hand with the true knowledge and understanding now that they have something special in their hearts for each other.

When the doctor leaves, Lucas looks at Isabelle and then kisses her on the lips for the first time since her illness. Isabelle accepts the kiss, and they start kissing passionately; they both feel their love for each other after more than a year apart. Lucas has known all along in his heart that he could never give up on his wife.

CHAPTER 30

As Lucas tells his life story to his daughter, Lucy, he hears people talking in the hall. He listens intently because he thinks he knows the voices.

"Lucy, your children have arrived. I can hear them talking outside the room," says Lucas as he pats her on the shoulder, wishing for her to wake up. "I hear Danny and Ryan's voices. They must be waiting for Dwayne and Johnny to arrive because I don't hear them."

Lucy lies there with no response to her father. Lucas stares at Lucy and then starts to feel a pain in his chest. As he gasps for air, he feels relief from the pain.

"Lucy, your boys will be coming in soon, and it would mean so much to them if you would just open your beautiful brown eyes to see them walk in. Please, Lucy, come back to us! There are so many reasons for you to live, and one big reason is standing in the hall worrying about you right now," expresses Lucas. Then he takes her hand, looks at her and kisses her hand. "You want me to finish my story before—that's why, Lucy. Promise me you will open your eyes when I finish my story about your mom and me."

Lucas smiles as he bargains with his daughter; then he kisses her on the cheek. "Lucy, at that point, I thought our lives would be a success story, but it wasn't that simple. There was a twist to it. I can remember that day clearly," says Lucas as he goes back to the day he took his wife back to their home for the first time after her depression.

Lucas looks tenderly at his pretty daughter as he clears his throat.

Weeks have passed, and Isabelle is getting better. She slowly starts remembering her children, even their births. Lucas is so proud of Isabelle, of her willingness and the improvement she shows every day. One day, Lucas thinks Isabelle is ready to meet the children. He asks Dr. Jones if it would be a good idea to take Isabelle home for the day. Dr. Jones thinks it would be all right, but he cautions Lucas that it could be overwhelming for her, especially the first time at the house.

Lucas explains everything to Isabelle and asks if she thinks she is ready to meet their children and his parents. Isabelle agrees to go, so Lucas tells the children that their mommy is coming to visit but just for a day. The children are excited to see their mother, and Isabelle wants so much to see them. Lucas is ecstatic to reunite his family together after such a long time.

The next morning, Lucas heads to the hospital to get Isabelle and tells the children that they should be back within the hour. Isabelle is in her room, getting ready and trying to look her best for her children and her husband. Lucas opens the door and walks in with a gorgeous smile as he sees his pretty wife. He goes to her and gives her a passionate kiss.

"Are you ready to see our children?" asks Lucas as he kisses Isabelle again on her cheek with his arms around her waist.

"Yes, I want to see our children, but I'm feeling very nervous. I'll also be meeting your parents, and it all seems a little overwhelming," says Isabelle as she processes the fact that today will be a big day for her.

"The first time can be extremely challenging. If you're not ready, we can stay here," replies Lucas as he puts his hand under her chin. "Isabelle, the day is yours. I'm just happy that you got your memory back and that you are my wife."

"Lucas, I want to do this, but if it is too much for me, can you support me, please?" requests Isabelle as she gives Lucas a kiss and then hugs him.

"Okay, let's try this. If at any time you feel afraid or anxious, just tell me, and we'll leave," says Lucas. Isabelle agrees. He gets her jacket, and then they go.

As they arrive at the farm, the children are watching them enter the laneway. They are sitting on the stairs overlooking the huge picture window. They sit there patiently, with excitement in their eyes but without words. They stare as they watch their dad bring their mom back home to them, as he has promised he would. Elizabeth and John wait anxiously in the kitchen as Elizabeth brews coffee for them. She has baked cookies for the children.

Lucas parks the vehicle, stops the engine and takes his time as he looks at Isabelle. Isabelle gazes back at Lucas and then at the farmhouse. She takes a deep breath.

"I remember this house. We made so many memories," says Isabelle as she reaches for Lucas's hand. "Thank you, Lucas, for not giving up on me. I love you," she says and squeezes his hand.

"I love you, Isabelle," replies Lucas, and then he kisses her hand. "Our children are probably watching us, and they are anxiously waiting for you, their mommy." Lucas brushes Isabelle's hair. "Are you ready to go in?"

"Lucas, I'm scared. I feel anxiety coming over me, and I don't know why," says Isabelle as tears roll down her cheeks, "but I do want to do this. They are my children, and they need a mom."

"Isabelle, don't overdo it if you're not ready. I can go in and explain what's happening to the children. We want you to get better, and this is crucial for you. It is a very delicate situation, and we don't want to put too much pressure on you right now," says Lucas in a soft voice as he gently holds her by the shoulders.

"Lucas, I want to do this, but if I panic, please help me. I want to get better and come home to you and our children," says Isabelle as she wipes her tears and gets ready to see the children.

Lucas opens the door for Isabelle, and she enters and greets his parents. He offers Isabelle a chair, and she sits down and starts to look around. As she turns toward the hall, all she can see is children running toward her, and she starts to panic. Her heart starts beating rapidly, and with no control of her feelings, she starts to cry and becomes very frightened.

Lucas and Elizabeth react quickly. Elizabeth heads off the children and tells them softly that they thought Mom was ready to come home, but she is feeling sick again and Dad has to rush her back to the hospital to get better.

Lucas gets Isabelle out as quickly as he can so she will not further panic or lose control and seriously hurt herself. In the past, he has seen days when Isabelle became very violent to herself. He looks back and sees the sadness in his children's eyes as Elizabeth tries to comfort them. Lucas's mouth goes dry; he is torn between his wife and his children. He carries his wife to the vehicle and sits her in the seat. Isabelle cries harder and harder, to the point of screaming.

"Isabelle, Isabelle, it's okay. You're with me—it's me, Lucas," says Lucas as he tries to comfort her. "Isabelle, you just had a panic attack because you got so frightened. It hit you before you could control what was happening. This is also new to you, honey. Don't feel bad. The next time will be much better."

"Lucas… Lucas… Where am I? What just happened? Why am I crying?" asks Isabelle in confusion. She doesn't remember what just took place.

"Isabelle, we were at the house, and the children came running toward you. It scared you, and you had a panic attack. You're not ready to have the children run to you right now; we need to take it slowly," replies Lucas in a soft voice. "We need to go back to the hospital because you need your rest." Then Lucas closes her door and goes to sit in the driver's seat.

"Lucas, I'm so sorry!" cries Isabelle. She is starting to realize what has just happened.

"It's not your fault, Isabelle," says Lucas as he tries to comfort her. Then he starts his engine and heads toward the hospital.

As they leave, Lucas looks back at the house and sees the children at the window, staring toward them with gloomy faces. He feels so sad for what has happened, but there is no one to blame, not his innocent children who want their mother back home nor his wife who is very fragile at this time in her life.

Once Lucas takes Isabelle back to the hospital, he helps her settle in and comforts her. Lucas kisses Isabelle goodbye and tells her he will be back in the morning. He is going to see the children and explain why Mom became sick so fast that she had to leave.

Isabelle looks at Lucas just before he leaves and tells him that she doesn't want to give up. In a few days, she wants to go back and see the children. She wants to make this work, she tells Lucas, because they are her children, and they deserve to have their mom home with them. Lucas walks back to Isabelle, kisses her on the cheek and tells her that they will be back together as a family soon and not to worry; it will all work out.

When Lucas arrives back home, he gathers the children in the living room. They sit there and listen to what their dad has to say. They are happy to have him build their confidence that their mom will be back soon and that they just have to be patient with her illness. He also reports to them that Mom is not giving up and wants to recover to be with all of them. Then Lucas sends them to brush their teeth and settle down in their rooms for the night. It has been a big day.

Once the children are settled, Lucas talks with his parents for a little while about Isabelle's behavior. He describes to them how bad she feels about what took place that afternoon and also how she doesn't want to give up. Lucas tells his parents that Isabelle is a fighter, and he feels they will get through this very soon. He kisses them good night and goes into his room. He is so beaten up from his day that he hardly has any energy; he sits on his bed, puts his head down and breaks down.

A few weeks pass, and Isabelle is getting better and gaining strength. One light, snowy afternoon, she tells Lucas that she wants to go back to the farm and reunite with her children. Lucas looks at his wife in shock.

"Isabelle, please repeat what you just said," says Lucas, surprised at what he has heard. "Did you just say, on your own, that you want to go back to see the children?" Lucas is amazed because it is the first time that Isabelle is making her own decision without having input from Lucas, the doctor, or the staff.

"Lucas, I want to go back and see my children today, if that is okay with you. I am ready for them; even if they run at me like they did last time, it will not bother me. I have given it a lot of thought, and I want to be back home with you and the children before Christmas Day. I want to be there to put up the Christmas tree with our children. On Christmas morning, when they open their gifts, I want to see their beautiful faces," explains Isabelle with confidence. "Lucas, I have thought about this for a few weeks, and now I am ready. Let's surprise them."

"Isabelle, this is what I've wanted for so long—to have my family back," replies Lucas. He walks toward Isabelle and hugs and then kisses her passionately. He now believes again that they will be together for Christmas.

"Lucas, I love you and our children, and I know that I am getting better now with the help of Dr. Jones's therapy. He has suggested for me to try again because when I am in therapy, I can easily talk about my childhood abuse and about the death of my sister without crying all the time. I have come to grips with the whole ordeal of my depression and I don't feel so anxious or nervous. I also feel less tired and more relaxed with the medication. Lucas, I feel we can be a family again," she says, smiling as she holds onto Lucas and feeling safe in his arms.

"Let's go, Isabelle. We have a family to attend to before Christmas morning comes," says Lucas as he picks up Isabelle and swings her around. Then they kiss, for they are both happy to have found their way together again.

When Isabelle and Lucas arrive at the house, no one knows they were coming, not even Elizabeth. It is a surprise. Lucas stops the vehicle and asks Isabelle whether she is ready to do this, and with a huge grin, Isabelle nods yes. They both smile at each other and then Isabelle tells Lucas that she is feeling great, that she was not tense at all nor anxious. Lucas is thrilled to finally have the chance to have his family together for Christmas.

Lucas walks in first and Isabelle follows. They find no one in the kitchen, not even Elizabeth, who usually spends most of her time there. Lucas listens, and he hears the television playing in the living room. He slowly walks toward the sound and sees his children and his parents sitting quietly watching television.

"Hi, guys," says Lucas beaming. Isabelle stands behind him with the same shy smile that she's had since her youth.

"Hi, Dad," replies Richard and, as he looks up at his dad, exclaims, "Mom! Mom is here too!" He gets up and hugs his dad and his mom.

"Mom! Mom! Mom!" shout the others as they jump up and run toward Isabelle. The children are so happy, and they only now realize, deep within themselves, how much they have truly missed their mother during her lengthy hospitalization.

Isabelle opens her arms to hug them all, and Lucas watches them unite. It is an incredible sight for him to witness. Elizabeth and John look and can't believe their eyes. Isabelle is home and hugging her children with Lucas by her side.

As a family, they are all so happy that Isabelle was able to recuperate from her psychotic depression and have the ability to remember her family after such a long time. Even the doctor didn't think she would recover, but thanks to Lucas and his persistence, now she is home with her children.

Isabelle sits down with her children around her, and Lucas stands beside them, looking at his mom with a grin. Elizabeth grins back; she can see so much joy in her son's eyes. John pats his son's shoulder with pride for his determination.

They are all having such a marvelous time that Isabelle looks at Lucas with warmth and asks him if it would be okay if she stayed over for the night. She doesn't want to go back to the hospital, and perhaps Lucas can call and tell them their situation. Lucas calls the hospital to convey her request, and they approve it. The children are ecstatic to hear that their mom will be spending the night, and they will be able to see her in the morning as well.

The next morning is so much fun. Elizabeth and Isabelle make pancakes, and Lucas brews the coffee as John sits near the radio listening to the morning news. As the children slowly wake up, they smell the aroma of coffee brewing and pancakes in the kitchen. They all gather in the kitchen for breakfast as a true family, just like old times. Lucas and Isabelle explain to the children that Mom has to go back to the hospital to sign her release form, but they promise they will be back before supper. Isabelle assures her children that the next day they will put up the Christmas tree.

After breakfast, the children kiss their mom and dad and then watch them leave. Elizabeth stands with the children and smiles as they all wave goodbye. Lucas and Isabelle arrive at the hospital and are pleased to see the nurses at the nurses station for the last time. As Isabelle signs the release form, Lucas picks up her last items from the room. The nurses wish Lucas and Isabelle the best, and Dr. Jones tells Isabelle that he is proud of her recovery; she is an amazing person and very lucky to have a husband like Lucas, a man who never gives up.

A week before Christmas, Lucas has not yet bought a gift for Isabelle. He wants to do something special. Lucas tells her to get ready; they are going out Christmas shopping for her gift. Isabelle tells him that she doesn't need a gift; her gift is to be with her children for Christmas, which he has made possible for her. Lucas kisses Isabelle and tells her that she is his Christmas gift. They both laugh as Lucas gets Isabelle's jacket and leave together. Lucas has a little money left from his savings, so he takes Isabelle shopping for a new bedroom set of her choice for her Christmas gift. Isabelle is excited as she looks around the furniture store and sees the most beautiful bedroom set. The bed has beautifully carved head posts, the woman's dresser has wood carvings all around the mirror that matches the post carving of the bed, and the men's dresser is set high with beautiful carvings to match. It will be the first brand-new piece of furniture they have ever bought. Isabelle thanks Lucas for everything he has done for her.

On Christmas Eve, Isabelle puts on a fabulous Christmas Eve party with Lucas's family. After the party is over and everyone has left, Lucas and Isabelle tuck the children in. The children are so excited that they have a hard time falling asleep. Lucas and Isabelle have a cup of tea with John and Elizabeth, and they enjoy a few goodies left over from the party. Lucas kisses his parents good night, and Isabelle follows. Tomorrow will be a big day.

Early on Christmas morning, Lucas and Isabelle can hear the children running toward their room. The door opens, and the children run in and jump on the bed. Lucas and Isabelle kiss their children. The children are so excited to have their mother at home on Christmas!

"Mommy and Daddy—Santa brought us gifts! They are under the tree! Come see, Mommy! Come see!" says little Thomas.

"Yes! Yes! Let's go!" giggles Lucy as she hugs her daddy.

"Did Santa bring Mommy a gift too?" asks Lucas as he laughs and starts play fighting with his boys while hugging his little girl.

"Yes, Santa brings everyone a gift on Christmas," replies Thomas as he jumps out of the bed and points toward the living room at the tree. "See, Mommy, right there."

"Yes, honey," says Isabelle as she also gets up. "Let's go see what Santa brought us."

Richard and Johnny walk with their mom toward the living room; little Thomas runs with Steve. Lucas carries Lucy on his back with her arms wrapped around his neck. Elizabeth and John hear all the laughter, and they get up. Soon everyone is gathered in the living room. Lucas reads out the names on the gifts, and Isabelle hands them out. As they all open up their presents, Isabelle takes a second and stares at her children. *It is a Christmas miracle,* she thinks in her head, and she smiles. Lucas hugs his wife and kisses her; he is thinking, *what an amazing Christmas it is,* as he thanks God for his wonderful family and for restoring his wife's health after all the hardship she and the family endured.

CHAPTER 31

It is 1979, and Lucas is now thirty-nine years old. He does not go back to work for the cable company, choosing instead to be home with his family. He has used up all his savings to help Isabelle with her illness, so he goes back to work in the logging business. Lucas buys bushes from farmers, cuts trees down and brings his logs to Domtar, a paper company in Cornwall. He doesn't like his work, but he is eternally grateful for having a healthy family and having Isabelle back as his wife. Isabelle has gone back to work for the shoe company that she worked for before her depression. She is doing much better at coping with her depression but will always need to take medication.

They do not live a rich lifestyle. They both work hard to pay their bills, but their life is rich with the love they share with each other. Isabelle always enjoys being with Lucas, especially when he smiles, and she adores watching her children grow. Lucas has tremendous respect for his wife and loves seeing his family together and enjoying life. They have been through tough times, and he is grateful that things are easier now even though they are not perfect.

Lucas gives up on his dream job and focuses on making sure Isabelle is well cared for. He is protective of his wife and does not want another repeat of her illness, as she will always be delicate. Once in a while, she has a recurrence, but never major, just a few days of feeling exhausted. Lucas makes sure she rests, and the children are also understanding of their mother's illness. They know how to handle situations when their mom needs time to herself to recover.

Lucas is proud of his children, as they became teenagers. They are into sports and also play the guitar and drums. Richard and Johnny have formed a little band with friends, as they enjoy rock music. Richard is becoming a great artist; he has won many art contests throughout his childhood. Johnny is more into sports, and he plays football at his high school. His dream is to someday become a professional player, but he also loves sports cars and is knowledgeable about car models and styles. Steve is shy, just like his mother, but he loves to learn everything about cars, just like his dad. Lucas has taught Steve all he knows about mechanics from old beaten-up cars that he buys for parts to sell. Then he brings the rest of the metal to the scrap yard for extra cash. Lucy is growing fast. At only thirteen years old, she is blossoming into a beautiful woman, like her mother. Unlike her mom, she is very sporty and enjoys hanging with her brothers instead of cooking and cleaning. Lucy's passion is reading books, and she adores caring for children; she often babysits her cousin's children. Thomas is a happy little boy, who loves to hang around his sister. His favorite sport is soccer. He is a child who asks many questions because of his inquisitive mind. Lucas and Isabelle call Thomas their little scientist.

Lucas and Isabelle enjoy parenting, especially watching their children grow. They know that the children will persevere through life's obstacles because of their strengths and uniqueness; both parents have been incredible role models in terms of overcoming adversity, particularly Lucas with his persistence in helping Isabelle to get well, but Isabelle played her part by never giving up. They have taught their children to believe in themselves and to fulfill their own dreams in life. Lucas has one big rule as he raises his children and that is to respect each other. It is also important for Lucas to teach his children, at the end of the day, to each say something special about his or her day at the supper table. Isabelle is also strong on respect, and she loves how Lucas is a gentle but tough disciplinarian. He knows how to show their children the difference between right and wrong.

A few years later, it is not sports and music but cars and girls that excite Richard and Johnny. As for Steve, he is too busy learning about mechanics to have time for dating. Lucy starts dating one of Richard's friends, Justin, when she reaches sixteen. She goes steady for a short time, and then she becomes pregnant. Lucy cries when she announces to her mother that she is pregnant. Isabelle is conflicted to hear the news, and she remembers the fear she went through when she was expecting for Richard. She especially recalls being so frightened about her mother finding out. Isabelle is happy that Lucy can confide in her as a mother. Lucas doesn't know what is happening because Lucy is too afraid to tell him. Isabelle feels the pain her daughter is going through, as she can relate, so she tells Lucy that she will be the one to tell Lucas about the pregnancy.

The next day, Isabelle and Lucas are camping at Loch Garry, where they love to spend their summer camping with friends. Lucas is ready to start his day; as he finishes his breakfast, he gives Isabelle a kiss. He opens the door, ready to step out to go for an early morning boat ride with his friend Fred, when he notices Isabelle has tears in her eyes.

"Isabelle, is there something wrong? You look as if you're about to cry," says Lucas as he steps back into their camper and closes the door.

"It's Lucy, our baby girl," says Isabelle in a trembling voice, as she reaches to hug him.

"Is there something wrong with Lucy?" asks Lucas with a worried look. He hugs her back and tries to comfort her; so many things go through his mind. He is bracing himself for the worst.

"Yes," replies Isabelle as she starts to cry on Lucas's shoulder.

"Isabelle, what is it?" questions Lucas. Worst-case scenarios run through his mind.

"Our little girl is pregnant… she's pregnant, Lucas," cries Isabelle. She is going back in time and feeling the pain she went through when she found out she was pregnant the first time.

"What! Did I hear you right?" replies Lucas in a confused tone as he tries to put his thoughts together.

"Yes, Lucy is pregnant, Lucas, and she is only sixteen years old," cries Isabelle.

"This is not happening! Not my little girl! This is a lot to take in right now," says Lucas he sits down and rubs his forehead. "Isabelle, how can we help our daughter?"

"We have to support her through this, Lucas," says Isabelle as she sits down beside him. "Lucy was very shaken up when she told me about her pregnancy, and she was afraid to tell you. It reminded me how I felt when I got pregnant twenty years ago."

"Isabelle, Isabelle—I want Lucy to be happy. She has so much potential! I thought she had a bright future. My little girl has grown too fast, and now she is going to be a mother. What's going to happen with her education? What about Justin? Will he stay with Lucy and raise their child? Isabelle, there are so many unanswered questions. Where do we go from here to help our daughter?" Lucas asks rhetorically because he knows that Isabelle will not have all these answers.

"Lucas, Lucy and Justin are coming here this afternoon to see you because I promised Lucy that I would tell you first, and then they want to talk to you," replies Isabelle sniffling. Looking at the clock, she gives Lucas a kiss. "I have to pick up Thomas, and you'd better get ready for your boat ride before Fred starts knocking on the door."

"You're right, Isabelle. I better get going. Fred will be waiting. I'll see you later, and we'll talk with Lucy and Justin to see what they are planning to do with their lives," says Lucas. He hugs Isabelle and leaves to go boating with Fred. Isabelle freshens up to pick up her youngest son for an early soccer practice.

When Lucas returns from his boat trip, he settles down on a lounge chair with a hot beverage while waiting for Isabelle to arrive. He sips his coffee and thinks about his little girl and what she must be going through. He then ruminates about Isabelle and what she went through when she was pregnant with his child. How could history repeat itself? *What could I have done to prevent this from happening?* he thinks as he finishes his coffee. *Should we have talked to the kids about contraception or having sex before now? Or did Isabelle's absence and illness have an adverse effect on Lucy?* Lucas doesn't know the answer to these questions, and he has to stay focused in the moment. There is no use looking back.

Within the hour, Isabelle arrives with Thomas. Thomas comes running to Lucas and tells his dad what a great game he has had and that after the practice the coach asked him to be the team captain. Lucas smiles and pats Thomas on the shoulder. He tells him how proud he is. Isabelle watches them interact with a sense of joy in her heart because Lucas always has a way of showing his love to his children. Thomas runs off, full of confidence, to go swimming with his friends.

Isabelle sits beside Lucas, and they stare at each other in silence for a few seconds as they try to put their thoughts together. Lucas is about to say something when they hear a car driving up. He looks up to see Richard and Johnny and their girlfriends.

"Hi, Dad. Hi, Mom," says Richard as he gets out of his vehicle with his girlfriend, Chelsea. Johnny and his girlfriend, Angie, also say hi to them as they follow Richard and Chelsea.

"Hi, guys," replies Lucas, as does Isabelle, while they look at their children with pride.

"We're going for a swim," Richard informs them, holding Chelsea's hand.

"Dad, do you want to come with us?" asks Johnny as he reaches for their beach towels.

"No, not today, son," says Lucas, looking at Isabelle. She knows why Lucas is not in the mood to go.

Lucas loves swimming with his children. However, Isabelle has a fear of water, especially large bodies of water. She doesn't like boating either; she has only gone a few times. She only trusts Lucas to drive when she is on the boat. As for the children, they are all like their father: they enjoy swimming and boating, and they all can water-ski.

Richard and Johnny glance at each other, wondering why their dad doesn't want to go swimming, but they respect his choice. As they are leaving to go for a swim, Chelsea tells Richard she'd rather not go today because she doesn't feel that great, but she is happy to sit at the beach to watch them swim. Thomas is already there, swimming with his friends. Not long after that, Steve arrives and asks his parents where the others are; Lucas tells him where they have all gone, so Steve heads for the beach too.

Lucas and Isabelle can watch the teenagers swim from a distance. As they sit there, Lucas asks Isabelle, "Where has the time gone? It was not long ago the children were little, and now they are young adults."

Isabelle looks at Lucas with tears, saying, "Soon we will be grandparents! Our little baby girl is having a baby herself." Isabelle starts to cry. "Lucas, where have I failed in being a mother? How could I have prevented this from happening?"

"Isabelle, please don't blame yourself for what has happened to Lucy," says Lucas in a soft voice. "What could we have done differently? We always tried to provide our children with the best. We protected them and gave them a happy childhood. And was there anything wrong with my parents? Look at us. We got pregnant very young. And it turned out fine." Lucas does not want to mention to his wife that her lengthy illness may have affected young Lucy; he doesn't want Isabelle to feel responsible, and he's not sure if it's a factor in the pregnancy either.

"Lucas, we never told our children that I was pregnant with Richard before we were married. I feel ashamed because if I had said something, maybe this wouldn't have happened to Lucy. Perhaps she would've been more careful, or maybe she would have come to me for advice," says Isabelle sounding wracked with guilt.

"We never mentioned it to our children because we never thought of it or found the right time to tell them. We can think of 100 things that we could have done differently and beat ourselves about what we should have done, but it won't change the fact that our little girl is pregnant," observes Lucas, grabbing hold of Isabelle's hand.

"Yes, you're right, Lucas," says Isabelle as she wipes her tears. "We need to be there for Lucy. And we need to stay in the present moment. No looking back."

Lucas has always had a way of talking to Isabelle to make her feel confident about herself. Isabelle is happy to have Lucas by her side; she can always trust him for encouragement. Isabelle gets up, kisses Lucas and thanks him for his support.

"Isabelle, we will get through this—we've been through worse—and we will be there for our daughter. She needs us. We'll always be there for her and our grandchild," expresses Lucas as he looks at Isabelle with confidence and strength.

Late that afternoon, Lucy and Justin arrive at the campsite; they look exhausted. Lucas sees his little girl looking sulky as she walks toward him. Lucy kisses her dad and mom and then sits beside them with Justin. The whole family chats as Isabelle starts preparing supper and Lucas cooks the steaks on the barbecue. Lucas stares back at his children as they continue to converse with each other. He is thinking to himself what a wonderful family he has. He goes back in time to when they were little; they loved camping then and still do as young adults.

Once they have finished supper, the girls help Isabelle clean up while the boys play horseshoes with Lucas. While Chelsea and Angie are gathering dishes outside, Lucy is inside with Isabelle, putting the food away. Lucy looks at her mom. "Mom, did you tell Dad?" she questions. She sets the food she is carrying on the table and sits down in despair.

"Yes, Lucy, your dad knows, and he wants what is best for his little girl," replies Isabelle as she puts the food away. She sits beside Lucy. "Your father and I are shocked to hear that you are pregnant because we thought you would finish high school and move on to university. You have so much potential, and we, as parents, wish for our children to grow up doing what they love best. Now you will have to give up your education to become a mom. Are you ready to become a mother and wife?"

"Oh, Mom! I'm so scared right now. I know there will be lots of responsibilities soon for me; my life will change. Justin and I talked about our future, and he will stand by me. We're very young to start a family. Mom… Justin says he loves me and wants to marry me as soon as we can," cries Lucy. "I don't want to have to marry Justin just because I'm pregnant. I want to marry him because I love him."

"Everything has a way of working out in life, and we will be there for you, Lucy," says Isabelle as she kisses and hugs her daughter. "Your dad will want to talk to you and Justin to see what your plans are. You know your dad is full of surprises; when he wants answers, he has ways of getting them."

Lucy feels relief being in her mother's arm but stills feels she has brought grief to the family. She also knows she will have to grow up fast because she will become a mother soon. Isabelle and Lucy get up and continue to put things away as Chelsea and Angie walk in with the dishes.

Once everything is cleaned up, the girls sit down with a cup of coffee. The guys smell the coffee and come running over. Lucas doesn't follow; he goes to pick up four life jackets and then looks at Isabelle as he walks toward her.

"We're going for a boat ride with Justin and Lucy," says Lucas to Isabelle, and then he gives her a life jacket. He knows Isabelle is frightened of water, but Lucas doesn't know any other way to have this important conversation.

"Okay," replies Isabelle, feeling a little nervous but putting her trust in Lucas. She knows that he wouldn't ask her to do something that makes her uncomfortable without a good reason.

"Justin and Lucy, let's go for a boat ride," says Lucas as he hands them two life jackets, averting eye contact.

Justin looks shocked and scared as he takes the life jackets and helps Lucy put on hers. He is only a child himself, and yet he finds the strength within to act like a man.

As the four of them head toward the dock, Lucy's brothers wonder why their father is so determined to do this, knowing their mother's fear of water.

They get in the boat, and Lucas drives slowly because of Isabelle's fear. He stops the boat in the middle of the lake, turns around and looks at Justin and Lucy. He stares at them for a few moments; Justin looks terrified.

"Justin, my daughter is pregnant with your baby," says Lucas in a serious but soft voice. "What are your plans for Lucy and your child?"

"Mr. Clarkson... Lucy and I have talked about what we should do, and I plan to marry your daughter," replies Justin. His voice is shaky as he looks at Lucy and holds her hand.

"Lucy, do you want to be with Justin? Are you planning your life as Justin's wife?" Lucas asks his daughter, seeing her tear up. "Lucy, I'm not trying to be hard on you, but you have decisions to make. I want you to know that you have a choice—you are not trapped. I will help support you and my grandchild if you don't want to get married."

"Dad, I've thought about it, and I want to marry Justin. I want my child to have two parents," replies Lucy as she cuddles toward Justin, and he holds her tight.

"Justin, will you take good care of my little girl and my grandchild?" asks Lucas in a sincere tone. He has been worrying about the answer to this question since he learned of the pregnancy.

"Absolutely, Mr. and Mrs. Clarkson. I'll take good care of Lucy and our baby. I'll provide for them and give them a home. That I can promise," replies Justin as he reaches over and puts a supportive hand on Lucy's knee.

Lucas is content with that response, and the corners of his mouth turn up slightly. He takes a deep breath and says, "Thanks, Justin. If there's anything I can do for you both, I'd be glad to help."

"Justin, I am proud of you for being there as the father of my grandchild," says Isabelle as she takes Justin's hand.

"I'm not proud of what I did, but I love your daughter, and I will care for her. I want to be a great husband and wonderful father, just like you, Lucas," Justin says with a smile; then he gives Lucy a tender peck on the cheek.

"I love you, Justin. I love you, Mom and Dad! And I hope that we can be great parents like both of you," says Lucy, feeling relief as she smiles at her supportive parents.

"Let's get back to your brothers, Lucy, before they wonder what we're doing here in the middle of the lake," says Lucas jokingly, and they all feel the tension lift after the strained conversation.

"Yes, please—let's go," replies Isabelle, looking at the water and feeling anxious to be back on land.

They all chuckle as Lucas starts the engine and heads slowly back to the dock while he comforts Isabelle.

Weeks pass, and the family learn about Lucy's pregnancy. Her brothers all support her. Then Chelsea also opens up and tells Richard that she is almost six months pregnant. Richard is in total shock. He finally realizes why Chelsea has been wearing loose clothing and seems to be gaining weight. Chelsea is very shy, and her parents would not be as understanding of her situation as Lucas and Isabelle are with Lucy. Richard tells his family right away, as there are only three months left to prepare themselves for the arrival of their baby.

Lucas and Isabelle are baffled at what is taking place in their lives. Now they will become grandparents twice, only three months apart. They also have a talk with Richard and Chelsea about their intentions with each other and help them settle into an apartment not far from the family home.

CHAPTER 32

Lucy and Chelsea become even better friends as they chat about their pregnancies. The time is near for Richard and Chelsea to become parents; they are counting the days. On a November morning, Isabelle and Lucas get a phone call from Richard saying Chelsea is in labor. Isabelle excitedly gets ready and goes with Richard and Chelsea to the hospital. Lucas wishes them the best as he watches them leave. On the morning of November 12, 1979, Chelsea gives birth to a beautiful girl. Richard is proud when he holds his little girl and gives Chelsea a kiss as she watches them bond. Isabelle is grateful to be able to witness the birth of her granddaughter. She watches Richard and Chelsea bond with their little girl, whom they have named Paige. Isabelle starts to reminisce back to the day she gave birth to Richard as she smiles and enjoys the moment.

Lucas and Isabelle are extremely happy to become grandparents. Paige is the highlight of the family. As Christmas approaches, Isabelle is excited to have Paige with them that she puts up the Christmas tree early. On Christmas Eve, Isabelle and Lucas take Elizabeth to church. Once they return home, the kids are waiting for them to open the Christmas gifts. It is a great time; even Paige is there, sleeping by Grandma's side as everyone opens their gifts. Lucas is proud of his children as he sits beside Isabelle watching them and thrilled that his wife knows who they are and the whole family is together. John and Elizabeth sit on the couch. Even though John is on an oxygen tank, he is grateful to see his grandchildren open gifts, and he glances at Paige, his great-granddaughter, with a smile.

The next morning, they have a special breakfast, and Richard and Chelsea go to her parents' place with Paige. Johnny goes to visit his girlfriend, Angie, at her parents' house, and Steve goes to spend time at his best friend's as Isabelle and Lucas prepare supper for the Clarkson family. The children all promise they will be back for supper. Thomas stays to help his parents, as he is still young. Lucy tells her mom that she will have lunch with Justin's family but will be back early to help out. Isabelle and Lucy have a wonderful mother-daughter relationship, although she has always been Daddy's little girl in Lucas's eyes.

Christmas supper is a feast, as Isabelle is an extraordinary cook. Everyone thanks Isabelle for the wonderful food; they are all stuffed after the delicious meal. They sit down in the great room by the Christmas tree and listen to Christmas carols. John and Elizabeth are proud to see their children gather together with their grandchildren and their great-grandchild, Paige, the newest addition to the family.

The evening is wonderful as Lucas and Isabelle host the party. James and Debra always love to gather at the farmhouse with Donna and Scott, along with their oldest son, Paul, with his wife, Linda, and their two children, Tommy and Lisa. Mary and Joe are also there. Joe is not drinking, but his health is diminishing; he has cirrhosis of the liver. Mary loves to be with her family; although her children are all grown up and raising families of their own, they all drop in to see their grandpa, John, and grandma, Elizabeth, and taste their aunt Isabelle's cooking.

Once everyone has left, Isabelle and Lucas sit down with John and Elizabeth for a coffee, and soon Elizabeth is helping John go to their bedroom, for he is exhausted. Lucas and Isabelle continue to clean up after the big Clarkson Christmas gathering. Lucas smiles at Isabelle and thanks her for the wonderful meal she has prepared for his family. He kisses Isabelle and hugs her; he has never taken their love for granted nor her renewed health. Lucas is proud of being Isabelle's husband and always displays the love he has for her. Isabelle smiles back as she stops picking up the dishes, and tells Lucas how wonderful he is as a father and husband. Isabelle strokes Lucas's face gently and kisses him on the cheek. They finish tidying the house, and then they head to bed, feeling joyful but exhausted after the big event.

Around three o'clock in the early morning, the phone rings. Lucas is half-asleep as he reaches for the phone. It's almost never good news when someone calls at that time. "Hello," he says in a soft voice, yawning.

"Lucas! Lucas! It's me, Chelsea. Something is wrong with Richard—he can't breathe! Lucas, help me—please help me!" She is in a panic.

"Chelsea, slow down. What is happening to Richard?" asks Lucas. His heart starts racing; he is not quite clear on what Chelsea is saying.

Isabelle hears all the commotion, gets up and walks toward Lucas. She hears Lucas's voice trembling. She stands beside him and takes hold of his arm as she waits to be informed. She knows something is terribly wrong.

"Lucas, Richard is having a hard time breathing, like his throat is swelling. Can you come over and take us to the hospital, and can Isabelle keep Paige? Richard is gasping for air—we don't know what is happening! I'm afraid that he will choke," cries Chelsea.

"Okay, Chelsea, stay calm. We'll be there soon," says Lucas. He tries to keep himself calm as he hangs up the phone.

"What is wrong, Lucas?" asks Isabelle as she looks at him intensely.

"I'm not sure, but Richard is having a hard time breathing," replies Lucas as he rushes to the room to put on his clothes. "Isabelle, come with me; you need to take care of Paige so Chelsea can go with me to the hospital."

"Maybe he is having an allergic reaction to something he ate?" questions Isabelle as she hurries to the bedroom with Lucas to get dressed. "He is such a healthy young man. What could it be, Lucas?"

"I don't know, Isabelle. When Richard left here, he was perfectly fine," says Lucas as he grabs for his keys and heads out.

"It is not like Richard; he usually has so much energy," replies Isabelle in confusion as she follows. She stops quickly to inform Elizabeth about what is happening while Lucas goes and starts the vehicle.

When Lucas and Isabelle arrive at Richard and Chelsea's apartment, which is only ten minutes away, Chelsea is waiting near the door with Paige in her arms, and Richard is sitting on a chair fighting for air with every breath he takes. Lucas runs in and helps Richard to the vehicle as Chelsea hands over Paige to Isabelle and then runs to the car with Lucas and Richard. They rush off to the hospital.

Lucas runs in with Richard, and Chelsea follows behind. Lucas sits Richard on the nearest chair and shouts for help. The nurses hear the shouting and disruption near the emergency doors, and they run to help. One nurse hurries to the patient, and another gets a gurney, while the nurse at the nurses station calls for the doctor. The first nurse attends to Richard as she asks Lucas and Chelsea questions on his status. At the same time, the doctor rushes in and takes over. While the nurses help put Richard on the gurney, the doctor checks him over. He orders oxygen to stabilize Richard's breathing. Then they wheel Richard into the emergency room to observe his condition. One nurse stays behind to take information about Richard. Lucas and Chelsea go to the nurses station to give some information.

Lucas asks the nurse, "How long will it take before we can be with Richard?"

"Once the doctor has your son's breathing under control and determines what is causing his respiratory problems, he will see you in the waiting room to talk to both of you. You can wait over there until the doctor comes," replies the nurse.

"Thanks," says Lucas to the nurse. He gets up, as does Chelsea, and they walk to the waiting room. They sit together in silence, both deep in thought and worry, and anxiously they wait. They feel helpless. There is nothing for them to do but pray.

It is over an hour later when the doctor enters the room to tell them about Richard's condition. Lucas sees him and stands up apprehensively as he watches him approach. Chelsea also stands up nervously beside Lucas, with tears rolling down her cheeks.

"Hi," says the doctor. "I'm Dr. Franklin," as he shakes their hands.

"Hi, Dr. Franklin," says Lucas in a concerned voice. "How is Richard doing?"

"We have Richard stabilized. His breathing is under control, but we're still concerned about why Richard's respiratory tract was swollen. We did tests, and the results will be in tomorrow. For now, he is doing well, and he is breathing on his own, but we want him to stay here for the night, in case he has another attack. We will have more answers tomorrow when we get the test results," explains Dr. Franklin.

Enormously relieved, Lucas says, "Thanks, Dr. Franklin." He is grateful that they have stabilized his son even though they don't really know what's going on yet.

"Can we see Richard before we leave?" asks Chelsea as she wipes her tears.

"Yes, you may certainly have a visit before you go. He is still in the ER for observation. Come with me. I have to go that way, and I will take you directly to his room," says Dr. Franklin as he gestures to the left.

"That's very kind of you, Dr. Franklin," replies Lucas as he walks toward the doctor with his arm around Chelsea. "Thank you."

The next morning, Lucas and Isabelle take Chelsea and Paige to the hospital to visit Richard. Everything seems fine; Chelsea tells

Lucas and Isabelle that she had a phone call from Richard early in the morning telling her he was feeling great, but the test results were not in yet. He wants to ask the doctor if he can be released from the hospital. As the family arrive, they head toward the emergency room where Richard was last night. Lucas can hear a familiar voice, which he recognizes as his son's. Chelsea, with Paige in her arms, checks the room, but the bed is empty. Richard is down the hall, chatting with other patients in the lounge. They walk toward the lounge until Richard notices them. He excuses himself, gets up and walks forward to greet them. When he reaches them, Richard kisses Chelsea, and then he holds his little girl and kisses her. Isabelle and Lucas reach out to hug and kiss Richard. They walk to his room as Richard says goodbye to his new friends. Richard is a social person and loves to talk and joke with people. He is the fun-loving joker of the family, and everyone appreciates the joie de vivre that he always brings to the table.

"How are you doing, Richard?" asks Lucas, as they walk toward the room.

"I'm feeling great compared to last night," replies Richard as he holds Chelsea's hand and carries his little baby. "It felt like I was taking my last breath."

"I'm so happy you are feeling better," responds Isabelle, thrilled to hear the news.

"Did you get your test results from Dr. Franklin?" asks Chelsea as she cuddles on his shoulder.

"No, not yet, but he should be here shortly," says Richard. He and Chelsea gaze into each other's eyes, and even at this difficult time, he seems to be in good spirits.

They arrive in the room, and within seconds, the nurse walks in to tell Richard Dr. Franklin will be coming soon with the test results. She checks his temperature and then tells him and Chelsea what a beautiful baby girl they have. Richard and Chelsea smile with pride as Richard repositions Paige for the nurse to see his daughter better. The nurse fusses over the baby and then leaves the room. She is smiling to see the joy of a young couple with their precious baby.

Lucas talks with Richard as Isabelle and Chelsea chat about Paige and what a wonderful and peaceful baby she is. Chelsea is grateful because Paige is incredible; she hardly fusses and sleeps well through her nights for a newborn. Lucas takes a minute and observes the joy in the room. Then he smiles at Isabelle as he puts his arm around her. Richard also becomes silent for a few minutes and stares at his daughter while she sleeps. Then he looks tenderly at Chelsea for the beautiful little girl she has given him. He thinks how delicate life is with every breath the baby takes.

Shortly after that, Dr. Franklin walks into the room with Richard's test results. Richard looks up and notes that the doctor is looking serious.

"Good morning, Richard," says Dr. Franklin as he opens up the file and greets Chelsea, who is sitting beside Richard on his bed. Then he nods at Lucas and Isabelle. "Richard, I received your test results, and we found an explanation for why you felt your throat tightening and weren't able to breathe. I'm not a specialist in this department, and I want to make sure that this diagnosis is right, which means you need to go to Ottawa for more detailed tests."

"What are you talking about, Dr. Franklin?" replies Richard in a concerned voice. "I feel good—why would I have to go for tests in Ottawa? What did you see in the test?"

"Truthfully... Richard, I saw dark spots on your throat, which could be cancerous. But, don't panic. I don't want to diagnose you, Richard; I'm not an otolaryngologist, so I could be wrong. That is why I want you to go to Ottawa for specific tests that will determine whether it is cancer of the throat or not. You may feel well right now, but you could have another attack, and next time, you may not be so lucky. For that reason, I want you to stay here for observation until we can get you to Ottawa for more specifics on your situation. I don't want to scare you, but I want to make the right and responsible choice about what we saw in the test results," explains Dr. Franklin in a tense voice. It is hard to announce this kind of news to a young father.

"Cancer! That's a lot to take in, considering I was going to ask you to go home because I am feeling fine," says Richard. He tries to comfort Chelsea as she starts to cry. "No disrespect, but I am a very healthy person—you must be wrong!"

The tension is mounting, and Lucas senses his son's increasing agitation. He diffuses the situation by interrupting. "You mean the cancer unit in Ottawa?"

"Yes. I am just waiting for confirmation from the hospital as to when they can do the tests. Because of the holidays, it might be a few days before the arrangement can be made, but I will put a rush on the appointment," says Dr. Franklin as he closes the file.

Richard stays in the hospital for observation, and the next day, Ottawa Civic Hospital confirms they have an opening for him at the cancer unit. Lucas drives his son to Ottawa, along with Chelsea and Isabelle, which takes about one hour. They all feel in shock at what the doctor announced: the possibility of a tumor in Richard's throat. The drive is very quiet. Chelsea snuggles in Richard's arms in the back, and Lucas holds Isabelle's hand.

CHAPTER 33

Richard spends part of the week at the Ottawa Civic Hospital waiting for test results on his condition. He is still having a hard time breathing and has been on oxygen for most of the day. Swallowing has become an issue, and his voice has started to become hoarse when he talks. Lucas and Isabelle take Chelsea every day to visit Richard at the hospital while Lucy takes care of Paige. The doctor explains everything to Richard as he undergoes intensive tests and tells him that if there is a tumor, they will have to operate.

On December 31, the new test results are in. The doctor visits Richard and tells him that he definitely has a tumor, and it is cancerous. The doctor explains that he has already scheduled surgery for the next morning. Richard is feeling depleted and saddened as he attempts to digest the truth about his diagnosis. But he tries to pick up his strength and stay positive because the doctor tells him if they remove the tumor, he has a fifty percent chance of surviving and becoming cancer free. Richard asks the doctor to call his family to tell them the results; he is feeling too weak, and talking is an issue for him.

Lucas and Isabelle have been anticipating the call from the hospital with the results of Richard's tests. Late in the morning, the phone rings and the whole family happens to be there. Even Chelsea is at the farmhouse with Paige. As the baby sleeps, the family gathers around the kitchen table drinking coffee when Lucas gets up to answer the phone.

"Hello," says Lucas, nervously waiting to hear who is calling.

"Hello, may I speak to Mr. Clarkson, please?"

"This is Mr. Clarkson speaking," replies Lucas; at this point, he knows the phone call is from the hospital. He silences his mind so that he can take in each and every word.

"Mr. Clarkson, Dr. Reid speaking. I am the surgical oncologist who reviewed Richard's test results, and Richard requested that I inform you of his condition."

"Yes, please go on," replies Lucas in a low voice. He can hear his own heart beating and feels that it might explode out of his chest soon. He instinctively places his hand over his heart to calm it down.

"Your son has a tumor lodged in his throat, on his thyroid, and it is cancerous. I have to operate. We can't wait; it has to be done quickly. Richard is scheduled first thing tomorrow to undergo the surgery. The nurses will prep him so he is ready. The surgery is scheduled for 6:00 a.m. If you want to see him before the surgery, I will advise the nurses of your arrival around 5:30 a.m.," says Dr. Reid.

"Yes, we'll be there. Is it a complicated operation, and how long will it take?" questions Lucas as he wipes the tears rolling down his cheeks.

"It's hard to say, but on average, this kind of surgery should take a few hours, depending on the size of the tumor. It should not be very complicated—again, depending on the tumor and where it is located on his thyroid gland. We will keep you informed as the surgery progresses and let you know if there are any complications or other issues concerning the cancer. I'm sure this must be very difficult for you, Mr. Clarkson. Hang in there, and let's see what tomorrow brings. Hopefully, we will get it all," Dr. Reid says kindly.

"We will be at the hospital early tomorrow, before Richard goes in for the surgery," says Lucas barely audible; he feels all his energy draining out of his body.

"We will see you tomorrow, Mr. Clarkson," replies Dr. Reid. "Good day."

"Bye, sir," says Lucas as he hangs up the phone. He inhales deeply and wipes his tears before going to the kitchen. He tries to summon his strength before he announces Richard's condition to the family.

Lucas walks into the kitchen slowly, and at that moment, Isabelle looks in his eyes, and she knows that their son has cancer. Lucas puts his hand on Isabelle's shoulder, and with a gentle squeeze, he announces to the family that Richard definitely has throat cancer and has to have surgery early the next morning.

Everyone tears up in disbelief at this news. Chelsea drops her head onto her arms at the table and sobs. Isabelle turns to Lucas; as he hugs her, she cries in his arms. Elizabeth hugs Thomas as they cry together, and Justin reaches out to hold Lucy as she weeps. Johnny and Steve put their heads down in disbelief, tears rolling down their cheeks, too. Hardship has hit the Clarkson family as they sit in their kitchen absorbing this heartbreaking news. There isn't a New Year's Eve celebration that night; instead, everyone stays at the farm to support each other.

New Year's Day begins very early for Lucas and Isabelle, as they get ready. They hardly slept that night. Chelsea slept over with Paige; she also gets ready, and she gives her daughter a goodbye kiss on the forehead as the baby sleeps. Everyone else is still sleeping at 4:00 in the morning. Lucy is the only one up because she will be taking care of Paige.

"Please, Dad, call me as soon as Richard comes out of surgery, and I'll make sure the boys and Grandma and Grandpa get the news," says Lucy as she tearfully hugs her dad.

"You'll be the first to know after Richard's surgery, I promise," replies Lucas as he kisses Lucy on her wet cheek. "Be strong for Richard, honey. There is a fifty percent chance that he can beat this," Lucas says, trying to reassure his daughter.

"Thanks, Dad," utters Lucy as she tries to smile. Then she hugs her mom and Chelsea before they leave for Ottawa.

Lucas arrives at the hospital, looks at Isabelle and then takes a deep breath as he parks the vehicle. *New Year's Day 1980,* Lucas thinks to himself as he takes the keys out of the ignition. Isabelle looks at Lucas's family. She opens the passenger door and takes a few moments as she glances at the hospital, wondering how many mothers are in the hospital right now feeling the way she feels. Lucas helps Chelsea out of the backseat, and they both walk toward Isabelle. For a few seconds, they all stare at the huge hospital.

"Let's see Richard; he must be waiting for us," says Lucas as he reaches out to hold Isabelle's hand.

"Yes, Lucas, our baby needs us right now. We have to look positive for him," replies Isabelle as she starts to walk forward with Lucas and Chelsea.

When Chelsea walks into Richard's room, she sees him lying there, looking fragile; she notices a change in him after only one day. Chelsea gets closer before Richard even notices her.

"Hi, Chelsea," says Richard, smiling weakly. Incredibly, the lively twinkle in his eyes is still detectable. "Hi, Dad. Hi, Mom."

Chelsea kisses Richard, saying, "Hi, sweetie." The young mother is emotionally drained, and her exhaustion and anguish are visible in her expression and her body posture. *These were supposed to be the best years of my life,* she thinks. Her main concern should be the new life they produced, not the threat of death.

"Good morning, buddy," says Lucas as he hugs his son.

"Good morning, dear." Isabelle looks lovingly at her boy as she kisses and hugs Richard.

"How's my little princess doing?" Richard asks Chelsea. "I miss her so much." He looks at Paige's photo on his nightstand—Richard's family is his life, just like his father.

"Paige is doing great. Lucy is taking care of her for the day," replies Chelsea as she sits beside Richard on the bed.

"Paige is in good hands with my little sister, Lucy," Richard says with a smile as he looks toward Chelsea and his parents.

It is not long until the nurses come into the room to prep Richard and move him from the bed to a gurney. Chelsea kisses Richard, and Isabelle walks over and runs her finger through Richard's hair, smiles gently and kisses him on the cheek. Lucas follows. As he watches, he wipes his tears and then takes hold of Richard's shoulder with a comforting hand, and Lucas whispers to him that everything will be okay. "I promise you that as you open your eyes, we will be right there," Lucas says as he softly kisses his son on the cheek. Richard smiles as he is comforted by his dad. Then he takes hold of his father's hand, and at that moment, the nurses start to push the gurney away. Lucas releases Richard's hand. He stands beside Isabelle and puts his arms around her and Chelsea as they watch the nurses wheel Richard away.

Hours pass, and there are still no answers from the doctor. Chelsea falls asleep on the lounge chair, and Isabelle puts a blanket over her to make her more comfortable her. Lucas asks Isabelle whether she wants a coffee. Isabelle sits down near Chelsea and nods yes to Lucas. Lucas goes to get coffee for both of them, and as he is walking back to the lounge room, he sees the doctor from a distance. Lucas enters the room and looks directly at Isabelle with a nervous expression as he holds the coffee cups in both hands. Isabelle looks up and sees a concerned look on Lucas's face.

"What is it, Lucas? You look like you've just seen a ghost," says Isabelle, worried.

"I just saw the doctor, and he's coming this way," replies Lucas anxiously as he gives Isabelle her coffee and then takes a sip of his own. He looks toward the door, hearing someone talking.

"The doctor is coming!" says Isabelle as she jumps up from her chair with her coffee in hand.

At that moment, Chelsea hears all the fuss and wakes up. "What is happening?" she asks as she sits up and rubs her eyes in confusion.

"The doctor is coming!" Isabelle repeats as she, also, looks toward the door.

Chelsea stands up quickly as she sees the doctor walk in. They all stand together nervously as Dr. Reid approaches them.

"How is Richard?" asks Lucas, trying to calm his racing thoughts as he puts his arm around his wife.

"Mr. Clarkson, Richard is doing fine. We removed the tumor from his thyroid. As of now, your son has no more cancer. We were able to take it all out," says Dr. Reid, with a smile.

"Thank you so much, Dr. Reid," says Lucas as he takes a deep breath of relief.

"Your son is a trooper. He needs his rest, but you can all see him now briefly," replies Dr. Reid with a proud smile.

"Dr. Reid, you have saved our son's life," says Isabelle in gratefulness as her eyes brim with tears of joy.

"Thanks, Dr. Reid, for saving my daughter's father's life and giving us a second chance as a family," Chelsea says, her voice full of gratitude. "This is wonderful!"

"You're all very welcome! The nurse will take you to Richard's room," replies Dr. Reid as he leaves.

"Go with the nurse," says Lucas as he kisses Isabelle. "I'll meet you there. I promised to call Lucy."

Lucas calls his daughter and tells her with great happiness that her brother is doing great and is now cancer free. Lucas takes a moment and thanks God for a New Year's miracle. Then he goes to see his son.

A few days later, as Richard recovers, John takes a turn for the worse; his breathing becomes intolerable. Elizabeth calls an ambulance to take John to the hospital, as she is alone with him. Lucas has gone to Ottawa with Isabelle, Chelsea and Paige to visit Richard. Elizabeth calls James, and he takes her to the hospital in Cornwall.

Lucas arrives home from Ottawa to find a note on the kitchen table stating that his dad has been rushed to the hospital. Lucas turns and looks at Isabelle as she takes off her coat.

"My dad has been hospitalized. James has taken Mom to the hospital, and they're there with Dad," says Lucas as he rereads the note in disbelief. He can't believe that his life has turned into such an emotional rollercoaster—he was just in the hospital tending to his son and now his father is ill? They seem to be moving from one crisis to the next. It's too much for one family to bear. But Lucas has always been strong and resilient and stood up in the face of adversity.

"Is it your dad's emphysema—his breathing?" questions Isabelle as she puts her coat back on. "Lucas, let's go to the hospital now."

"Yes. I need to be there," replies Lucas.

Lucas and Isabelle arrive at the hospital and ask about his dad at the nurses station. The nurse tells him that his father is in room 214, on the second floor. Lucas thanks her as they rush up to see John. Lucas enters the room and sees Elizabeth sitting by his dad's bed, with James by her side.

"What happened, Mom?" questions Lucas in confusion.

"Your father had a bad attack and couldn't breathe. I called an ambulance, and here we are. The doctor took tests, and they just told us your dad's lung has collapsed, and it is putting a strain on his heart," says Elizabeth as she starts to cry. "The doctor told us it will be just a matter of days... Lucas, your father is dying."

Lucas hugs his mom as she sobs and feels her whole body trembling in his arms. "James, is there anything they can do for Dad?" asks Lucas in the hope of finding a solution to save their father.

"Sorry, Lucas. Dad is dying," replies James, his eyes red and moist like everyone else's.

Isabelle comforts her brother-in-law and sits beside Elizabeth as she watches Lucas kiss his father and tell him how much he loves him. As Lucas holds his father's hand, he can feel John squeezing his

Path of Lucas

hand in return. Lucas looks into his father's eyes and takes in this precious moment as John makes eye contact.

On January eighth, Richard comes out of the hospital. He asks Lucas to drive to Cornwall because he wants to see his grandfather. When they arrive at the hospital, Richard walks to the door of his grandfather's room and watches him lying there for a few minutes. He slowly approaches his grandfather's bed, tells him he loves him and holds his hand. He tells him how he is now cancer free. John opens his eyes for a few seconds, and smiles. He is thrilled to hear this news about his grandson. Richard smiles back and then kisses John. Elizabeth hugs Richard and says how good it is to see him, especially with the great news of him being cancer free. Lucas notices Richard becoming weak, so he tells him he should go home to rest, and Richard agrees. Lucas kisses his father goodbye and hugs and kisses his mom. Lucas and Isabelle say goodbye to Elizabeth and take Richard back home with Chelsea.

Early the next morning, Lucas and Isabelle leave to pick up groceries. With so many things going on, they have not had time to shop for food. Lucy is home alone, cleaning the house, when the phone rings.

"Hello," says Lucy.

"Hi, Lucy—it is me, Grandma," says Elizabeth in an unnaturally shaky voice.

"Hi, Grandma. How is Grandpa doing?" questions Lucy. She hears her grandmother weeping at that point, and Lucy has a gut feeling that her grandfather has died. "It's Grandpa... Is it, Grandma?"

"Yes, Grandpa just passed away. He took his last breath as I was alone with him. I called James, and he is coming to pick me up, and we're heading home," replies Elizabeth as she weeps.

"Grandma! Are you okay?" asks Lucy, crying too.

"Yes, dear, I am okay. Is your dad around to tell him?"

"No! Dad and Mom left to get groceries, but they should be back soon," replies Lucy. She hears a vehicle and looks out to see Lucas

311

and Isabelle driving in. "Grandma! Grandma! Dad and Mom just got home. I'll get him—just wait a minute, Grandma," calls Lucy, and then she runs out to get her dad.

"Dad! Dad! Grandma is on the phone... She wants to talk to you," says Lucy as she opens the door.

Lucas runs to the door, knowing that something serious has happened to his dad. "Thanks," he says to Lucy as he enters.

"Welcome," replies Lucy, holding the door open for her mom.

Lucas answers the phone; his mom tells him his father has passed away and that she is coming back home with James. Lucas hangs up the phone and bows his head as he sits on the couch. Isabelle and Lucy walk toward Lucas; they both sit beside him and comfort him. He stares down in silence, thinking about the great life he has had with his father. He is also glad that although he didn't want to do it at the time, he made immense sacrifices for his father over the years, giving up a career in mechanics that could have made him extremely happy. Lucas did everything he could for his father and he takes solace in that fact. He had been a good son to John and vice versa; John had always been a wonderful father.

The funeral is on a cold, snowy day. Lucas, James, and Mary give a eulogy for their father, and six of the Clarkson grandchildren are the pallbearers. Paul and Johnny carry the front of the casket; Richard and Scott are in the middle because Richard is still weak from his surgery and Scott is not too strong; and Steve and Thomas are at the end of the casket. This has been John's request for many years.

The following month, Isabelle helps Lucy prepare for her big day; she will be giving birth at any time. Lucas and Isabelle prepare a room for Lucy and her new arrival to stay in until Justin and Lucy get married. The time comes, and Justin takes Lucy to the hospital and then calls Isabelle and Lucas to tell them she is in labor. Isabelle rushes to the hospital to be with her daughter. Early that evening, on February 10th, Lucy gives birth to a beautiful boy, weighing seven pounds and twelve ounces. Justin is so proud to have a son, and Lucy is thrilled to hold her son for the first time with her mother by her side. When Lucas arrives to see his daughter and grandson, Lucy and Justin tell him and Isabelle that they will name their son Daniel.

Spring finally arrives. It has been such a hard winter for Lucas and Isabelle; they have gone through so much but have always maintained their love for each other, regardless of the hardships. Lucas and Isabelle were always proud parents and are now proud grandparents. The family gets together frequently with the babies at the farmhouse; they are a close-knit family. They often speak about John, especially Elizabeth, who always mentions his name at the supper table, for example, commenting on how he loved her desserts. Things become normal around the home.

May is a beautiful month. Everyone is happy and enjoying the beautiful weather outside. But then Richard takes a turn for the worse. He starts with a sore hip and has a hard time walking. Lucas takes Richard to the hospital where they perform tests and find cancer cells again. This time it has jumped into his lymph nodes. He has to go for chemotherapy, along with radiation therapy, and take many different kinds of medication. It takes a toll on Richard; after his treatments, he is sick for days.

Lucas and Isabelle stay strong for their son, but the reality is that Richard has only a year to live. They do everything to help him. Lucas finds a mobile home and brings it to the farm for Richard and Chelsea to live in with the baby. That way they can have a home and live independently as a family but still be close for Lucas and Isabelle to be there if Chelsea needs help with Richard.

It is Lucy and Justin's wedding day. Isabelle helps Lucy into her beautiful gown. As she walks down the stairs, Lucas watches his little girl become a woman. It is a touching moment for Lucas, as he remembers not too long ago Isabelle in her wedding dress. Lucas takes his daughter to church in a beautiful white Cadillac. As he walks her down the aisle, he becomes very emotional inside but keeps his cool as he smiles. The evening is beautiful; it is a dream wedding, thanks to Isabelle and Lucas, who have made their daughter's wedding day possible. Lucas has paid for his daughter's wedding. Even Richard is feeling great; he dances the night away with Chelsea. Lucas takes a moment and observes from a distance all the fun his family is having, and it leaves a good feeling in his heart.

Christmas soon comes around again. Isabelle wants to make it the best Christmas because she knows it will be Richard's last with them. Lucas helps Isabelle with all the preparations, and together they make the holiday the best and the most festive time they can have together as a family. Richard thanks his parents for such a fantastic time; he feels at his best that day. Lucas and Isabelle are extremely happy to see their family together, although deep down, they are sorrowful knowing it will be their son's last Christmas.

Early in the spring, Richard's health starts to decline. He asks his dad if he can sleep back at the farmhouse because he wants to be near his parents for his remaining days. Lucas prepares Richard a room, but within weeks Richard's pain becomes so extreme that he has to be hospitalized. Lucas carries his son to the vehicle, puts him in the backseat with Chelsea, and with Isabelle in the front, they head for Ottawa to the emergency department at the Civic Hospital. Richard is put in a private room, where he is on intravenous and morphine for his pain. Lucas and Isabelle dedicate all their time to being with Richard. On May 14, 1981, Richard takes his last breath with Isabelle by his side. Chelsea is lying down on the couch in the lounge, and Lucas has just stepped out for a few minutes when Richard dies. Isabelle holds her son's hand and starts to cry, and when Lucas walks into the room, he knows at that moment that his son is gone. Lucas looks at Richard, and with great sobs, he closes his son's eyes and kisses him on the cheek. Then he breaks down. Chelsea wakes up to find out Richard has just slipped away, and he is at peace. Chelsea cries on Lucas's shoulder.

The funeral is extremely painful for the whole family. Lucas stays strong for all of them, especially Isabelle. Lucy finds the inner strength to read the eulogy for her brother. Everyone tears up as she gives a beautiful speech. Lucas is proud of his little girl.

At the luncheon after Richard's funeral, Lucas needs to get a breath of fresh air. He can't believe that at the young age of forty-one, his firstborn son is now gone. He goes outside to be by himself; it has been a disturbing day. Lucas takes a walk toward the nearby forest and sits under a tree, thinking of his son. He notices a monarch butterfly flying around him—and he knows it is Richard.

CHAPTER 34

Lucas looks at Lucy lying there, and at this point, he remembers his son's death and thinks he can't face losing another child. Lucy remains motionless while Lucas speaks. Lucas feels nostalgic and helpless as he looks at his daughter clinging to life and thinks of the anguish he felt losing his precious son Richard—it tears him apart. He would give anything to turn the clock back and have both his children healthy and strong again. Lucas becomes silent and listens as he hears voices in the hall coming toward the room. Lucy's children are coming to see their mother. He takes a deep breath as his pain recurs. Still holding Lucy's hand, Lucas suddenly smiles as he feels a sign of life from Lucy.

"Lucy! Lucy! I felt your hand squeeze! You can hear me!" says Lucas with excitement in his voice. "I know you want me to finish telling you the story of my life before the kids come in. Lucy, squeeze your hand one more time, and I'll continue the story."

Lucas takes a few moments to put his thoughts together. As he does so, he feels another squeeze from Lucy's hand. Lucas is excited. This time he knows for sure it is not just a nervous twitch—it is really Lucy communicating with him. Lucas chuckles, as he now knows his daughter has been listening to him all through the story.

"Lucy, you remember your brother's death and how it took a toll on your mother and me. There were many sleepless nights," says Lucas as he kisses Lucy's hand and continues his story.

Lucas and Isabelle sometimes talk about Richard all night long: how he was a natural comedian and the way he entertained the family. They talk about the different times he made them laugh. Lucas's favorite was the time Richard and Steve recorded a funny song about their old neighbor friends. Isabelle laughed so hard she cried, recalls Lucas. Talking helps ease their pain.

Lucas is trying to pull his strength together, but it is very hard on him. He just has to live life day by day. He thanks God every day for his wife, his other children, and his two precious grandchildren. Lucas knows the importance of family; since his son's death, he appreciates and acknowledges their importance every day.

Isabelle spends her days caring for Paige while Chelsea goes to work. Paige and Isabelle are inseparable; they have a strong bond. Lucas is happy to see Isabelle enjoying her granddaughter and seeing how Paige runs to her grandmother every chance she has.

Paige is about two and a half years old when Chelsea finds a boyfriend. Lucas and Isabelle are happy for Chelsea to start a new fresh life, except the boyfriend is not a good choice. He doesn't have a job, and he spends the day driving Chelsea's car while she works. One day he drives up the laneway very quickly as the two grandchildren are playing outside with Isabelle. From the spinning wheels, the gravel goes flying and endangers the children. The boyfriend has no respect for the little toddlers in the yard. Lucas sees this action, and as a gentle person, Lucas privately goes over to Chelsea's boyfriend and tells him not to drive up the laneway so fast because of the children playing in the yard.

Two days later, Chelsea's boyfriend is back, driving at full speed up the laneway, blaring Ozzy Osborne, with no respect for what Lucas has told him only two days prior. Lucas, for once in his life, starts to fume. He goes directly to Chelsea's boyfriend and shouts, "If you can't drive decently up the laneway, don't drive at all!"

Path of Lucas

Chelsea's boyfriend gets offended and makes up a story that Lucas has kicked him off the property. Chelsea gets so frustrated that she takes all her belongings, sells the mobile home and goes off with her boyfriend—taking Paige away from Lucas and Isabelle.

Isabelle is so devastated that she goes into another depression. Lucas can't bear to live through this again, but his love for his wife is so strong that he holds on. Isabelle begins to gain weight; she comforts herself and eases her pain with food. She is starting to look like her sister France; Isabelle is now obese. She now has many health issues and cries all the time. Lucas tries to comfort his wife by taking her on trips. Isabelle loves to go on trips to Florida with Lucas; it feels like a different world. But once they are back home, she becomes depressed all over again. She has been through too much over the last several years.

Years pass, and Lucy has another baby boy; she names him Ryan. Not long after that, Johnny gets married, followed a few years later by Steve. Thomas finds himself a lovely girlfriend. The family keeps on growing. Lucas and Isabelle love seeing their children start families of their own. Isabelle always makes Christmas fun, especially for her grandchildren.

Elizabeth's health is deteriorating; she is starting to show signs of Alzheimer's disease. Isabelle has to care for her mother-in-law, and her own health is not great. Lucas is always worried; if it isn't his wife, it's his mother. He spends more time in hospitals than at home. Elizabeth is hospitalized until they can find a nursing home for her. Her Alzheimer's is much worse now, and she has no recollection of her children. She doesn't even know her own name at this stage. She just sits there without an expression when Lucas and Isabelle visit. Even though Isabelle is in and out of hospital for depression, she dedicates time to feed Elizabeth, as she has always adored her mother-in-law.

Two years later, on August 17, 1990, Elizabeth dies at the nursing home, with her children by her side. She looks peaceful in death, as she has a smile on her face when she takes her last breath. James,

Mary, and Lucas make arrangements for their mother's funeral. Lucas is torn apart by the loss of his mother as she has meant so much to him; since he was a young boy, Elizabeth has always been there for him through all the happy and sad times. She has been a tremendous support and he loves her dearly. Lucas tells Isabelle that he feels he has lost his mom twice: once to Alzheimer's and the second time to her actual death. Isabelle comforts her husband as she sees him break down and cry.

This is an eye-opener for Isabelle. As she sits there holding Lucas, she realizes the burden of pain and suffering he has been carrying his whole adult life without ever complaining. Lucas stops crying, takes a long look at Isabelle and kisses her.

"Sorry, Isabelle; so sorry for breaking down like this," says Lucas as he takes out his handkerchief.

"It's okay, Lucas. You have been through so much in your life and never broken down. You have always stayed tough so that you could be the family provider and take care of the rest of us. You have earned the right to break down and cry," replies Isabelle. It is her turn to be strong for him. "You helped me through my darkest hours, and you never gave up on me."

"Isabelle... I love you," cries Lucas and gives her an immense hug, as if he never wants to let go. "You mean so much to me, Isabelle."

"I love you, Lucas Clarkson," says Isabelle with a smile. They kiss passionately, driven by thankfulness that through all of the suffering, they still have each other for support.

Isabelle takes a good look at herself. After all the pain and suffering she and Lucas have endured, she knows she has to do something with her life. She wants to give the biggest gift to her husband, so she is going to regain her former health.

Isabelle takes control of her life. She doesn't get depressed as often now that she is working hard on healing herself. She also watches her diet, thinking back to the past about the tips she learned when she received help with dieting and lost lots of weight. Isabelle digs back in her files to retrieve all the information she kept for losing weight. A month passes, and Isabelle is doing extremely well with her new health project.

"Isabelle, you're looking great! I notice you are slimming down," says Lucas with his adoring smile. "Whatever you're doing, keep it up! You look happier than I've seen you in years."

"Thanks, Lucas. I feel incredible, like I've been reborn!"

"Isabelle, your birthday is tomorrow, and I have something special planned for you," he says before kissing her on the cheek.

"Lucas, you know I don't like surprises," replies Isabelle shyly.

"Your sons and daughter have it all planned. Because you are turning fifty years old, I promised them that we would do something special. They love their mother so much; they just want to express their appreciation for you," says Lucas, laughing with joy.

"Lucas, what is your plan? I'm getting a little nervous," Isabelle jokes.

"I'm not telling you what we're doing, but it will be fun—that I promise," says Lucas as he continues to laugh.

The next day, Lucas gets ready, and then he shouts, "Isabelle, are you ready? We have to leave soon."

"I will be right out," Isabelle shouts.

When Isabelle comes out of the room, Lucas takes a good look. He is amazed at how gorgeous she looks; it takes his breath away.

"Isabelle, you look so beautiful."

"Thank you. Where are we going?" asks Isabelle.

"Sorry, I can't say," replies Lucas. "Just follow me. Trust me, you'll love it!"

Lucas takes Isabelle to their son Steve's house. As they enter the driveway, Isabelle looks around. Everything seems quiet.

"Steve wants us to stop here for a few minutes because the grandkids want to wish you happy birthday before we continue our night out of town." Lucas grins as he gets out; then he goes and opens the passenger door for Isabelle, as he always does.

"Thanks," says Isabelle with a smile. She is always excited to see her grandchildren.

Lucas knocks on the door. Steve answers and invites in his parents. Everything seems normal to Isabelle, as the grandchildren come running to wish her happy birthday. Then they invite Isabelle to come out into their backyard to see their new pet. Isabelle walks around the house with her grandchildren, and to her surprise, that's where she finds her birthday party. She is in shock to see so many people there.

Everyone yells and sings happy birthday. Lucy brings a beautiful birthday cake trimmed in pink roses, which are Isabelle's favorite color and favorite flower. Isabelle is at a loss for words for minutes. Tears of joy come running down her cheeks. Lucas walks toward her and wishes Isabelle a happy fiftieth birthday. Then he kisses her passionately, and everyone claps hands with joy to see Isabelle and Lucas so much in love with each other.

It is the most fabulous backyard birthday party that Isabelle could ever imagine. She thanks Johnny, Steve, Lucy and Thomas for the beautiful party they have thrown for her. Isabelle thanks everyone for coming, but most of all, she thanks Lucas, not only for the birthday party surprise but also for always being there for her.

A few years pass, and it is now 1993. Isabelle is back to her regular weight and feels proud of her hard work to get small again. Lucas is amazed to see his wife bounce back to better health. Life is starting to look bright for Lucas and Isabelle. They often take trips, and they go to Florida every year with James and Debra. Lucas has bought a Winnebago to travel across Canada. His favorite part of the west-coast trips is finally getting to stop in Alberta to see where his old friend Steve used to live before he died.

Isabelle's favorite part is British Columbia. She admires the mountain views and the friendliness of the people. She especially likes Vancouver Island and all the beauty nature has to offer there. The overall trip is great, and then the following year, they travel to the east coast. Lucas and Isabelle enjoy being in Newfoundland, except Isabelle is not too crazy about taking the ferry there. But putting her trust in Lucas, she manages to conquer her fear of water.

Path of Lucas

Traveling is their joy, and they love going to Florida every spring. Lucas and Isabelle start enjoying life to the fullest as their love grows stronger for each other.

One night as she and Lucas are enjoying their evening together, Isabelle feels an uncomfortable pain in her chest, so she goes to bed early. She does not sleep that night because of her discomfort. The next morning, Lucas asks Isabelle how she is feeling, but she tells him she is fine, so Lucas goes off to work. Later that morning, Isabelle's daughter-in-law, Amy, comes over to help her with her flower gardens. As they are playing in the ground, putting in flowers, Isabelle tells Amy that she has started to have chest pains. So, Isabelle sits down for a few minutes to catch her breath, and a few minutes later, she gets up and starts gardening again. Amy is worried and asks Isabelle whether she wants to go to the hospital, but Isabelle refuses to go.

Later that evening, Isabelle decides to cook a delicious supper for Lucas. Their favorite is sirloin steak with baked potatoes and sour cream. Lucas is happy to see Isabelle feeling better and making supper as he walks in. He knows Isabelle always makes fantastic meals. Isabelle smiles and tells Lucas to wash up because supper is almost ready. Lucas kisses Isabelle as he greets her with the beautiful smile she loves so much.

Lucas and Isabelle are having a great evening planning their next summer trip. Lucas mentions to Isabelle that he would like to take her back to the area where she was born.

"Quebec City!" cries Isabelle with excitement in her voice.

Lucas nods, and they agree it will be their next trip. Isabelle has many family members there that she has not seen in many years with whom she has always kept in contact by letters and phone calls.

After supper, they decide to settle down and get ready for bed early that evening because Lucas has to start at sunrise the next morning to haul a load of pulp to Domtar in Cornwall before he goes back to the bush. In the middle of the night, Isabelle starts again to have pain in her chest, but this time, it is severe. Isabelle tries to get up from the bed to ease her pain, but the pain becomes more intense. She has no choice but to wake Lucas.

"Lucas, Lucas! Please take me to the hospital—I have severe chest pain," says Isabelle, crying.

"What's the matter, Isabelle?" replies Lucas as he wakes up in confusion and sees Isabelle suffering.

"I don't know, but it hurts, and I'm having a hard time catching my breath," says Isabelle as she puts her hand to her chest and gasps for air.

Lucas jumps up fast and rushes Isabelle to the hospital. The whole time he is driving, he is worried for Isabelle as she sits there holding onto her chest. As soon as they arrive, Lucas helps Isabelle into the emergency unit, where the nurses attend to her as he watches.

Lucas gives Isabelle a kiss on the forehead. "I'll wait right here for you, Isabelle," he says softly as he watches them wheel her away.

Isabelle looks back at Lucas tenderly.

Lucas sits in the emergency waiting room until the doctor is finished examining his wife. Soon the doctor arrives with a nurse, and they walk straight to Lucas.

"Mr. Clarkson?" asks the doctor.

"Yes!" replies Lucas.

"Hi, my name is Dr. Lynch," says the doctor as he shakes Lucas's hand. "This is Nurse Fox," he says, motioning toward the nurse. "She will be caring for your wife."

"How is my wife doing?" asks Lucas as he nods to the doctor and the nurse.

"Mrs. Clarkson has had a mild heart attack. She is stable now and resting," explains Dr. Lynch.

"Heart attack!" says Lucas, perplexed. Regardless of how many times Lucas has heard difficult news in his life, it does not get any easier to hear. "Will she be okay?"

"Yes, Mrs. Clarkson is doing well, but she will need her rest and must stay here tonight for observation," replies Dr. Lynch. "Otherwise, Mrs. Clarkson is fine."

"Thank you, Dr. Lynch; thank you so much," says Lucas as he wipes a tear from his eye.

"No problem, Mr. Clarkson. We will keep a close eye on her tonight, but I think she will be fine," replies Dr. Lynch.

"Can I see my wife?" asks Lucas, feeling anxious.

"Yes, but remember that Mrs. Clarkson needs her rest," says Dr. Lynch. "Nurse Fox will take you to her room." Lucas follows the nurse to Isabelle's room.

Lucas spends time watching Isabelle sleep and thanking God that his wife is all right. Lucas knows enough to understand that heart attacks can be fatal. The nurse walks in to change Isabelle's intravenous and tells Lucas he should go back home to sleep, that Mrs. Clarkson is doing fine and in stable condition. She shows him the heart monitor. Lucas agrees because Isabelle needs to sleep, and so does he after this taxing night.

Lucas arrives home and goes straight to bed. He dozes off, but after about an hour, the phone rings. Lucas jumps out of bed to answer.

"Hello," says Lucas in confusion as he tries to wake himself up.

"Mr. Clarkson?" says a woman's voice.

"Yes," says Lucas. Now he is really confused. "Whom am I talking to?"

"I'm Nurse Fox, your wife's nurse," replies the nurse.

"Nurse who?" questions Lucas as he slowly awakens.

"Mrs. Clarkson's nurse."

"Yes, yes, now I remember. Nurse Fox, is there something the matter with my wife?" says Lucas as his heart starts to beat harder.

"Mr. Clarkson, your wife is very ill, and we need you to come to the hospital right away," says the nurse.

"What? What's wrong with her?" asks Lucas. He feels extreme pain, as if a knife is stabbing him in the chest.

"Please come to the hospital right away!" repeats Nurse Fox. "There is no time for questions."

"I'll be there as soon as I can," says Lucas. He hangs up the phone and rushes out the door. While driving, he feels a tremendous sadness that his wife is sick. He remembers the times they spent driving around in his Studebaker, listening to Johnny Cash and Chuck Berry. At the time, he felt invincible and totally content with his beloved girl by his side. It is strange to him that so much time has passed because it feels like that was just yesterday. The contrast between his former happiness and how he feels right now is too much to bare; he forces himself to focus on the road.

At the hospital, he runs straight to the nurses station. "I need to see my wife—Mrs. Clarkson!" says Lucas, trying to catch his breath.

"Mr. Clarkson… Mr. Clarkson, your wife had a major cardiac arrest," says a nurse at the station. "Come with me, Mr. Clarkson. Follow me."

"What's going on?" demands Lucas; he is baffled by their behavior.

"Mr. Clarkson... Mrs. Clarkson had a major heart attack, and she did not make it," says the nurse as she opens the door of Isabelle's room.

"What! Isabelle is dead? She died—is that what you're telling me!" shouts Lucas. "No way, she is only fifty-three years old—she's too young to go! I just left here a few hours ago! This can't be—what will I do without her?"

Lucas barges into the room and looks at Isabelle. She looks at peace; there is no sound of the heart monitor or any intravenous in her arm. He stands there for a few seconds and then walks toward Isabelle. During this time, Nurse Fox is disconnecting all the machines around her.

"I am sorry, Mr. Clarkson, for your loss," says Nurse Fox. "Is there anything we can do for you?"

Lucas is silent. He just stares at Isabelle, unable to believe this could happen. *Why! Why! Why!* Lucas asks himself, and then he starts to cry. He holds Isabelle's hand and kisses her on the forehead as he continues to sob. Both nurses leave Lucas alone with his wife.

Lucas cries even more as he puts his head down on Isabelle's chest. His sense of loss is unbearable and only paralleled in intensity by his immense love for her. In all their years together, he now realizes, his love for her has only grown stronger and stronger.

Lucas gets up from the side of Isabelle's bed and goes to the nurses station to call Johnny, Steve, Lucy and Thomas. He tells them their mother has just died of a massive heart attack and then returns to Isabelle's room. As Lucas sits beside Isabelle, waiting for his children, he notices a monarch butterfly flapping its wings outside the hospital window. Lucas can't believe it—it looks just like the monarch butterfly he saw at Richard's funeral. Then he sees a bird, a rose-breasted grosbeak, fly around and perch on the windowsill for a few seconds. Then they fly off together toward the dark-blue sky.

Soon the children arrive at the hospital, in shock as they enter the room where Isabelle is lying peacefully in the hospital bed with Lucas by her side. It is June 10, 1993. The children stand by their mother's side in silence as they say their last goodbyes.

Lucas tells his children about the monarch butterfly and how this time he has also seen a rose-breasted grosbeak perched on the window. He describes to them how they both flew off together toward the sky.

CHAPTER 35

As Lucas stares at his daughter, he thinks of his wife, and he becomes emotional. He again feels Lucy squeezing his hand, and then he also sees Lucy's eyes starting to twitch, as if she were trying to open them. At the same time, he can hear the door opening slowly.

"Grandpa! Grandpa!" cries Danny as he enters with his wife, Emily. He walks toward his grandfather, gives him a hug and then looks at his mom hooked up to so many machines.

"Danny," replies Lucas, tearing up as he gives his grandson a hug. Then he hugs Emily.

Ryan is walking behind his brother, with his wife, Kayla. He has tears in his eyes to see his mom lying in bed. He, too, hugs his grandfather. Dwayne and Johnny follow their big brothers, and Mark trails behind all of Lucy's sons.

Lucas finishes hugging all his grandsons and their wives, and then he hugs Mark, as Mark tears up. Then they stare at Lucy, and they all hope and pray that she will come out of the coma.

With a smile, Lucas lets Mark sit beside his wife, knowing that Lucy will squeeze his hand and that Mark will then know what is really happening with her. Mark sits down and holds Lucy's hand, while all her children stand around her quietly crying. Lucas stands at the foot of Lucy's bed. He understands and empathizes with the children's extreme pain because of what has happened to their mom and because of all the losses he has endured.

Lucas smiles as he concentrates on Mark holding Lucy by the hand. It isn't long until Mark feels a squeeze. He looks at his wife and then at her hand, and he feels another squeeze. Lucas glows when Mark smiles with amazement.

"Hey, guys! Your mom just squeezed my hand!" says Mark with excitement, and he continues to look at Lucy's fingers.

"Lucas, did you see what just happened?" repeats Mark as he turns and looks at him.

"Yes! I saw that." Lucas smiles, and there is immense joy in his heart.

Danny takes his mother's other hand, and he also feels a squeeze. "Wow!" says Danny, "here, Ryan. You try."

"Yes! I can feel her clinch," says Ryan joyfully.

Dwayne gets excited as he sees his mother's hand moving. He knows she is trying to wake up. Johnny also realizes that his mother is coming out of the coma. They are all smiling because their mother is attempting to communicate with them. Mark gives Lucy a kiss, and as he is kissing her, he notices her eyes struggling to open.

"Look, guys! Look!" says Mark as he stares at Lucy. "Your mom is trying to open her eyes."

They stand around Lucy with amazement, waiting for her next move. Lucas watches them all gather around and sees the joy on their faces while they watch over Lucy. As he smiles, he feels tension around his chest. Lucas holds onto the footboard of Lucy's bed as he tries to ease his pain. Mark sees him bending over slightly and asks Lucas if he is okay. Lucas smiles and tells Mark he is fine, just a little tired. Kayla goes to comfort Lucas, and as she puts her arms around him, everyone hears Lucy start to moan. They all look toward Lucy as she moves her head slowly.

"Lucy! Lucy!" says Mark as he places his hand gently on her cheek.

"Mom! Mom!" utters Danny as he holds his mother's hand.

Lucy moans again as she tries to open her eyes to focus.

"Lucy! It's me, Mark," explains Mark as he continues to rub her cheek. "Your boys are here also, with your daughters-in-law and your dad."

"Yes, Mom, we're all here," repeats Ryan with a smile. He touches her knee. "Wake up, Mom. Wake up."

"Mark... Mark," says Lucy in a very feeble tone.

"Yes, Lucy. We're all here with you, sweetie," Mark tells her.

"Mark, what happened? Where is my dad?" asks Lucy in confusion. Her voice is very low; she is so weak.

"Lucy, you were in a car accident," explains Mark. "Your father is at the end of your bed."

"Yes, honey, I'm right here," says Lucas as he walks toward her side of the bed and reaches out to hold her hand.

"Dad... Dad... I had the most vivid dream about you," Lucy mumbles faintly as she tries to open her eyes.

"You had a dream about me?" whispers Lucas as he kisses his daughter on the forehead. "What kind of dream?"

"You were talking about your life," replies Lucy as she tries to focus on her father's face.

"Really!" As Lucas smiles, he gets another jolt to his chest; he keeps trying to hide his pain.

"Dad... it was a great dream!" says Lucy in a low voice.

Lucas runs a finger through Lucy's hair. "I'm so happy you came through for us. Lucy, you're such a strong person. I'm so blessed to have a daughter like you." Lucas smiles even as he starts to become short of breath. "Love you, Lucy."

"Love you, Dad," replies Lucy as she tries to lift up her arm to touch her father, her rock, the one who has been the stable force in her life since she was a child.

Lucas reaches out and helps Lucy lift her arm to touch his face.

"Lucy, I'm going to call your brothers to tell them what has happened to you and how you are a true survivor," says Lucas. He tries to catch his breath; at this point, he feels the pain crossing through his arm.

"Okay, Dad. Don't be long," says Lucy gazing at him with adoration.

Lucas looks at Lucy, and at that moment, he sees Isabelle's last gentle smile before she died. Lucas kisses Lucy and reassures her he won't be long. He tells the boys he will be right back; he is just going to make phone calls to their uncles. Lucas leaves the room, and as he walks toward the phones, he has another chest pain.

Lucy is more awake now, and the doctor comes into her room to monitor her actions. With incredulity, the doctor tells Mark and Lucy's children that Lucy is starting to make progress toward a full recovery. As he tests her reflexes, he knows that she is not paralyzed. Mark takes a deep breath and a sigh of relief; then he thanks Dr. Wright for everything he has done for Lucy. Her children take turns thanking the doctor for saving their mother's life, and they shake his hand with joy.

Lucy starts to focus better now. She sees everyone around her, and despite some confusion, she begins to comprehend what has happened to her. She starts to remember the car accident and how she was heading to see her father to spend the weekend with him. Lucy looks around and then asks Mark where her father is. Mark tells her he has stepped out for a few minutes to call her brothers. Lucy tells Mark that she had a dream about her father's life and how he went through so much pain but never once complained. It was a dream, yet it felt so real. Mark tells her that she has been in a coma; it must have been just a dream.

Lucas finishes calling his sons, and as he hangs up the phone, he feels another shock in his chest. He turns to head back to Lucy's room. As he walks, another jolt hits his chest; it really takes his breath away. Lucas folds in two and tries to catch his breath. Feeling the lack of oxygen, he grabs onto his throat. Finally, he catches his breath. He takes a few seconds and starts walking toward Lucy's room again.

Path of Lucas

Back in Lucy's room, Mark smiles at Lucy, knowing she is starting to recover from her coma. The children hug each other, feeling blessed to have their mother back with them. As they celebrate their bliss, Lucy looks around the room.

"Where is my father?" she asks, and this time there is concern on her face.

"Don't worry, Lucy. I told you that your dad just stepped out for a few minutes to tell your brothers that you're recovering from your accident," says Mark as he grabs her hand and kisses her on the cheek.

"He's been gone too long," says Lucy, as she gets a feeling of fear deep inside her.

"Mom, Grandpa will be back in a few minutes," reassures Danny as he tries to comfort her.

"If he's not, Mom, I promise, I'll go get him," says Johnny.

'Thanks, Johnny," says Lucy. She smiles, as she looks at her children. "Thank you all for being here for me. It means so much to me."

"Mom, you mean so much to us," replies Dwayne as his eyes fill with tears of joy.

They all gather around Lucy's bed, chatting and making Lucy laugh, as they always do. Mark smiles as he watches the children interacting with each other. The best part about loving his wife is seeing Lucy and her children loving each other.

Lucas is almost to Lucy's room when another jolt hits his chest, and this one brings him down to his knees. Lucas tries to get up, but he doesn't have enough strength to even move his hands. He knows this is serious and that there is something very wrong as he falls flat to the floor. The moment Lucas hits the floor, he hears beautiful music, and then he sees bright lights. At the same time, he can feel himself leaving his body. As Lucas leaves his body, he looks up and sees Isabelle reaching her hand toward him, with an angelic smile. She is so beautiful. Lucas smiles and reaches his hand to hold Isabelle's. They hold onto each other's hands, and then Isabelle tells

Lucas to follow her. Lucas agrees, and he follows Isabelle. He sees his body lying on the floor as a nurse runs toward it.

When the nurse notices a man face down on the floor, she runs to him and immediately calls for backup. The nurse turns Lucas over, not knowing who the person is at this point. Once she repositions him, she realizes it is Mr. Clarkson. *Lucy Ferguson's father,* she thinks as she reaches for his wrist. When there is no pulse, the nurse starts CPR. Other nurses run to help with a defibrillator. The nurses work on Lucas's lifeless body for a while until the doctor comes to take over. The doctor works on Lucas too, but he isn't able to revive him. Lucas is pronounced dead.

After all the hard work of trying to revive Lucas with no success, the doctor and nurse have to go to Lucy's room to announce to her that her dad has died. As they walk in, they can feel the joy in the room. This is obviously a close-knit, dedicated family. They love each other so much, and the nurses know that this news will be devastating. The doctor walks toward Lucy, and everyone thinks he is coming in to check up on her. To the children and Mark's bafflement, what he has to say is not about Lucy. It is about Lucas.

"Mrs. Ferguson, I am so sorry to have to tell you this, but your father had a massive heart attack. He was in the hallway, and by the time that we found him, he had already passed away. I am sorry… We did everything we could," says the doctor in a low voice; he has difficulty breaking this news.

"No! No! Not my dad! He just left to call my brothers about me," cries Lucy. She tries to get up, but her body is too weak after what she has been through.

Mark and the children are in shock. *Lucas was such a strong man,* Mark thinks. The boys gather around their mom to comfort her as she cries.

As Lucy looks out the window, she stops crying as she suddenly notices something unusual. She sees two beautiful rose-breasted grosbeaks singing on the ledge and a gorgeous monarch butterfly flapping its wings above the two birds. Lucy can't help but smile as she looks out the window. She feels a magical experience has just taken place right before her eyes. Lucy feels in her heart that at that moment her father and mother are together, along with her brother Richard. *Love is magical,* thinks Lucy. While she grieves the loss of her father, she realizes that her parents have always had such a strong bond for each other, so it is good that they are together again. Lucy remembers her father seeing a monarch butterfly at her brother's funeral and a butterfly with a bird at the hospital when her mom passed away. Lucy looks back at her family with a joyful smile, knowing loved ones are being reunited.

The following week, Lucy's remarkable recovery has taken everyone by surprise; even the doctors are impressed. Lucy is determined to be at her father's funeral. Somehow she finds the strength to read the eulogy that she wrote.

> *Dad was a strong man with a big heart. Everyone knew his wonderful spirit and his great kindness. His smile would light up every room; the stories he told, we will always remember and share; his jokes will never be forgotten. He has given us the greatest gift—his wisdom—we will cherish and carry in our hearts.*
>
> *Dad, you have been a man of strength; you have shown us in many ways. You had to go, but you are not gone. We love you, Dad; in our hearts, you will always stay. We can find you in a ray of sunshine or in a drop of rain, even in a grain of sand. We know you will be there.*
>
> *We will all miss you, but now you are set free.*
>
> *You were once my father; now you are my angel. Shine for me, Daddy, until we meet again.*
>
> *Thank you for being my dad.*
>
> *Love you, Daddy,*
Your little girl

Mom and Dad, you are both an inspiration in my life. With all my heart and soul, I believe you guided me in the right direction and shaped me into being the person that I am. I want to thank you from the bottom of my heart for being my parents.

Until we meet again!

Based on a true story

I dedicate this story to Roger Bellefeuille.
My father, my hero!

These were his last words to my sons before he died:

Cry when you're happy. When you're sad, fight it.
—Roger Bellefeuille

*First picture is Roger with Maurice (Rocket) Richard,
Second and third picture is Roger at the age of nineteen,
Fourth picture is Roger and his wife, Gisele.*

342

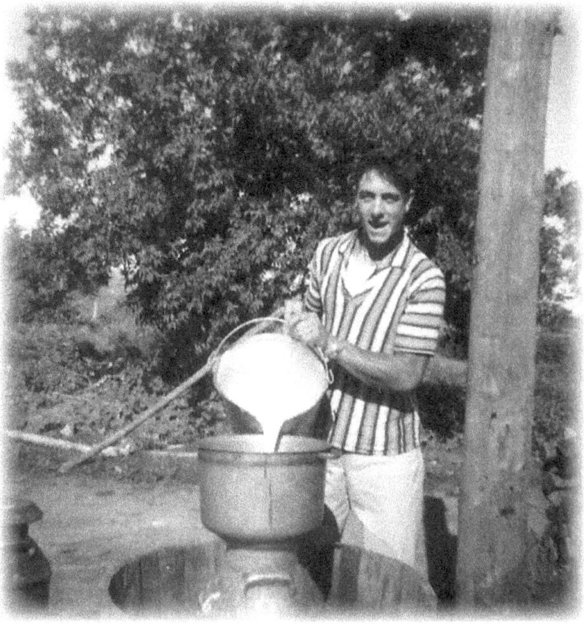

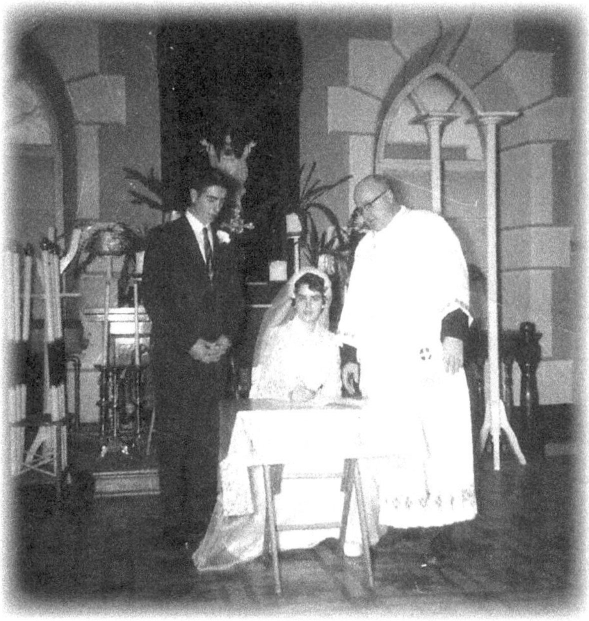

"Cry when you're happy.
When you're sad, fight it!!"
~ Roger

In loving memory of
Roger Bellefeuille
1939 - 2015

Milton Keynes UK
Ingram Content Group UK Ltd.
UKHW011930140823
426877UK00012B/305/J

Faust

Also by Sandeep Parmar

The Marble Orchard
Eidolon

Sandeep Parmar

Faust

Shearsman Books

First published in the United Kingdom in 2022 by
Shearsman Books
P O Box 4239
Swindon
SN3 9FN

Shearsman Books Ltd Registered Office
30–31 St. James Place, Mangotsfield, Bristol BS16 9JB
(this address not for correspondence)

www.shearsman.com

ISBN 978-1-84861-827-5

Translations copyright © Sandeep Parmar, 2022.
The right of Sandeep Parmar to be identified as the author of
this work has been asserted by her in accordance with the
Copyrights, Designs and Patents Act of 1988.
All rights reserved.

Contents

I

Faust / 11

II

A Winnowing Shovel / 47

An Uncommon Language / 57

III

The Nineties / 67

IV

On Desire / 75
'Vivien With Household Gods' / 78
Nightmares at the Waldorf-Astoria / 80
A Good Wife / 83
Something Particular / 84
Krampus / 85
Elsewhere / 86
Queens Astoria / 88

Acknowledgements / 90

For my daughter, Gaia

I

FAUST

But see how, rising from this turbulence,
the rainbow forms its changing-unchanged arch,
now clearly drawn, now evanescent,
and casts cool, fragrant showers all about it.
Of human striving it's a perfect symbol—
ponder this well to understand more clearly
that what we have as life is many-hued reflection.
   —Goethe, *Faust*, Part II, Act I, 4715–4727, trans. Stuart Atkins

Yes, he can say to himself: Here on the most ancient, the eternal altar, built directly on the foundations of the world, I bring a sacrifice to the being of all beings.
   —Goethe, 'On Granite', trans. Norman Guterman

…that queer amalgamation of dream and reality, that perpetual marriage of granite and rainbow.
   —Virginia Woolf, 'The New Biography'

i.

I'd be but a shadow   seed of clay
    turned earth   blown onto the path of shadow

    Want or indigence   Debt or shame
      sisters of Distress   whose midnight phone calls
        light the bedside lamps
          you take the coverlet with you
to the next room, Care, sister of Death
    where grief is not an abstraction but an inheritance   a waiting for

another dawn   a being   with sisters

      sageless arrows of grief

we rain down our fury

      the devil whistles while he works

ii.

I am the fifth sister
    whose striving lays an ocean
        between the shadows of our dead

        quarrelling shores
          a great distance apart

        here is your image
    a swan unfolding its wings
        a river of blood down its back
          its beak preening at arterial speed
            red feathers   foaming   unstopping flow

    we cross a mudded field of apple trees   in its dwindling harvest
        a circle of blonde heads   murmurous clutching arms
          crouched webwork of ground

what magic is this   a conspiracy of daughters casting in daylight
    red and white   making sacrifice   of abject girlhood
        how have we come
          to be here   sister

    the Autumn banks   the exile   of a grasslaid river

iii.

If I drew a line   through all our births   over five centuries
    from the Silk Road to the Sutlej
      through the woolly Khyber   its dark resin
        wending towards Lahore
          pockets of carved stones
  at one end would be the seed   ferrous imbricate hybrid
    yellowing thorn of wheat

At the other   distance   the June waking the July waking
    to inedible sheaves   to age
to our hair falling out, our eyes clouding with disease
    and the children   that keep on never coming

Father wild logic scythe in hand
barefoot harvesting all night
high on opium

iv.

You ride the elevator to the eleventh floor of a hotel
    the tallest in our seaside town
        pale yellow or coral or white
            no lighthouse but an abrasive plinth
                chartered to the shore by cement.

Holy fathers, beatified men   their bronze or wooden statues dot the coast
    from San Diego to San Francisco
Up El Camino Real—
    where curved poles topped by soundless bells
        hang like sickles.

A river, a mission, a chapel, its garden.
    An ocean, a boardwalk, mountains, a freeway.
The town's Franciscan priest,
    Junípero Serra, once had his hands
doused with red paint. Genocidal
    churches, arable lands. A museum
with pieces of or whole Chumash
    bowls and other poorly-handled things.
School children appraise them. It is an annual ritual.

            *

You request a room overlooking the Pacific.
The elevator does not stop; the hotel is never full.

A wooden pier—once of remarkable length—
    extends towards the Channel Islands,
draped in fog, reachable by boat

      if you wake with the fishermen before dawn.
A novel was set in those islands about the sole
      inhabitant of San Nicolas. The facts are:
a native woman alone for eighteen years
      spotted on the beach skinning a seal;
hauled ashore to the mission where dysentery
      killed her and her language off. She was given
a Christian name. We read it in school
      but remember nothing except
the word Aleutian and a numbness
      sharpened by no response. It was written
by a descendent of Sir Walter Scott.
      Scott was, among other things, an early translator
of Goethe. Dear sister. What you have learned is a dying craft.

The elevator opens onto a quiver of directions.

*

You drift back to a rose garden, a small women's college
      where each girl is permitted to pick and take
all the roses she can carry back to her room.

*

The pier, battered by storms, is rebuilt. A catafalque
      decked in American flags from sternum to navel.
From this angle, the sea is a parade of elbow length satin.
      Excavating the cave of the lone woman at San Nicolas,
diggers were halted by the Navy. It lies half-dug,
      disputed, full of sand, making distress calls.
You run towards the end of the pier with your arms
      open, lodging in its sights like a gale or target.

*

The room's ceiling is shot white powder,
    liable to yellow and stain.
Someone later recalled seeing you taking
    in the view from your balcony.
The sun is flattening into the sea and below
    there are families fishing or striding
in the dimming orange light. It is well-beyond
    happy hour in the tiki-themed bar,
the seafood restaurant we thought was so sophisticated.
    There's a revolving ballroom,
long since closed, where high schools held their proms.
    Corsages, rented limos, hairspray,
saliva drying on gums in windy sunroofs. The sun
    is a gold disc over the grey-blue waters of the Pacific.

*

    To strive, you think, to know. You've brought with you a copy of *Faust*. What is it to want to know everything. The light sharpens to a point to a full stop to an ingot of gold at 7.30 p.m. This alchemy. Do you open *Faust*. Do you leave it in the dingy room, on the beige bedspread, a wager of its own in our Eden this Arcadia. Faust's strip of coastline, a paradise built in his dotage, unbegun but in his imagination, an inner light. Now you remember everything. You are in a state of sudden alertness. You find your aim you strive. There is the sun, blinding all the summer day. There is the cliff, where Euphorion dropped into blackness marching heroic. You think of the roses and how you carried them all in your arms. Striding full of hope into another century. To want, to owe, to feel shame. Dear sister. To wish to know everything Faust says you must become nothing Mephistopheles says to extend beyond what is human you must become the Spirit of Eternal Negation Faust says you must be willing to die but I am not afraid to die Mephistopheles says I will route your indentured soul from an eye an ear a navel a fingernail for the jaws of hell are always open Faust love has waded through my many dreams and orchestrations Mephistopheles opines we were all girls in another century baring our arms in an inhabited garden Care slips through the keyhole like smoke a kind of being without a kind of alchemy Faust you will never fall where love can be seen from a great height rising above these hills like a memorable star.

v.

Go home then—

Why did you come here

To study (you tell the officer)

To retrace my steps part way home

Across a burning field

To stand in the smoke and to locate its source

To conquer this country back

To watch the black dog circle with its tail of fire

    The snares of our future bondage

To stand between a grandfather and his meat cleaver

Across a burning street

Where men carve flames into a glass shopfront and debouch into

Another burning street

A memory you steal or borrow

Heavy in my hand like a defunct currency

    A language

    To learn

vi.

Kernels of rain   or *seeds* of rain
    is how raindrops translate

so that even the rain is not itself
                                when you wait mouth open
                                looking sceptical or just pulling
                                at the dry earth with broken lips.

Who will plant the rain   in a hearse so that the moon blooms
                                                    from his heart?
Grandfather, laid out and burnt like a stoic length of chaff,
his mind a prophecy of smoke.
    Two rupees in his breast pocket and a slip of white, neatly folded,
        with his son's address on it.

Smoke that is not rain nor wheat but leans
into them both like a fever
unmatched by the living.

There   he says, in a blue of white,
that is all you ever needed to know about wheat.

vii.

The wheat came apart in her hands

her hands came apart in the grass

her body a field

the field her body

innumerable hands would bury

Carry the charge

the imprisoned lightning
of her name

viii.

A landscape that repels description   this counterfeit Eden
    whose surfeit demands   you catalogue

but did not think to note its variety   merely its similitude
    of bougainvillea, agave, eucalyptus, orange wildflower

A cartilage of succulents, yellow synovials of kelp popping under
                                              your feet
      where nothing ages or dies

First I waited with a shovel   then I threw the shovel and ran

Lilac Creek overflowing
Romero   San Ysidro
    cottages roll into the sea over a cliff

   A child chokes on a deluge of mud
      slides into a living room
         on a wave
         under a coffee table
         his mouth a breach of tides
         someone gently empties

the sand and clay from his fists
A woman and her clever dog float to the surf

ix.

        Who will we become
    across several oceans—Arabian to Pacific—

rude stars
    in an arc bending over Kyiv, Belarus, Astrakhan.

    This ear that recognises its name and the words for water, hunger
                                           learns

the cold sum   the clean sum.

You say   where there is water.
And the obvious truth of god.

A long long homecoming
across a field of ash
grain spilling a trail
from an unsealed urn.

x.

by soft coincidence
        by a chance crossing
of wild river grasses
        by seizing threshing seeding
by training the eye on green
        green wild soft unfolding
the seasonal miracle named
        by its naked composition
its durability also female
        by sowing and harvesting
incidentally woman given shape
        by burning off its chaff
by haploid shedding its goat
        face stricken by no word
for spring only weather
        coincidence of chance
the periodic flight
        from the sun's long shadow
by a known path
        which is why you take
your elders with you
        or else lose your way

xi.

Who will tear at their faces   for the Levantine or Persian
    extraction   the lost wheat   hold vigil at the pyre
    for whatever remains at dawn

To return home is to choke on the bread
    risen   that is no longer made

    this desi kanak like ash
    that carries your diurnal
    blood in its whiteness

You cling to it   or you don't   falling out of use

Someone else bows   touches fire to the feet
    of your dead

Gone
    the seed holds
        lodged in its thin neck
           head swaying   driven out to

where your ancestors
were cut down   empty handed   crossing a border without shoes
where one day   you will sit   on dry earth with them

and eat your own flesh
shaking with pity

xii.

botanist	grass
chemist	organic compounds
geneticist	a challenging organism
farmer	a cash crop
hauler	freight
laborer	employment
merchant	produce
miller	grist
baker	flour
banker	chattel
politician	a problem
animals	feed
parasites	sustenance
conservationist	ground cover
religion	a symbol
artist	a model
a livelihood	lifegiving food

(cf. *Wheat and Wheat Improvement*, Karl Spangler Quisenberry, 1967)

In the book of dowries
everyone in its handwrit
ledger is in debt to each
other which is why
marriage must continue
so neighbours mither
sit crosslegged over
generational accounts
of poor past harvests
and dream of burning
the heavy handling

25

                                    of ancestral losses
                                    like a stubble of reeds
                                    along with the thin man
                                    whose family is charged
                                    with preserving them
                                    in carefully inked rows
                                    but when otherwise
                                    would the village gather
                                    to listen to the given
                                    names of their forefathers

Sonora, Lerma Roja,
their descendants took indigenous names
so each could be traced like male heirs
to caste family faith district acre season

Kaliyan meaning   the solution

A seed is not a jewel   a prized son   a golden interloper
to set in a collet
deposing all others

xiii.

                The grain as hands   her hands as grain
                  The grain as light   dust as grain
                    As light as dust   her hands as seed
                Grain as weather   as moving through
                  The earth where   grain falls she falls
            Here as water   sweetened after a fast
                  The grain she saw   growing not as grain
                    Is your father   in the marketplace
                     Grain cursed   penniless, auctioned
                    Shuffling home   unseasonable yields
                  Indelible shame   and hunger its own
                shame sets fire to   grain plots a loss
                 standing over a   jute sack of seed
                  that is his body   and they appraise it
                between fingers   for the going rate
                 father if I could   have bought a year
        of wheat exchanged   for bread you'd
                stride powerfully   as a boy as grain
                  in the hands of   a mother regained
                  from the earth   where she fell into
            Bitter yellow   rattle light this chance
                                            harvest

xiv.

The plough carves fate into flames that split your skull forty-six years after your birth. The *douleur,* the *gham,* the *tragedy* of six harvests overseen as the tumours weave like fire in your gut and the seventh, final crop you will never see breathes gently under the frost of Punjab. Shadows step inside you, capacious as a groom apprised of all he's won. Debt sown into the skin like disease, like one who, mad from silent protest, hapless, runs and runs into a headwind of bullets.

This is how it takes root, brother. You were too busy to notice. The bottle of Johnnie Walker exsanguinating between your palms like the prophet who squeezed blood from a rich man's bread into the sand refusing his table for the peasant's humble spread. *These potatoes, these onions, I have planted and dug for centuries and you bring me—an Englishman?* Sisters, stones in the soil at the best of times, crown your threshold carelessly on the day you die.

xv.

How is your family life? [my uncle]
You are living a half life. [my drycleaner]
You are living a stupid life. A stupid life. [a poet]

xvi.

The Traveller returns to the cottage on a hill of Philemon and Baucis, old childless couple. Years prior, they rescued him and his ship of goods strewn on the rocks, his eyes half-dead. Baucis wound her shawl across his chest and dragged him lifeless to the tall linden trees circling a chapel. Or was it Philemon who bellowed with his last drop of youthful vigour at the man to stand, palms open, making the Traveller stumble like an unborn son through sand dunes. Perhaps their charge grew familiar as the hearth lit his profile, coming to, or on forming early words, an ocean stirring in his chest, they turned away unsettled and blinked and bit their lips. *I have returned*, he said, seeing them so aged and the shore transplanted from their door to a distant port by technology. Chance or misfortune will not bring you twice to your destiny. This time the Traveller strove to throw himself into their arms, trudging up the leeward slope across forest and marsh. To strive to make his way home. *You will remember me from long ago.* Baucis prepares a meal and Philemon pours a shortage of wine. *Whom do you love?* How often the Traveller thought of being so saved. The fire's embers whirl into the sky. The smoke churns the far off covetous and lonely. Together, they pray. The chapel bell sways in a funerary dance. The devil and his strongmen stride up the narrow path. Silently, the three of them break their fast.

xvii.

On Walpurgisnacht   in the land of monsters   of half-women
    Lamiae cocottes admit the devil to their dance
    a murmuration of Sirens shift like a veil
    and other birds—goose-footed mouths of vultures—prophecy
    atop a primordial peak, flecked by fire

The Sphinx asks for your name
        an unsolvable riddle

You, questing spirit
    hewn from granite
        you war-storied obelisk
        you unripe grain of corn
        you daughter of abominations
        you sister of Mephistopheles
        you Faust lusting for Helen
        you who cannot stand your ground
        you who mount—and then cling to—a horse that never stops

xviii.

You held the long-forgotten cup to your lips
    a sharp reasoning   to lessen your striving

Old magician, doctor, survivor of plague,
    hypocrite scholar   whose strangulation cure

Gave fame to his mercy. Knowledge-maker, spirit
    of the Earth, of the sky   inscriber of pentagrams

Inviting in he who rings the bell   for Christ is risen
    knocking the wine from your hand   whose poison

packs your suitcase, waves goodbye to your kin, burns
    every house   eternally   within arm's reach

xix.

We see the flatterer   coming up the path   through a single eye
    We sisters, monsters grey from birth, keeping counsel in our cave
        We graceless Graeae, kin to Gorgons, Fates, we Phorcides
            who pass between us one eye, one sharp tooth
                We who cannot see the devil all at once
                    But know his many guises

He, the procurer of certificates.
He, the forger of passports.
He, who is paid only in cash.
He, a forgetter of faces.
He, a registrar, a bursar, bank manager,
        a purser, a pilot, border patrol officer,
        a suitor, a celebrant, senior doctor.

Scatter yourselves
over the earth,
he ordered.
Go at once
you seedless
women;
you beasts.

So I have taken the eye, and left you our shared tooth.

What I have seen, dear sister.

    If you can name yourself, no riddle will remain

xx.

Faust: There is no past or future in an hour like this, the present
                                            moment only

Helen: is our bliss   [Goethe]

Child, whose name is abundance
   who leans into a drift rising
      heroic into a war
         across a wingless ocean   this rumour this child
           whose very happiness depends on battle
           whose body will disappear into the body
               of a man and then into the unholy
               darkness that unknowable shore
               of the ground descending
               alone or into the wide sky
               as mist the body whose leaving
               is untouched gleaming untarnished
               whose parents lean into a present becoming
               quickly past whose name means everywhere
               a loss I catalogue each moment its noble fall
               holding fast—mother—to these clothes that scorch
               and draw up like smoke clouds this body is the last child
               these clothes sewn by my hands you have long since
                                         outgrown

xxi.

I mulched the roses for your physic,
the Doctor says, lopping each head
into a good sterile jar. Tomorrow
I will sow these fermented blooms
back into your lungs, its opal tincture
an apotheosis of rainwater injected
into the body on trial. The townsfolk,
drawn by some popular ritual or by an
unharvested crop will macerate spring
bulbs back into the earth, ploughing
on a saint's day, dancing in a beerish
circle, claiming I am their protector.
—I confess to you what salves are poisons
what passes for heroism, I weep, I laugh
loudly, knowing only the devil knows—
that sharp-elbowed CEO at the lectern
scalding the lawn brown like herbicide.
I signed a contract in my blood to strive.
A reporter starts up, corrects himself,
gets my name right, right again, wrong.

xxii.

That we cannot recall a single dinner conversation
That we always ate cross-legged on newspaper
That we (sometimes) had a dining room table
That our tables were (sometimes) cardboard boxes
That boxes were half of everything we owned
That none of our dinner tables would survive
That no conversation prepared you for my leaving
That we were so unprepared for what we endured

xxxiii.

Even the wives and children of the prophets are not spared the return of fire

—it is late I cannot show you where I have thrown the good seed

Who would trust the white devil to fetch a pail of water to break his crown

—it is late you cannot harvest what has taken root among the thorns

Even the mothers of mothers walked through flames to spare his namesake

—who lit the weeds and wheat refusing the bargain it is too late to know

        a *knowledgeable unknowing*   a girl breaking loose running

xxiv.

the language of the saints (Gurmukhi)

the language of the king (Shahmukhi)

cross this burning line

hot sticky mustard seed

a late winter crop

whose meaning

clings inseparably

to the melting skins

of my devoted

xxv.

He that hath ears, let him hear. [Matthew 13:9]

In a palmed square, staged for an ancient drama
you appear as Old Iniquity, a man of shrunken
goat-hoof in a riddle of circadian spheres. Pour
the fino—flowering a fist that turns bread to wine
wine to bread—vain general trained at rhetoric
by ancestral magnates in provincial misericords.
In the tall shadow of the archaeological museum
you are every busted remnant of war under glass
that once pertained to great civilisations. Come
fire, its purge, with you at the bellows. Turn blood
to vapour. I am certain that with your cold blue
eye you sized up our village, its grasses lodging.
You weighed the iron and sold us back its alloy
cheap, melting down family names etched there
for dowries. An object is only worth its use—
and what use is memory. You, whose forgetting
pawns itself in grief. I remember how at the wall
you pissed an apology over ruined stones, a white
road leading you back to England. Drawing a line
that we must cross and cross again towards you,
old enemy, dragging dark symbols into the sun.

xxvi.

*Warning, in music-words / devout and large, /
that we are each other's / harvest*
                            —Gwendolyn Brooks

Wretched girl, there you go
        flashing in beads of glass, a silver-

laid comb, a mirror, gifts of the devil
        from your disguised suitor, who

wanting nothing but to break your striving
        in faith, in love, in youth

would make your family crawl
        on his orders or be flogged—*O*

*you think I am a beast? I will marry you
        and your daughters and make*

them crawl and their daughters having
        disbanded their sons will crawl

on their bellies like the worm and gather
        your hair like sheaves every April

a mystery rite, a crime scene, cupped palms
        burning with an inedible seed.

                *

*Psyche made my work easy, so did Helen,
but you are a girl so simple that destroying
you loses my interest. Throw yourself
from a cliff, the ramparts, where no wind
will save or split your body from its skin.*

*

She, honestly risen on the singing ash of her
neighbours, makes a poor offering to Faust.
Her first death was beauty, her second that
he should replace her god, her third by her
own hand. O, to be an ecstatic field of grass.

*

I married the devil but he brought me back.
Shadow woman wearing a collar of knives.
Separable from all that is mine or was hers.
Every circle cries like a starved, angry child.
Even my slippers with their red velvet eyes.

*

The tributaries of the Indus—fingers across
a throat or arm of a girl bolting through
grasses. *Landrace* is that the word for her
slow dying. A box of scent from the queen
of the underworld. O, mothers, wash me.

xxvii.

Your heart packs up its mismatched syntax

In another room your husband

Is typing typing

The ladies in Barbour jackets are so nice

They sing to themselves on their morning walks

Go back to sleep he says

Streetlights go off one after another

It is some ritual

Come to pieces

Like a mausoleum

For a first wife

At the altar a third figure

Burned who you also married

He is in another room

Sterilising the linens in a churn

Singing his goatfoot steaming

Go back to sleep he says

I re-read the book of myths

The ash falling from my hair onto its pages

—*You were young and beautiful once, too, ho ho hee hee*

xxviii.

'…civilization is a process in the service of Eros, whose purpose is to combine single human individuals, and after that families, then races, peoples and nations, into one great unity, the unity of mankind.'
[Freud, *Civilization and its Discontents*]

You're pathetic, a joke—

See this line

  You can't see

Crawl over it

  On your belly

Like the snake   a degenerate race

  You will know by my tone

When you've crossed it

  this mudded field   a holy shrine

  turned over   the Devil knows

I do God's work   keeping you in line

It   it is   this shape

  A shadow

Your very best side   your very last words

  Tightening around your throat

xxviv.

Faust: What happens now?
Mephistopheles: Direct your strivings downward.

Follow the river, sisters. Follow the beasts
who walk the threshing circle, doomed, blind
beside the man who put out their eyes. Follow
the mist-sacred ground, the *bad coin of fear
inverted*, to the last home we would ever know.

II

A Winnowing Shovel

In 2002, the Spanish cultural psychiatrist Joseba Achotegui developed the term *Ulysses Syndrome* to describe a set of stress-induced disorders seen in migrants suffering harsh living conditions in their adopted homelands. In otherwise mentally healthy individuals, Achotegui noted the prevalence of symptoms such as migraines, insomnia, recurrent worrying, nervousness, irritability, disorientation, fear, and gastric and osteo-physical pains, symptoms that aren't uniquely experienced by migrants but are linked to complex migration: to the struggle to survive, to belong, to a sense of failure, to social isolation and cultural loss, to acculturation in a hostile host nation. He calls it a picture of 'extreme migratory grief' and, citing Odysseus's reply to the cyclops Polyphemus (that he is no man), suggests that if you must become nobody to survive you become permanently invisible. But to be a hero may be the precise opposite of this, and I am reminded of the classicist Jane Ellen Harrison's *Ancient Art and Ritual* (1913) which draws a bridge between the communal, spiritual desire in ancient ritual to the impulse towards the creation of art—both differently serve the emotional needs of their society at critical moments through enactment and representation. Harrison compares them thus, writing that 'In the old ritual dance the individual was nothing, the choral band, the group, everything, and in this it did but reflect primitive tribal life. Now in the heroic saga the individual is everything, the mass of the people, the tribe, or the group, are but a shadowy background which throws up the brilliant, clear-cut personality into a more vivid light.' Harrison's primary interest in ritual is at odds with the heroic impulse, for it is in the shared ritual that we come to understand human society and its fears and hopes, not in its exemplars, those heroes bathed in light and literary glory. For her there is no such thing as a heroic society. In her synthesising both ancient and modern worlds, Harrison writes 'in a word, the heroic spirit, as seen in heroic poetry, is the outcome of a society cut loose from its roots, of a time of migrations, of the shifting of populations.' The wandering hero, whose glorious deeds guarantee his fame, is of course nowhere in evidence in the mass migrations of the twentieth and twenty-first centuries nor in its literary representations. Such involuntary migrations tethered to world wars, empire, genocide, climate crisis, globalisation, economic drivers, etc, if made heroic or exceptional commit a kind of violence on its subject. And yet conversely, the body of the migrant is perceived as plural, invasive; this multiplicity is a dehumanisation built into the very language we use to speak about migration. To be a hero in the modern sense is to be someone who anyone could be and is therefore, also, no one.

But what of the case of voluntary migration? The self that makes itself heroic by remaking, in striving away from home, striving for gain, whose journey is chosen but whose stresses and grief are in some ways not dissimilar to Achotegui's figuration of complex migration? How is striving itself, as an idea built into literary models and real-life stereotypes of the good immigrant or the model minority, how might striving—in the Faustian sense—provide a way of thinking about heroism, tragedy (modern and ancient) and migratory grief? Who chooses to leave and why, who attempts to return, who stays on, who, to borrow from Bhanu Kapil's image of reverse migration, is made psychotic in a national space, who is this hero who journeys, who strives and for what? To be visible or invisible? As others have looked to the Faust legend for ways to explore the insatiability of man's appetites, the questions I put to Goethe's version specifically bring together three strands: striving as a fear of and countermeasure against mortality; a critique of globalisation and technology; and the female element counteracting male aggression, destruction and desire.

For me, these questions emerge from a personal, ancestral misery. On both sides of my family—who are linked closely by tribal bonds, a caste-bound brotherhood of intermarriages going back centuries—we have moved further and further from home for as far back as can be traced. In the early part of the nineteenth century, my ancestors had a flexible existence—they made their home on the banks of the Chenab river in what is now Pakistan; they farmed a little, largely for their own use, they made their living twisting reeds into rope and baskets. It wasn't until, as I understand it, the British apportioned forest land to those who would commit to clearing and cultivating it in the mid-19th century that my family became bound to agriculture. A network of canals was built in Punjab, the land of the five rivers, what would become the breadbasket of a newly-independent India. Drawing from a somewhat romantic, orientalist viewpoint, Marx critiqued what he saw as the colonial degradation of rural village life by colonial systems of governance and bureaucracy as the onset of capitalism, of farming driven by profit rather than the benefit of the community. A denaturing of the old ways, Marx foresaw, would lead to famines. In the *New York Daily Tribune* in 1853, Marx decries the 'spectacle of the crumbling of an ancient world', a sort of nostalgia for a world order that had already crumbled in the West. He ends somewhat ambivalently by quoting from Goethe's capacious, orientalising poetic dialogue between east and west, the *Diwan*: "Should this torture then torment us / Since it brings us greater pleasure? / Were not through the rule of Timur / Souls devoured without measure?"

What is gained when one home is lost, and another is offered in its place as you walk and as you are driven over the earth in such torment? The British would relinquish the cultivation of their land, to be farmed and taxed and nominally owned, until their withdrawal in 1947. Partition, for those who managed to stake a claim in an imaginary new nation for an equivalent land holding, meant exchanging your farm for another farm of equal size over an imaginary line. If you could reach it. Here the story accelerates: industrial farming on the scale promised by the Green Revolution of the 1960s led to bigger harvests, more technology, expensive machinery, irrigation canal and dam building, pesticides, fertilisers. Nothing could be further a hundred years later from life on the banks of the Chenab. This is how I understand it. That in the edible grasses growing under your feet you might remember the harvest you never made on the land from which you fled. That you arrive to harvest someone else's abandoned season and find that on leaving they destroyed all of their wells. That one year's harvest—some five thousand rupees—might buy a plane ticket for a son to go to England and to eventually send money home—that if he failed, you ate seed borrowed on credit for as long as you could to survive. That you make heroes of your children because someone set fire to your house across an invisible border and you can't stop running. So you start striving. A better house, a better job, more money. You disband, are disbanded. The shadowy background of the choral band recedes like ghosts in the underworld.

To return to Ulysses: in Homer's Book XI, Odysseus recounts meeting his mother in hell. He hasn't gone looking for her; he didn't know she was dead. He digs a pit; he sacrifices two sheep; their blood runs into the trench; the hero holds the assembling ghosts at bay who are drawn to drink from it with his sword. Asking how she died, his mother replies 'my longing to know what you were doing and the force of my affection for you—this it was that was the death of me' [tr. Butler]. Odysseus repeatedly attempts to embrace his mother and each time she dematerialises, a phantom form, unreachable. It is the blind prophet Tiresias who Odysseus seeks, and he instructs him how best to make the passage safely back to his kingdom; but follows this up with a further labour: to make peace with Poseidon who he has angered and who torments his return home after a twenty years' absence.

> But once you have killed those suitors in your halls—
> by stealth or in open fight with slashing bronze—
> go forth once more, you must…
> carry your well-planed oar until you come
> to a race of people who know nothing of the sea,
> whose food is never seasoned with salt, strangers all
> to ships with their crimson prows and long slim oars,
> wings that make ships fly. And here is your sign—
> unmistakable, clear, so clear you cannot miss it:
> When another traveller falls in with you and calls
> that weight across your shoulder a fan to winnow grain,
> then plant your bladed, balanced oar in the earth
> and sacrifice fine beasts to the lord god of the sea,
> Poseidon—a ram, a bull and a ramping wild boar—
> then journey home and render noble offerings up
> to the deathless gods who rule the vaulting skies,
> to all the gods in order.
>   [tr. Fagles, XI, 136–152]

This final task feels unnecessary, even unfair. An added labour onto the hero's journey now ended that extends the narrative's natural resolution of return, conquest, the restoration of the king. The work of return is never done. And perhaps this is the migrant's striving: to make home where home can never be made, to carry what is familiar into a place of unfamiliarity and to repurpose it in a place of unbelonging, a place where you risk being no one. Perhaps this is the migrant's grief-sodden task, sent on an errand to sate forces greater than themselves, to never tarry, to distrust happiness, beset by longing. My mother's first memory is of a grain harvest in Punjab, of a winnowing shovel throwing freshly threshed wheat into the air and the hot chaff sticking to her face. I have never seen a wheat harvest up close—the combines that roam the fields in August around where I live in semi-rural Lancashire are decidedly joyless. The pain of false recognition builds a temple in its own image to satisfy what angry god. Yet we continue to build.

*

On the night of August 15th 1947 my grandfather climbed to the roof of his house. From where he stood he could see his city burning. To one side were the fields he owned in the dark distance. And the sound of unhoming, forcibly or voluntarily taking whatever you could carry or tie onto a cart. But he felt no urgency to leave. Anyway, what is fire. It will extinguish itself by morning, he might have thought. No one alive remembers his house. What were his children doing and his second wife, the first taken by death in her childbearing years? His eldest son urged them to run, to fight, to stand their ground. What is fire anyway for the young. What is it for your elders.

On a night in December 2017, my father spotted a fire spilling down the hillside in Ventura, California. An alchemical line to a scientist is oxygen, fuel, toxic fumes in parts per million, wind speed and probabilities—proximities to death. He and my mother lay in bed watching it, wondering whether to sleep. What is fire but a chain of reactions waiting to exhaust itself. We should go, he said. My mother, unpicking passports and photographs from what might reasonably be left to burn, refused. We should stay and fight, she insisted. What is fire to a mother who has walked through death for each of her children. She knows the weight and composition of the house, how combustible every corner is and could arm herself with a shovel and tie back her hair. Fire is also her own mother crossing a newly-drawn border through fire and leaving everything in her home behind to burn.

On the night of [redacted] my childhood friend's elder sister [redacted] rented a hotel room in our hometown with a balcony overlooking the Pacific. From where she stood she could have seen as far as the Channel Islands to the west, to the east in the hillsides were both our houses. Her house yet unconsumed by the fires of 2017 that were captured by a security camera mounted on an eave. She took nothing with her but a copy of Goethe's *Faust*. From there, around sunset, she jumped. I remember her and her love of the German language. That in the '90s, she was a goth. I remember her great kindness and how elder sisters are like gods. How her family had fled the Holocaust. How much I have wondered about her love of the German language.

What is home but a waiting for, a fire to which we must return. The myth of another century bearing down on the horizon like a galleon. Once you leave home you can never be at home anywhere; someone will always be quick to point to a road or a mountain assuming you hadn't already spilled blood there so know it intimately. Something set us going that won't let go.

*

In Marshall Berman's reading of *Faust* as exemplary of the modern condition, he posits that Faust's development of self is tied to economic development, that Faust's story is indeed the *tragedy of development*. In one way, we see this most clearly in Faust's ambitious final project—a canal system that fights the force of the ocean to reclaim a coastal strip of land. Faust, who begins as the scholar in Goethe's part one, ends as an imperial figure appropriating land for an imagined project of development as both philanthropy and avarice. Having made a wager over his soul to never tarry, to never stop and enjoy the beauty of the moment, to ceaselessly strive, Faust loses… but this is not the tragedy of Goethe's subtitle. It is not in the classical sense that *Faust* is tragic for the modern and hence more reflective post-Enlightenment Man doesn't suffer in the pattern set forth by myth or divine design; he suffers his own choices with full knowledge of their consequences (Kierkegaard). Faust's self-development is also a series of tragic failures to grasp the moral and at times social dimensions of his own wish for omnipotence.

As Freud would lean on Goethe's *Faust* to develop his ideas of the Death Instinct, of Mephistopheles as aggressor and antithesis of creation (he calls himself the spirit of negation) and finally in *Civilisation and its Discontents* to link narcissism with the Nazis, we see the individual's wish for omnipotence (a kind of heroism) as the enemy of mankind. On the female presence in *Faust* there is much, really too much to say. But three groups of women interest me most: the Mothers, a shadowy group of ancients who provide Faust the means to retrieve Helen of Troy from the afterlife is the first, the second are simply referred to as Four Women ghosts, sisters who precipitate Faust's downfall: they are personifications of Want, Debt, Distress and Care. Faust is in the process of completing his land development project and has just had the elderly couple Philemon and Baucis, whose house stands in his way of total conquest, killed by Mephistopheles and his henchmen. The conversation between Faust and Care results in her blinding him, having promised him unending torment and dissatisfaction with any achievement. One might well argue that Faust throughout the play is already driven by this constant anxiety and dissatisfaction, this 'companion-cause of fear' by striving for material gain in the present moment. But what changes is Faust's will for a legacy, a hoped for afterlife through his deeds on earth, fame and remembrance. And this thought triggers the end of his wager. Ultimately Faust is saved from damnation by god's grace and female intervention—the wronged Gretchen from *Faust* Part 1 and Christian female figures of the divine, the third group of women significant to Faust's story. Whatever creative or erotic impulse Faust's earth-bound feats demonstrate—from seductions to diplomacy to marshland retrieval to the invention of paper money and the expansion of empires—the play ends with the chorus proclaiming 'Woman, eternally, shows us the way'. They are the not just the physically beautiful but idealised forms on which truth relies, as Walter Pater's essay on Johann Joachim Winckelmann and Goethe naturally associates a marrying of the romantic with the Hellenic in the figures of the Mothers. The Mothers, even their mention, makes Faust shudder.

Faust parts 1 and 2 took Goethe sixty years to write from an early sketched-out version we know of now as the *Urfaust* to its final posthumously published version. The idea of *Faust* haunted him for almost his entire life—he first witnessed *Faust* as a puppet play in childhood, so common was the myth of the magician and necromancer—and we know that amid his other many works including scientific treatises on colour, plants, geology, *Faust* was always in his mind, always ready to spring into action as Goethe's world view and quest for understanding science and art became more and more insatiable. We see the imprint of this expansive learning—some of his theories proved to be foolish, others prescient—throughout his *Faust* in rainbows and granite—Woolfian binaries not far from Goethe's own imagining. Goethe's life bridges, it has often been said, many crucial rendings from the old to the new world of industrialisation, secularism, empire, and capitalism. We return continually to his version of *Faust*, second only in English to Marlowe's version and a distant cousin to Thomas Mann's dark reworking of the legend. Serendipity and a life of learning guide Goethe's play, the force of it pulls anything even remotely close to it into its orbit.

And, finally, another serendipity—serendipity as a mode of poetics is how I generally work and how this essay, too, is shaped. Among the many translators of Goethe's *Faust* was the Northern Irish poet Louis MacNeice who, along with a literal translator, adapted it for BBC Radio in 1949 to mark the bicentenary of his birth. MacNeice wrestled with the task not because he found it linguistically challenging but, as his notes to the Faber edition of his translation state, because so much of *Faust* is digressive, lengthy and unrelated to the central plot and characters. MacNeice set about trimming Goethe, drawing the listener's attention to Faust the man, his actions and desires. With an eye for a hero. I read his *Faust* with interest, note the staging of good and evil, of action rather than context. I turn to MacNeice, his life and homeland, his measured political stance as a poet and BBC features reporter for the Home Service. MacNeice in 1949 had not long returned from India, where he made a few documentary features about the end of the Raj and on Partition. His letters to his wife Hedli and indeed a poem called 'Letter from India' give us a sense of what he saw—mixing with intellectuals, political figures like Nehru and the poet Sarojini Naidu, Krishna Menon—and his anxiety at the coming violence. Poignantly, at the lavish final party given by Lord Mountbatten at Viceroy's House in Delhi, the band plays 'Old

Man River', a song about the pain of enslavement most famously sung by actor and anti-imperialist Paul Robeson. The silence of the river, its indifference to human suffering, is history's ambivalence to the individual.

The producer accompanying MacNeice in India, Vaughan Thomas, recalls the violence they saw as they crossed a dividing country:

> I remember once driving with Louis to a little village called Shakpura. We got there to find that there'd been a terrible massacre that very morning… and suddenly I saw a totally different Louis, one I never imagined existed. Louis the man of action. He ordered those people into a nearby lorry, we got some sort of structure going of a way to get them out of the refugee area into something like safety and suddenly he was ordering people about, they were obeying him—a totally different Louis I suddenly saw revealed and also a Louis that was no longer the detached observer but one deeply and profoundly involved in the human dilemma.

MacNeice writes about this moment in the aforementioned 'Letter from India':

> I have seen Sheikhupura High School
> Fester with glaze-eyed refugees
> And the bad coin of fear inverted
> Under Purana Kila's trees
> And like doomed oxen those and these
> Cooped by their past in a blind circle;
>
> And day by day, night upon nightmare,
> Have spied old faults and sores laid bare,
> Line upon lineless, measureless under
> Pretended measure, and no air
> To feed such premises as where
> A private plot would warrant shelter.

MacNeice never mentioned or wrote about his actions as Vaughan describes them and instead retains the position of detached observer in his poem. Did he carry this inward sense of horror at human suffering, violence, evil, imperial power, into his remaking of *Faust*? It is impossible to say. But I cannot read his version of *Faust* without this knowledge. And with that, too, I bring the personal story of my own family seeking refuge in tents on the grounds of a different high school during Partition, some miles away, bound to their migratory fate across three continents like their abandoned bullocks locked in a threshing circle. I imagine what these refugees, turned economic migrants would finally wager their souls for. Think of how progress, how striving, is so encoded into the life of the immigrant that we find ourselves turning into any usable, familiar object. How they might plant their oar. For whom they would build a temple.

Sources:

Joseba Achotegui, *Ulysses Syndrome: The Immigrant Syndrome of Chronic and Multiple Stress* (Ediciones el Mundo de la Mente, 2015)
Marshall Berman, *All that is Solid Melts Into Air: The Experience of Modernity* (New York, NY: Simon and Schuster, 1982)
Sigmund Freud, *Civilization and its Discontents*, trans. by James Strachey, ed. by Peter Gay (New York, NY: W. W. Norton & Company, 1989)
Johann Wolfgang von Goethe, *Faust Parts 1 & 2*, trans. by Louis MacNeice (London: Faber & Faber, 1951)
—— trans. by Stuart Atkins (Princeton, NJ: Princeton University Press, 2014)
Jane Ellen Harrison, *Ancient Art and Ritual* (London: Williams and Norgate, 1913)
Homer, *The Odyssey*, trans. by Robert Fagles (New York, NY: Viking Penguin; London: Penguin Books, 1996)
—— trans. by Samuel Butler (London: Longman, 1900)
John Henry Jones, ed., *The English Faust Book: A Critical Edition Based on the Text of 1592* (Cambridge: Cambridge University Press, 2011)
Bhanu Kapil, *Schizophrene* (New York, NY: Nightboat Books, 2011)
Louis MacNeice, *Collected Poems* (London: Faber & Faber, 2007)
Louis MacNeice, *Selected Letters of Louis MacNeice*, ed. by Jonathan Allison (London: Faber & Faber, 2010)
Rüdiger Safranski, *Goethe: Life as a Work of Art*, trans. by David Dollenmayer (New York, NY: Liveright, 2019)
John Stallworthy, *Louis MacNeice* (London, Faber & Faber, 2011)

An Uncommon Language

> The doctor says it's an empty room in there
>
> And it is
>
> A pale sack with no visitors
> I have made it and surrounded it with my skin
> To invite the baby in
>
> But he did not enter
> And dissolved himself into the sea so many moons ago
>
> (Dorothea Lasky, 'The Miscarriage')

It is said that 1 in 4 women miscarry at some point in their lives. Yet why are there so few poems about miscarriage, something that many women evidently experience? Why is this private and unseen loss near invisible or taboo, to speak or write about? Dorothea Lasky's poem was a discovery for me. And it is stark, perfect, detached, even. Its refrain, 'Work harder!' speaks to the exhausting demands on women's lives and bodies from a (western capitalist) society bent on the forward momentum of (re)production. Likewise, Fiona Benson's lyrical poems about miscarriage from *Bright Travellers* reframe human loss via the natural world in 'Sheep' and 'Prayer'. Sharon Olds and Lucille Clifton boldly describe the visceral experience of miscarrying. From this memory, both poets retrieve the lost child and imagine them into a (racial, marital, personal) history, where they otherwise have no physical presence in lived time.

> you threw off your
> working clothes of arms and legs,
> and moved house, from uterus
> to toilet bowl and jointed stem

and sewer out to float the rivers and
bays in painless pieces.

(Olds, 'To Our Miscarried One, Age Thirty Now')

the time i dropped your almost body down
down to meet the waters under the city
and run one with the sewage to the sea
what did i know about waters rushing back
what did i know about drowning
or being drowned

(Clifton, 'the lost baby poem')

These are some examples among what I suspect is a minor note in the canon of women's writing. There has been, of late increasingly so, what seems like a flowering of poems and whole collections about motherhood. But how might poems about miscarriage, its silence, broaden our picture of maternity, a range of experiences, too often co-opted by the logic and language of productivity?

Sylvia Plath's poem reflecting on her own miscarriage, 'Parliament Hill Fields', I already knew but had not read attentively. It is not the 'bald hill' or 'faceless' sky where the lost child's 'doll grip lets go' that stopped me on re-reading it this time, but the line: 'I suppose it's pointless to think of you at all'. This teaches us something about grieving, perhaps, and its point. Although I also recalled reading Plath's radio poem drama, *Three Women*, at least fifteen or more years ago, I never listened closely to the three voices in it. Perhaps I flipped past it, thought one day I might return to this poem about maternity when its consequences applied to me. Back then, I couldn't differentiate clearly between the 'happy' mother of a son; the 'reluctant' mother who gives her daughter up; and, of course, the woman in between, the 'second voice', who miscarries. Now, for me, the second voice is the most compelling. She identifies as dying, dead, death. She has lost a 'dimension'. She is pointless, flat, has created no new face. But other faces, the 'faceless faces of important men', nations, society, governments, all conspire against women who have the power to produce new living dimensions. Who are not otherwise pointless.

> I am not ugly. I am even beautiful.
> The mirror gives me back a woman without deformity.
> The nurses give me back my clothes, and an identity.
> It is usual, they say, for such a thing to happen.
> It is usual in my life, and the lives of others.
> I am one in five, something like that. I am not hopeless.
> I am beautiful as a statistic. Here is my lipstick.

But grief is not pointless, its mourning or melancholy offers something when there is nothing to show for death. Where is the special language of grief given to women who miscarry? Does the expression of this particular grief rely on a borrowed tongue, more so than any particular love, or especial happiness, grief's necessary antecedents? I look everywhere for a way to wrench it from the mouths of doctors and nurses. Stillbirths, yes, there are brave books. The deaths of children, too, who have taken breath. But so little I find beyond the 'author unknown' postings on websites—a pop up asks if I want a 'grief friend'—and the exchanges between women who carry a secret death that make friends and family flounder for *the right words*.

In Helen Charman's powerful essay, 'Parental Elegy', she explores Complicated Grief Syndrome in poetry via Denise Riley's *Time Lived, Without its Flow* and both Jahan Ramazani's and Andrea Brady's works on the elegy. Charman writes that 'The relationship between productivity, parenthood and mourning reinforces, rather than alleviates, the 'complicated' problem of grief and narrative.' What are the ethics of producing poetry from grief, if that grief is pointless, finds no point, speaks back to death with an illegitimately and imprecisely acquired language?

§

You are no philosopher. Every time you speak of this kind of death you fear you are exaggerating. Death is real; what happened to you is not this but some unspeakable loss. A fact that cannot be explained by the framework of life, its order. You have no language of your own only a remote vocabulary, borrowed from mourning mothers, hoarse as Demeters, each heroic—and you are not this fact at all.

When a woman with certain privileges is about to give birth there's a slog of learning. Guides in print and thousands of websites. Most of which do not entertain other outcomes. Gradually, you pick it up, the knack of counting your life in weeks. Consider buying one of the many new books on motherhood, mostly by middle-class white women. You learn what it means to [redacted]. You feel the energy quietly being sapped away from you and the plurality of an internal conversation. When you inform the midwife you're opting for a consultant-led birth, she's surprised that 'an intelligent woman like you would make that decision'. You throw her a forced smile. What must it be like to see you or some version of you over and over day after day. Making the wrong decisions. Not quite English. The NHS leaflets piled thick in your palm. The hostile posters on the wards threatening those without legal status. This woman of the State is disappointed in you. But, anyway, you never see her again. You stop talking to your selves.

The woman's body is adrift. You find sisters to nurse you. *Her body is a graveyard*, A says. M explains: *miscarriages haunt women down generations*. S, who suffered a stillbirth, messages: *this is a minor moment in a woman's life that, at the time, feels major*. B emails you a spell. D and V are both Americans; they advise on the right drugs and procedures. P, blood sister, doctor, keeps you talking: *don't go quiet on me*. Miscarriage is its own language—clinicians keep it alive whereas women listen to its cold music and then forget, or try to. What would it be to keep this language in common use. To claim it back. Did women ever share ways to explain this to each other and to themselves? 'Language cannot do everything', Adrienne Rich advises in her 'Cartographies of Silence'. The scream /of an illegitimate voice // It has ceased to hear itself, therefore / it asks itself // How do I exist?'

M notes that in India even men know what a *D&C* is. Why is that? Your family would never acknowledge the shame that is pregnancy.

Aunties moving heavy with sin that gave your sister and you nightmares for at least thirty years. Neither would they speak of female feticide or amniocentesis, an antenatal means by which one can determine sex. But you know your Aunties have heard this language misused against them. Those Uncles who bluntly ask their wives or mistresses to cut into their insides by the right name.

You say, to your husband, 'if all goes well'. You say *you* because it's not your body. You imagine time reeling forward.

And, when the future stops, all is not well. You say 'I', but not aloud—an unspent curse. What is language anyway. An agreement. To make reparations. With whom. For what.

§

A world gone quiet must be this fact.
For which there is no precise language.
The monitor goes off and you are led
past a succession of mothers to a room marked 'empty'.
Taxonomies of grief elude the non-mother,
the un-mothered, the anything-but-this-fact.
No face no teeth no eyes or balled up fists.
To light the dark with a particular breathing.
A black lamp beats its wings ashore.

In the dark there is breathing.
After five visits to the hospital, the bruising
of inner elbows stitching themselves to themselves
in obsolescence, the nurses stop saying: *sorry for your loss*.
I may come to miss these laminated hallways.
I know my way there, to the artefact of losing.

Loosened from the factual world into a silence
where there is no grave but your own self stumbling
from floor to ceiling without an inch of your life.
Or mine. Or this particular absence.

The Lancastrian nurse is matter of fact.
Her metaphors are agrarian; the language of slaughter.
If you start bleeding like a stuck pig.
Under those thick white fingers an ancestry
of collapsing valves and bleating
transfigure into notes. You look familiar.
Why have you come here, again,
to my door with your metaphors of slaughter.

A folder, yellow, the word *baby*
on its cover, re-filed as miscellaneous.
What grew in you is not you but a shroud
and any idiot knows a shroud.
A ghost who wakes you up five times a night
stands undecided between rooms
shivering in its thin shadow.
I know my way here, to the language of loss.

My grandmother, who died giving birth,
explains what makes carnelian so red.
I assumed it was the iron in its veins
that made the Romans stamp their profiles
onto its brittle clots. Pulse of empire.

Don't say that / I never visited you.
A ghost is as good a family / as you may get.
Va, itni der baad thusi aaye hai?
After all this time, you've finally come?
The child that clawed you towards death is my kin.
His bones are a line pressed into the earth

you never wanted to cross, transfigured on the back
of a convoy somewhere else. It must be this fact.

A village and its farms and its wells
On an ordinary day in August
smell of blood and panic
carrying a child from this and that
disease, whose death is on your hands.

You look familiar. Why have you come here.

Blighted or to *blight*. What gives up gives over
is absorbed back into itself like a harp gone quiet
imperceptibly in the night.

Sources:

Lucille Clifton, *How to Carry Water: Selected Poems* (Rochester, NY: BOA Editions, 1987)
Dorothea Lasky, *Milk* (Seattle, WA: Wave Books, 2018)
Sharon Olds, *Stag's Leap* (New York, NY: Knopf; London: Jonathan Cape, 2012)
Sylvia Plath, *Three Women*, in *Winter Trees* (London: Faber & Faber, 1971); *Collected Poems* (London: Faber & Faber, 1981)

III

The Nineties

This is our fear of 'the other'
– Indians, blacks, Mexicans, Communists, Muslims, whatever –
America has to have its monsters,
so we can zone them, segregate them,
if possible, shoot them.
     —Robin Robertson, *The Long Take*

i. April 29, 1992

This is not your city. What burns and whose likeness with the earth burns with it. When did you arrive only to leave again? Walking through wet cement. What does your longing mean. The sky asks who made a season as wretched as this. A man stands on his shop roof with a rifle pointed at the crowd. Another 'stood his ground and did his duty'. He 'got caught up in the frenzy'. You watched it on T.V., the suburbs greened and rolling. Over and over, a man, many men, they are all men, this much you think. 'Can we all just get along.' Wash and repeat, your mother says. Latasha Harlins, three years older than you, shot dead by somebody's Asian grandmother. A grandmother not unlike yours. She gets community service. Money in her hand. *Empire Liquor,* 91st and Figueroa, one of the first to go. The city is far away, the city is in your living room. A two-bedroom apartment in El Rio, California, once 'New Jerusalem'. America must have its monsters. It would take a long decade to change you from an American to an immigrant to a monster. Your likeness burns with it. The event is not itself but who is watching themselves being watched with relief. 'U just had a big time use of force', the cop types into his car dispatch, driving a victory lap round the precinct. *Officer officer overseer* (KRS-One). Chances are you have been looked upon with thoughts of violence. Not guilty. Devils. *Filthy* (Ice-Cube). *Today, the jury told the world that what we all saw with our own eyes was not a crime.* (Tom Bradley) *At the end of the small hours* (Aimé Césaire) *Everyone cried for himself / As the great noise descended / The beat of a thousand wings* (DS Marriott). For all that is yours. For all you have taken. Take this. This is not your city.

ii. April 17, 1993

You climb, arms over you, arms over your head. 188 feet into the air to drop and ply yourself from land again in loops of steel painted red. In the two and a half minutes this takes, two kinds of screams split the air from the ground. This is personal. Below, 'a mob' of black teenagers is angry about an oversold TLC concert. *Magic Mountain spokeswoman Eileen Harrell said park officials did nothing wrong. She blamed the violence on a crowd attracted by "that type of music"*. Dropping 171 feet at an angle of 55 degrees, you go round again. Yesterday, a Federal court imprisoned Stacey Koon and Laurence Powell. This is not personal. You will have due process. You will have equal protection under the law. It was never personal. Running under a man's overcoat to the school bus, you lie down on the green vinyl seats and wait to be counted. Some of you are missing, others are crying. One is focused on a tennis ball-sized jaw breaker seized in his fist. A refugee from El Salvador whose first memory is a low flying plane you wrongly guessed was a crop duster. Luis believes he is a mutant, a saviour, a polymath, a Professor Xavier. He is waiting for his father who was disappeared. The park is emptying but he concentrates on it the white ball melting between his palms. Is personal. Helicopter searchlights flood the windows and rotate over your low breathing. Serpents of light and glass upend themselves in the dark, riding empty cars into the night.

iii. January 17, 1994

The old fault shakes our mountains, and rolls the San Fernando Valley's avenues into its song of buckled stucco and drywall. The smell of Vermont, Fairfax and Sepulveda burning. Folds of stone slither along a fissure that opens on your doorstep. A tremor, a riot, a verdict. Your step widens across the pavement. On the bank between sleep and death, you find your life at once to be so orderly. Unpatriated as you are by the parting of granite. Earth falls from an axe handed to your enemies in turns. Its dark soil burning. No reason then, to watch your well-built house, duly peopled, whiten to ash except that you might otherwise have refused to leave. Successive tremors fly. Dishes thick as cataracts wheel over the linoleum starboard hard and smash in the pitch. Something disturbing itself in the night has cracked the mock Tudor mould of your exile. An overpass crumbles out of view. Valley Fever beds into your lungs with the rising dust. It is Martin Luther King Jr. Day; it is Robert E Lee Day; it is almost 5 a.m. in the thin doorframe juddering between two rooms. That year, the neighbours wouldn't rebuild and left. What clings to you, you carry into another century. The cheapness of all you are obliged to call home. This is not personal. You recall without disgrace the borders you crossed, invisible but alive. Wrong question, you say, pointing your body to the west.

iv. April 11, 1994

This is not your history. There are two doors at the Museum of Tolerance: one, for those with prejudices and the other for those without, which is permanently locked. Inside, a whisper tunnel hurls prerecorded epithets at your classmates as they file through. Some giggle; some shout back. The thing you remember most clearly is eating a brownbag lunch as your eyes adjust. A white hot cement parking lot near Beverly Hills. This is personal. The film director Steven Spielberg is visiting Castlemont High School in Oakland at the request of state governor Pete Wilson, who is up for re-election. Earlier that year, on Martin Luther King Day, 69 mostly black Castlemont students were kicked out of a screening of *Schindler's List* for laughing at a concentration camp execution scene. A Nazi soldier casually shooting a Jewish woman. Psychiatrists were hauled in over the public uproar. The students wanted to watch *House Party 3*. Governor Wilson will be remembered for Proposition 187—a law denying illegal immigrants healthcare and education. At the assembly, Spielberg insists the kids received 'a very bad rap for what happened'. He'll come back, he promises, without the cameras. Most applaud the director of *E.T.* and *Jurassic Park*. Wilson has just signed the Three Strikes, habitual felon statute, into law. A campaign ad—grainy footage of people running across the Mexican border—warns, 'they're coming'. On the way home from the museum the school bus is rowdy. This is not personal. Your history teacher is visibly annoyed. Diane is not a natural blonde. She is a liberal feminist. She proudly poured coffee one summer for MLK in a southern diner, voted for every Kennedy. The LA freeways throw everything out of scale. 'I don't think I should have to take that history', Castlemont student Laronnda Hampton, 17, reportedly said. 'I don't even know my own history'.

v. October 3, 1995

This moving quarry on which you have landed carries on burning. Seneca, the only black student in the twelfth grade, bursts from the classroom, shouting—*my n***** is free, my n***** is free*—circling the school annexes where you sit in a row figuring the terminal velocity of a car travelling at speed against a wall without casualties. Your heroes are not good, your teachers proud; they pull the doors shut and let Seneca run himself tired. You gather your books and wait for it to be over. The physicist doubles as the girls' tennis coach. Holds court. He is a sentimental Europhile in a household of women. Every morning, he joins the prayer circle around the flag pole. They quote Pat Robertson into the onshore breeze. This is personal. The door is still shut. Outside, transplanted eucalyptus trees stand guard, dropping their tan sun-hardened skins. Parallax of shade and milk, axes x and y, the perfect state of *standard temperature and pressure* to whom all laws equally apply. Who is under siege. Who rattles the wall with their footsteps, fractures the cement. Who longs for the door to open, a leading out. Tracks that appear in the blood. Intersecting nowhere. A victory. A quarterback. Who stays on like this, until they die.

IV

On Desire
(*after Winckelmann*)

What is *the gift?* To receive—she is touched,
or the scuttle of her heart is mollified by its touch.
O to be *touched* by the gift, like being singled out
and blessed by infirmity. The gift—
simulacrum of love—and he who gives it does so
knowing that by giving it to me nothing
could really be gained.

>Black corollary of love—
>*go trouble younger hearts.*

The man who wrote that phrase the breadth
of a single hair: *noble simplicity and grandeur*
also boasted: 'Ich esse gut und ich scheisse gut'.
He could articulate it, and wanting it, had that gift
of seeing that somewhere between these vivifications
of 'consummate' and 'evacuate'
is the completion of desire.

Eugenics of Art—
Homer mentions no pitted face, no pox. Arcangeli,
who would disembowel the Abbé, was not
the tone-deaf Olympian Alcibiades, fondling boys
in the gymnasium, but a disfigured man of no account.
Winckelmann wrote, much before his fated friendship:
The Archangel of Concha's *face*
'glows with indignation and revenge.'

*

Turning over rubble in the Villa Albani,
Winckelmann observes the broad repose of time.

Gleam of white light on a stone neck, on a pedestal of bone.
Perhaps some conquest, in a preternatural hour,
had carried off her head? Or trampled her face to dust.
Either way, he is sure that finding it is beyond his office.
The absence makes her animal.
He does not note this in his catalogue.

*

What had Rhodopis said, all those hours, to the ugliest of men?
When she heard his fables, what love stiffened
in the folds of garments that could hook itself
to the promise of one wayward slipper?

Chewing her thumbnail through his long-winded tale,
she may have at last excoriated:
'Enough of your riddles!'

Here is the apple and *there* is the tree, appearing ordinary.

*

Where is the tree? Despondent wife of Socrates
young and ancestrally equestrian.
Xantippe (meaning 'blonde horse') whom the old man
would not woo. He, a coquette in the world of men—
A gadfly—she could only buck.

*

True art in imitation
or true propaganda?

David's *Death of Socrates* alarmed the salon of 1787.

The scroll at Plato's feet. Death warrant… or versifications of Aesop?
Wise son of a midwife, who in his final hours
Reared like the horse of Napoleon Bonaparte.

      *

Slave of Samos, gnarled hunchback, deformed fabulist.
Your animal phrase soils the footstools of Europe.
There—and also there—a fleet of eyes, each identical
out-minister the other.

An unctuous industrialist pats his thorax.

Dissolute parthenogenist,
man vis-à-vis his instincts—
we sniff our own blood.

How you have multiplied in us
like an incandescence that hauls itself
up from the dark
to colour a woman's cheeks?

      *

Slave-girl, Cinder-girl, Horse-of-a-Different-Colour.
The wise busts of Herculaneum
angle the torsos of headless girls.

Withdrawing the candle from his window
that opens onto the Porta Salaria
Winckelmann carries thoughts of his pupil's contours
Down tapestried corridors to bed,
Following his moral windmill.

'Vivien With Household Gods'
[HB/PH/241-57: Photo Album of 57 Chester Terrace 1924–1929]

It is a matter between two wives, living and dead,
and who can guess where one ends and the other,
in shortened, enumerated breaths, begins
that loveless phrase of emptied rooms
and unpeopled letters:
yours in eternity.

One, colloidal with dust,
is powdering in upstairs rooms
by fireside lanterns of vinegar and gin,
desiccate widowhood mealing itself in air.
The other, besmattered and freaked with decay—
her face, razed by sunlight to purest whitewash,
turns towards her mantelpiece of household gods:
a silvery plate, pewter candlesticks and Hellenic vase—
its heroic scene a spear in the fist, muscular and poised to strike—
candles, a portrait of a lady in high-collars, jet beads, faraway in the eye.

V's hands are clasped
(as if she is trying not to touch them)
Her elbow rests lightly.

There can be only one priestess
at the altar of the fair husband.
Her prayerful look is excised
en toto, clean from the ears.

Tom & Polly & Peter (the dog and cat)
invigilate the changing of the shift.

V crumbles, inverts, wanders the streets in blackshirt
repeating the childhood question up to Stoke Newington
it's raining it's pouring and all the King's horses and all
in my lady's chamber and couldn't get up in the morning.

O O O all the King's men in Lancashire, in Hampstead,
in Compayne Gardens ringing me thin and ransacking
the house tedium deus protracted life ringing me thin
bring me gin by the fire on the lawn of Ottoline's garden.

[A Letter dated 14 September 1939 from TSE in London (on *Criterion* letterhead) to Richard Jennings: 'Your letter arrived timely to cheer me up: I have been plunged in dust, going through and destroying old papers which ought to have been destroyed years ago: turning up unanswered letters from people who are dead, a photograph of a man who has been in an insane asylum for years, and such cemetery matter.']

Nightmares at the Waldorf-Astoria

After Marilyn Monroe/Wallace Stevens

M enters, a golden imbricate
of mythic beauty. Stunning serpent
in the long grass of fluted columns.

She slept here. Semblance of the woman
one loves or ought to love.

Marble equipoise anxious
at the grand entrance.
Unaccustomed to the flop-house
or to God's long, long face.

On the ceiling, dead center,
tragic muse with a mask
of golden ringlets—

And yet, Marilyn is not a wild poem, fresh from Guatemala.
    Aqua Sancti—she dreams of excavation—
dark adventures into the whole of her creation.

> *to bring myself back to life*
> *has prepared me—given me*
> *whatever the hell it is.*

After the Fall—after a bottle and another bottle—
a woman sacrificed by her own hand or husband
to her pupils' black circumference.

> *and there is absolutely nothing there—*
> *there was absolutely nothing—*
> *finely cut sawdust—like out of a*
> *raggedy ann doll—the sawdust*

spills all over the floor & table
& hopes for theater are fallen.
Arthur is
disappointed—let down

(I stole four teaspoons from room 1614 and slept well)

there was absolutely nothing

Come to the Waldorf-Astoria!

Penitent arcade   of the Guerlain Spa
    where a man with enormous eyebrows
        dabs glycolic acid ecumenically
            Adieu, adieu mia cupola!

Once-brass bell-plates papered over in the 80s
    doors erupt onto dead porticos
        and valets emblazoned 'WA' approach
        gentlemen tendering ticket stubs,
        wrapped and civil in their livery.

Faces dipped in camphor: the Duchess Wallis, three Elizabeths,
(Windsors and Taylor), Princess Grace, lunatic and orchid-breasted.
All culpable Guineveres.
Does Mademoiselle—
who is very wealthy—
do borders?

In the wild country of the soul revolving
mirrors swing apart from fair forearms.
Despotic tableware fillets M's psyche, turtle-necked,
aqueous, framed in monochrome by books.

They serve swell board here.
Elsa Maxwell looks tired.   *O This terrible dis-ease.*

A sound in an adjoining room
an imagined body pacing lengths
of tired flesh.
        For what, M wonders?

Woman has no natural home.
Return her floral tributes c/o.
At the edge of the mind someone's father—
    is that you, unlikely man of letters,
    dreaming of the tropics
    under an Imperial timepiece?—
    He waves a huge spray of greenbacks, agreeing.

A Good Wife

O Lord of the world, this is your lamplit service. You are the Arranger of the affairs of those humble beings who perform your devotional worship service. [Pause.] Lentils, flour and ghee—these things I beg of you. My mind shall ever be pleased. Shoes, fine clothes, and grain of seven kinds—I beg of you. A milk cow, and a water buffalo, I beg of you, and a fine Turkestani horse. A good wife to care for my home—your humble servant Dhanna begs for these things.
—Guru Granth Sahib

I am the snake in the box. You married me
after I strangled your horse. What service
was the wringing of its throat. This I beg
of you, your humble servant. The noise of
its two dry hind bones knocking together—
what a noise. The grain falling unripe from
its long stalk. Your continuous pleasure—
shoes, fine clothes, a buffalo—these things.

In the lamplight, any horse will do. But
you are particular, my Lord. Your home
is the shattering of glass bangles, drawing
blood. Colour. [Pause.] Lentils, flour, ghee.
I should have stripped the milk cow of
her soft, white buttocks. Who beguiles you,
heavy-eyed, with her sullen daily worship.

Something Particular

My aunt is in the kitchen. On the counter is a cup of tea. It is not precisely tea, but a boiled mix of leaves and spices with milk and sugar. Some would say this is another drink, an elsewhere. How my aunt makes it isn't a family secret but it is unique and no one not her mother not my mother not me makes it like she does, pinching and tearing as she swaps through the jars and into the water already simmering. Now it is green. And the house smells differently. She lifts the cup and pours it into the sink. It isn't cold. Her daughter falls out of the sky from an upstairs window onto a box, lately flattened for waste. She did not exactly drop in like an origami crane on a scatter of rough toys. In this way my aunt forgets her drink of no abstract use so quickly. A baize door slams like thunder. One corner of the picture this woman with her foreign drink. Another, the child swinging against an open window at play. Her husband, my uncle, is also my cousin but they are not really related by blood. The daughter is no primitive taboo whose shattered idol fears nothing in a back garden like this where no one saw her fall. Except her mother the tea already sweetening the metal socket of the drain. *I draw a black dot under your ear every morning to ward off evil and praise.* This means nothing or something particular to her.

Krampus

On the banks of Lake Fuschl the butter-coloured Schloss is ringed in snow. Emerald edged, glacial blue at its depth, a lakeside luxury hotel smothered by a valley of tall black pines. For a period of fifteen years in six hundred or so its fortress walls entertained officers making stiff one-armed salutes between courses of venison and sole at circular tables overlooking the wooded banks of the See. An old hunting lodge brushes up for the upright swine barking in their sunken pen of floor to ceiling windows as von Ribbentrop toasts the ear of the Führer over a bonfire of foreign gossip—Edward, he is sure, and Wallis stand firmly with the Reich. The dining room is almost level with the lake. You feel you could walk on it, the last unchanging vista on earth. The Schloss curates its losing. Its battlements are decorative; thick walls did little to deter the Anschluss and deportation of the house's previous owner— also a fascist. Von Ribbentrop, Hitler's man in Britain, is a champagne dealer by marriage, and the first Nazi to be hanged at Nuremberg. None of this features in rapturous descriptions of the hotel's fine aspect. You learn, only on returning home, facts that complicate the idyllic Salzburger charms of Christmas markets, Mozart marzipan chocolates that roll as both ball and bullet in your mouth. But didn't they point— you joked to your friends at home—like parody racists at you, your father, your mother, in the main square, in the restaurant, even the Schloss where you'd paid a migrant's ransom for the smallest room? And pointing, metamorphose into bearded devil-goats rampaging the streets, whipping tourists? Children at play; tradition for some, a ritual that sends you three fearful indoors. A vintage shop: iron plates, antique pistols, mishandled brooches and there, too, a porcelain bust of von Ribbentrop in military regalia, miraculous, honest as a slur.

Elsewhere

In Westwood, California, our professor,
whose name was, he told us proudly,
Yiddish for *fucker*, careened through Merrill.
Goethehaus I pronounced 'goathouse'
and the professor's modus
operandi was startled. Farnoosh scrawled
it wasn't me
on our copies of 'Lost in Translation'.
Who is Gunmoll Jean? We were too shy
to ask. But she did. Lee was all baseball.
Every verb was nude, and every girl extra innings.
It was 1999. Ty Warner was our D.W. Winnicott.
We stank of booze up and down Sunset Boulevard.

In Westwood, California
we were not Elizabeth Bishop, nor were we
her Aunt whose name is fiction.
As for Osa and Martin Johnson, *dressed in riding breeches*,
they were scheduling a sweet date while the *fucker*
yodelled on. *'Long Pig', the caption said.*
My dear F, it never occurred to us,
that yellow border around our necks.
Our modus operandi was shackled
to the knife in those *horrifying* breasts
we'd come to inherit without question.

I wish I'd known then about Osa and Martin.
The plane flying into the side of a mountain
queer as an animal appearing from the brush
regarding us like familiars. Death meant nothing
as we trampled through Lowell's *Life Studies*
never hearing the hesitation in his voice reciting

'For the Union Dead'—*that's what the despatches said*
—it might have meant something.
Flash. Bang.

In Newhall, Santa Clarita, the 'incident' that choked
in the throat of Stacey Koon in the decade
of our education no *pith helmets* could save
was not the crash but a blessing for violence.
How had I come to be here, / like them
and not know the century just beginning
would be our last. Together, this strangeness
would engender an earth's worth of unfamiliar
pictures, all unframed. The sound of telephone
lines going soft in a generation without
the children we birthed or didn't. Did we?
The family voice. Staring out into the Pacific alone.
But that moment *held us all together*
like the quiet before an exodus.
That *cry of pain* gathering in the margins
where one alights on what is worth taking—
carried through fire, my ancestors, a reliable syntax—
and what must be left behind.

Queens Astoria

Not one but two both useless. Women who have no use, evade use, betray use you women are these useless creatures. Useless where use is not determined, indeterminately useless women subpar all over the shop with your useless wittering on so useless is such uselessness. Flat in the face useless, over the edge, peculiarly useless from your palindrome of uselessness I read useless in many antiquated and extinct and exonerated defunct languages. Whatever uselessness you trade on the open market, however useless your synonymic imbricated functions of lack of use, the end of use the use that sees no other use but to drain heavily into the drain of uselessness that is you woman you are useless. I shout at your lack of present use, the hitching post of your uselessness the downtrodden borderline and bivalvic uselessness of your seafloor uselessness soundless as the ocean, the core principle of use. Back of the taxi useless, fine ermine useless what use is the figure of another woman dressed in the figure of my primarily female body that we inherit our uselessness from this kind of logic can have no use and makes for no useful conclusion. Concussive uselessness, uselessness that befits the stature of women in their unorthodox cheek sucking this is fine this is poor this is where I imitate a younger woman uselessness that evades the livery of useless clothing all women are in fact out of use if not out of fashion. We get swindled out of 10 dollars by a man of our own tribe. How useless are we not to scent our own after he told us we were without much use and then this man the prosecutor wants us to testify over the telephone against our taxi driver *well now there's a story*

Acknowledgements

Thanks, as ever, are due to Tony Frazer at Shearsman for letting me get on with things without much interference.

I am grateful to the editors of magazines and anthologies that published these poems before they found this book shape: Ilya Kaminsky for *Ploughshares*, Emily Berry at *The Poetry Review*, guest editors Richard Scott and Andre Bagoo at *The Poetry Review*, Alex Houen and Adam Piette at *Blackbox Manifold*, Gboyega Odubanjo and Joe Carrick-Varty at *bath magg*, Jeet Thayil for *The Penguin Book of Indian Poets*. And to Helen Tyson for inviting me to the University of Sussex to speak about *Faust* and (sort of) modernism.

Thanks also to those who generously offered feedback on these poems along the way: Valzhyna Mort, Bhanu Kapil, Sarah Howe, Ilya Kaminsky, Anthony Anaxagorou, Fred D'Aguiar, Fiona Curran, Sara Crangle, Dinah Roe, Nuar Alsadir, Deryn Rees-Jones, Rachael Allen, Sam Solnick, David Hering, Anne Enderwitz, Vidyan Ravinthiran, Forrest Gander. To James and our beloved Gaia. And to my parents and my sister, Parveen, for many lifetimes of striving.

Finally, thanks are owed for permission to quote lines from Dorothea Lasky's poem, 'The Miscarriage', from the volume *Milk* (2018), to the author and to Wave Books; likewise, thanks are owed to BOA Editions for permission to quote an excerpt from Lucille Clifton's 'the lost baby poem', from *How to Carry Water: Selected Poems*. Copyright © 1987, by Lucille Clifton. Reprinted with the permission of The Permissions Company, LLC on behalf of BOA Editions, Ltd., boaeditions.org.

Lightning Source UK Ltd.
Milton Keynes UK
UKHW010717130722
405782UK00001B/39